For Frances and Forde Good,

affectionately,

Victor White

THE DOMINANT NOTE

Victor White

The Dominant Note

The Bobbs-Merrill Company, Inc.

Publishers

Indianapolis • New York

FIRST EDITION

THE DOMINANT NOTE

CHAPTER ONE

Relentless Errand

THE train slid discreetly to a halt with hardly any jolt or noise, as if it were a luxurious nursery and the children in it had to be kept from waking at any cost.

Kansas City!

The porter flung open the Pullman door and stepped importantly out onto the platform. Peter followed the two men who had been talking together in the club car during the last couple of hours. The short, tubby, loquacious one who had tried to pump him before dinner still seemed to bear him a grudge for not satisfying his curiosity. Peter saw the resentment in his eyes as he met his glance, like a child's, almost, that had been cheated out of some game.

For a moment he sympathized with the tubby man. It must have been annoying to hear—without hearing a great deal more—that he was twenty-four but was thinking of retiring, that he had worked in steel mills and by now, by 1926, in a mere three years, had made his fortune manufacturing radios. No wonder the sawed-off man had scowled when

3

he had told him that he was just back from a vacation in Europe and was planning to take another vacation in Santa Fe! It all had the sound of a gross imposition on anyone's credulity.

He thought, Well, what was I to tell him? I suppose I should have said, "I'm going to Santa Fe to see my father whom I've never seen before, whose name is Geoffrey Middlemas and who is an English painter whom I went to France to track down. I went there first because that's where he lived when I got his address out of my mother in 1919. This happens to be an errand that was planned years ago—one afternoon when I was not even fifteen, in Vienna, in the cold, rat-infested cellar of a hardware store where I was an apprentice and half starved. I had just had my frostbitten hands scrubbed with mechanic's soap by a bookkeeper who was a bit of a sadist. You see, I'm a bastard and my mother dumped me on her sister in Vienna and went off to America with a theatrical company and presently got herself married. It was Aunt Kathi, who disapproved of everything about her flighty young sister who, she had known, would come to no good in the theatre, that brought me up after her own children—after Franz and Poldi were pretty well grown up.

"Of course, I needn't have gone into the hardware store. Not that there was any getting away from the constant gnawing hunger during those war years, but I could have starved more elegantly as an apprentice in a bank or in a haberdashery shop. But there wasn't really any choice, not after I'd applied to get into a cadet school the previous spring and had passed all the exams and had got as far as the board of officers which sat on admissions in a beautiful old room. After I'd heard the commandant whisper to the colonel next to him that one word, 'illegitimate,' I'd felt a need to plunge down into something dark, to get away from all the officer elegancies of which I had dreamed. I wanted only to get my hands on something real and get power until eventually I could get revenge on Geoffrey Middlemas."

Well, it had taken him until now in 1926, until he was twenty-four— he thought with a grin—before he was actually on his way. Power, that had been his dream. But one's concept of power changed. One got sidetracked. One got seduced.

First, when he had finished his apprenticeship and had started to make a quite respectable little pile trading on his own like everybody else in the hardware business after the War, after everything had gone to pot in 1919, there had suddenly been the engrossing demands of

America. Mizzi—well, his mother!—had wanted him to join her in Westchester, and he had half cynically and half eagerly agreed. There had been that whole new world to challenge his foreignness!

There had been the friendly overtures of Mr. Thorson who was much too nice to be thought of as stepfather, and the callow dog-in-the-manger hostility of Bob, who didn't have it in him to be anything but a stepbrother, and the enchanting confidingness of little twelve-year-old Anne, the little sister he had dreamed of and miraculously found. And there had been Mizzi's determination to make him over into a nice innocent American boy who had never known the precocious casehardening of the wartime years! There had been the constant friction with Mizzi which after only two weeks had made it impossible for him to stay.

Then there had been Pittsburgh and the two years at the puddling furnace and the open hearth—and at his algebra and physics books after the twelve-hour shifts. Then there had come the spell in the laboratories; and finally the switch to the new radio industry, with John Hearn and Stelle and him starting their small factory, each with a few thousand dollars to put in—and he with a little more, thanks to what Cousin Franz in Vienna had insisted on calling black-market profits.

After that it had been work, work, work—first in Pittsburgh and then in New Jersey—as they had grown and grown, until this spring after the merger with Federated he had pulled out—it still seemed a little incredible—with quite enough money to last him the rest of his life. To say nothing of the royalties he might eventually collect on his record changer and on the chrome-plating process. Two patents that promised to pay off out of five wasn't too bad.

It was almost dizzying to look back. Only Hearn's genius in the laboratory and the fact that they had got in at the beginning of a fantastically growing new industry, and Stelle's gifts as a salesman, and his own success in handling production had made it all possible. But in that arduous climb he had almost forgotten about revenge, or rather his whole notion of revenge had become subtly modified with every step that had brought him nearer to it, had become more refined and tame— until it seemed embarrassing to remember that at fifteen he had thought of killing Geoffrey Middlemas, until now only a vague desire to punish him remained.

But that much was still there all the same. *Let's not get too fancy and forgiving!* he admonished himself. For there still remained the fact which could make him go hot and cold with humiliation and rage that

Geoffrey Middlemas had walked out on Mizzi—and on him. "Six months before you were born," Aunt Kathi had told him once when he had asked. "As soon as he had got her into trouble he couldn't get away fast enough. I warned her. I knew no good was going to come of it, acting in the theatre and going out with a foreigner, an artist and a Protestant, a man without any religion. . . ."

And Geoffrey Middlemas had so courageously walked out, it appeared, because his father in England had threatened to cut off some allowance if he got married on the Continent, presumably to an adventuress. As if he couldn't have gone to work and supported himself if he had been as heartbroken over having to choose between Mizzi and his career as Aunt Wetti had claimed.

No, the fact remained that as far back as he could remember there had been the crushing consciousness of his inferiority to other children because of some inherent flaw in him somehow connected with his birth. There had been Aunt Kathi's frequent, tart reminders of it. There had been the made-over clothes which were all he had ever had to wear, the endless hours spent with Aunt Kathi in church while other children were allowed to play, the good school to which Aunt Kathi had refused to let him go because French and algebra might encourage the vicious bent in him. In a way his childhood sufferings had been worse than the festering frostbite sores and the ravening hunger of his apprentice years.

All that had been Geoff's fault.

And there had been Sibby! . . .

He could not have told a chance acquaintance on the train about Sibby either. It would have been too painful to say, "I was wonderfully lucky once. You see, there was the daughter of the head of the American Quaker relief committee, whom I met in Vienna in 1919 and who became a symbol to me of everything that was beautiful and exciting about America, whom I dreamed about all those years in Pittsburgh and who was the bright goal of all my ambitions. But I made a mess of that."

No mere chance acquaintance could have possibly understood his joy last fall when he had found Sibby still unmarried, settled in her own apartment and studying art in Greenwich Village, nor the poignancy of his fight for Sibby with Lyle, the poet. Nor could a stranger have understood the peculiar frustration of that other fight against a much more baffling antagonist than the brilliant Lyle: his own perfectionism, as Sibby had called it—asking too much of everyone because he had always asked a great deal of himself.

Though that was oversimplifying it, too. He had had a right to his suspicion that Sibby had taken him only as second best, because she couldn't have Lyle. He had had a right to bridle at the condescension shown him by Sibby's mother because he was a foreigner. He had had ample cause to feel that Sibby for all her rich-girl sophistication and her flirting with the arts and for all her sweetness was disturbingly shallow and inept.

But that did not lessen the sharp pain of remembering how—just five weeks ago now—he had broken it off, with almost brutal abruptness, from fear of hurting her worse by letting things drag on. Nor did it lessen the subtle panic that went with the memory of her accusation that he was incapable of loving anyone because his romanticism made him expect too much.

It had not helped to say that even if there was a grain of truth in her accusation, if he had acted a little like a schoolboy in idealizing her too much, it was because he had never had any time for calf love. It was perhaps the ultimate frustration of being self-made, the most cruel part of the price one paid, that one never had had time to be young. There had been only this much good about the fiasco with Sibby—that it had reminded him of the account he had to settle with Geoffrey Middlemas. . . .

Poor tubby man who thought himself snubbed, he wouldn't have understood much of it. He didn't know what he had been spared, Peter thought with a grin as he watched the short man try to keep up with his long-legged companion.

Peter bought a paper from a newsboy merely because it promised some contact with the city of which he was not going to see anything. He watched the few passengers getting on, the man with the broad-brimmed Western hat, the long rows of blinded windows along the night-quenched cars, the two conductors returning from inside the station somewhere. The porters were beginning to slam doors. There was a perfunctory "All aboard!" He went back to the club car and was all by himself this time. The two talkative men had evidently gone to bed. The train began to move as softly as it had stopped.

After a few minutes he could see the lights of the city again. Then the lights fell behind. There was a full moon. Rolling hills, farms, here and there a silo or windmill sticking up with prankish Halloween ghostliness although it was much too soon for that, and everywhere the immense and fertile plains. How vast it all was!

He opened the Kansas City paper, read about a scandal at city hall, about a big wedding and what all the women wore, about wheat and cotton futures and the price of beef and pork, and presently found himself looking out of the window again.

In the end it was the vastness, the exhilarating vastness, that gave one such a sense of freedom! Elbowroom. Everything still to be made and shaped, a glorious vacuum waiting to be filled, still some wilderness left to be tamed. Was that why Americans were so strikingly alike and did things exactly as their neighbors did, so that the wedding in Kansas City sounded just like a wedding in New Jersey, right down to the sweet peas —because pioneers needed a compass in the wilderness and assurance that they were not alone? Now in Europe where everything was already charted and built and fenced the only freedom lay in rebelling against the familiar, in pretending that the walls were not there. Perhaps that was why Europeans differed so sharply from one another, almost to the point of eccentricity. A puny kind of liberty!

Still, his week in Vienna had been wonderful. How lucky he had decided to go after he had discovered that Geoffrey Middlemas was no longer in Arles—no longer in France at all. He wouldn't have missed it for anything!

The amazing thing was how gay everyone had been in spite of the poverty left by the War. Not so surprising in the case of Cousin Franz, perhaps, who had always had that infectious gift of gaiety, but a little to be marveled at in Bianca, who had so cheerfully forgotten her title and the aristocratic country houses and the servants and carriages she had known as a girl. She had appeared radiantly happy with her little boy, who had Franz's blue eyes and blond hair, out in the modest apartment in Hietzing, which was all Franz could afford on his government salary.

It gave him a glow of satisfaction to think of Aunt Kathi and of the mortgage on the little house in Hütteldorf which he had been able to pay off. It had taken a lot of arguing with Poldi to accomplish even that. Poldi had bravely bought the charming little villa for her mother and herself, but it would have taken her forever to pay it off. Poldi, turning rather old-maidish, a little mannish with the important job she held, so unlike her brother Franz and yet so loyal and generous still, he thought affectionately.

But the big surprise had lain in Aunt Kathi. Incredible that he should have felt so much warmth for her whom he had hated so as a child, who had seemed the bane of his life, a constant cloud. Was it she who had changed so much, or he? No matter, there had been this irresistible tenderness in him, this smiling indulgence for her plying him with one of her herb teas. "After a long journey one should always drink *Mutterblätter* tea," she had explained half apologetically. It had been one of those bits of herb lore she had brought with her from her childhood in the Tyrol, some ancient simple that probably went back to the days when people got all cramped up from riding in a stagecoach all day. He smiled now as he thought of her solicitude and of a kind of awed shyness she had shown with him and of her festive attempts to cook all the things he had liked as a child.

No, he wouldn't have missed it for anything!

It was time to go to bed. He walked forward through the darkened cars. When he was in his berth he raised the shade and looked out. The moon was setting and the veiled vastness was suddenly a little frightening. It struck him all at once how like the moment was to the time when he had looked out of the porthole almost exactly seven years ago, the night before they had docked in New York. He had had almost the identical feeling then of expectancy and apprehensiveness.

Was one always caught in the same situation a second and a third time? Was there a pattern one had to follow because of the sort of person one was and because of one's past? Occasionally—now that he thought of it—in the past, the sense of repetition had frightened him and had prompted him to rebel violently against the pattern in order to escape from it. Yet at other moments he had welcomed the strangely familiar configuration of mood and circumstance because it had seemed a guaranty of success, and he had been aware of a superstitious need to do things exactly as he had done them before.

It was never, of course, the exact same thing. The circumstances were different. The identity consisted rather in one's somehow sorting out the circumstances in the same way, so that there appeared to be a striking similarity. More like a spiral perhaps: the circle was there, but the level of the circle changed. As now, for instance. To be sure, he was heading into the unknown as he had been the night before he had first seen Mizzi and America, and certainly he had even then been bound for Geoffrey Middlemas. Yet there was this difference: that this time the unknown—the West, where even his young sister Anne had been—could hardly be considered very formidable. It was enticing rather with its promise of a new variation on the American theme. There was this difference, too, that he was no longer fumbling his way toward Geoffrey

Middlemas but knew precisely where to go. Tomorrow or the day after, whenever he chose, he'd be able to walk up to him.

"La Junta," the conductor said. "Colorado."

But it was not the name of the place with its aggressively new, low-roofed, concrete station that mattered, or which state they were in; it was the quality of the air. He had noticed it as soon as he woke up in his berth, and out here on the platform it was unmistakable: that thin, exhilarating edge to the air—mountains! One could even see them now in the distance: massive peaks shouldering into the blue sky—the Rockies. The baffling thing was that for miles and miles in every direction there should be nothing but tame low hills, parched-looking and barren. Yet the air had that exciting, nose-tingling smell of snow.

In the dining car at breakfast the man with the broad-brimmed Stetson who had got on at Kansas City explained with proprietary pride, "That's the altitude you're feeling; you're up some five thousand feet. Wait till we get up to the Raton tunnel, where we cross over into New Mexico; there you'll really feel it. That's seventy-six hundred feet."

The same joyous anticipation that he had known as a boy, standing beside Franz at the train window on his first visit to the Tyrol, possessed him. He waited impatiently for the mountains to draw close. His expectation of precipitous spruce and pine forests, of rushing mountain streams tumbling down rocky ravines, of mountain meadows fragrant with the pungent scent of mint and wild strawberries, quickened him with an indefinable promise of happiness.

But when they came out of the tunnel and were presumably as close to the mountains as they were going to get, he was disappointed. There were no dark forests, no sheer rock walls rising right beside the railroad tracks, no soaring peaks arrayed in majestic palisades such as he had seen only two weeks ago in the Alps. No ice and no snow. There were only blandly sloping hills, sprawling in lazy succession and mottled with scrub growth. Nor was there any sign of the lush mountain meadows which his imagination had dangled before his eyes. "The gray stuff's sage," the rancher from Albuquerque said. "Those evergreens? That's piñon—haven't you ever eaten piñon nuts?"

Even the woods on the distant slopes appeared sparse and the trees not very tall. Once, right alongside the tracks, he noticed a whole stretch of tangled cactus, and the discovery made up for his letdown because the mountains were so unlike the Alps. Why, they must be very far south if there was cactus, real cactus growing wild! Two or three different

kinds at least. It explained why there was no snow on those blunt moun-
taintops, why everything looked so dry.

They passed another small village of straggling, flat-roofed houses.
Those must be the adobe houses Anne had talked about. They were
square, slovenly, drab. An occasional porchlike arrangement—nothing
more than a row of roughly dressed logs stuck in the ground to support
a projecting roof—along one side of a house, to relieve the monotonous
lines. Weeds growing on the flat roofs. Always a row of beam-thick pegs
sticking out a foot or two below the roof line. Ungainly shacks! He
wondered what Anne could have seen in all this, for she had been
enthusiastic even about the houses when she had come back in July
from visiting her friend from Smith College. He voiced his disappointment to the genial, soft-spoken rancher who liked to talk.

"That's right. Good old dobe mud."

"But don't the houses wash away when it rains?"

The rancher's eyes twinkled under his sparse, pale brows which hardly showed against the bright-pink, leathery skin. "That's the first question every tourist asks. When you get to Santa Fe, ask them to show you
a few old houses. Some of them have been there a couple of hundred
years. Dobe lasts pretty good. You mix the mud with straw and dry
the bricks in the sun, and they get as hard as cement. "Cee'-ment" he
pronounced, just as he said "hoh'-tel" and used such odd expressions as
"I like to have died" when presumably he meant that he had nearly lost
his life.

"What are those wooden pegs sticking out from the walls?"

"Those are the beams that support the roof. They've got boards laid
over them for the ceiling and then a couple of feet of dirt on top of the
boards, and that's the roof. The Mexicans call them "vigas." Peeled pine
logs is what they usually are. The Mexicans always let them stick out a
little way. In the fall they hang up their chili on those butts on the south
wall to dry. In a couple of weeks you're going to see those red strings of
chili all over the place."

"The mountains aren't very heavily wooded, are they?" he asked.

The rancher chuckled. "After we get down from Las Vegas a little
bit, I'll show you the Truchas Peaks. That's virgin forest—real wild
country still. Trees that a couple of men can't get their arms around. A
bunch of us packed in there last fall to shoot some elk and we got caught
in a snowstorm and we like to have never got out. We had to hole up
under some rocks for four days."

"Is there a lot of game?"

"All you want. Everything from turkeys to brown bear, and mountain lions thrown in."

"The mountains don't look very high."

"Don't let the distances out here fool you. On a clear day like this you can see eighty or a hundred miles—that's why everything looks kind of small. You take the Truchas Peaks—they're thirteen thousand feet. I call that pretty high."

It was. Elk and even bear; cactus and desert side by side with mountains as high as the Alps! Gradually as he sat looking out through the window, he began to grant that the landscape had a certain impressiveness.

His thoughts veered abruptly to something else: that girl's ranch—how close was it to Santa Fe? He had been full of belated curiosity about Anne's trip during the few short days he had had at home between getting off the boat and getting on the train, but that had been prompted chiefly by his desire to know whether Anne had by any chance run into Geoffrey Middlemas in Santa Fe or heard about him. She hadn't, and apparently she and Aleida had got to Santa Fe only once or twice from the ranch during Anne's stay. At any rate, he had no desire to run into Aleida Gibbs and her airs of older-sister competence!

"Pecos? That's no distance," the rancher said. "Only about twenty-five miles or so. You can see it from the train. . . ."

He felt relieved. Twenty-five miles and over dirt roads that became impassable when it rained or snowed, according to the rancher. He ought to be fairly safe. All the same, what a nuisance that of all the places to come from she would have to pick Santa Fe, this paragon of Anne's who was so wonderful at skiing, at horseback riding, at everything! And according to Anne, she was brilliant and beautiful besides, this glamorous senior last year at Smith whom Anne had been determined he must meet! He smiled in spite of himself: what passionate admiration girls could develop for one another, especially when they were generous by nature like Anne.

It had worked out just as he had known it would. When he had finally run up to Northampton in May to visit Anne and incidentally had met the paragon, they had rubbed each other the wrong way from the moment he had mistaken another girl for Aleida and then for some unfathomable reason had persisted in calling Aleida "Adele." He had been perfectly willing to admit that she had looks and style and that she was bright and probably good at many things. It had hardly been enough to make him fall in love with her or make him jealous of her Amherst escort or to do away with the subtle friction that had lasted all through the picnic Anne had arranged.

Poor, delightful Anne who had schemed so stubbornly all last year to have them meet, only to have it all fall flat. Of course, it was only fair to remember that he had just then been in the throes of the breakup of his love affair with Sibby and not exactly in a state to do justice to anyone. Still, he had not been wrong about that irritating poise—that older-sister air.

No, while he didn't say that it mightn't be interesting to see her again sometime he had not the least desire to run into her now. There was Mizzi to consider in all this! If he did bump into Aleida he would quickly have to take Anne into his confidence about Geoffrey Middlemas, just in case Aleida by some fluke got hold of something and without knowing what it meant wrote to Anne, who might in all innocence mention it at home. In her blind devotion to him Anne had never shown any awareness that there was the least problem about his father: Geoffrey Middlemas might merely have been dead! No need for Mizzi to be upset—now that he had more or less made his peace with her and could even call her "mother" without too much self-consciousness! And Mizzi would be upset if she heard that he had looked up Geoffrey Middlemas!

He saw the Truchas Peaks and then Pecos—no more than a few scattered ranch houses nestling among ancient cottonwood trees in a steep-walled, charming mountain valley which made him question his earlier superciliousness. Or was it, he wondered, his nearness to his goal that filled him with this mixture of eagerness and something very like stage-fright and inclined him to admire rather than to scoff?

But it was after he had transferred to the lumbering little two-coach train that took him and the few other passengers from the main line to Santa Fe, that he became aware of a steadily growing enthusiasm for everything he saw. The landscape appeared all at once rooted and uncompromisingly there—no longer a mere series of pictures on the window pane which he could accept or reject. The mountains were suddenly challenging in their tremendous solidity. The piñon bushes which from the distance had appeared scrubby and drab proved to be ten and fifteen feet high and a rich, deep green, and they might have been planted by a skillful gardener, so satisfying and dramatic was their spacing on the majestically rising slopes. The sage, which before had looked dusty and gray, turned out to be an exquisite silvery green.

Nor was there any letdown in his secret excitement when he reached Santa Fe. The adobe houses here in the city at least were charming. They were squat and massively built and yet had grace. It was the arcades, Peter decided, the surprisingly stately rows of peeled and weather-darkened pine logs with carved wooden corbels on top to support the arcade roofs, which gave the streets their air of mellow elegance.

Small shops, two men on horseback, a farm wagon slowing half a dozen cars to a crawl. A small town and yet in some indefinable way with the feel of a minor metropolis. Was it because the town dated back before Plymouth Rock, as the rancher had explained, or because its isolation up here in this high mountain valley gave it an air of haughty self-sufficiency. And there was something more striking still: the gaiety of the streets!

Bright colors everywhere. The swarthy-faced men with the wide-brimmed, almost feminine straw hats must be Mexicans; and there, the man with the bright-red shirt, driving a donkey laden with firewood across the square—that must be an Indian. Presently he saw another one, with a saffron-colored bandeau circling his forehead and coal-black hair, walking past the hotel entrance just as the taxi stopped. Even the hotel struck him as interesting. It was new but built in the style of the old buildings they had passed, with a handsome lobby, brisk efficiency at the desk, oddly delicate and angular water colors which he took to be Indian in his room.

He kept going to the window to look down into the street while he unpacked and was getting cleaned up. How exotic it was! One could hardly believe that one wasn't abroad. Why, the bus boy who had brought up his bags had talked in Spanish to the two chambermaids in the corridor. He could not bear to stay in his room. He felt that he was wasting time. He must explore!

But in spite of his eagerness to get downstairs he lingered for a few seconds in front of the mirror after he had knotted his tie. He looked and for the first time in months had a sense of seeing himself as a stranger might. Leaner than a year ago, he thought as he ran his hand over his cheek and jaw to see whether he really did not need a shave. His eyes seemed to have grown a darker gray and to have less of a level stare. His forehead seemed softer, too, where it bent around to the temples, and his mouth seemed more ready to smile. Or was all that only because he was conscious now of his dark eyelashes which Sibby had always teased him about and had called indecently long for a man? Still, he really did look more boyish than before. Oddly enough, considering the last few harrowing months with Sibby and the strain of endlessly stepping up production at the factory all last year and at the same time keeping Stelle and his clique from getting too complete control of the company.

Though really nothing about his looks was changed: still the same straight nose and passable chin and mouth and long upper lip and unruly, mouse-colored hair which would never lie straight, no matter how hard he bore down on the brush. At any rate—he pursued his swift inventory —good shoulders, and he was lean and trim, less heavy than when he had worked at the furnaces. Funny that he had never managed to grow that one extra inch to bring him up to an even six feet. It still gave Bob an edge: the inch and Bob's Sheff degree and the fact that he had Mr. Thorson—a father to be proud of, documented, and always there to be produced—would always allow Bob to patronize him. Would allow him also, Peter remembered with a grin, to forget about the twenties and fifties Bob had borrowed during the past spring with his Yaleman-about-to-graduate-and-sure-of-a-big-job breeziness.

He realized all at once that his scrutiny of himself had been prompted by a remnant of his old obsession that he had to grow and grow before he would be ready—be big, powerful, important enough—to confront Geoffrey Middlemas, just as a year ago he had a little fearfully scanned himself in Montclair before starting out for New York to meet Sibby for the first time since Vienna from a sudden uneasiness that she might no longer care for him. The phrase he had used then came back to him. He grimaced at the mirror and said out loud, "What a mug!" Then he slipped on his coat and hurried downstairs.

Across the street from the hotel there was a large curio shop, its windows enticing with colorful woven blankets, earthenware bowls and jars decorated with the same bizarre designs he had noticed on some of the woodwork in the hotel, much silver and turquoise jewelry. He went inside. A middle-aged man with a leonine head and a cultured voice was showing two well-dressed women around the shop, telling them about Indian pottery, about Indians. Two men and a girl, who also did not look like clerks, were sitting on barrel-shaped, thong-laced, presumably Indian drums by a rear window, drinking tea and talking animatedly.

He looked around and strained not to miss the explanations and bits of history the two women tourists drew from the man with the impressive head. He learned a lot: the blankets were woven by hand by Navaho

Indians and dyed with vegetable dyes; the bizarre designs on blankets and baskets and pottery were Indian symbols for rain, lightning, corn, squash; most of the Indians lived in pueblos, which were small towns, but the Navahos were nomads and depended on their herds of sheep for a livelihood instead of on agriculture, like the pueblo Indians; the little carved and painted wooden statues of saints were called "santos" and had been made by Mexicans; the baskets came from the Zuni pueblo; the turquoise-studded bracelets and rings and belts were Navaho. . . . He bought a bracelet for Anne and asked a few questions himself. He discovered that the adobe plaster on the houses was applied and smoothed with bare hands and that this was what gave it its charming unevenness. He was told of half a dozen things he must not fail to see.

He started with the reddish-stone cathedral at the head of the street. It proved no more than a large church, Romanesque in style, unpretentious to the point of bareness in its clean lines and freedom from gilt gimcrack inside, and yet strangely appealing and imposing, too, by reason of what the man in the curio shop had said about the first archbishop's struggle in the last century to carry out his dream of a cathedral in this mountain-desert diocese of impoverished Mexicans and Indians. He knelt for a while in one of the pews, vaguely wishing that he could pray, then thought of Geoffrey Middlemas and went back outside. He passed the plain archbishop's palace and a convent school, came to a bridge over a creek which had gone dry, and followed an unpaved street that seemed to wind at random up a slight slope.

As he strolled and looked, his enthusiasm grew. Lovely old houses set back from the street behind waist-high garden walls; rows of towering, sentrylike poplars fronting the street; enticingly secretive gardens glimpsed behind a thicket of lilac bushes or over a high wall. Instead of a sameness about the houses which he had expected after his first view of them from the train, it was their delightful variety which struck him here: those pine-pillared arcades—"portales" the man in the shop had called them—and the patios they sometimes enclosed could evidently be used in an infinite number of ways. But what enchanted him most was the texture of the adobe which held the light like some subtle velvet cloth. Why, one might be in France—in Arles—on this poplar-lined, quaintly rustic and yet urban street patterned with the rich shadows cast by the trees! And what an amazing light! No wonder artists came here to paint.

He returned pleasantly tired from his walk. It was only a little after five. While he had been gone the lobby of the hotel had taken on a remarkable air of coziness for so sprawling and exposed a hall. Small groups of people stood or sat around everywhere, laughing and talking. Local people obviously. One could tell the mere visitors—especially the women—by their city clothes and their isolation in the midst of the surrounding gaiety. The local women were all without hats. They wore much brighter colors than the visitors. Some of them wore Navaho bracelets and necklaces, and one of them even had around the waist of her purple velvet blouse one of the heavy silver belts he had seen in the curio shop. The men were in tweeds, in blue denim jackets, in bright-colored wool shirts. A good many of them wore those oddly cut Western pants he had first seen on the rancher on the train, narrowing down to the ankle and without cuffs, made of some tan whipcord or twill. Without exception they all had more or less wide-brimmed hats. They all seemed to know one another, drifted from one small group to another, made their farewells and were hailed by somebody else. It was like a party almost.

He started to look at the pictures on the walls. There were paintings of desert landscapes with startling rock formations that looked as if some giant had carved them to amuse himself, and several paintings of Indians. All the artists showed the same preoccupation with the problems of catching the incredibly brilliant light. He noted the names. Nothing by Geoffrey Middlemas!

He saw that one of the settees by the three big French windows which gave on the patio was unoccupied except for a bald, large-faced man in a leather jacket and riding breeches and puttees. He sat down at the other end of the settee and looked around again. Already the furniture and the decorations—the square, heavy chairs, with cowhide laced with thongs to the frame to form the backs and seats; the elaborate tinwork candelabra which were Mexican; the stylized Indian symbols carved and painted on the woodwork everywhere—no longer appeared as strange as they had at first.

The two women whom he had seen in the curio shop were sitting now with another woman and a man by one of the writing desks, talking with forced vivacity and stealing frequent glances at the lively groups all around them, their envy parading as faintly patronizing curiosity. The tourists generally looked well-to-do, but that was to be expected in a hotel of this sort. What interested him was that a good many of the local people showed signs of somewhat more than ordinary prosperity: fine wool shirts under the frayed tweed coats; obviously expensive boots below the faded denim pants; wrist watches which plainly had not come from some busy-corner jewelry store. Their voices and manners betrayed breeding and a certain amount of boredom underneath their apparent zest. Santa Fe, then, belonged to the category of swank rustic retreats, like a lot of old villages in Connecticut, where the wealthy who were tired of big-city elegance could make a hobby of simplicity. Gentleman ranchers instead of gentlemen farmers as in the East!

The man at the other end of the settee finished reading the last of the letters he had been opening one by one, slipped it back in its envelope and turned to him. "You just get in?"

"Yes, a couple of hours ago."

"Going to stay or just passing through?"

Peter tried to size up the man while he answered his blunt inquiries. His breeches and puttees and his hat were old and not very clean; only the brown leather jacket looked new—too new; the two paper sacks on the floor held groceries. Was he a real rancher? Still, he spoke like an Easterner. He sounded intelligent and there was something sensitive about the broad, faintly bloated face, behind the gruff voice. Was he an artist perhaps? But his hands looked coarse, with thick fingers and corded veins, and there were half-healed scratches and gashes on them, as if he had recently done some hard outdoor work.

"What are you doing out here?"

It seemed somehow frivolous with this gruff, humorless man to claim that he was just another tourist who'd come to gape. "I thought I might do a little painting. I'd heard about the light."

"You a painter?"

"No—no, I'm not a painter." Already he was all tangled up! "I've done a little drawing, that's all. I thought I'd take some lessons with somebody in Santa Fe."

"Lessons in what?"

"In oil painting. I'd like to learn the oil technique."

"Whom did you study with back east?"

"Nobody. I palled around with some young artists in New York and that's how I came to draw." Nothing about the drawing lessons when he was a boy. He had already said too much. Vienna mustn't be mentioned; the man might know Geoffrey Middlemas, say something to him. "Heck, I don't know the first thing about art," Peter laughed at himself.

Wryness, but not the least amusement, showed in the big, puffy face and in the hard, brown eyes. "That's what I thought. There's no such thing as a little painting. If you want to paint it takes all you've got."

A painter, unquestionably, although he did not look like one!

"Yes, I think I can understand that. Are there many artists out here?"

"The woods are full of them."

"Are there many good ones?"

"Just look around," and his head indicated the walls. "You can see for yourself. Been over to the museum?"

"No, I'm going there tomorrow. Which artists would you say are the best ones?"

"I wouldn't say. That's up to the critics. There's Henri and Davy . . ."

Half a dozen names, but not the one he was waiting for. He asked cautiously, "Is there an artist out here called Geoffrey Middlemas?"

"Yes, he's here. Are you going to take lessons with him?"

"Why, no, I don't even know him. I just happened to hear about him in the East. Is he any good?"

"He's all right." There were all kinds of reservations and secret strictures in his tone. "He's a portrait painter."

He's got a chip on his shoulder, Peter thought. He asked, "Is it bad to be a portrait painter?"

The husky shoulders in the leather jacket hunched aggressively, then relaxed. The big head—brusquely uncovered and proving to be bald—waggled once from side to side in an amusing dumb show of resignation and reckless impartiality. "Nobody said it was. It's just dangerous. A portrait painter has to please his clients and their families, while an artist has first of all got to please himself. You can't do both."

"But wasn't Sargent a good painter? He painted a lot of portraits, didn't he?"

"Sargent didn't have to please anybody but himself. People liked what he gave them or he told them to go to a society photographer. There aren't many Sargents around."

Peter did not dare continue his inquiry about Geoffrey Middlemas. The man was quick—touchy, too. He asked, "Where do most of the painters in Santa Fe live?"

"All over. A lot of them live up on the Camino. I don't suppose you know where that is? You walk down here to the cathedral and turn right until you come to the Santa Fe River. The first street after you cross the bridge is Canyon Road. You walk up Canyon for about half a mile and you'll come to the Camino del Monte Sol."

"Is that where a painter like Middlemas, for instance, lives?"

"Yes, he's up there. He's got a little house next to the one that looks like a church. There are some old tamarisks out in front. Do you know what a tamarisk tree looks like?"

"No," he said, got himself instructed in the feathery appearance of the tamarisk, and immediately plunged into further questions about Santa Fe to dispel any impression that he was particularly interested in Geoffrey Middlemas. The man in the leather jacket, for all his bristliness, was gruffly eager to be of help. Another of those rough diamonds, Peter thought as he listened to his description of an Indian dance. There was no longer any question in his mind whether the man was an artist. Not only had he spoken with authority about painting, but all his descriptions evoked sights rather than sounds.

A part of him was not listening at all, was wholly taken up with secret exultation. He knew now that *he* was here and even where he lived—Camino del Monte Sol.

People were beginning to drift toward the dining room. He was getting hungry himself and a little worried that he was taking up too much of the man's time. But just as he was about to thank him for his helpfulness and get up, the brown eyes came back from the lively group by one of the pillars and the man said abruptly, "There's Middlemas right now over at the desk. I'll take you over and introduce you to him."

Alarm froze Peter like a bath of ice. An unbearable excitement succeeded his alarm. It cost him an effort to turn his head slowly with pretended indifference. Two men were standing by the desk, both about the same height, both with their backs turned and their hats off, exasperatingly alike except that the nearer one had gray hair and looked somewhat heavier.

"No," he said quickly and with such urgent refusal that he realized he sounded rude. "Thanks, but I don't want to bother you."

"No bother. I thought you wanted to meet him."

Peter tried to joke. "I don't know that I'm so keen on it after what you've said about portrait painters. Anyhow, I'll be here for a while. There's lots of time." But he had to look again—he wanted to look toward the desk. "By the way, which one is Middlemas?"

"The one in the riding getup—the one that's talking to the clerk."

The dark-haired one! He was free now to look, but his seething excitement, his very need to devour him with his eyes, curiously blurred his vision, just as it had done seven years ago when Aunt Wetti had shown him the photographs of Mizzi and him. He caught a glimpse of a tanned, high-colored face—not so lean as he had thought—without gaining any impression of its quality or character, an unrelated glimpse of a hand stretched out to take a telegram blank from the clerk, a still more random glimpse of a greenish tweed jacket and gleaming brown riding boots. That very instant even the side of his face was withdrawn as Geoffrey Middlemas bent over the desk to write, and Peter had a sense of mingled triumph and loss. Then this was *he.*

Irritation, as if he were somehow responsible for Geoffrey Middlemas, stirred in Peter after his final glance. He had not missed the faintly caustic inflection with which the man beside him had referred to the riding togs. Why did he have to wear shiny boots as if he were going riding in Central Park?

Peter asked, "Who is the other man?"

"That's Piggot, the writer—Ralph Piggot."

He was still there, pausing in his writing for a moment, raising his head to say something to Piggot, who was talking to the clerk. Very white teeth; he drew his lips back when he talked; a deep furrow down to the corner of his mouth and another down to the jaw; dark hair graying at the temples, but an almost youthful face because of its pinkness and the white teeth. But he must not look too long. Nor could he stay here if by any chance he and that fellow Piggot threatened to come over to the settee! Peter poised himself for instant retreat, ready to jump up and mutter an excuse—bathroom, anything. Also—it occurred to him while he pretended to observe the two girls and the man with the beret by the pillar—dangerous to stay here at the hotel too long! If he ran into this painter again who obviously knew Geoffrey Middlemas——

"I've been wondering about the chance of renting a studio or a small apartment."

"You aren't going to find any apartments here. What you do is to rent a little house."

"I see," he said, swiftly docile. "I sort of thought I'd like to be a little away from the center of town."

"You might find something on the Camino."

"I don't think that would be the right place for me. Isn't there some other section? Fact is I'd rather be a little way out."

"Did you come by car? Because if you haven't a car you can't go too far out; you've got to come into town for your groceries."

Geoffrey Middlemas, he saw out of the corner of his eye, was leaving— yes, making some final remark to the writer by the corner of the desk, giving an odd little jerk to the hat in his hand at his side, briefly listening to Piggot, nodding again and then heading for the door. He had already acquired one of those Western hats! Peter strained for a last look at his back. . . .

"No," he said, "I came on the train but I like to walk. I wouldn't mind walking back and forth."

He felt himself subjected to a sudden sharp scrutiny by the blunt brown eyes. "If you really want to be out of town I might be able to find something for you in Tesuque. That's five miles north of here. It's where the old archbishop used to live and it's nothing but a small native village. There's a good hotel out there—Bishop's Lodge—where you can go for some of your meals if you don't want to do all your own cooking; it's in easy walking distance. But five miles in and five miles out every time you want to come to town is quite a walk. I drive in a couple of times a week, and you'd be welcome to come in with me then."

It had been thrown out tentatively, grudgingly, like a challenge almost. Half of Peter's attention had been on Piggot who had stopped to talk to a very gaunt man, with a red silk neckkerchief caught in a silver buckle below his cadaverous chin by way of a tie. Now that Geoffrey Middle-mas had gone it was Piggot whom he felt irresistibly compelled to watch. The very nearness of the writer made the five miles to Tesuque sound less far. He said, "That sounds like just the place. Are there any painters there?"

"Well, I'm a painter. Yes, there are a few painters out there. I'm Dave Buell. What's your name?"

None of the pictures on the wall had borne that signature; yet the man had undeniable air of being of some consequence. A more pressing concern flashed into his brain, alarmed him for an instant: with Piggot so near, with all these people knowing one another, *he* might find out that he was here! And the hotel register—he had never given that a thought. Too late now for that.

He smiled hastily and said with the glib eagerness with which some of the men had invariably introduced themselves at the engineering society meetings in New York, using their blustery formula, "Peter's the name. I'm certainly glad to know you, Mr. Buell."

Buell gave a brusque nod. "Well, Peters, there's a house that I know you can have because the fellow who's been living there has just moved out. There is furniture of a sort, though it won't be anything like you've probably been used to. The important thing if you want to paint is that the living room has a good north light. The last fellow had that put in.

Another good thing—the Mexican family that own the house live right next door, and the woman would probably do your cleaning for you. You could have her come in a couple of times a week."

"Is there any place where one can rent a car by the week or the month? I wouldn't want to bother you for rides all the time."

"Yes, you can rent a car if you can afford it. Two or three garages in town that'll rent you a car." A note of irrascibility and the dubious look on his face again, as if he already questioned Peter's seriousness and his fitness to take it and regretted having spoken at all. He warned, truculently almost, "You aren't going to find any modern conveniences out there. No bathrooms and no central——"

"How are you, Dave? How are things in Tesuque?"

The writer had come toward them so quickly that there had been no time to get away. Nor was there any reason for him to leave, Peter felt. There was no real danger now. On the contrary he might learn something more about Geoffrey Middlemas. He merely withdrew half a step and tried to efface himself.

"How are you, Piggot?" the painter said without much enthusiasm.

"I saw your canyon picture in the Chicago show. It was right in the center of a wall and it looked fine. How's the work coming?"

Piggot had a pasty complexion and a broody, sagging face but fine eyes. Something compelling about the eyes, which quarreled with the down-turned corners of the mouth. Good clothes and that strenuously well-bred—or was it, well-heeled?—Riviera English which one got to hear on boats and in Paris and at Connecticut parties sometimes. A husky physique, and yet some physical assurance lacking; voice pitched too high or too theatrically low; too much ravaged sensitiveness and not enough healthy sensuality perhaps. Were all writers and painters as taut and unsmiling, Peter wondered, as these two?

"No work," Buell grumbled. "I've been putting a new roof on my studio." As if to put a decisive end to the questions about himself, he said, "This is Mr. Peters, Piggot. He's come out here to paint."

Piggot shook hands and to Peter's surprise proved capable of an astonishing amount of warmth. "And you're a painter?"

He denied it quickly. "I'm just trying to learn."

"He's going to live out in Tesuque," Buell said as if it were all arranged.

"That's a good place to work. One needs a quiet place. This is a violent country which makes unusual demands. . . ." Without warning,

Piggot launched into a dissertation on the difficulties that confronted the creative artist who wanted to live in Santa Fe. It appeared that the sparse population and the lack of things to do created a sort of spiritual vacuum in which some individuals went to pieces—exploded like toy balloons. It appeared that a good many artists or would-be artists who came ended by drinking themselves to death. "That's one aspect of the frontier never sufficiently stressed. A man may have failed back east and if he comes out here and succeeds in making a new start, he is all right. But if he fails out here, he's through. Well, good luck! I hope I'll see you again." He ended his bewildering discourse as abruptly as he had started it, nodded to Buell, and went to join the group by the pillar.

What a passion to instruct older men had! And with what proprietary gusto everyone he had met so far said "out here," as if this were a paradise to which only he had the key, and at the same time a treacherous wilderness against the perils of which he had to warn. As if this were an island in the Pacific somewhere, thousands of miles from telegraphs and hotels. Why, it was ludicrous!

Buell was saying, "I have to be in town Saturday morning anyway. If you want to I'll take you out to Tesuque and let you look at the house. Then I'll bring you back." He was picking up his mail from the settee, stuffing several letters into the pocket of his leather jacket.

Peter took it for his dismissal, promised to be in the lobby on Saturday, thanked him, and walked away toward the staircase and then on a sudden impulse out of the hotel into the street. He had seen Piggot head for the dining room and he felt reluctant all at once to expose himself so soon again to Piggot's scrutiny. No use pressing one's luck too far. The writer might just happen to mention him to Geoffrey Middlemas, bragging how he had given a young painter some tips about living "out here," describe him perhaps. After a while, he could go back and find a table where he would not catch Piggott's eye. He was much less hungry now anyway. . . . He decided to walk for a few minutes, just far enough to make sure that by following Buell's directions he could find the Camino del Monte Sol.

After he had passed the convent school and crossed the bridge over the dry riverbed once more and turned into the first street on the left, he saw that it was the same street he had walked that afternoon. He checked with two little Spanish boys who giggled and had difficulty in understanding him at first, so that it took a whole minute to extract an answer from them, to make sure that he was on Canyon Road.

It was beginning to be dusk. Here and there lights showed in the windows beyond the garden walls. He noticed a delicious, incenselike fragrance which had not been in the street that afternoon, realized that it came from the chimneys, and resolved to ask what wood produced the aromatic smoke. A sleek touring car passed him and jounced gaily over the ruts as it disappeared around a mild turn screened by the rows of poplars.

How amusing, he thought; an hour ago when I walked by this same tree with the twin trunks, I was a complete stranger in town and so free to do as I liked that I even felt a little lost. Now I've practically agreed to take a house in a place I've never seen and mayn't even like, I've put myself down as a guy who wants to paint, I've as good as committed myself to taking painting lessons I don't want—all because of a conversational maneuver, because I had to produce quickly some reason for being in town. One always talked too much! No, he chuckled inside himself, it was the price he had had to pay for information he had to have.

Hoofbeats behind him were coming closer. He stepped out of the road toward a crumbly adobe wall, turned curiously to watch the two horses—one fawn and one black—coming up at a smart trot, found himself for one split second looking right into Geoffrey Middlemas' eyes, not fifteen feet away! A cursory, politely impersonal inspection—no more. He himself helped to make it that by instantly, almost too hurriedly, withdrawing his glance, brushing over the woman on the fawn-colored horse, pretending to need all his attention for the low-growing cedar branches sticking out over the wall. The cedar sheltered him and allowed him to steal another glance as they went by. The woman—riding breeches, loose-hanging, tasseled chamois jacket over the white blouse, white-and-black-beaded leather gauntlets—presented a delicately modeled profile under the Western hat with the bead-embroidered band. Geoffrey Middlemas had long lashes, just like his own. He heard the woman say something in a clear voice, the sounds drifting back tantalizingly along with the staccato clopety-clop of the hoofs. For an instant he heard Geoffrey Middlemas speak as he turned to her. "Eleven o'clock"—unemphatic but very clear and distinct.

Peter went out into the road again, to keep them in view as they drew ahead. The woman looked rather tall, slim. She sat very erect in the saddle and yet looked at her ease—no doubt what Anne meant by a "good seat." Geoffrey Middlemas held himself rather stiffly, compared with her, but his shoulders and back had had something of that same brittle tenseness even in the hotel.

Who was the woman? Was *he* married? It was the one thing it had never even occurred to Peter to ask. He must find out!

He lost them around a bend although he had quickened his step. He walked even faster and saw them once more when he got past the bend, far up the road. Then they disappeared for good. His curiosity would not let him stop. He found the Camino del Monte Sol, turned up that, recognized the big house from Buell's description, saw the feathery tamarisks and the little house set back some fifty feet from the road. The two horses were tied to a rail beside an old roofed-over well. Behind a large uncurtained window, lights were on.

He walked past the wide opening in the garden wall through which the uneven driveway led down to one side of the house, went on up the road a little way, and came back. The horses were still tied beside the well, and the lights in the house were still on. Reluctantly he forced himself to walk back to the hotel.

He felt elated over his jaunt. He felt that the house with the lighted window and even the woman were allies which held Geoffrey Middlemas safely tethered and tied. But before he was halfway through dinner uneasiness insinuated itself into his self-congratulation. He inquired first of the waitress and then of the desk clerk where he could find saddle horses for rent, and he did not rest easy until he had walked to the livery stable a few blocks from the hotel and had assured himself that he could rent a horse by the hour or the day. He asked for a gentle one for next morning at ten.

Apparently—he half mocked at himself—I still have to go on proving to myself that I'm as good as he! There's a degree of cowardice in that. What's knowing how to ride got to do with my going up to Geoffrey Middlemas?

His memory of the woman on horseback answered him. Supposing they asked him to go riding with them: he would not want her to think him a clumsy fool! .... He fell asleep amid a profusion of comforting images of himself boldly sitting a horse, dashingly galloping over the sage, coolly dismounting on the Camino del Monte Sol.

CHAPTER TWO

O My Father, O My Father!

HE realized only in the morning how eager he was to sit on a horse and learn how to ride.

I'm as excited as a kid that's just read his first cowboy story and can't wait to get near a horse, he thought as he put on the gray wool shirt and the pair of blue denim pants he had bought on the plaza as soon as the clerk had opened the haberdashery store.

The livery stable on Don Gaspar Avenue, with its air of outlived grandeur and stubborn persistence in the face of the motorcar, appeared to be a favorite meeting place for idlers of every sort. Half a dozen Mexican youths and several cowboys lolled against the low wall. Two spry old men had stopped by the gate to pass the time of day. Some prosperous-looking ranchers stood laughing together inside the yard.

The horse was ready for him: a dirty-white mare with a shaggy mane and the lumbering proportions of a draft horse, her bloated belly lazily straining against and then sucking away from the saddle girth, one hind leg crooked under her as if she were waiting between the shafts of a milk wagon. Yet his initial disappointment was quickly swallowed up by ex-

27

citement when the Mexican groom handed him the reins. Almost volup-
tuously he put off the moment of getting on. "What's her name?"

"Compoun'."

"What?"

"Compound."

He could make nothing of the name, but his possession of it gave him
a sense of mastery like the reins. As nonchalantly as he could he swung
himself up, groped and found the other stirrup with his foot, heard the
pleasant creaking of the saddle under him.

"Ees th-ee stirrup long enough?"

It seemed to him that, if anything, the stirrups were far too long. The
knees of the horsemen in Central Park had been much higher up. "You
tell me," he said. "Do they look all right?"

The Mexican squinted at the stirrups, shrugged, displayed his gold
eyeteeth. "Ees all right."

Only half reassured, Peter flicked the reins and clicked his tongue. The
horse started obediently, took four or five steps, then stopped. He tried
again and added a prod with his knees; once again a few reluctant steps
ending in a halt. He cajoled, "Come on, Compound," and hit the big
rump behind him with the flat of his hand.

So far no one had paid much attention to him or at least he had been
able to pretend to himself that he was not being watched, but now there
was no escaping the fact that an increasingly open hilarity was spreading
from the Mexicans along the wall to the ranchers by the gate.

A short, bandy-legged cowboy called, "Why don't you build a fire
under her?"

One of the ranchers advised, "Kick her. She'll go."

He tried it. The mare exploded into a jarring trot. There was a boisterous chorus of "Ride 'im, cowboy!" and laughter from the men along the
wall.

The trot lasted only as far as the gate. A few feet this side of the little
group of cowboys the mare slowed down and stopped. He looked around
angrily for the groom who was taking his time coming up and not even
bothering to conceal his enjoyment of the scene. "What's wrong with this
nag? She doesn't want to go."

The Mexican showed his gold teeth. "*Quien sabe, señor?* Maybe he eat
too much."

The bandy-legged cowboy said, "What you need is a quirt. She's just
lazy. You gotta whup her."

The tall, lean cowboy with him, the one with the baby face, said in a soft Texas voice, "Kick her. You ain't gonna hurt her."

He said, "I thought the horse was supposed to do the work." He got off, handed the reins to the stableboy, and walked over to the burly old man with the leather waistcoat and the big Stetson who had rented him the horse.

"You didn't go for much of a ride!"

He tried to keep his irritation in check. "That horse isn't very lively. She won't go."

"Well, you asked for a gentle one."

"Not that gentle. Haven't you got one that'll move?"

"Yeah, I got one livelier. You don't want one that's too lively, though, if you say you haven't ever been on a horse before. Lobo'll be about right for you. Joe," he called the stableboy, "saddle up Lobo for this fellow."

Peter strolled over to the two cowboys while he waited for the new horse. He said, "That dobbin's like a double bed—good to take a nap on maybe."

The bandy-legged cowboy chuckled. "She's a good pack horse. She goes up a hill like a truck. That's why they call her 'Compound.' You want to watch how you get off a horse," he warned. "You always want to get on or off on his left, or he may rare up on you. Left's how every horse is trained."

"I see," he said gratefully. "I didn't know that. What else did I do wrong?"

"Well, you want to hold him pretty tight. If he feels any slack in the reins, he's liable to take out for the tall timber. Not too tight," he warned; "tight enough to let him know you're boss."

"Hold him," the lanky cowboy said in his soft voice, with a faintly derisive air of explaining the obvious.

They were after all meaning to be helpful and not trying to lead him on as he had suspected for a moment. He stayed with them until Goldtooth came leading a reddish-brown horse into the yard.

He liked the new horse. Smaller than the other one, trim, something skittish about its head. He patted its nose and said, "Hi, there, Lobo," passed one rein around Lobo's neck and swung himself up. Almost instantly the horse reared, rose up so high that he felt the pummel dig into his stomach and felt himself ignominiously sliding off over the back of the saddle. In alarm, hastily, he jumped off.

Guffaws from the gallery around the wall greeted him as soon as his

feet touched the ground. He grinned back as good-naturedly as he could.
The two cowboys had become strangers again in their glistening-eyed
enjoyment of the fun. Worse than that, several passers-by out on the sidewalk had stopped to watch.

He scolded, "What the hell is the matter with you, Lobo?" and gave
the reins a sharp downward jerk. Lobo looked disarmingly docile but
started to do a little sideways dance the moment Peter attempted to put
his left foot in the stirrup again. Two little Mexican boys shouted ecstatically, "Mira!" just as he got a new grip on the pummel and swung himself off the ground. This time the horse rose before he could even get his
leg across the saddle. He landed on Lobo's hindquarters, lost even his left
stirrup, and slipped off. The merriment became boisterous along the wall.
Hastily, to escape his ludicrous isolation out in the middle of the yard
and meet any excessive laughter head on, he led the horse toward the
two cowboys.

"What do you do when he acts like that—shoot him?"

"Aw, he's just payful," the short cowboy said. "He's all right. Hit him
between the ears and he'll stay down. Hit him with a stick, that wagon
spoke over there's about right. Want me to show you?"

He said eagerly, "I wish you would."

He had avoided looking at the two or three passers-by who were still
lingering hopefully by the gate. But now while the stubby cowboy bent
over to pick up the heavy spoke from the ground, something insistent
about the way the young woman in the light-gray tweed suit was looking
at him made him glance at her. The smiling challenge in her eyes became
an open smile.

Oh, no! he rebelled indignantly as he recognized the arched brows, the
smile, the way she held herself. Not *she!* Of all the places to pick between
Pecos and Santa Fe, she has to pick this one to come to this morning!
Just my luck, he thought sourly even while he returned her smile and
started toward her with the reluctant horse tugging back on the reins.

"Hello," she said altogether too brightly for him, her exuberance and
the gaiety in her hazel-colored eyes due—he was sure—to the ridiculous
spectacle he had made of himself.

"Hello, Aleida." He said it very carefully. Not likely that he was going
to call her 'Adele' again; this was already quite sufficiently like those uncomfortable moments in Northampton last spring when she had so neatly
and emphatically put him in his place for not making an appearance on
either of the two week ends when she had been Anne's guest in West-

chester—for not showing enough enthusiasm to meet her. And this was her own bailiwick even more than Smith College had been. As if to impress him with the fact, she called every bit as gaily as she had called to him, "Hello, Curly! Hi, Shorty!" to the two cowboys who greeted back with flattered alacrity, "How-do, Aleida?" and "Ha-ow you, Miss Aleida?" an unmistakable male homage in their voices to her glow and self-possessed attractiveness in the gray tailored suit and the pert cloche hat, and to her legs perhaps.

She had turned back to him. "I had no idea you were in Santa Fe. I got a letter from Anne only two days ago—she didn't say a word about your coming."

"Anne didn't know, I guess. I'm just stopping off—and putting on a free show learning how to ride."

She politely refused to admit that she had seen him teetering in one stirrup and sliding off Lobo's rump. "How long are you going to stay?"

"Not very long—a few days maybe."

"What a shame! You might have liked to see the ranch, and I'm just going away. I have to be in Dallas for two weeks." Sincere, yes; conscientiously gracious like a hostess at a large party to a guest of a guest who's tagged along; warm because enthusiasm and a lurking exuberance seemed to be part of her temperament, so that even now she had something about her of a skier triumphantly poised on the brow of a hill before the breath-taking descent; but also cool and pointedly aloof, to remind him that her interest in him did not go beyond the fact that he was the brother of Anne. Perfect with me, he thought. . . . "If you're still here two weeks from now, perhaps you'd like to come out to dinner sometime. We're in Pecos. You'll find Father listed in the telephone book."

"Thank you, Aleida. If I'm still here I'll certainly call." Just catch me doing it, he thought.

"Good luck with the horseback riding!" She gave him an annoyingly lighthearted farewell smile and went.

He turned with a mixture of irritation and relief to Shorty, who stood waiting with the wagon spoke in his hand. "You going to show me?"

"Yes, sure—nothing to it."

At least she had not seen him on that first horse: that would have been even worse! . . . He watched Shorty land heavily in the saddle and look immediately as if he were fused to the horse. Lobo tossed his head but did not attempt to rear. Only once, after Shorty had walked him around the yard and pulled him up short, his forefeet rose from the ground. The spoke cracked down hard between his ears. After that Lobo trotted and walked exactly as the chunky cowboy wanted him to.

"He ain't going to give you any trouble," Shorty assured him as he turned the horse over to him. "If he rares up just hit him with this. . . ."

Lobo started out of the gate at a lively trot, found that too slow after only a couple of blocks, and lunged into a somewhat terrifying gallop which became suddenly exhilarating when Peter saw that he need not hold on so hard with his knees and thighs, that there was a reassuring sameness to each forward plunge. He began to enjoy the speed. He began to wish that Aleida could see him on the horse now.

But he did not wish it for long. Lobo was displaying an inexplicable tendency to shy at a mere rock or a piece of wood by the side of the road, to give sudden sideway jumps that threatened each time to pitch him out of the saddle and land him on the ground. He was only vaguely aware that there was a pungent fragrance to the scrubby sagebrush crushed under the pounding hoofs and that the tiny leaves of the sage were not gray but silvery. His knees ached from gripping so tight. He experimented but could not decide whether it was better to rest all his weight in the saddle or to rise in the stirrups on each downward plunge. . . . There must be a more comfortable way of doing all this, he told himself angrily when after three hours he at last allowed the horse to head back toward town; I'm going to learn how to ride if it's the last thing I do!

No one was around to watch him get off at the livery stable. The little boys and the Mexican idlers had evidently all gone to lunch. He ran into the two cowboys in front of a small eating place a few doors down the street, Shorty twisting a toothpick between his puckered lips and the lean, handsome one rolling a cigarette.

Shorty took the toothpick out of his mouth. "How'd you get along?"

"Fine; he didn't rear up once. But he has another cute trick: he shies at every piece of paper in the road or even at a white rock, and then he jumps about three feet to one side." He watched Shorty's bushy, straw-colored eyebrows twitch and saw the lean cowboy grin. "I'd like you to give me some lessons. I'd want to pay for it."

Shorty said, "Curly's got some horses."

"Yeah, we can give you some les-sons—" the word seemed to amuse both of them—"if you want to come out to my place."

"Where's that?"

"Out Canyon Road."

"Anywhere near the Camino del Monte Sol?"

"Beyond the Camino, all the way out. Ask for Curly Davis—anybody'll show you."

The prospect of the cowboys' expert tutelage elated him all afternoon. It was like a pleasant mist that blurred the figure of Geoffrey Middlemas and at the same time sharpened his enticing memory of the woman in the chamois jacket on the fawn-colored horse. He glanced into the window of the curio shop across from the hotel, saw that the man from whom he had bought the bracelet and whom he had intended to ask about her was busy with customers, and with a sense of saving something agreeable for later went to the museum instead.

No picture by Middlemas—he noted with disappointment, with a glum sense of loss almost, as he scanned the list of exhibitors handed him by the attendant—but there was one by Buell, a mountain scene. He studied it carefully. The color was subtle and lyrical, astonishingly sensitive for so blunt and cross-grained a man as Buell appeared to be. There was no sentimentality. Great boulders lay in the morning sun on a desolate mountain slope and looked immensely massive and stark; a few stunted pines stuck up stubbornly here and there; a tiny Indian came riding out of the purple shadows of a canyon into the sunlight but the minuscule Indian had clearly not been put into the picture to convey some trite message about the awesome disproportion between man and nature or about the rebirth spelled by the sunrise but solely for the brilliant splotch of red his blanket supplied. Nothing but rocks; yet the whole thing sang, Peter told himself when he finally turned to some of the other pictures.

It was too late when he came out of the museum to see much of the old Palace of the Governors which the man in the curio shop had advised him to go and see. He contented himself with a stroll up the street which continued the north side of the plaza, saw from a sign that it was called Palace Avenue, rather liked the more modern and pretentious houses that made the wide street seem like a haughty city cousin of the Camino del Monte Sol, walked to the end of it and saw that it crossed the dry river and came out on Canyon Road. Immediately he turned around. There was no sense in letting Geoffrey Middlemas see him too frequently, become aware of him and start asking perhaps who he was. Not till he was sure of not making a laughingstock of himself on a horse, especially if the woman who sat a horse so elegantly was going to be around! *Not till I'm ready to go to him!*

The excuse, once he had put it into words, kept him from going into the hotel dining room—where the sallow-faced writer with the too-knowing eyes might be having dinner again—and drove him to eat in a drab little restaurant outside. It made him glance cautiously around the lobby before he went up to the desk for his key; made him spend the rest of the evening in his room, hiding almost, writing first to Anne to tell her that he had stopped off in Santa Fe and meant to stay for a few days— "Oh, yes, I ran into your friend Aleida; she was just going away"—and then to the factory in Harrison to have his mail forwarded.

It was the riding lesson the next morning that gave him back a sense of having the upper hand—of being the one to play the tune to which Geoffrey Middlemas was going to dance. After the first half hour he actually began to enjoy himself. The cow pony which Shorty, who seemed to be at once Curly's friend and his hired man, had saddled for him was not only eager to go but responded to the slightest touch. Half the game was in having a decent horse, he told himself delightedly as he loped along between the two cowboys.

They did not volunteer any advice, but if he asked for help they told him what he did wrong. He learned to sit out a trot and he discovered that the easy gallop which they called a "lope" was the smoothest and most exhilarating pace of all. His legs were only a little sore after four solid hours in the saddle when Curly took him in an old pickup down to the hotel. Why, it was as easy as sitting in a rocking chair; a couple of more lessons and he'd know how to ride, he assured himself during lunch.

He had walked boldly into the hotel dining room and he looked calmly around. He had become the hunter again. There was no one he knew either in the dining room or in the lobby afterward. He looked into the curio shop, saw that the man he had talked to the first day was nowhere in sight, strolled over to the plaza and got to the far corner just in time to realize that the slim woman—tan polo coat; dark, almost black hair gathered in a chignon low at the nape of her neck; ends of the white scarf fluttering—getting out of a bright yellow roadster and going into the grocery store was the woman he had seen riding with Geoffrey Middlemas. No mistaking that mouth and chin and that unconsciously haughty, unbending way she carried herself. She walked exactly as he had known she would: with her body very erect and yet with a fluid, gliding step, so that one had the impression that she was tall and exquisitely graceful in spite of it.

He sauntered past the grocery-store window and saw her unfold a tiny shopping list she had taken from a small silver-mesh purse, saw her smile at something said by the clerk. She stood clear of the counter, her elbows slightly thrust out, her eyes returning frequently to the list as if she had trouble in reading it, her head rather than her body turning to follow the movements of the chubby clerk. Everything about her betrayed that this was an infrequent visit to the store, that she was shopping for somebody else. Slim legs, he noticed, almost too slim. An exciting pallor, because of the dark hair. Why those dangling, old-fashioned amethyst earrings? Why earrings at all with that beautiful, strikingly pure jaw line? . . . He waited at a safe distance until she came out followed by the clerk with a carton full of groceries, watched her get into the car and tuck the ends of her scarf into her coat. She was gone much too simply, too quickly for him.

He went back to the curio shop. The large, fleshy man with the leonine mane and the pleasantly modulated voice remembered him, inquired whether he was enjoying his stay. It was easy, in between looking over some Navaho saddle blankets like the one he had seen that morning on Curly's horse, to let his interest in the Santa Fe painters appear as mere idle tourist curiosity. He was able to learn something about all the painters whose work had struck him at the museum; where they lived or what they looked like or what their hobbies were—tart little odds and ends of information that every once in a while gave him a sudden glimpse of a tantalizingly close-knit social life which apparently embraced the artists and some rich people who gave large parties in town. Not all the artists though! A subtle gradation of enthusiasm hinted at a social hierarchy and placed each one. Buell's name, Peter noticed, evoked impartiality rather than warmth.

"Buell's a good painter. He's won some important prizes."

Apparently that was not enough. The condescension in the lion-maned man's tone was unmistakable. Peter said, "I thought his color was beautiful."

"Oh, Dave's a fine colorist. He's in the Fonda quite frequently. You can't mistake him: he always wears leather puttees and an old cavalry hat."

"I've met him. He spoke to me the first night I was here and introduced me to a Mr. Piggot."

"Oh, Ralph. You've also met one of our writers then."

"And he pointed out another painter, a man named Middlemas, but I couldn't find anything by him in the museum."

"Well, no, you wouldn't. Geoffrey Middlemas hasn't been here very long. He's an Englishman who's painted mostly in France. It always takes a while for an artist to get used to the light here in New Mexico before he can hope to paint this country. Geoffrey has done some fine water colors since he's been here but I don't believe he's ready to show those yet."

The man's approval of Geoffrey Middlemas was as obvious as his cool-ness in speaking of Buell had been. Peter was aware of a secret thrill of pride deep inside himself. He asked, "He lives on the Camino, doesn't he? I think I saw him riding there with his wife."

"His wife? Oh, I think I know whom you mean. That must have been Cristina Day. They go horseback riding together quite a bit."

"She drives a yellow roadster, some kind of foreign make. I'm pretty sure I saw her just now in the plaza."

"Yes, that's Cristina Day. That's her Isotta-Fraschini which she brought over from Florence this year. She calls it 'The Turtle' because it's built so low and because—" he chuckled as over a family joke and its probable meaninglessness to an outsider—"it doesn't look very fast. But, of course, it wins every race."

"It looks as if it had a beautiful motor in it."

"It does. In a way it seems a shame to drive a fine car like that on these roads, but Cristina says the car is six years old and she couldn't get anything for it if she tried to sell it, so she might just as well drive it out here."

"Is she an artist, too?"

"I don't think Cristina does anything. She comes here for part of the year, as a lot of people do. She has a beautiful house out on Cerro Gordo Road, but most of the time she's in Italy."

"Is she Italian?"

An invisible curtain dropped between them. "I believe not. Cristina's family are New England and New York. I think her stepfather is an Italian, though."

It was as far as he dared to pursue his questioning. Reluctantly he turned his attention to saddle blankets and got himself instructed in the virtues of vegetable dyes and the various Navaho weaves. As soon as he could politely get away, he hurried down the street alongside the hotel to the big garage where he had arranged after lunch to rent a car for next week. His pretended worry whether the Chevvy would have a good battery in it was sufficient excuse to stop in again so soon. The mechanic knew all about Cristina Day's car and about her house on Cerro Gordo Road—about a mile up Alameda Street or up Palace Avenue if he pre-ferred.

He walked very fast up Alameda for what he judged to be a mile, found the hilly, winding Cerro Gordo Road, and began to keep an eye out for the yellow roadster. With an absurd quickening of his heart he suddenly caught sight of it, sticking part way out of a garage which was itself half hidden by trees. The long, low house, though not set back very far from the sidewalk and only partially screened from view by lilac bushes and pine trees, presented the bland and slightly forbidding aspect of many of the Spanish houses which faced away from the road. There was no portale and no door along its entire length.

He tried to catch a glimpse of the patio inclosed by the two wings that ran at right angles from the house toward the rear. His only reward was the gay gleam of a bright-red beach umbrella through a wrought-iron gate set in a jog in the far wing. Behind the house, all the way in the back, there was a corral. He distinctly saw the fawn-colored house.

No question that it was her house. What was she to Geoffrey Middlemas? Buell would be the one to ask! He waited impatiently for the painter to show up in the lobby the next morning at ten.

Buell was fifteen minutes late. Instead of apologizing he blustered when they got into his ancient, hearselike sedan which was packed to overflowing with rolls of chicken wire and with crated pictures and cartons of groceries. "Good thing you were there. I was going to look in the lobby and if you weren't there I was going on."

Peter was amused. "Did you think I wouldn't show up?"

"Lot of young fellows like you turn up each year, full of talk about the painting they're going to do. All it usually amounts to is talk. Next thing you know they're out every night partying and getting drunk until their money is gone. This is a great town for parties if that's what you want." He nodded toward a grove of cottonwood trees that extended far over to the right. "That's Tesuque village. The Tesuque pueblo is a few miles farther on, to the left of the road. I'd take you to see the Indians but today I can't spare the time. Bishop's Lodge, the hotel I told you about, is over there on the right. You can't see it from here on account of the trees."

It was in any case the village that interested Peter, the scattered adobe houses that began to appear between the trees. "Is it a Mexican village?" he asked.

"Except for half a dozen Anglos, all you'll see is natives. And there is one thing you want to learn if you're going to live out here: 'Mexican' to a native means 'dirty Mexican' because that's the way the Texans always used the word in the early days. The natives call themselves Spanish-Americans. You mayn't like it out here at all; a lot of people don't. That's

Carol Praither's house right here. He's a painter. Back in there, with the blue garage doors—that's Phil Banta's. This is my place. We'll come back here afterward."

He liked the village—the freshly plastered houses with broad portales running down one side, the bare adobe yards baking in the sun, the ancient cottonwood trees and the small orchards, the crude log sheds with the great piles of hay on the roofs, the corrals, the black-eyed children playing in the road. It was primitive—one hardly had to look a second time at the rough pine-board housing over each well and at the buckets used to draw up water to be convinced of it—and yet everything had an oddly seductive, laughing, sun-washed charm. Just like the square little house sitting squat in the middle of a bone-bare yard where Buell stopped his car. Just like the snaggle-toothed landlady with all her family who had to be summoned from the next house.

His first reaction was one of incredulous dismay when the plump daughter who acted as interpreter and to whom all the children belonged unlocked the door and stood solemnly aside for Buell and him to go in. A big kitchen range, recently blacked, its nickel doors glistening, loomed importantly against the opposite wall. Starched red chintz curtains on the two low windows; a crude set of shelves with another chintz curtain over it and two or three battered aluminum saucepans on top; a table with a blue-checked oilcloth and two chairs painted a bright red; an insurance-company calendar depicting a mawkish woodland scene tacked on the wall beside a rickety cupboard with carved doors and stippled tin sheets by way of glass.

It was obviously the biggest and most important room in the little house. As if he could have missed any of the few paltry furnishings in his stricken survey, the snaggle-toothed crone—not so old as all that; she still had black hair and intensely alive, malicious black eyes—whispered vehemently to the plump woman and pointed to the range. The handsome younger woman with the little girl snuggling against her skirt translated, "My mother says the stove is new. It come from Denver this spring. It ees very good."

He said politely, "It's very nice."

Buell said, "You got a good range there. You can heat all the water on that you need when you want to take a bath. In here is the studio and living room. You couldn't want a better light."

He admired the four-by-six-foot window for Buell's sake, but the very brilliance of the light that came flooding through it made him uncomfortably aware of the exuberantly flowering geraniums in the coffee cans on the window sill, of the garishly painted earthenware pot beside the fireplace, of the horrible paper flowers in a brass vase in a niche. The bedroom was at least no worse. He rather liked the huge homemade bed with the massive posts and the incongruous paisley spread, the single window that looked like a small door in a rustic church, the two low chests. . . . A lot of the stuff, he reflected hastily, could be thrown out. But would he want to stay out here?

Yet even while he was telling himself that it would be grim, the geraniums winking from the window sill, the sunniness of the rooms, some challenge in the stark pine-board floors and the freshly whitewashed walls stirred a sudden eagerness in him. For everything was clean, pridefully austere rather than drab, engagingly stiff and starched with expectancy, somehow amusing like the malicious-eyed hag in the glossy black dress and her plump daughter and the jovial, broad-bellied son-in-law and the bright-eyed children.

"You've got everything here you want," Buell prodded gruffly.

"Where could I keep the car?" he balked in a last flicker of uneasiness over the problem of baths and the uninviting prospect of the outhouse far in the back between two cottonwood trees.

Buell consulted for a minute with the Mexican in a jargon that seemed to contain as many English words as Spanish ones. "Crecencio here can build you a shed out of pine slabs."

"Si," Crecencio agreed, "I can build th-ee shed. Maybe next week."

Within a few more minutes he had taken the house, engaged the plump woman to come in every other day to clean, and paid her mother the rent for the first month—not because all his misgivings had been stilled, but because he found himself curiously anxious to convince Buell of his seriousness.

They stopped at Buell's place. It was a comfortable old native house that looked as if it had been built around the gigantic willow tree in the patio. It was at once solemn and gay with its thick walls and dark ceilings and heavy Spanish furniture and the bright, small windows like laughing eyes, each one winking from its deep recess, and the colorful Navaho blankets scattered everywhere as rugs on the floor. There was no evidence of any wife. A pair of boots had been left in front of the couch and a tangle of ropes and old overalls were piled in a corner on a chest and argued an untroubled bachelor untidiness. There was a huge studio, obviously added to the house fairly recently. There was a dining room in which a very dark, plain-faced Spanish girl was setting the table for two. There was also a perfectly modern bath, Peter noted wryly and could not help commenting on it.

Buell cut him short. "If you stay long enough and decide to buy a place you can build all the bathrooms you want. That's not important if you want to paint. I got along without one for years." Nor was he less gruff in the studio. He rebuffed even honest praise of his work as if from some jealously defended crag of self-criticism from which he scowled at his insufficiency. "The color's all right," he growled at a still life of apples and gourds, "but the composition is all wrong. I'll show you the pictures another time."

On a sudden impulse Peter said, "I've been wondering whether you'd be willing to give me some lessons in oil technique. I'd like to pay, of course."

"I don't know about that. I haven't much time to teach. You do a few drawings, and we'll see. Now we better have something to eat. I have breakfast at half past five and I get hungry by this time. I think the girl's ready for us."

He felt both warmed and embarrassed by this new proof of friendliness. "I'd hoped you'd have lunch with me in town, Mr. Buell, if you didn't mind my leaving right afterward because I have a riding lesson at half past one."

"Matilda has got lunch for us right here. What time do you have to be back in town?"

"If I could get there about one . . ."

"Then we better not waste any more time."

They talked mostly about art materials while they ate. Buell told him where to go in town for stretchers and canvas and oil paints and what brushes to buy. He also offered useful advice in connection with the house: there was a place in Santa Fe which delivered ice; a man named Abelardo—second house from the split cottonwood tree—was the man to go to if he wanted an honest load of piñon wood for his fireplace; a Mrs. Martinez took in laundry and knew how to iron shirts. . . . It was only when they were again in Buell's car and nearly back in town that Peter found an opportunity to say, "I suppose you know Mrs. Day. I've been seeing her around a lot. Does she paint?"

"She plays the piano, is all I know. Yes, I know Cristina Day. She's a fine woman."

"I was just wondering because I've seen her out horseback riding with that painter Middlemas."

There was a stubborn pause while Buell's attention was apparently all taken up by steering around a farm wagon. "Society painters are always chasing rich women. That's how they get portraits to paint."

"Is he chasing her?"

"You'll have to draw your own conclusions. All I know is that she came here first and that they knew each other on the other side. . . . What do you want to take riding lessons for? With a Western saddle all you do is get on and ride. A little practice is all you need."

He explained about his mishaps at the livery stable and the help given him by the two cowboys. There was a delicious sense of secretiveness in allowing himself to think for an instant of the real reason for his impatience to learn how to ride.

"You want to watch yourself with that fellow Davis."

"Anything wrong with him? He seems all right."

"He's a professional gambler and he's been in the pen for dealing in stolen cars. He'll do you if he can. Don't let him sell you anything. . . ."

He thought of Buell's warning two hours later when he was galloping between Curly Davis and Shorty over a fairly even stretch of ground and there was a sudden "Whoa" from Davis close by him on his left. He felt a sharp jolt and was still wondering how his horse could have stopped so abruptly when he felt himself sailing through the air. It was the scratchy sprig of sage sticking into his neck rather than the sharp pain in his shoulder and the memory of the thud that angered him as he lay stunned for a few seconds before he could gather himself together and get on his feet. It took him a little while to find his hat. His horse stood where it had stopped and was nibbling at some grass as if nothing had happened at all.

He went over to Curly Davis, stood challengingly by his stirrup and let his anger flare. "What the hell is the big idea?"

"You wanted to learn how to ride. You got to know how to stop."

"When you're roping steer, you got to stop sudden, boy," Shorty, his round face still swollen from laughter, supplied earnestly.

He ignored Shorty. "You called to the horse."

"Sure. You couldn't stay on."

He could see suddenly that while he was up against Curly's humor—a crude kind of humor not unlike that responsible for the often savage practical jokes in the steel mill—Curly had a point. He gathered up the reins of his horse. "All right, try it again."

"Bet you that saddle blanket you can't stay on." It was the black-fig-
ured Hopi blanket he had admired the day before.

"Against what?"

"Ten dollars."

"O.K."

Again they lashed into a gallop over the sage. He sat with his feet
poised in the stirrup this time, angrily ready for the "Whoa," prepared
to grip instantly with his knees. But for all his determination to hold on
he was too late—or rather, he thought as he picked himself up after
what seemed a long time alone with the throbbing in his hip, he had
clutched the pummel and that had been wrong. He had turned a complete
somersault.

Davis wore his bland smile when he limped back, trying to ignore the
ache in his shoulder and hips. Shorty looked a little concerned. "You
want to kick up your feet and lean back when he stops."

"That's what I was trying to do," he said irritably. "I'm going to stay
on this time. What you going to bet?" he challenged Davis.

"Bet you this saddle against fifty bucks."

Though it could not be called a new saddle, it had not been used much
and it had some silver inlay on the pummel and a good deal of tooled-
leather work. But he hardly gave the price Curly had put on it a thought.
"All right, fifty bucks. Let's go! . . ." When the shrill, treacherous whistle
came instead of the "Whoa" for which he had been prepared, he kicked
up his stirrups toward the horse's head and flung himself back. He hurt
his crotch against the pummel but he stayed on.

Curly grinned. "By damn, you did it!"

Shorty praised. "You done all right."

He felt as elated as when the superintendent of the puddling mill in
Pittsburgh had let him have his own furnace the first time. A warm affection for the two cowboys glowed in him during the whole ride back.
He thought of asking them to have dinner with him. He thought: I like
the West! Curly is a good gambler. He can take things in his stride. He's
just as cheerful as if I hadn't now won his saddle away from him.

Both the cowboys came along downtown, Shorty joking all the way
down Canyon Road. When the pickup passed the Camino del Monte Sol,
Peter looked up the climbing road with a defiant surge of pride. It was as
if a barrier that had blocked his way had been swept aside. . . . In front
of the hotel he paid Curly the ten dollars he had lost and offered him
twenty dollars for the Hopi blanket and insisted on paying that much.

He said, "I won't be able to come out for a lesson Monday. I'm going to be busy moving to Tesuque. I'll pick up my saddle, though."

It was Curly who said, "You can get your saddle any time you want. You don't need any more lessons anyway. Just get you a horse and ride some every day. . . ." Buell had been completely wrong: nobody had tried to milk him or sell him anything.

He soaked for fifteen minutes in hot water, then examined the bruises on his hip and twisted his back experimentally. He was all right. The tenderness in his bones only added to his exultant mood. He felt too restless when he was dressed to think about dinner yet. He felt as if he must flaunt his triumph on the Camino del Monte Sol. At least he could see whether the yellow car was there!

Once he had started he could not get there fast enough. The Isotta was not out front. There were no horses beside the well. But someone was in the house: smoke was coming out of the chimney over the room with the one large window, and in a far corner of the room an electric lamp was turned on. He thought irritably: what am I waiting for?

He walked quickly through the gate in the wall, past the tamarisks and the rail where the horses had been tied, up to the door. There was a cast-iron knocker shaped like a miniature Indian mask. For an instant the knocker paralyzed him. *What was he going to say?* The tumultuous shyness at the pit of his stomach was like the mingled awe and expectancy he had known as a little boy on Christmas Eve just before the living-room door had been pulled open and had revealed the lighted Christmas tree. He fought down his dry-throated panic indignantly and knocked.

The door opened almost at once. He stood looking at Geoffrey Middlemas: double-breasted blue suit—pigeon-colored tie—head held stiffly in polite inquiry.

He thought: *I could hit him and make him sit there on the floor. I could talk to him there. . . .*

"Mr. Middlemas?"

"I am Mr. Middlemas."

His voice as he said it—warm baritone held in reserve, noncommittal, dry—was like an arm guardedly extended in a wrestling match. One could lay hold on it by matching one's own inflection to his.

I could also back him across the room with neat little jabs on the chest until his skull cracked against that wall. But there's no need for that.

"I'm Peter Domanig."

The bluish-gray eyes seemed suddenly to have trouble focusing on him.

The stiffly held shoulders remained very still. It was all at once more revenge than he had ever dreamed of to watch this frozen irresoluteness. Could Geoffrey Middlemas be afraid that he would actually assault him with his fists? How ridiculous! . . . Geoffrey Middlemas said at last with precipitate warmth as if to give the lie to his indecision, "Do come in!"

The door opened directly into the living room. Peter let his eyes sweep to the fireplace in the center of the end wall on the right and realized with a mixture of annoyance and hot-surging shame that they were not alone, that in the armchair beside the big floor lamp with the mottled parchment shade, wearing a black tafetta dress and a single string of pearls, looking steadily at him, sat Cristina Day. She lowered her eyes to the magazine in her hands but without haste or embarrassment.

Geoffrey Middlemas said, "Will you excuse me for a little while, Tina? I want to see this young man. We'll go into the studio."

She put down the magazine. "I think I'll call the garage again. They promised to have the car here by now." Her voice was not so much warm as subtly vibrant and clear. There was an indefinable foreignness in the way she pronounced "garage"—the long *a*'s haunting and musical.

"We have a quarter of an hour yet," Geoffrey Middlemas said. The next instant his eyes met Peter's with the beginnings of a smile, urging him toward the door on the left. "We'll go in here, shall we?"

Oh, anything at all, mocked the caustic voice inside him, which was part of himself and yet somehow irreconcilable and not to be commanded.

A short, dusky passageway led to the studio. Peter walked as far as the model stand halfway across the floor toward the big north window. Behind him Geoffrey Middlemas softly closed the door, hesitated for one moment, then switched on a single powerful bulb on the ceiling.

It was a fairly large studio. A number of packing cases had been pushed close together in one corner. A tall, ponderous easel stood half turned to the window, so that it was impossible to see the picture on it. Several stacks of unframed pictures were leaning face to the wall. A massive, thronelike, carved oak chair—French or Italian perhaps—had pieces of brocade and tapestry and a magnificent old red chasuble flung over its arms.

Geoffrey Middlemas nodded toward a Mexican leather chair between the window and the small corner fireplace in which the crumbling embers of a log were still glowing fitfully. "Won't you sit down?" He himself reached for a high, three-legged stool beside a table littered with paint tubes and jars with brushes in it, pulled it closer to the fireplace, and stiffly sat on it. "This is rather a surprise, of course. A very pleasant surprise," he said. "I had been hoping . . ."

A surprise I had been planning ever since I saw the word "illegitimate" on my birth certificate as a little boy and found out what it meant!

He was older, Peter found time to reflect, than he had looked at first. His hair at the temples was quite gray and there were wrinkles on the side of his neck. He must be at least fifty or fifty-one! It was only his high color and the dark hair on top and the lean line of his jaw that made him look so young. I like his seriousness, Peter thought; it almost amounts to awkwardness and makes one like him. But maybe that's also his technique with women! . . .

"Have you been in Santa Fe long?"

"Just a few days."

"Did you know I was here or did you find out after you came?"

"I'd heard you were here."

Small talk—the amenities. How long was this chatter going to last? Well, he'd put up with it for a while.

Not for too long, the voice inside warned. *We've got a long score to settle, he and I. There were those festering sores that cracked open all over again every morning on the backs of my frostbitten hands when I pushed up the shutters that first winter in the hardware store. And there were the grubs that floated in the barley soup on the days we had that instead of a plateful of watery turnips at the apprentice home. . . .*

"I'm very happy you did. How long will you be able to stay?"

The feeling that he had allowed Geoffrey Middlemas to gain too much of an advantage made him say coldly, "I've no limit. I'm taking a vacation. I've always wanted to see the West. I'll stay as long as I find it interesting."

"Then we'll have a chance to see something of each other—Peter." His smile groped for assent. "Have you enjoyed your vacation?"

Not so fast, the inexorable voice, which seemed to speak for a myriad moments of hate and rage, balked. *Not so much coziness all at once. I'm not used to such a tender interest in my vacations. I didn't have it as a child.*

"I've been doing some riding and I plan to do a little painting while I'm here."

"If you ride, then perhaps you'll join us sometime. Mrs. Day and I ride every afternoon. We usually start at three and stay out until five. There is a man just below me here who has saddle horses for rent." He spoke more rapidly, zestfully almost, as if he had shaken off some constraint.

After all, I'd be jittery, too, in his place, Peter excused him. I knew what was coming, but for him all this is like a bolt out of the blue. Rather a pleasant British accent, he noted as he watched the marked drawing back of the lips from the white teeth; more distinct than most American speech but not a very noticeable accent at all—a very hard *l* sound and occasionally a faintly theatrical *r* at the beginning of a word. . . .

"And you paint?"

"All I know is how to draw."

"That is already a great deal."

He felt that he had made himself ridiculous. "I don't mean that I'm any good. I just draw."

"Where have you been studying?"

Studying—vacations! the voice jeered. *At the time he must think I was in art school I was putting in afternoons like the one when I was dragging the heavy handcart with the four big rolls of steel wire on it across the endless Danube bridge through the slush and over the icy stretches, six miles in all in the knifelike wind, that first year as an apprentice, and the biggest boon in the world seemed to be allowed to hitch onto an empty brewery truck—only, I wasn't allowed to! The driver used his whip on the horses and the truck got away from me.*

"I haven't been, except that in Vienna in grammar school an art teacher once gave me lessons for a year. I'm really a mechanic—an engineer."

Geoffrey Middlemas suddenly grinned. It was an engaging grin, rueful with self-mockery. "That's very much better than being a painter."

Just because he felt himself soften to the grin, Peter felt a need to probe and thrust. "Lately I've got interested in drawing again. I thought I'd like to take lessons with Dave Buell."

"Buell?" There was no missing the faint distaste. "Do you know him?"

"I ran into him the first day I was in town. He's been very nice to me." It gave him a sharp satisfaction to goad Geoffrey Middlemas with Buell even while he wondered at the certainty with which he had known that Geoffrey Middlemas would dislike him. "I find him exceedingly interesting."

"I'd be happy to teach you anything I know." As if to forestall a possible refusal, he went on hastily, "I tried—ah—get in touch with you before you left Vienna in 1919."

When I was already seventeen and had come out on the other side of the hell I'd been through and had already been doing a man's work for three years and had enough good solid currency in the bank in Switzerland from my private trading to get out and go all the way to China if I wanted to! Even then you didn't rupture yourself trying. If only you had tried when I was a little boy and used to have one persistent dream— of a grand lady who was supposed to be my mother arriving from America to rescue me! That was because I didn't know yet that every little boy had a father, too. . . . If only later, after I knew, you had given some sign of life—just a post card, just a snapshot of you, looking as you do now— I'd have been so proud! Instead you left me with that later dream—that bright ambition to cheer me—of cutting you to ribbons with a knife, with a whip, with anything, as soon as I could get my hands on you. . . .

"Yes, I know."

"I suppose your mother told you."

"No, she didn't." He made it emphatic, like throwing open a closet door to show that there was nothing hidden inside. If Geoffrey Middlemas had any naïve idea that he was under Mizzi's thumb and had perhaps been sent by her, he'd better be disabused of the notion at once. "Aunt Kathi told me because I made her tell me a few things!"

The almost imperceptible twitch of Geoffrey Middlemas's left eyebrow, which was a little higher than the other, showed that he had heard. He shied away from Aunt Kathi and the "few things." "How is your mother?"

"She is fine. I don't see her very much. I was in Pittsburgh until last year and since then I've lived in New Jersey."

This time it was as if Geoffrey Middlemas had decided to face the inevitable. His lean, trim jaw gave a little jerk to one side. The gray eyes became vague and yet watchful in the shadow of the dark brows.

"You must have thought me pretty unspeakable."

Peter had an indignant sense of being maneuvered out of position, of being robbed of the initiative by this self-accusation. He looked back bluntly into the dusty blue eyes. "I didn't exactly love you for leaving me in a place like Vienna during the War."

"Vienna isn't such a bad place."

"It was a hellhole during the War, with everybody starving."

"But here you are with obviously a decent education and a fine physique, so that I'm rather proud of you."

He was actually smiling. Peter felt his anger gather into a ball. Was he trying to kid him out of what had happened? "The only education I had was in starvation and wearing paper shoes."

"Still, Vienna had good schools."

"Not for me. My peculiar status kept me out of military school where there would have been food and where the tuition was free. So I got my education in a hardware store, wrestling with tons of horseshoes and carriage springs and with miles of stovepipe."

"I don't suppose it helps to tell you that I am sorry, that I—well—longed for you. As I said, after the War, when I was in a position to, I did try."

"After the War I no longer needed anybody. It's when one's little that things hurt."

Although he did not actually move one inch, Geoffrey Middlemas seemed to have come indefinably closer. "I know," he said. "I lost my mother when I was very young, and my relationship with my father was not all that it could have been. Not that I mean to plead that as an excuse. Life—" he seemed uncertain whether to go on—"is not easy on any of us. We can't always do what we like."

It was a reference presumably to what Aunt Wetti had told him: that Geoffrey Middlemas' father had threatened to cut off some monthly allowance if he married Mizzi. As if he couldn't have painted posters and done illustrations to earn his own living, same as any other artist!

"I think I'd have found it a little difficult at the time to work up much sympathy for your difficulties."

"And now?"

And now, said the voice which had suddenly turned traitor, *I'm happy to be sitting with you here like this, watching where the razor has gone very close over the pink skin in front of the ear and along the jaw and across the chin—happy, though we aren't going to tell you that.*

He pretended to size up the studio, the house. "You don't seem to be in any particular difficulties."

"Is that why you came, to tell me that?"

"I wanted to have a look at you."

"And is that all you want of me?"

I don't want to lose him again, the voice said and the next instant was suddenly caustic and glass-hard with revenge and as relentless as he had been at sixteen. *Who knows, I may still want to push him under a car.*

He said, "What could you give me now?"

"We could at least give each other a chance to get to know each other."

He felt cheated out of another bit of revenge. Geoffrey Middlemas was looking at him expectantly. There was the woman in the other room! He thought: I want to find out about her!

"All right."

The gray eyes lighted up. The warmth was also in Geoffrey Middle-mas' voice. "How did you discover that I was here?"

"The man in Arles—" I'll be damned if I call him "sir," he thought, but the awkwardness of not calling him anything made him uncomfortable, so that he talked faster than he wanted to—"told me. I'm just back from Europe. By the way, Mr. Anson said something about sending some water colors and a roll of canvas you had left behind."

"Oh, yes, I asked for those." With an air of dismissing the water colors to talk about more important things, he said, "I'm sorry I didn't know sooner that you were here. I made a dinner engagement for tonight. I could cancel it, of course, but perhaps you'll forgive me if I don't since you are going to stay. There is no hurry," he said hastily when Peter started to get up. "Please don't hurry. Where are you staying here?"

"At the hotel, but after tomorrow I'll be in Tesuque. I've taken a little house near Mr. Buell."

"Will you have a telephone?"

"I'm afraid it's pretty primitive. Mr. Buell has one and he would probably give me a message." He blamed his uncomfortable knowledge of Geoffrey Middlemas' dinner engagement for harping on Buell like that. He started to move toward the door.

Geoffrey Middlemas kept alongside of him. "We'll manage. Perhaps you will call me. . . ." It was almost a plea. "How is—ah—Aunt Kathi?" he asked as he opened the door into the passageway and stood aside to let him go out first.

"She's all right—thank you." He realized that the unnecessary "thank you" had been drawn from him solely by his awareness that Cristina Day could already hear. She was still in the chair by the big lamp but she had evidently grown tired of looking at the magazine. She watched them come in, the tiny gold pencil with which she had been writing in a small notebook in her other hand dangling from a silk loop slipped over the tip of her index finger.

Geoffrey Middlemas took two short steps toward her, so that Peter felt compelled to face her, too. "Cristina, this is Peter Domanig. Mrs. Day . . ."

Her "How do you do?" was crisp, bell-clear and subtly vibrant with flattering interest, welcoming as if she had been waiting for precisely this, compelling because of that remarkable voice of hers. Not an act, he told himself as he moved forward to acknowledge the introduction. Her whole being had been committed in one instant to this unreserved atten-tiveness. Did she *know* about him? No, he decided almost regretfully;

there was not the least preoccupation with checking him off against some previously formed image in the steady candor of her silvery eyes.

Beside him Geoffrey Middlemas was saying, "Peter has just returned from Arles."

"Oh, you saw the Hutchinsons," she said eagerly.

He hated to disappoint her. "I'm afraid I didn't get to know anybody. I was there only a short time."

"Are you going to stay in Santa Fe longer?"

"Yes, I intend to."

Nothing had been funny, but they both had to smile.

"We shall see you, then."

A polite formula, yet the exquisite clarity of her voice made it sing. He allowed himself one more glance at the vivid pallor of her skin and at the black-chestnut hair parted in the middle and drawn back from the forehead Madonna-style to the chignon at the nape of her neck. He said, "I'm pleased to have met you, Mrs. Day," and she gave him another smile.

At the door, holding it open for him, Geoffrey Middlemas put out his hand. "Well, we shall see each other soon."

"Why, yes, I hope so—sir."

The yellow roadster was parked on the other side of the street. He walked rapidly to get down the Camino del Monte Sol before they caught up with him and perhaps felt obliged to stop and offer him a ride. It was only when he was safely on Canyon Road that he remembered how briefly Geoffrey Middlemas' hand had stayed in his. Wooden was what Geoffrey Middlemas had been—all desperately summoned small talk and awkwardness and constraint. He grinned at the memory of it. The next instant his glee deserted him. He was aware that he was hot with secret perspiration and that his exuberance was due not to triumph but to a sense of unbounded relief.

Of course it had been a strain, he excused himself, especially with that woman there. She was much younger than Geoffrey Middlemas—thirty-four or five at most. What was she to him anyway? She had seemed completely at home in that chair by the fireplace. . . . It must have been hell on wheels for him, he found himself excusing Geoffrey Middlemas. He seemed pretty shaken a couple of times underneath that shy, twitchy, dead-pan façade of his. Just as I almost lost my grip a few times and all but apologized for sounding so rude! I had no idea I'd find anything about him I'd like. Not that I'm going to run after him! It's up to him now to make the next move.

CHAPTER THREE

Music by Mozart

THE zest that gained on him with every new kitchen utensil he bought and every new shelf he put up and coat of paint he brushed on, made him chuckle at himself from time to time. Imagine me buying oilcloth and chintz and worrying about what groceries to lay in! Pretty soon I'll be taking up knitting and wondering how one tats.

He attributed his gaiety to the novel experience of keeping house. Except for the third evening when he took Buell to dinner at Bishop's Lodge, he did all his own cooking. He told himself that it was part of an art student's life: painters were supposed to be good cooks. But there was also the reason that he did not want to eat in town, not even at Bishop's Lodge which was only half a mile down the road, for fear of running into Geoffrey Middlemas. The very liking, the shy affection, that had so unexpectedly stirred in him during his call at the house on the Camino, made him insist now that Geoffrey Middlemas must come to him. It was his move! He saw it as a point of honor to which he clung with increasing stubbornness. Every new touch that added to his sense of permanence in the little

51

house had the same secret core of defiance in it. I'm entrenching myself as if I meant to stay here for life, he thought. Sooner or later I'm going to force him to come merely by being around.

But there was also in his eager shifting of furniture and in his hammering and painting until late at night a growing joy in the primitive little house and in his neighbors and the countryside. He liked the Spanish children who watched intently while he built a better housing over the well. He liked their mother who came in and scrubbed the floors when he was at last through with sawing and unpacking things—their plump twinkle-eyed father who had begun work on the shed—the hag-faced grandmother with the alert black eyes. He loved the ancient trees all down the street and the unobtrusive, mellow houses and the exhilarating peacefulness that was like a gay question posed each morning at dawn.

Buell came in on the way to Bishop's Lodge on Wednesday night, approved of what he had done, and warned: "Very nice. You're comfortable now. A fellow can spend too much time getting ready. When are you going to get to work?"

"Tomorrow," he said.

He gave up his plan to get a gasoline pump for the well—if the Spanish people could draw up their water with a bucket at the end of a rope, so could he!—and instead started out on Thursday morning with his sketch pad. He drove to the Tesuque pueblo and looked for the first time at an Indian village: at the sun-baked little square, the freshly plastered 'dobe houses that adjoined one another and inclosed the plaza as if it were a fortress yard, at the few Indians who crossed the square and who—except for their white deerskin boots and the gaudy cotton shawls the women wore over their shoulders and heads, and except for their dark and faintly reddish skin and the long black hair twisted into a knot on the head of the men—were merely drab. He felt disappointed that they were so unlike the feather-bristling savages he had read about in *Leatherstocking Tales* as a child. There was nothing to sketch.

He drove a little distance up the road and tried his hand at drawing the rocks and clumps of piñon trees, but he had never been good at landscape and he gave it up and drove back. He realized as soon as he got home that he had been restless every minute he was away. It was a restlessness, he had to acknowledge to himself, that had had to do with his fear of perhaps missing Geoffrey Middlemas.

He sketched the little boy from next door, walked home with him when he was through, and got Josefita to talk her mother into posing for him in the afternoon. The old woman came somberly dressed in black, with a black lace shawl loosely laid over her hair and hanging down over her shoulders in front, with a prim, small gold cross on a thin gold chain by way of sole ornament. She came with the oldest of Josefita's children, little Dolores, obviously kept home from school for the afternoon to act as escort and interpreter.

He posed her against the blank wall in one of the high-backed leather chairs he had bought in Santa Fe. She sat stiffly as if at a funeral. She remained frozen in a kind of stony formality. Only the black lace rebozo down along her cheeks was interesting. The pose was no good to him. In paint perhaps, he thought, one could do something with all that black. . . .

He tried to loosen her up. He asked through the child whether she had always lived in Tesuque, found out that, no, she had been born in a place called Mora, that Mora was on the other side of the Truchas Peaks, that her family had always lived there—found out a few trivial things more. He offered her a cigarette. She took it and smoked it half greedily and half politely, holding it with daintily stiffened thumb and forefinger close to the end which her lips had soon made wet and brown.

There was still no conversation from her. He asked whether her husband had built the house he was renting now. *"Quiere . . ."* the child began to translate when suddenly the woman's face tightened into a vicious grimace, the tip of her tongue shot out under the crooked teeth, and she spat fiercely on the floor. She mumbled rapidly to the child: her husband had not built the house; her brother had! But she made no move to get up out of the chair and fling out of the house, as Peter had feared. She kept right on sitting with stiff complacency and decorously sucking at her cigarette.

In one instant the grimace and the spitting had made her come alive for him. He started to draw. The mixture of explosive rancor and stodgy decorum challenged him. So did his determination to keep out of his drawing any traces of the "Munich school" which the young artists had spotted so quickly in New York. No need for Buell to know about Vienna yet. . . . He drew with lean, simple lines, resisting any temptation to niggle and shade. Again as in New York, in Sibby's studio during sketch class that time, the ease with which he succeeded in drawing an old hag delighted him. He caught the magnificent ugliness of the splay teeth, the rocklike propriety with which she sat on the chair and the prissy greed with which she smoked, and something of the flashing-eyed malice with which she had spat. She came to look at the drawing when he was through.

"*Es bueno*," was all she vouchsafed him, but her eyes glinted with satisfaction at the sight of her militant ugliness.

That evening a gray disappointment settled over him: five days now and still no sign from Geoffrey Middlemas. Had he deceived himself about Geoffrey Middlemas' sense of guilt, his warmth? Perhaps Geoffrey Middlemas was waiting there on the Camino del Monte Sol for the telephone to ring. Well, if Geoffrey Middlemas had any notion of bullying him with father-and-son proprieties he was in for a rude awakening! He could step up the pace somewhat. . . . He went out although it was close to nine o'clock and bedtime for the Mexicans and lined up the man from whom he had ordered his firewood, a gaunt man with an ascetic face and singularly delicate hands, to pose for him all the next day. He felt impatient all of a sudden to get enough drawings to go to Buell with, to get started on lessons with him—and annoy Geoffrey Middlemas.

He made two drawings of the Mexican and a sketch of his team of Clydesdales in the afternoon. At half past three Buell dropped in. He looked at the drawings, neither praised nor criticized but said only, "Uh-huh. Keep on drawing till you get the feel of the country." He stalked once around the room in his heavy boots and then said abruptly, "Reason I came down—Chet Orr and his wife are giving a party tonight. Orr is a painter and there'll probably be a lot of artists there. I thought you might want to meet a few people since you're going to stay awhile. You're invited if you want to come."

The more people he got to know who might mention him, the greater the pressure on Geoffrey Middlemas! Geoffrey might even be at the party himself. . . . He accepted with alacrity.

"Better take your own car," Buell warned. "I don't stay late at these parties. You can either follow me in or find it without any trouble by yourself. It's on the Camino."

"I'd rather go in with you. I'm being asked only because of you."

"Suit yourself, but we aren't so touchy here about formalities. You'll find that out after you've been here a while, Peters."

He said quickly, "Mr. Buell, I've been meaning to tell you: 'Peter' is my first name—my last name is 'Domanig.' "

"Why didn't you say so before?" Buell squinted at him. "You're a foreigner, aren't you?"

Only yesterday he had been concerned with keeping any trace of European training out of his drawing, to prevent this very question. Yet now all of a sudden it seemed desirable to have Buell and as many others

as possible know where he was from—to harass Geoffrey Middlemas.
"I was born in Austria," he said.

"I thought there was something foreign about you. You're too damn
polite! You'll get over that. I'll pick you up around half past five. . . ."

In the car when they were already on Canyon Road, Buell said, "I've
got an extra easel you can have when you start to paint. Save you buying
one."

Buell had liked the drawings, Peter interpreted it. There were going
to be lessons with him! He felt increasingly in a party mood.

A long line of cars was already parked in front of the poplar-sentried
house with the rose tint which he had noticed several times on his way
up and down the hill. More cars in the driveway, lights under the portale,
an engaging hall, a wide doorway into a crowded living room. . . . Their
hostess—small, middle-aged, sprightly-eyed—ebulliently took possession
of him, took him over from Buell and proceeded to introduce him to the
nearest clusters of people before she was called away by a plump servant
girl in a Mexican fiesta dress. Two women and a man on a couch and
another man standing up with whom he'd been left asked the usual polite
questions about his stay and presently when he had told them about his
primitive house in Tesuque fell to talking about Bishop's Lodge, so that
he was free for a few seconds to glance around.

No Geoffrey Middlemas! But in the corner by the big potted plants on
the long window sill, facing the baby grand with the tall vase of gladioli
on it and talking to Piggott and another man beside her on the low, upholstered bench—was Cristina Day. She wore a dark-green velvet evening
gown. Her throat and face were an enthralling muted white in the soft
gleam of the parchment-shaded lamp between her and the fireplace.

A couple of dozen people in the room, his second hasty survey assured
him while he listened to the man on the couch tell about a Spanish adventuress who had run a famous gambling den in Tesuque in 1848. Most
of the women were in evening dress, but the men wore tweeds or at best
dark suits. The members of the pleasantly boisterous groups sat crowded
together on settees and drawn-up chairs and even on hassocks, like the
red-headed woman in a gold-embroidered, black silk Chinese coat which
she kept drawing over her knees.

The handsome woman on the couch interrupted the story about the
adventuress and looked up at him with her deep-set gray eyes. She said,
"But you haven't a drink!"

"I guess Chet's in the other room, and the girls are passing hors d'oeuvres—hey Lupita!" the lanky man beside Peter called and failed to catch the attention of the Spanish girl with the tray. "No chance. Do you want a refill, Pat? Don't tell me—I remember: just half!" He nodded to Peter. "Come on, we'll get you a drink."

It was noisier, livelier in the dining room with the red-tile floor and the massive refectory table which was already laden with stacks of plates and arrays of silver and neat piles of napkins for the buffet supper. Most of the guests were clustered around the sideboard where their host— rough-hewn, with a surprisingly urbane voice and wit—was mixing drinks. Peter's eyes failed to find Geoffrey Middlemas, locked for an instant with the laughing eyes of a homely but vivacious woman on the other side of the room.

The lanky man introduced him to some people by the kitchen door, then to a rangy, fine-featured man with a nervous twitch to his eyebrows and an overemphatic grip. "Carol Praither is a neighbor of yours in Tesuque."

"So you're the fellow," Praither said. "You must come and see us. Do you hunt?"

He did not have to answer. A girl had called, "Oh, Bill!" and Praither, who looked about forty, had spun around with flirtatious schoolboy eagerness. The lanky man, balancing the highball in his left hand over the heads of two women who were squeezing by, managed to take a drink out of the glass in his right. He did not seem in any hurry to get back into the other room. "How do you like the liquor we make out here?"

"I like it fine." Peter hurriedly took a second sip. It was strong but not raw. "Better than the stuff we've been getting in the East."

"That's 'Taos Lightning.' It's got a history. They used to make it up in Taos in the old days and sell it to the mountain men. Now the bootleggers have started to make it again. Well, here we go ...

In no time Peter was separated from him by a bunch of new arrivals in the crowded hall. He helped hunt the crystal beads that rattled on the floor from a woman's necklace when she took off her coat, joked with the woman and the others while they hunted on all fours, felt suddenly at home at the party when they all introduced themselves and laughed together when one last bead fell out of the woman's dress just as Mary Orr came rushing out of the living room to welcome her new guests. He decided not to go back to the couch.

Cristina Day was still on the upholstered bench, but with the man from the curio shop beside her now. She was smiling at something he said, answering, and then listening again, the gleaming highball glass in one hand, her head held very high on the slim, white neck. She looked altogether gayer than before when Piggot had been talking so intently to her; she had an air of having been suddenly let out of school. Only the fear that the man from the curio shop might make some playful reference to his inquiries about her checked his yearning to move nearer to them— near enough to catch her eye. Piggot, he saw, was with the woman in the Chinese coat—dress, smock, whatever it was—talking earnestly again.

He lighted a cigarette to mask his aimlessness and looked unobtrusively over the largest of the groups, in the rather cosy corner of the bookcases. Nothing like a party in Connecticut, he told himself; none of that desperate week-end hysteria. For one thing most of these people were older, between thirty and fifty somewhere, but even apart from that, they appeared much more relaxed, mellow, content. It couldn't all be just middle age and weariness, for there seemed lots of zest, and the voices were at party pitch—only, festive without being shrill. Was it because a lot of them were supposed to be artists and therefore more satisfied with their lives, or did they have more money and perhaps fewer worries than people in the East? At any rate Chet Orr seemed to be doing all right, owning a handsome house like this. He glanced once more around the room, not at the people this time but at the walls and furniture, and took pleasure in the fact that already he was getting used to the sight of Navaho blankets on floors, to leather and split-wood and wicker Mexican chairs, to the big Indian drums used for coffee tables and to the gleaming Mexican tin-and-glass light fixtures on the walls, to 'dobe fireplaces and to the vigas overhead, so that a ceiling like this would have looked bare without the trim round beams every two feet.

He was just lowering his gaze to look at what appeared to be a Picasso hanging beside an embroidered and evidently native tapestry in blue and white when a man beside him asked in a humorous voice, "The ceiling coming down?" It was one of the men to whom Mrs. Orr had introduced him when she had started to take him around. He was carrying a drink in each hand and his eyes twinkled behind his spectacles as he pretended to inspect the ceiling with mock concern.

"No, I was admiring it." Peter grinned back at him. "I'm still getting used to the architecture."

"The vigas, I suppose. I guess they do strike you at first. Have you seen any latilla ceilings or split-cedar ones? Come on over and join us. . . ."

He followed the man to the lively group by the bookcases, met more people, found himself the center of attention for a few minutes while several of them told him about latilla ceilings—peeled aspen sticks laid herringbone fashion over the vigas, it appeared—and about a very old split-cedar ceiling at the Ryans' which he simply must see, until one of the women gave him a rest from being all taut attentiveness by asking the others, "Have you seen Regina's new guesthouse? She's doing the most exciting things! . . ."

By degrees, pleasantly, as if each new person he talked to—the blonde girl with the jangling bracelets; the bald painter who seemed to have a grudge against critics; Piggot, who remembered him from the Fonda—was an amiably helpful roller in a genial conveyor system, he was aware of moving past the piano and closer and closer to Cristina Day. He realized that it was only seconds while he stood half with his back to her, only a few feet away, listening to her voice rather than to the woman who was saying how darling the dachshund puppies were, yet he tingled with the strain of putting off the moment when he would turn around. When he did—pretending a sudden alarm that he might be cutting off somebody's view—he saw that she had been calmly watching for him to turn even while she was talking to the man beside her on the bench. She finished her sentence without hurrying but held him with her eyes. "Hello!" This time she held out her hand. "Do you always walk so fast?"

"Fast?" He was puzzled and caught off guard by her flattering intimacy in front of the other two who, however, had begun to talk to each other and somewhat to his regret were no longer listening. "When?"

"Last Saturday when you left. I wanted to give you a ride, but when we passed you you were just going into La Fonda. We couldn't have started out more than a few minutes after you left."

We! How much had Geoffrey Middlemas told her about him in those few minutes?

"I like to move along when I walk."

"So I noticed." Her smile—in the fur-gray eyes, so luminous as to seem almost black, rather than on her lips—and the caressing clarity of her voice took the place of a laugh. "Are you all settled in out in Tesuque?"

If she knew that then she knew all the rest about him! The hot flush that mounted in his chest teetered between embarrassment and relief, became relief—even happiness.

"I'm getting there. I——"

He was about to tell her about the snaggle-toothed Seferina and the delicate diplomatic negotiations involved in persuading her to take back some gaudy china and vases she had sent over to him today, hoping to make Cristina laugh, when a gawky, gray-haired woman came bearing down on them. "Oh, Cristina, I've been hoping you'd be here. I want——" There was nothing to do but turn away.

A few feet to the right, by the piano, a dumpy, vivacious woman with fluffy brown hair curled into much too youthful ringlets on her forehead and a perky, birdlike face protested shrilly, as if appealing to everyone around her for support, "I don't believe it. Nobody is as good as that."

"It's true, Gladys," the younger woman between Gladys and Piggot said. "Marguerite told me herself."

"She said she'd take him back? After what happened at the fiesta?" Gladys' voice squeaked with delicate, faintly comical outrage, but immediately slid several octaves lower into a confiding baritone. "I suppose you heard that the father of that Spanish girl tried to kill him last week? I don't mind about Ned's drinking and not even supporting Marguerite and those darling children—you know Judge Keffer fined him for contempt of court because Ned was just reeling when he got up in court to plead a case—but making that horrible scene at the fiesta, really, that was too much."

Largely because Piggot seemed to be taking part in the discussion, and because even being near Piggot, who had talked so intimately with Cristina before, gave him an illusion of still being in contact with her, Peter moved closer to the group.

The man with the neat Vandyke beard said soothingly, "Ned's been on the booze route for years."

"I know that. Marguerite should have ended it years ago. First begging her not to divorce him, then asking her for a divorce, and now Marguerite is going to take him back. I like Ned—everybody does—but I think he's behaved disgracefully to Marguerite. Don't you agree?"

The sudden shift from deep-toned indignation to the purring appeal addressed to him, left Peter floundering. "Why, yes—I suppose so—it sounds like it. . . ."

The younger woman said to Gladys, "Well, you know what an angel Marguerite is."

"I simply adore Marguerite. I think she's the most perfect human being I've ever known."

Piggot broke in, a little didactically, humorlessly, the way he had sounded the first afternoon in the hotel lobby, his moody face with the fine eyes somehow sullen with knowing too much: "Perhaps that's what's wrong with her."

"Why, Ralph, what do you mean?" Gladys' voice soared in a school-girl crescendo, and her eyes widened incredulously.

Peter was amused. Quite a histrionic gift!

"Well, I can conceive that a woman like Marguerite—never one hair out of place, never ruffled, all statuesque poise—might be poison for Ned. Perfection can be a constant reproach."

"But you are saying Marguerite is smug when you know she isn't. She isn't just statuesque; nobody could be sweeter than Marguerite. She's never complained to any one about Ned, and look how many times she has forgiven him."

"Perhaps he would have preferred not to be forgiven so much. For-giveness can make you feel like a worm. The very thing that makes Mar-guerite appear so admirable to the rest of us may be what Ned is protest-ing against because it makes him feel dwarfed. Jealousy, if you like."

"Now you're saying Marguerite is putting on an act. That's just not true, Ralph! I've known Marguerite for years and——"

"And she's always been the perfect mother, the perfect wife, the same gracious and even-tempered and beautifully groomed Marguerite. I quite agree. No, I don't think it is an act. It's possible perfection may have been forced on her by the fact that she is tall and probably even as a little girl always was the 'big one' who was held responsible for every-thing and couldn't be grimy and hide the way the other children did. At any rate precisely because it isn't an act it may be hard on Ned."

"Then you think Ned would have been happier if Marguerite had been a bitch?"

"It's possible, yes."

"Oh, I don't agree with you at all! Do you?" Again, Gladys' eyes swept indignantly around the little group, insisting on support.

"Ned——" the man with the Vandyke beard started out cautiously. Peter did not hear the rest. Where the crowd was thickest, over by the doorway into the hall, someone—a woman—had called, "Hi, Geoff!" He turned with taut discreetness, with one eye on Piggot, to look. Geoffrey Middlemas was shaking hands with Praither, saying something to Mrs. Orr, looking constrained and slightly ill at ease—either because he was arriving so late or because the two women alongside of Praither were making a fuss over him—but distinguished, too, with his politely inclined head and the brittle urbanity and guarded reluctance with which his shoulders were set. He was clearly about to move up the room toward Cristina Day.

It irritated Peter to feel himself so tense—all tremulous again inside, as if he still had to knock on his door and talk to him for the first time. He felt exposed where he was. Geoffrey Middlemas would think he was thrusting himself into his path! He stiffened defiantly, told himself, what of it? Let him come! But the impulse to gain time was too strong. He caught the eye of the bald-domed artist who had been so caustic about the shortcomings of art critics before, saw a chance to murmur, "Excuse me," to Gladys and Piggot, and slipped away toward the group by the bookcases.

Except for one surreptitious glance after a couple of minutes, which showed him that Geoffrey Middlemas had joined Cristina Day and stood in front of the upholstered bench along with Piggot and Gladys and the man from the curio shop, he resolutely kept his back to the upper end of the room. He listened eagerly to the bald painter, who was expatiating on the sins of art dealers now. He persuaded himself that he was engrossed by one of the women's descriptions of the native markets in Old Mexico. He made himself agreeable, smiled flagrantly, he felt, plunged into the small talk of the group until Mary Orr interrupted and got them to join the procession into the dining room.

Buell came up to him while he stood with the others by the step up into the gaily crowded passageway, laughingly dodging the first few people who were already returning from the dining room with heaped plates, and asked, "Getting along all right?"

"Yes, fine, thanks."

Neither Geoffrey Middlemas nor Piggot beside Cristina Day, he saw in glancing swiftly past Buell, seemed in any hurry for dinner. Piggot was just lighting another cigarette.

"I thought you'd be all right."

"But he's not all right, Dave. Look at his empty glass! Have you been carrying that around all this time?" The handsome woman with the deep-set eyes, who had been on the couch before and had worried about his not having a drink, young-matronly—thirty perhaps—and with something girlish about her still, had come over from the fireplace to join the line. "I can see I'll have to look after you!"

He grinned at her, happy to notice that Buell was turning away. "I wish you would. Just what I've been looking for." She was beautifully dressed in a very simple, frilly, ever so faintly and delightfully stodgy, black gown with a scalloped neck which allowed one to see the soft shadow of her collarbone. Her heart-shaped face had a charming sobriety. . . . Something warned him that he was going too fast. He corrected himself: "Praying for, I mean."

Her deep eyes took note of it. She obviously wanted people to be well-bred. That air of daintiness about her was a fence. "I'm Dorothy Lambert, in case you've forgotten."

"Not likely!" His gaiety, he realized, owed something to his consciousness of Cristina Day—there, behind him still, watching perhaps. "Look, may I get you a plate? Then you won't have to stand in line."

"Oh, no, I'm going to see that you get something to eat."

"Do I look so——"

Someone was clutching his elbow—Buell. "Here, come here a minute!" Buell tugged him toward Geoffrey Middlemas, who had left Piggot and Cristina Day and was coming across the room, evidently to join the line. It was too late to stop Buell. There was only time to give Dorothy Lambert an apologetic glance. "Middlemas," Buell was saying, "here's a young fellow has been wanting to meet you. His name's Domanig."

Geoffrey Middlemas said woodenly, "We have met." The side of his jaw looked bonier than the other day, slightly drained of color. The almost imperceptible flush on his cheeks might be due merely to the light. It was hard to tell whether the brittle stare of the mist-blue eyes was caused by annoyance or discomfort. "How are you?" he said.

Instead of answering him, Peter said hurriedly, "Yes, we have, Mr. Buell. Thanks."

Buell, looking nettled and vaguely suspicious, grunted, "Oh, well, then . . ." and stalked off.

"I have been meaning to get in touch with you," Geoffrey Middlemas said. "I've had some trouble with a tooth."

Perhaps that accounted for the whiteness around his jaw and the drawn look of his face. "I hope it's better—" and he added out of common sympathy, he told himself—"sir."

"It will be." He could grin, and his face became oddly boyish and engaging when he grinned. "I had it out today. I understand you are all settled in?" Cristina and he had talked about him again!

"Well, at any rate I've moved in."

"It may be some time before I'll be able to get out to Tesuque. I'm waiting for my car to be fixed. Are you doing anything tomorrow evening?"

"No—I'm not."

"Perhaps you'd like to have dinner with me at La Fonda. If you come to the house first, we could have a drink of sorts. At five—will that suit you?"

"Why, yes—sir, thanks."

"Geoff, I heard you had a bad tooth," Dorothy Lambert called from where she stood. "I'm so sorry."

"Quite all right now, thank you," he assured her. "At five, then. . . ."

"You see, I've kept your place for you," Dorothy Lambert greeted him when he returned to her from Geoffrey Middlemas. "I'm just determined to look after you." She laughed softly at herself, smiled at him, shut out the cheerful voices all around them which were like a shelter for their privacy.

Not a flirt, Peter thought happily, his whole being kindled still from the talk with Geoffrey Middlemas. Too forthright and open for that, and somehow too proper, though without prissiness—just very nice.

He liked Dorothy. He liked the whole party while he sat beside her on the couch with his plate and with dessert and coffee afterward: the warm hum of voices all around them; the jokes; the woman in the mandarin coat, who was telling about a trip in an oxcart through Outer Mongolia; Praither sounding boisterous over by the bookcases; the bald-headed Furfey, who had joined them and was telling a story about Sargent and a scowling tycoon whose wife had bullied him into having his portrait painted—"Cost you? If you promise to look like that, it won't cost you anything!" He liked even the little man with the flamboyant silk tie and the affected way of talking which managed to scan "New York" in seven syllables; but most of all he welcomed the fact that he had a clear view of Cristina Day and Geoffrey Middlemas in the window seat.

He got an opportunity to talk to Dorothy while Furfey and the gaudytie man fell to discussing scene designing and the theater—nostalgically at first, both of them having apparently once worked for the stage, and then more and more lackadaisically and waspishly, as if each of them became dissatisfied with having only another talker for audience. The woman in the Chinese coat, who had already secured herself another drink and had settled cross-leggedly on the floor by Dorothy's corner of the couch, was letting her head sink lower and lower over the glass she was holding in her lap. Peter listened happily to Dorothy.

Her husband was a lawyer and late for the party on account of some meeting downtown. She was giving a party next week, Wednesday—would he come?

"I'd love to," he said.

"But don't say much about it, do you mind? I can't ask everyone that's here tonight. Santa Fe is getting so big, one can ask only a few people at a time."

"I won't. I understand." He wanted to prolong the feeling of closeness evoked by her smile and whisper a question about who the noxious man was with the sunset tie, but Furfey and the pompous little man had almost stopped talking now, and he did not dare. "Tell me, who is the nice fellow with the glasses, talking to Mary Orr?"

"Larry Collard—haven't you met him yet? He is a sculptor. Would you like me to introduce you to him?"

"No, I didn't mean that. I talked to him before dinner. I just wondered who he is."

"He's very brilliant. He's really a scientist. He was the youngest full professor at Harvard and he had to give it all up on account of his health. I think he got t.b. when he was rowing in college and he got all over it; and then it started up again, and he had to come out here."

"He certainly doesn't look as if he were sick."

"Oh, it's in his spine, not in his lungs."

"What kind of scientist?"

"I don't know exactly. It was something to do with biology or maybe physiology. I think he is an M. D. That's why I can't understand why he won't go to a sanatorium and take care of himself. He doesn't! He says he's going to die anyway and until then he's going to have fun. I think it's a shame! . . ."

The two Spanish girls were coming around to collect the dessert dishes and refill coffee cups. Mary Orr was handing out glasses of ice water from a shiny tin tray on the coffee table and asking who would rather have a drink. Praither had sat down at the piano and was playing popular songs, skillfully modulating from one into the other, exuberantly improvising every now and then. The woman in the mandarin coat raised her head with a soft jerk, looked up brightly when Peter bent toward her with concern because the barely held highball glass in her lap threatened to tip over and roll out on the floor, and explained, "I wasn't asleep! When I get tired, I just draw into myself and relax completely. I learned that from a Chinese monk." Dorothy Lambert listened to the explanation with an air of having heard it before and of being too well-bred or too kind to wink. Gladys and another woman and Chet Orr had gathered around the piano bench to sing snatches of songs and join Praither in boisterous choruses. People were again moving about and forming new groups.

Dorothy's husband arrived, a rangy, likable man of about forty, and Peter was introduced before Mary Orr whisked the lawyer off to the kitchen to get him something to eat. Dorothy insisted on introducing him to Collard, too—"Dr. Collard," she said—while they were by the doorway into the hall; but there was nothing about Collard's conversation that betrayed any particular brilliance—only a nice tartness and an occasional hint of a caustic wit. They talked about vigas and ceilings again and about carved corbels and doors which could still be found in outlying villages. Dorothy Lambert excused herself to join her husband and Mary Orr. The woman in the Chinese jacket had again let her head sink in a tipsy doze. Collard saw him glance at her and said, half to Piggot and half to him, quizzically, "Jeannie has deserted us."

Piggot, with the same somber intentness with which he had been discussing "Marguerite" before, without gaiety, corrected him, "Journey into inner Mongolia."

"You're too hard on Jeannie, Ralph." He had a nice smile. "She isn't a character in one of your books. She's——"

Mary Orr was back in the room, up by the window seat, urging Cristina to play. Gladys was noisily chiming in, "Oh, yes, Cristina, you must!" Praither had already slid out from the piano bench and was saying, "Your turn, Cristina." Chet Orr was propping up the gleaming piano lid.

Peter watched: she was neither eager nor coy. Her reluctance ended in a smiling giving in. She sat down at the piano simply, put a tiny green silk purse on the corner ledge, collected herself for a few seconds, and played.

"Oh, I love this," a woman was confiding to the man with the Vandyke beard. "Schumann—I love the part with the 'Marseillaise'!"

Romantic music, cleanly played; not dripping with soulfulness—rather gay. The room was stilled and rich with sound. Only from the kitchen there came the distant tinkling of glass. Piggot scowled and tiptoed down the hall. Someone struck a match during a rippling run, and Peter felt a wave of annoyance pass over him; he wanted to frown. It delighted him to be able to observe her at his leisure for once. From where he stood he could see every strand of her dark hair drawn back from her forehead into the elegant chignon, the dark lashes lowered over her eyes, the pale nostrils faintly quivering when she took a breath, the somehow heightened, compelling pallor of her face, her bare left arm moving coolly across the rich green velvet of her dress in front as her left hand chased the other one. No contortions and no artistic agony. She played, he realized, beautifully. And there was the "Marseillaise"! How old would she be—thirty-five? No, she couldn't be. There was an utter youthfulness to her waist when she twisted to reach the treble end of the keyboard, as now. She might be my stepmother, he thought and looked for Geoffrey Middlemas, who stood with his gaze fixed somewhere beyond the fireplace and appeared to be only half listening. Tomorrow at five—would she be there, too? The "Marseillaise" again! Yes, beautiful. . . ."

Praither was the first to applaud. The others joined in. Cristina was about to get up. Mary Orr called out, "Cristina, won't you sing?"

She hesitated, with the green silk purse already in her hand. "Mary, not tonight! I can't—I ate too much."

Several people joined in the chorus to plead with her. Gladys begged shrilly, "Just one!"

"All right, just one." She played a brief introduction and then the sound floated out from her throat—assured, rounded, exciting, rich. Not a big voice—a mezzo-soprano, Peter told himself—but there was power to spare behind the notes and an instantly enthralling authority in the phrasing of the beautifully enunciated Italian words. An Italian folk song, apparently—deceptively simple at the start because of the captivating melody, and then decidedly tricky in the bravura passage at the end of each refrain. Oh, there, this was the last time—the end! He felt a poignant regret along with his enthusiasm, and he had to restrain himself to keep from applauding as wildly as he would have liked. He warmed to Collard for clapping so hard.

This time he forgave Gladys for her whinnying. However annoying her insistence—her blatant passion for being in the limelight—might be, it did succeed in keeping Cristina by the piano although she was already standing up. "Cristina, I simply must hear that Mozart aria again," Gladys wailed. "It's been going around my head all week. I simply won't be able to sleep tonight if I don't."

"Which one?" Cristina smiled.

"Oh, you know, the one from the *Marriage of Figaro,* the one that goes dah-da-dah," and she croaked a few hoarse notes.

"*Voi che sapete?* But that's really the last one! . . ."

Again her voice floated out into the room. Peter listened delightedly. Why, he knew that one! He had heard it before somewhere, a long time ago—in Vienna perhaps. It was as if something exquisite he had once had were suddenly restored to him, only so much more glorious than before. How lovely it was, especially when she pronounced that wonderful Italian "o"-sound in *"nel cor!"* If only it would last on!

But it was over. Cristina was picking up her green silk purse from the piano ledge, smiling at Chet, walking with him toward the corner of the fireplace. The talk had started up again. Praither was back at the piano with a drink, thumping out jazz. All as if Cristina's voice were not still lingering in the room! And yet he was not altogether angry with the humdrum that had reasserted itself, for it gave him a chance to work his way up to Cristina. He noticed out of the corner of his eye that Geoffrey Middlemas was talking to Mary Orr. He waited alertly until Gladys directed her gabble at Furfey and Chet, so that Cristina was for a few seconds free from the group. He said, "It was beautiful! I just wish there had been more."

She smiled. He noticed the fine wrinkles at the corners of her eyes, and they seemed to him exquisite, as rare as the pallor of her face and throat, an inextricable part of the enthralling richness of her voice. "Thank you—Peter."

Her calling him "Peter" was like a reward. It elated him. What did it matter how much she knew? The more, the better, in fact!

Buell picked that moment to interrupt—to compliment Cristina and turn gruffly to him. "I'm going now. Praither'll give you a ride out if you want to stay."

"No, I'll come with you. . . ." It pleased him that Cristina was there to hear and could perhaps guess the tribute to her that lay in his leaving now, while the party was still going on: everything being bound to be anticlimax after hearing her play and sing and after having had this rich moment with her. . . . "I want to get a lot of work done tomorrow," he said exuberantly to Buell in the car.

He was up early the next day, his zest to start a new drawing whetted by the brilliant autumn morning. He drove out to the Tesuque pueblo and found a gaunt old Indian with interesting facial planes and a challenging serenity who was willing to pose. He worked hard all morning and again after lunch, trying to blow up his initial sketches of the smiling old Indian with the twisted red cotton cloth around his forehead, like some sort of hieratic bandage, into a charcoal drawing. But his thoughts kept leaping ahead to five o'clock and Geoffrey Middlemas. Would Cristina be there, too?

She wasn't. Instead, when Geoffrey Middlemas pulled open the door and said with an air that was almost sprightly, "Good afternoon, Peter. Glad to see you," there proved to be a stubby, youngish man of about twenty-six or twenty-eight in front of the very chair where Cristina had sat last time. "Mr. Fettis," Geoffry Middlemas introduced him.

"Jack Fettis! Hi ya?" the stocky intruder immediately improved on it and stuck out a thick, red hand. He had a hot, overassertive grip. Peter was not taken with him. There was something of the big-city slums about Fettis, something brash and truculent about his chunky, uneven shoulders and thick, short waist and loud-checked shirt and about the rumpled beret on top of the portfolio on the table. His nose looked as if it had been broken some time in a fight. His small brown eyes were aggressive and naïvely eager and conciliatory all at once.

"I like that picture of the squaw. It's a dilly," he pronounced. "But I know I'm right about that bench. You gotta do something about that bench, Geoff! If you bring out that blanket you'll really have something!"

It was hard to figure out what his relationship to Geoffrey Middlemas was. He was handing out advice as if his opinion had been asked, and Geoffrey Middlemas was promising meekly to think about it. "I'll have another look at it tomorrow," he was saying patiently. Yet the very next instant Fettis was utterly docile and subservient. "Thanks a lot for the brushes. You think I ought to do it all over, then? . . ." One thing became clear to Peter and this was that Fettis was trying to say good-by but for some reason felt it to be a threat to his self-esteem to appear to be forced to leave, so that he had to bluster and delay awkwardly. He finally reconciled it with his dignity to pick up his beret and slap it on his reddish hair and to tuck the portfolio under his arm. "I'll see you on Tuesday— O.K.? Glad to have met you," he said noisily from the door.

Geoffrey Middlemas' face was blandly inscrutable when he turned around after seeing Fettis out. "Will you have a drink or would you rather have tea? I think it's not too late for tea."

"Whatever you'd rather have—sir." The vacuum that threatened if he did not call him anything sucked the "sir" out of him.

"Then we'll have a drink. I have a bit of Scotch left that I've been saving for some special occasion like this."

He did have charm, Peter noted to himself, half pleased and half disturbed by the fact. The quick grin, as now while he flicked open the lower door of the glass-top bookcase, could make his whole face look suddenly youthful and open and likable. The very furrows, from above the always faintly indrawn nostrils to the corners of the mouth and from cheek to jaw, looked attractive. But there was still something of the strained whiteness, which had been so marked last night, about the side of his jaw; it was even pleasant to have that to talk about.

"I hope you feel better than you must have done yesterday."

"Quite all right, thank you." His hand emerged from far inside the shelf with a bottle. "I suppose you like ice in your drink?"

Something warned him in spite of the casualness of the question. Perhaps it was a nuisance to chip off ice in the kitchen. "No, I'd just as soon do without it."

"Good! One gets into the habit of putting ice into everything here in America. It does help to kill the taste of Taos Lightning." A flicker of a smile again. "The soda is chilled in any case. I'll only be a minute. . . ."

No ice in Scotch, then? It's absurd how tickled I am, he thought, to have his approval.

He glanced around the room, at the fireplace, the chair where Cristina had sat last time, at the old-fashioned gilt-frame mirror and the rest of the furniture that must have come with the house. A car honked somewhere near by. There was the creak of a floor board. Geoffrey Middlemas appeared with a tray with glasses and a soda bottle on it. He set it down on the table and opened the brown whisky bottle.

"You didn't stay late last night at the party."

"No, I'd come with Dave Buell and he wanted to go home early. It was a nice party."

"Yes, very pleasant." He had started to splash soda into the first glass. He looked up questioningly.

"That's fine, thanks." Peter took the glass with slightly awkward fingers. Then he watched while Middlemas fixed his own drink. The vaguely ponderous emphasis with which Geoffrey Middlemas performed each motion all at once pleased him. It was perhaps worth while to invest each action with dignity, to slow oneself up and quite indefinably make a ceremony out of each moment. Or was it only his own extreme awareness of Geoffrey Middlemas, Peter wondered, that made his least gesture seem so deliberate and significant? There was nothing pompous or studied, certainly—only a delayed rhythm, an unconscious formality, that was as much part of him as the brittle set of his shoulders and the somewhat rigid tilt of his head—about his briefly poking the embers in the fireplace and throwing a chunk of piñon on it and then nodding to the armchair beside the floor lamp. "I believe you'll find that more comfortable than the other."

How often, Peter had time to wonder, had he sat opposite Cristina in this same chair?

The bluish-gray eyes were suddenly warmer than he had ever seen them. The long brows arched with the smile. "Here's luck, Peter!"

The odd shyness that had invaded him almost made him say "Thank you" again. He said, "Here's to you—sir!"

Geoffrey Middlemas took a sip, lowered his glass, met his eyes. He hesitated for a moment. "Uh, you don't have to call me 'sir.' It will simplify matters if you'll call me 'Geoffrey' as everyone does. This is an art colony; there is a certain amount of informality."

From one shyness into another! Still, if that fellow with the beret could call him "Geoff," what was there to be in such a fluster about? He said, "All right. Thank you," and then very quickly, "Is Fettis an artist?"

"Well, he paints. He intends to be a portrait painter."

The ludicrous lack in Jack Fettis of those social graces called for in a portrait painter according to Buell, made him say, "He doesn't have much polish."

"What has that to do with it?" There was a touch of tartness, as if Geoffrey had heard somehow what Buell had said about portrait painters. "He has talent. The poor chap's had to work extremely hard to get a chance to paint. He went to art school at night in Chicago and he drove a laundry truck during the day to save enough money to come out here."

"Is he studying with you?"

"He comes to me for criticisms."

Peter was almost certain that there was a veiled reference in his tone to the lessons with Buell. It was as if Geoffrey Middlemas had said: I'm quite competent to teach, as you can see! The infinitesimal reproach elated Peter, made him feel compensated for the irritating jealousy forced on him by Fettis.

"Is he so very talented that you took him on?"

"Partly for that reason, and partly—" the wide eyebrows lifted ever so little—"because he made me think of you, Peter." It was said tentatively, almost slyly, and yet with an air of naked confession; so that Peter felt a little guilty in letting himself listen only to his indignation which rasped: *he expected me to look and act like Fettis! Is he trying to put me in my place—is he trying to bully me?* It lasted only a second. Geoffrey Middlemas glanced at the fireplace where the burning log was crackling. "Have you begun to paint yet?"

"I've done a few drawings. They don't amount to much."

"I should like to see them."

"I can bring them in some time, or perhaps you'll come out to Tesuque to see the place I rented." They were on safely impersonal ground again, but enough of his jealousy of Fettis—who had seen Geoff's pictures!—remained to goad him into asking, "Could I see some of your paintings?"

"Now? There isn't much light left. Electric light isn't very good for looking at pictures. Still, if you'd like to see a few we can try it. Bring your drink."

The studio was darker than the living room. Geoffrey Middlemas turned on the ceiling light and a tall floor lamp with its reflector already twisted to throw the light on the canvas clamped on the easel. It was quite clearly the picture that Fettis had been talking about: a plump Indian woman in a faded lemon-yellow dress, sitting on an adobe bench that was partly covered with a blue and white blanket, bending forward to sift flour into a large black bowl on the floor beside a corner fireplace. In the wall above the bench, a tiny four-paned window. . . . The picture achieved an astringent richness. The color had been laid on with bold, short brush strokes, each note of color playing against the others, so that only the harmony counted. A kind of impressionism, Peter told himself. He hardly noticed the drawing. The color was all that mattered. What a bold viridian there in that shadow! But it was not the picture itself but the fact that Geoffrey Middlemas had painted it which excited him.

"I like it. The yellows against that blue are fascinating."

"It needs to have a lot more done to it."

"The texture of that adobe is beautiful. I like the bench especially." It was as close to openly contradicting Fettis as he dared to go without betraying his jealousy.

"There are some things about it that are pretty good," Geoffrey Middlemas conceded, "but I'm not satisfied with it yet." He raised the clamp on the massive easel, took down the canvas and replaced it with the nearest one of the framed pictures that stood face against the wall. It was a picture of an old Indian in a beautiful strawberry-red blanket, his elbows resting on the straight arms of the uncompromisingly plain wooden chair in which he sat, his ancient hands delicately holding a glossy black cane which had some red and green silk ribbons tied to its silver knob. The impression of primitive royalty was compelling. And those hands were drawn, no matter what Buell said! Peter felt his pride surge up again.

There was only one more painting of New Mexico, a picture of a Spanish girl. "That's all I've been able to do so far," Geoffrey Middlemas said, "except for some water colors. I can show you a few portraits if you like."

There was one of an elderly man—one of a woman in a blue evening gown—one of Piggot. Buell was responsible, Peter excused himself, for the jaundiced eye with which he looked at the portraits. Even their virtues, which made it possible to simulate enthusiasm for them, appeared only as faults to his secret strictures. Competent, yes; too competent, in fact—slick! Color used shrewdly to achieve rich flesh tones and warm Renoir harmonies—society paintings: self-consciously elegant, saccharine.

He had stepped close to the easel to examine the smooth picture surface and find something more to say about the portrait of Piggot. His eyes happened to fall on the dark slat that braced the two uprights of the easel just below the ledge that supported the picture. Printed on it in faded black letters that had become almost illegible on the dark wood were the words '*N'ayez pas peur!*"

Geoffrey Middlemas had seen him look. "Toudouze used to preach that to us when I was a student at the Académie Julian in Paris. He made us paint it on our easels. It's good advice for a young painter. I'll show you one more," he said. He tilted several large pictures away from the wall, found the one he wanted, and pulled it out deftly from between the others. "I can manage. Thank you." Peter wondered with an odd sense of deprivation how often in the past he must have lifted pictures from beside some wall just like this to the easel, to show to others. "This was done on the Riviera, near Vence," he said.

Bright-red roofs mounting like gay giant steps up a steep hillside, amid lush gardens that all but hid the summer-drowsy yellow houses, to a sky that was a blue canopy trapping an alluring sun-warm haze. A seductive picture, which drew one into its spell and made it seem churlish to resist and criticize. Involuntarily he compared it with Buell's painting in the museum. The color was much more engaging, but the houses and bits of garden wall that showed and the hill itself lacked solidity and weight, whereas Buell's boulders had an immense massiveness and thrust out defiantly into space. The charm here was all surface—illusionism—superior calendar art. Still, the purely flat pattern was lovely—Buell couldn't deny that. The paint, as in the portraits, had been brushed on much more smoothly than in the New Mexico pictures. There was no heavy impasto—

just a suave surface that barely allowed one to distinguish the brush strokes.

"The light on the Riviera must be almost like the light in New Mexico."

"Yes, very similar. It's a little warmer perhaps because of the haze from the Mediterranean. Well, I think you have had enough for one day; I don't want to tire you." Geoffrey Middlemas gave him a brief smile, turned out the floor lamp and picked up his drink from the painting table. "Daytime will be better if sometime you want to see any of the others."

"I'd like to very much. You've changed your technique in the New Mexico pictures, or am I mistaken?"

"No, you're not mistaken. I'm trying something now."

They were back in the living room. "I liked the technique in the portraits and the Riviera paintings, too. The colors are very luminous."

"That's underpainting that does that. It's the technique the old masters used. Have you ever worked in egg tempera?"

For half an hour, while they had another drink and sat by the fireplace and even after they got into the car and drove down the Camino, Peter alternately listened and prodded with more questions about painting, until he had persuaded even himself that nothing could be more enthralling to him at the moment than to learn about the priming of panels and about glazes and the superiority of stand oil to ordinary linseed. What he wanted above all, he realized, was to keep Geoffrey Middlemas talking—to observe him.

But in the dining room at the Fonda their roles were reversed. It was Geoffrey Middlemas who asked the questions, drawing him out about the years in Pittsburgh and the year and a half in New Jersey. "Then, you did do some drawing along with your work? . . ."

They had picked one of the small tables by the wall, where there was less likelihood of their being joined by some acquaintance of Geoffrey Middlemas. He had said firmly, "The little one over there perhaps," and had steered toward it after Piggot and the boisterous Praither and his wife and Gladys and a young couple had urged them to squeeze in at their already too crowded table and Geoffrey Middlemas had politely refused.

It was strangely exhilarating to sit in a public place like this, where everyone could see him with Geoffrey Middlemas. He felt himself secretly tingling with pride. It was Geoffrey's—*I'll have to try calling him "Geoffrey" some time soon!*—pink complexion, the faintly frowning pink forehead, his lean pink cheeks and slow-moving blue-gray eyes, rather than just the stiff way he held his shoulders and head, that gave him such an appearance of untamperable integrity, Peter thought happily while he told him about the puddling mill.

"And how long did you stay there?"

"Not quite a year."

"Where did you go then?"

He did not mind talking about Pittsburgh. What surprised him was that he felt so little urge to dwell on the hardships and even inclined to make it sound as if it had all been a game, and a lark to study at night, quite easy to stay awake. But it pleased him when every once in a while Geoffrey's questions betrayed some awareness of what it had really been like. "How did you manage that? Doesn't one need funds for that sort of thing?"

They were both careful not to go back into the past beyond his arrival in Pittsburgh, not to mention Vienna or to touch on Westchester. Their very caution made a bond, as if they were together in a fragile boat which must not be tipped. And Peter knew that he wanted above all to prolong the ride beyond tonight. He said quickly, as if to change the subject out of mere politeness, before Geoffrey could go on asking about the source of the money he had invested in the radio company since that would mean talking about his hardware-store apprenticeship in Vienna and his trading afterward, "Do you still go horseback riding every afternoon?"

Geoffrey grimaced ruefully. "I haven't been able to do much of anything this week. I usually ride with Mrs. Day, and Cristina has been busy herself with a new portale she is having built. We'll probably start again this coming week. You must join us if you aren't too busy painting."

Not much of a confession about Cristina; merely an acknowledgment of what everyone knew—that he and Cristina saw a lot of each other.

"I'd like to very much some afternoon if I can get a horse."

"Mrs. Day has an extra saddle horse, or I can always arrange to get one from the man who rents me mine."

"I guess I'd better practice a little more first. I haven't done much riding yet."

He watched Geoffrey take out the money for their dinner check from a black pocketbook, place it neatly on the little tray under the check, and slip the black pocketbook into the back pocket of his trousers as he stood up.

"It's been extremely interesting," Geoffrey said outside the hotel. "I'd like to hear more about the laboratories." "Laborrat'rees," he pronounced with his bizarre British stress, and his voice carried crisp overtones which announced that the evening was at an end. "Would you like to come back to the house?"

"I'm afraid I've already stayed too long. I'll just drive you back to the Camino and push on along to Tesuque." Peter revenged himself for the stiltedness Geoffrey had again imposed on them. "I hope I haven't kept you from doing something more important tonight."

"Well, you're important, Peter." In an instant his quick grin had restored the warmth that had been between them in the dining room for whole minutes at a time. But he refused a ride when they reached the end of the block, where Peter had parked the Chevrolet. "Call me up if you are in town. I'll try to come out to Tesuque as soon as I get my car back from the garage." Geoffrey held out his hand briskly. "It's been very pleasant. Good-by." A brief pressure, and the hand was withdrawn. He was already walking down the curving street, past the convent school.

Peter watched him for a second, then felt as if he were spying on him and hastily turned his back. He could still feel the brief touch of Geoffrey's hand. Was he going to see Cristina now? Well, none of your damn business if he is, he told himself.

He decided to walk once around the plaza before he drove out to Tesuque. He ran into Piggot in front of the hotel.

"Oh, there you are! Where's Geoff? I wanted to see him."

"He's just started home. He's walking."

Piggot looked undecided, as if he were considering whether to start out after him. "Well, it doesn't matter. I can get him on the phone." Now that he seemed to have made up his mind that there was no hurry after all, the pasty-faced writer with his saturnine brows and liquid eyes seemed inclined to chat. "I was waiting for you to come out of the dining room but I got hung up with some people in the lobby. I must have missed you. You seemed engrossed with each other during dinner. Did you spend the evening with Geoff?"

"Yes, he showed me his pictures."

"What did you think of them?"

Did Piggot know? He seemed to be Geoff's and Cristina's friend. They had been together nearly all the time at the party last night. Was he probing perhaps?

"I liked them—especially the New Mexico ones."

Piggot's face looked sullen almost. "Geoff is trying to work out his salvation," he said ponderously.

"What do you mean by that?"

"Solidity—Cézanne's apple! Geoff is looking for firm ground, like all of us. How are you and Buell getting along?"

"Fine, I guess. He's been very nice to me."

"I must run out to Tesuque sometime."

"I hope you'll drop in if you do."

Piggot said good night and walked off across the plaza.

What in hell had he meant with his "Cézanne's apple" and his "salvation"? He seemed given to cryptic phrases and a kind of lurid gloom. Of course Cézanne had painted a lot of still lifes of apples—it must have to do with that. He also seemed to remember vaguely that Cézanne had said something about apples. He must ask somebody about it!

He started the car and swung around in front of the cathedral. He thought of the pictures and of Geoffrey standing beside the easel and then, suddenly, of the faded inscription. Why would you remind yourself not to be afraid unless you *were* afraid? The pictures, now that he thought of it, had shown a curious kind of timidity. Even the new ones were still a little conventional. And he kept his change in a pocketbook and counted it out carefully—though that might be merely a habit he had brought from Europe with him and might not mean anything. But "working out his salvation" and "looking for firm ground" . . .

All at once as the Chevrolet jounced over the washboard road he felt himself lifted with exuberance. Why, it was easy! Why had he put it off so long? Geoffrey wasn't any giant! . . . He felt as if he had steeled himself to lift an enormous weight and as if now that he had begun to lift there was hardly any weight at all.

He smiled at the wavering beam of the headlights and at a rabbit that scampered across the road into the sage.

CHAPTER FOUR

"Feminine" Woman?

I OUGHT to bring the Buick out from Montclair, he thought buoyantly on Wednesday afternoon. Silly to keep it jacked up in the East and pay rent out here for an old wreck of a car!

He was standing by the well, watching Carol Praither drive off in his new Ford, waving back when Praither stuck his arm out of the window and hollered a noisy "Adios!" Two whole hours when he could have worked had been eaten up by interruptions and calls. First, a Santo Domingo Indian had arrived with strings of red chili which he had wanted to sell, and he had got rid of him by buying one to hang on the wall beside the kitchen door. Next, the gaunt Mexican with the inquisitor's face and the startlingly soft voice had shown up with his team of Clydesdales and a load of piñon which was not due until next month but which the tall Spaniard had brought today because this was "th-ee good time" for cutting firewood and because—"th-ee señor will understand"—he needed the money now, this week for his wife was sick, as he explained somewhat apologetically and yet without any loss of dignity. The difficult thing would have been to turn him down. . . .

No sooner had Saenz unloaded the wood and taken his leave with grave courtliness than Josefita's children had come trooping across the yard with a plate of cookies swathed in a starched white linen towel and he had had to spend the next quarter of an hour with the children because they were still fascinated by him and the house and he had not had the heart to send them away. And finally Carol Praither—a little disconcertingly boisterous and boyish, since he must be around forty—had descended on him for a neighborly visit, to make sure that he would feel free to drop in at their house—"any time! Come on up and have a meal with us."

Nearly the whole afternoon wasted! But he felt warmed all the same by the calls. He looked down the road toward Bishop's Lodge at the goldenly exuberant cottonwood trees, up toward the Truchas Peaks where a few white clouds seemed to wink in the laughing blue of the sky, at the clumps of yellow-centered wild asters along the ditch, at the pine-slab shed for the Chevvy which Crecencio had finished last week. Certainly I'm going to stay, he assured himself as if some challenge had been raised.

He went into the house and folded back the corners of the white cloth from the cookies with the poisonous-looking pink and green icing. He cautiously bit off a little piece of one, found that it was surprisingly good, and ate a second cooky before he shoved the plate into the ice chest. There was still a little time left to work on the folds of the blouse before he needed to heat the water and start getting dressed. He was aware of a stealthy elation at the thought of seeing Geoffrey again. He wondered, as he took the brushes out of the turpentine jar and wiped them on a rag, whether Cristina would be there and immediately told himself that it was Dorothy Lambert he wanted to see. Pity Praither hadn't been inclined to talk more about painting. . . . Geoffrey couldn't be too well off, to judge from that old Hudson he had driven past the drugstore yesterday afternoon. . . .

The mood of happy complacency was on him still when he drove past the spruce-studded lawn of the hospital beside the cathedral and turned into Palace Avenue. He liked the stately, peaceful, quaintly urban street, with the towering poplars like a drowsily whispering guard of honor down each side. Even while he tugged on the brake and got ready to lock the car, he realized that the party at the Lambert's would be as different from the one at the Orrs' as the houses here on Palace Avenue were from those on the Camino. Straight lines, blandly formal façades, slim, square, white columns, a brick coping on top—the Territorial style—in place of the mellow, wavy adobe surfaces, the crude pine pillars and corbels of the old native houses which the artists seemed to prize. Some of the neatly landscaped lawns could have been in Montclair. . . . Straight lines, too, inside the Lamberts' house: a trim front hall, a bright, high-ceilinged living room with a somewhat showy amount of window space, a combination den and bar and library—gleaming hardwood floors and oriental rugs, steam radiators and modern furniture, crisply matched pastel harmonies in the draperies and the upholstery. Only here and there a native touch, as in the Mexican tinwork wall fixtures and the white-and-black Navaho rugs in the hallway and in the fiesta costumes the maids wore.

There were delightful traces of snobbery and grave bourgeois reservations about the artist colony in Dorothy Lambert's selection of guests. Except for Cristina—already there and talking to a tall, white-haired judge who was full of Southern gallantry and mildly amusing jokes— and Geoffrey and Collard and Piggot and the Orrs, not any of the artist crowd were there. Neither Buell nor Praither nor the yoga-woman had evidently been socially acceptable enough to be asked. Instead there were several doctors and lawyers and a number of breezy, youngish business-men and their ambitiously dressed wives, two or three well-preserved elderly couples whose determined youthfulness and slyly expensive clothes and popularity with the others spoke of much party giving and idle wealth, and about half a dozen young people, glossy and faintly fatuous but gay, who clearly belonged to the fast young set one could not help noticing at the Fonda and at Bishop's Lodge.

The whole tone and tempo were different from the easygoing Bohemian informality on the Camino del Monte Sol. Dorothy Lambert's party was as deliciously prim and taut and flawless in every detail as Dorothy herself, with her impeccably waved brown hair, the orchid pinned to the shoulder of her blue taffeta dress, the seams of her stockings meticulously straight on her handsome legs. Buffet dinner, yes, but not eaten off a plate in one's lap as at the Orrs'. Little tables, already set and produced as if by magic from inconspicuous corners by the maids; gay linen cloths and napkins, crystal goblets, candles under charming parchment shades; even place cards—so that his maneuvering to draw Cristina into a con-versation just when they lined up for food, in the hope of sitting with her during dinner, proved in vain. He was allowed to stay with Cristina just long enough to help her find her card, at a table with Larry Collard and the flirtatious judge. Geoffrey, he noticed half proudly and half enviously, was at Dorothy Lambert's table in the dining room. He found his own place at one of the card tables in the hall, with Mary Orr and a likable chap who had flunked out of Yale in the spring and a rather pretty girl with an Eastern boarding-school voice.

Pleasant, chaffing talk after dinner and then, while the girls were still clearing away the tables and coffee cups, some of the young crowd turned on the radio and kicked aside the rugs and started to dance. Presently a good half of all the guests were on their feet—Geoffrey too, dancing somewhat woodenly with Mary Orr at the far end of the hall where there was less of a crush, Peter noticed with a rasp of irritation he was at a loss to explain. He danced with the girl who had been at the table with him, danced with her a second time and then with Dorothy Lambert—more attractive than ever with the faint frown on her forehead, her eyes darting softly this way and that, her body subtly taut with concern whether her party was going well. I bet—he told himself—she's been worrying over this evening for days! I must be a Philistine: I like all this bourgeois prissiness and propriety—I'm crazy about Dorothy! . . . Yet even while he drew her closer as they went into a turn, his eyes returned to Cristina in the gold-embroidered white wool gown, watched her finish the dance with the indefatigable judge and then escape him with some laughing excuse and turn down one of the doctors who was asking her to dance. She was alone for a second, snapping open her compact and dabbing at her face beside a tall floor lamp between her and a lively group on the couch. Someone cut in on him just in time. He was able to make his way to Cristina before she could quite join the hilarious crowd on the other side of the lamp.

She saw him and smiled. "It's a nice party, isn't it?"

"Perfect, except I don't see a piano anywhere! I've been hoping you might play again and maybe sing."

"Why, Peter, you're an outrageous flatterer." The luminous gray eyes under the dark lashes shone teasingly. "Shall we sit down?"

He followed her to a settee just beyond which Piggot stood talking to Chet Orr and another man. "But I'm not," he protested. "I mean it. I've always been crazy about Italian music. I loved those songs you sang last week."

"Mozart wasn't Italian," she said gaily and the silvery gray eyes gleamed with laughter over his predicament.

"I know, but the words of that aria were. It's such a beautiful language."

"Have you ever been in Italy, Peter?"

"No, it's just that I've always had an enormous liking for everything Italian. When I was a little boy I sang in a choir for a while, and the director was a man named Granini. . . ." And he went on to tell her about his childhood admiration for Herr Granini and about his infatuation with Bianca at sixteen and about his great liking for Moro, the Venetian steel worker whom he had come to know in the open hearth shed in Pittsburgh. He realized that there was a ludicrous incoherence between his description of Herr Granini's fiery black eyes and passionate musicianship and the attempt to evoke some picture of Bianca's charm and of Moro's gigantic shoulders and amazing gentleness. All he cared about was to keep Cristina listening and to prove to her somehow that he had things in common with her.

He was delighted when he saw something beside amusement, a tenderness, creep into her eyes. "And is Bianca your cousin?" she asked.

"No, she's married to a cousin of mine. I had a terrific crush on her." He succeeded in making her smile.

"Perhaps you should go to Italy, Peter."

"Oh, I'd like to! It must be a fascinating country, with all those famous cities—Venice and Rome and Florence."

She ignored his invitation—his plea almost—to tell him about Florence. She seemed to be making fun of him again. "How do you account for feeling that way about Italy without ever having been there?"

"I suppose it's a case of natural affinity. I mean, some places and people and sounds and things just seem to suit one somehow; there seem to be all sorts of secret correspondences between them and us. It's like—" he groped hurriedly for some illustration, mostly to conceal what they had been talking about from Ralph Piggot, who had sauntered over to them and was listening much too attentively—"well, like running across the right book just when you need it most. For instance this summer I was looking for some technical information and couldn't find it anywhere. There didn't seem to be any book on the subject, and then just by accident I ran across the very thing I was looking for in one of those bookstalls on the quay in Paris. I found a copy of a book by an English clergyman who had done some awfully interesting research a hundred years ago and who'd been entirely forgotten since."

"Sounds like mathematical heresy to me," Piggot said pleasantly. "If I understood you correctly, you believe in actively benevolent coincidence. Does that kind of mysticism include a belief in a guardian angel who suspends the laws of chance for our benefit?"

"But I wasn't talking about chance. I was talking about things and the way they have of coming to our attention sometimes just when we need them."

"Then you are attributing consciousness and intelligence to things. You're implying that that book you were talking about managed to get itself into a place where you couldn't help noticing it."

"No, I'm not," he defended himself, delighted to see Cristina so closely listening, elated still by those moments of near intimacy when they had talked about Italy, excitedly aware of her smiling eyes and the beautiful pallor of her skin. "What happens, I suppose, is that our subconscious is constantly hunting for anything that may bear on a problem that's bothering us. Then when we find the book or whatever else helps us with our problem, we aren't aware that we've been carrying on a pretty intensive search right along and it all looks like an uncanny coincidence."

"I know exactly what you mean," Cristina said warmly, as if to champion him against Piggot. "I've had the identical experience with music sometimes. I've run across a piece of music I hadn't known before at the very moment when it meant the most to me. You've known that feeling, Ralph."

But the writer would not be cajoled. His sallow, somber face with the fine eyes puffed out with weary knowingness. "You are both romantics," he said. "You aren't happy unless you can add devils and angels to the cast. Personally I find life quite hazardous enough without having to conciliate the stage furnishings as well. I like to think of the inanimate part of our environment as safely inert and untenanted by demons good or bad. The setting, at least, should show impartiality and be the same for all the characters."

What was he talking about? Peter wondered irritably and yet hardly cared since he had found something in Piggot's speech to fasten on and contradict, so that he had an exhilarating sense of holding Cristina as by some physical means almost. "I don't think that any given environment is ever the same for any two people."

"Oh? Is that some more of your mysticism? I seem to have heard somewhere that you're an engineer, yet here you go denying any objective validity to the material universe."

The old boy is riding me, Peter told himself, but so far he isn't being nasty about it. Geoffrey must have told him about the factory, or perhaps Cristina has told him—they are pretty thick, all three of them! . . . "It's precisely because I'm an engineer that I don't believe any given set of circumstances will have a constant value for different people who are exposed to it. I think we select our environment."

"Come now, how do you figure that?"

"Well, it's easy to prove. No two people will give the same description of a room or of even a simple accident. I think we all see what we want to see or perhaps what we must. We exaggerate some of the facts and ignore others—in other words, we select."

"And what governs the selection?"

"Heredity—drastic childhood experiences—inertia. I think we try to make every new situation conform to an earlier one with which we're already familiar and then to react to it the way we've reacted once before. . . ." He felt that he had never talked so much, yet Cristina's eyes on him made him go right on talking about the idea that had come to him on the train, that every human being was bound to act according to a characteristic pattern.

To his delight, Cristina said eagerly, "Oh, I know that's true. How often I've wished I could do things differently—one simply can't get away from oneself."

Piggot barely waited for her to finish. "According to you, Peter, we mayn't be the victims of our environment but we are the prisoners of a psychological pattern. That's a form of determinism that doesn't leave much room for free will, does it? I don't know that I don't prefer the tyranny of environment to being trapped in your pattern. Of the two, the struggle against environment would seem less hopeless."

"But I don't think we're trapped. Pattern is a predisposition to act a certain way and the compulsion is pretty strong, but the pattern itself can be changed."

"How can it be if it's the result of heredity and past conditioning?"

It was ridiculous that he should lecture like this—like Piggot—with people all around them gaily chattering about trivialities, with a good third of the crowd dancing out in the hall, with Geoffrey engaged in some genial discussion with Chet Orr by the fireplace; yet it made him extravagantly happy to be forced to go on.

He said, with his eyes on Cristina's faintly parted lips and small, even teeth enchantingly exposed by her encouraging smile, "By the mechanism of growth. If an individual grows, his characteristic pattern becomes modified. For instance suppose a man is very ambitious. He is then constantly trying to live up to some imaginary rival or antagonist—he sets himself goals. But as soon as he achieves a certain goal, the imaginary rival escapes to some farther reach, so that the striving starts all over again. That way the ambition itself changes in character and may become nobler at every stage."

He was furious with himself and felt the blood burning in his neck and stealing into his face before he was half through. How stupid to let his conceit betray him into saying that. Cristina and Piggot must both have guessed that he was talking about Geoffrey and himself, even though he had hastily beaten a bumbling retreat. No wonder Piggot didn't think him very clear. . . .

"I don't know that I quite follow you," the writer was saying. "Ambition doesn't usually carry with it a capacity for growth. If a man sets out to make a lot of money, for instance, he goes right on wanting to make money after he has reached some initial goal. There is no change in the nature of his ambition or in his pattern or in anything else about him. You must be thinking of some special kind of ambition rather than of the ordinary, uncomplicated lust for self-aggrandizement."

"There would have to be a capacity for growth," Peter conceded lamely while he chafed at the need to hide what was really in his mind. No wonder they couldn't understand! How could they know about the constant change in perspective in his old dream of revenge, about the curious phenomenon of the imaginary Geoffrey imperceptibly growing in stature all the time that he had been trying to grow up to him, so that his crude boyhood desire for revenge had changed from a mere wanting to maul him physically to a determination to make him suffer morally, to humiliate him and make him cringe, and from that to nothing more than a wish to make him feel ashamed and guilty perhaps, until now nothing at all of his once so burning hatred was left. No, nothing at all, he assured himself as his glance flashed for one instant past Piggot across the room to where Geoffrey was softly tugging at the lobe of his right ear with his thumb and forefinger—a habit he had—while he stood listening with bent head to Orr. Instead of hate there was only pride in Geoffrey. . . . "I imagine," he added cautiously, "that I was thinking of some noble rivalry growing out of what originally starts out as nothing more than envy or jealousy or hate."

"Couldn't it be love as well as hate?" Cristina asked.

"Of course. I just mentioned hate because it seems so much more powerful than love."

Cristina's eyes flashed with a silvery glint. "You don't actually believe that! Do you believe that evil is more powerful than good?"

He was saved from having to answer her. The tall, white-maned judge was bearing down on her with beaming certainty of his welcome. Cristina gave them a glance of whimsical despair and politely raised her face toward the booming voice. Piggot suavely turned his shoulder to the judge. "Dave Buell says you're quite a draftsman. I'd like to see some of your drawings sometime. Cigarette?"

"Yes, thanks. Buell must have been feeling good. I'm just a beginner. . . ." He lighted Piggot's cigarette and then his own. "I've been wanting to ask what you meant the other night by 'Cézanne's apple' and 'salvation'?"

"When we were talking about Geoff's painting?"

"Yes." It made him quiver with secret excitement to be leading Piggot on to talk about Geoffrey, with Cristina so close that she could hear every word if she chose not to listen to the judge, with Piggot perhaps fully aware of the nature of his relationship to Geoff, with Geoffrey himself still standing by the fireplace with Chet Orr, all unaware of being discussed. It was as if he were rewarding himself for having pointedly kept away from him all evening, except for a few words exchanged in the hall, so that neither Geoffrey nor anyone else could say that he was crowding him.

"We might as well sit down," Piggot was saying after a glance had assured him that Cristina could not be rescued just yet. He headed for two armchairs by the wall. "You're familiar with Cézanne's still lifes, of course?"

"I know that he painted apples a lot."

"Then you know that a few apples arranged on a rumpled tablecloth in a Cézanne still life can have the vital tension of an El Greco conclave of cardinals. Cézanne found his privileged vision and his idiom—that is to say, he learned to see an apple or a mountain or a tree as it exists most characteristically in itself and he found a way to put down what he saw in terms of pure paint, without faking and without sentimentality. Every painter is after such a profoundly personal vision and formula. If he finds them, you might say that the artist is in a state of grace and then an apple will suffice as a subject for celebrating life and the whole visual universe. If he doesn't achieve the rapport with the only reality that matters to him, then he either tortures himself or dopes himself with substitutes."

"What kind of substitutes?"

"Success, social or financial or academic. Or the substitute may be a sterile preoccupation with technique. Or it may be women."

Peter plunged boldly. "And is that Geoffrey's form of dope—women?"

"No, I should say a certain amount of success has been. But a man like

Geoff, who starts out with a considerable amount of talent and with inti-mations of genius but without actual genius, is almost bound to go through hell and to turn to women for help. Of course he is going to have a bad time there, too. Women can't help a man like Geoff because he hasn't it in him to be happy."

Piggot's dogmatic tone irritated him even while he drank in every new bit of information about Geoff. "Why couldn't he be happy?" he chal-lenged.

"For one thing because being an artist and therefore voracious by nature when it comes to emotional experience he goes through women too fast. For another, because having failed as an artist so far he has come to look to women for some revelation that will help him become the great painter he wants to be, and that's putting an unfair strain on any man-woman relationship. Then there is still another complication: Geoffrey has been hunting for a particular type of woman—the feminine woman. The subconscious quest for the mother, no doubt."

It couldn't fail. Piggot was bound to bring in the subconscious and Freud, just as he had the other night when he analyzed the lawyer fellow for the women at the Orrs'. But for all the wry antagonism Peter felt to-ward him for talking so possessively about Geoffrey, as if he were explain-ing the mechanism of a rather crudely constructed clock that belonged to him, he yet delighted in the fact that Piggot knew him so well. He asked, "Have you known him very long?"

"We got to know each other in France before the war."

That long ago! It seemed a little eerie, somehow outrageous, to Peter, to think of Geoffrey as leading an existence quite independent of his own before the war when he himself had been only a little boy—Geoffrey even then bearing himself, no doubt, with the same stodgy, muted elegance, talking to women as now. . . . "Feminine woman"! Was Piggot kidding, or was that just some more of his caustic whimsicality?

"What do you mean—feminine woman?"

The flicker of astonishment in Piggot's eyes as much as said: I'd for-gotten how young you are! He had an air of bridging a gulf. "I was re-ferring to the sort of old-fashioned woman modern man dreams about. A great many—shall we say older?—men feel that the modern career woman, who is inclined to be self-centered and arrogant and harsh, is perhaps not the ideal helpmeet, considering the exceptional stresses and strains of life in the machine age. Most men who feel like that are usually trapped beyond hope of escape in a situation they resent. They are the ones who account perhaps for the high incidence of heart attacks among American males. A few like Geoff are free to indulge themselves in a search for a woman with those psychological graces which are usually considered feminine."

He spoke with such rancor that Peter watched his sallow-jowled face suspiciously. Was he talking about Geoffrey or about himself? And was he making fun of Geoffrey or suddenly defending him? All that trite twaddle about "career women" and "older men" and "stresses and strains!" Obviously Cristina was one of the women of whom Piggot approved. . . . Feminine! Hadn't his mother been? Quite true that Mizzi had a will of her own and a certain matronly overbearingness now, but had she been arrogant and harsh at nineteen when Geoffrey deserted her?

He realized when he drove home from the party that there had been both an uneasy sense of guilt and a sharp pleasure in listening to Piggot discuss Geoffrey. Skirt chaser! he summed up all the finespun excuses Piggot had made for Geoff. He was aware of a sudden impulse—as he thought of the exquisitely white brow below the severely drawn-back dark hair and of the silver-gray eyes—to protect Cristina from him. The delicious conviction of her helplessness haunted his sleep. As if she could hear all the way in Santa Fe, he took a fierce delight in provoking Buell to air his scorn of Geoffrey's painting the next afternoon.

Buell dropped in after lunch to give him a criticism on the picture of the Indian. He stalked up to the easel in his heavy boots, glared at the canvas for a few minutes, raked the air with splayed fingers. "Your color is all the same intensity, here and here, don't you see that? You picked up the red in the blanket here in the band around his head. That's all right, but it's got to be a cooler red because it's in the shadow. . . ."

For half an hour Buell lectured to him about hot and cool color, about picture planes and modeling with color, showed him with dabs of paint how color could either recede or come forward on the canvas. It was exciting. The only thing that disturbed Peter was Buell's irascibility, almost as if he had been disappointed, as if Buell had expected him to do better even on his first try. Partly to reassure himself, and partly to soothe Buell's peevishness, Peter got him to talk about some of the other artists. Several of them, it appeared, could not even be called painters.

"How is Middlemas as a colorist?"

"All right if you like your Renoir secondhand. Middlemas is a decorator. He's cautious, and when he tries not to be cautious, he is self-conscious."

"But I saw a couple of his things, and they didn't seem bad."

"Of course they aren't bad. He's a competent craftsman who knows all the tricks. What his stuff hasn't got is vitality!"

"One canvas had a lot of punch to it."

Buell glowered at him. "You asked me, and I'm telling you—he's an academic painter. The more he tries to get away from it, the more you notice it."

"What about Praither?" Peter asked quickly.

"Praither could be the best painter out here if he worked once in a while."

"Is he that good?"

"Yep, that good. . . ."

After Buell had gone Peter set a fresh canvas up on the easel and copied off the drawing from the first picture. He stylized the folds of the red cotton blanket the Indian wore around his middle and he also gave more prominence to the bandeau knot over his right temple. The idea had come to him while Buell had criticized the picture to turn the blanket and the headband into symbols, to make them the focus of attention, to set up a stronger interplay of color between them. He went as far as he could without a model, so as to be all ready to start painting when the Indian came to pose in the morning. At four, feeling at a loose end, he decided to call on Praither, largely because Buell's high praise had aroused his curiosity.

Praither was cleaning a gun at one of the low living-room windows when his wife—a tiny, doll-like woman with enormous china-blue eyes, who never said very much and who seemed to be perfectly content at the center of her pacidly watchful silences—opened the door. Praither welcomed him ebulliently. "Just let me finish this, fellow. Sit down over there where you'll be comfortable. I'll rustle some drinks in a minute. Don't let the dogs bother you!"

Two vicious-looking bulldogs, all formidable bulk and teeth and dangling folds of skin, drooled with devotion and threatened to slobber all over his shoes when Peter petted them. Lily Praither finally had to entice them out into the kitchen, to save him from their friendliness. She had been embroidering a white fiesta blouse and quietly settled down to it again.

Praither was doing all the talking. "Ever shoot with one of these? It's a 44-40, an old Winchester carbine. I use it for bear hunting. Wonderful balance—heft it!"

He was as affectionate as one of his overgrown bulldogs, boisterous, high-strung. Now and again Lily Praither raised her blue saucer eyes from her embroidery, as if to show that she was listening. Not that Praither needed encouragement. He was all at once telling about the Santa Fe fiesta and a costume ball and a fight he had had with somebody called "Mike." "I'd gone as a cardinal and I wore a chain around my neck. The chain caught in a brooch she wore. I was trying to undo it when he comes up and swings on me. . . ." It astonished Peter to note with what earnestness Praither told about the fight, as if he had been a general reporting some major battle he had won or a little boy bragging about his first brawl. He could not get him to talk about painters or paint. Hunting and fishing and drinking and guns appeared to be all that interested him.

It was the same way when Praither took him to see his studio. They stayed only long enough for Praither to extract a box of cartridges from the litter of old paint tubes and loose shells in a drawer of his painting table. Then Praither headed outside again, loaded the carbine, and when Peter declined his invitation to try out the gun began to blaze away at a row of tin cans set up as targets on the sloping sagebrush land. He made the cans skip and roll on the ground with monotonous regularity. He did not quit until the entire box of ammunition was gone. Even when they went back into the studio, his mind still was on nothing but guns. Peter had to admire a rack full of rifles, shotguns, target pistols, telescope sights. At least half the studio was cluttered with things that had nothing to do with painting at all—a rowing machine, a punching bag, dumbbells, boxing gloves, a rubber boat, a shelf crowded with trophies Praither had won for marksmanship. It was only after Peter had shown a polite interest in a deputy sheriff's badge pinned to a holster hanging from the wall, that he felt free to edge toward the upper end of the studio.

Reluctantly Praither opened some portfolios and flicked out a few drawings and lithographs on the table for him. It was almost too dark to see anything. Yet even in the short time Praither allowed him to look at a sheet, even in the unsatisfactory light, he could tell how superbly Praither could draw. It was impossible to miss the sensitive line, the boldness with which Praither had rejected all the inessentials in the object he had portrayed. There were only two paintings to be seen: a small oil of an Indian girl, and a huge, half-finished canvas of a group of young men and women playing tennis, engaging in gymnastics, swimming and diving. It was a wonderfully decorative picture, beautifully composed. The young people were like gods and goddesses; everything was bathed in sunlight and joy; it was a glimpse of an athletic paradise. Even in the failing light of the studio, one could tell how excitingly color was being used. Yet when he tried to compliment Praither on it, Praither dismissed the picture with a curiously boyish shrug. "It's for a country club. Let's go build some drinks. Do you ever box? How about a workout sometime?"

They went back to the house, to the drooling bulldogs, to more of Praither's swaggering, to Lily Praither who had toasted some crackers spread with cheese and sardines to go with the overstrong highballs Praither presently fixed. But this time Peter was able to get him onto the subject of painting for a few minutes at least. He tried to check Buell's opinion. "What do you think of Geoffrey Middlemas?"

Praither hunched his rangy shoulders with nervous restiveness. "He's all right. He's an academic painter—Slade School and Julian's, but they weren't able to ruin him."

"You said Chet Orr's composition was weak. Does Middlemas know how to compose?"

"You bet your sweet life he does. There is no comparison between the two men. Chet arranges—he doesn't compose. Middlemas has an architectonic sense."

"How is he as a colorist?"

Praither fidgeted unhappily. It was clear that he hated to talk about art. "He's all right. It's not a palette I like but it's bold and it's sensitive. It's not embalmer's color and prismatic like you see in three quarters of the pictures in most shows. . . . Ever hunted elk?"

Peter wondered—while he sat in the dining room at Bishop's Lodge that evening—about the boxing gloves, the guns, all the talk of fights and shooting the rapids of the Rio Grande in a flimsy rubber boat. Why was Praither trying so hard to convince one of his virility? It wasn't as if he were a sawed-off Napoleon who constantly had to prove to himself that he was as good as the next man and twice as tough—though perhaps the sensitiveness written in his face, the very fact that he was an artist, was something of which he was ashamed. On the other hand, during the few minutes that he had talked about painting, he had sounded sure of himself and fiercely authoritative. He had not agreed with Buell about Geoffrey Middlemas!

As if Buell's strictures of Geoffrey's painting at once encouraged him to rivalry with him and at the same time made him want to defend Geoffrey by using his own work as a shield, he applied himself with consuming zest to repainting the picture of the Indian. He tried to use everything Buell had shown him about color and everything he had learned from looking at his canvases. He experimented, scraped off with the palette knife and tried again, did one of the hands over half a dozen times. He was proud of the interplay he thought he had achieved between the blanket and the bandeau around the Indian's black hair. On the fourth afternoon he could not resist the temptation to get Buell to come down and look at what he had done.

Buell dropped in at a little after four, studied the picture with narrowed eyes, scowled. "All right, get on with it. What do you want me for?"

"I wanted to know whether I was on the right track."

"You're learning something. At least you're showing that you're conscious of the different planes. The back of the Indian's head doesn't jump out of the picture the way it did before. You just don't think in terms of paint. Some people can't draw, and some don't handle color well."

"Does that mean that I won't ever be able to learn how to paint?"

"Certainly you can learn how to paint. I've known painters who were practically color-blind. Look at Ingres—he had no color sense. All I'm saying is that your talent runs to drawing. Have you ever done any lithographs?"

"No. Isn't that quite a difficult technique to learn?"

"Nothing much to it once you get used to drawing on the stone. I've got a couple of stones at my place if you want to come over and see what the process is like. Why don't you come to supper tonight?"

He had to beg off. "I'm sorry I can't tonight. I'm supposed to go to Jeanne Lauber's for dinner."

"And I suppose tomorrow you're going to Cristina Day's?"

"Yes, I got an invitation a couple of days ago."

"Well, I can show you some other time." Buell halted for a moment at the door. "I warned you about the parties out here! A fellow can get so he does nothing but bat around. . . ."

It was true—he told himself that evening in Jeanne Lauber's living room—that there seemed to be an amazing number of parties going on. Hadn't he got an invitation in the mail yesterday for next Thursday already, to a party at that elderly couple's he had met at Dorothy Lambert's house? It was true, too, that he enjoyed seeing each new Santa Fe house— as Jeanne Lauber's tonight, with its collection of Chinese hangings and bronze and jade and red-lacquered chests and Tibetan temple bells and playing cards and all the other loot Jeanne Lauber had brought back from her yoga pilgrimage. But Buell exaggerated the danger of his turn-ing into a party hound. What Buell could not know was that the excite-ment with which he went to each party had to do with his hope of meet-ing Cristina and Geoff. Once they had left—and Cristina had slipped away early tonight with the excuse of having a lot of work ahead in the morning to prepare for her own party tomorrow—Jeanne Lauber's place lost most of its charm for him, and he went, too.

Yet because Buell had got under his skin, he was up at half past five the next morning, shivering in the brisk October cold while he saddled the horse he had hired from the neighbor across the road. He stayed in the saddle all morning because Geoffrey had again mentioned his afternoon rides and he wanted to get in some practice before he joined Cristina and him, and because Buell's denying him any talent as a painter made him reluctant to go even near the half-finished oil painting. It was only after lunch, on a sudden impulse to prove Buell wrong, that he picked up the brushes again and presently was so engrossed in all the changes he wanted to make that he did not tear himself away from the canvas until it was almost time to leave for Cristina's party.

It was his first glimpse of the long, low house with the two wings ex-tending toward the rear since the afternoon when he had come prowling up College Street and Pecos Trail in search of the yellow car. He grinned to himself at the thought that this time he did not feel as if he were tres-passing and would be able to look his fill.

He caught sight of the Isotta again beyond the cedar trees while he parked behind the Orrs and walked with them down the driveway that was already jammed with cars. A short path lined with exuberantly blooming white chrysanthemums led through a tunnellike passageway cut through the wing into the patio. Two gay beach umbrellas were still open, as if to deny the tang of autumn in the air and the fact that now at six all that was left of the sun was a brilliant glow which gave a tender richness to the last few blossoms on the yellowing hollyhocks and to the banked dahlias and Michaelmas daisies and coleus around the wrought-iron gate set in the jog in the far wing. A wide portale ran along the main part of the house and down the two sides of the patio. Huge black Indian pottery jars filled with great bunches of white chrysanthemums stood be-tween invitingly placed wicker and cowhide tables and chairs. A Spanish girl was lighting a fire in the charming adobe fireplace in the angle be-tween the main house and the wing, where Praither and Furfey and Dor-othy Lambert and half a dozen others had come with their drinks.

But most of the warm hum of voices came drifting out through the screen door from what was obviously the living room. He followed Mary and Chet inside and down the two steps to the lowered floor, hastily took in the impressive size of the room, the small native windows, the huge corner fireplace, the ebony grand piano set at an angle to the wall about two-thirds down the length of the room, the relaxed elegance of the mingled Mexican and old Italian—or were those carved oak chests French?—and modern furniture.

There was almost the identical crowd as at the Orrs', except that several couples who had been at Dorothy Lambert's had also been asked, as well as Geoffrey's preposterous pupil, who was wearing a tie and a corduroy jacket in honor of the occasion but looked nevertheless as if he had just got off a truck and who presently grated again on Peter by addressing Cristina as "Christine," exasperatingly repatriating her with South Chicago chumminess. She did not seem to notice and smiled.

He had only a minute with her, just long enough to say hello and glance from her smiling eyes to the exquisitely wrought gold filigree necklace with the deep-red stones and back again into her eyes, before she was drawn away by some other guests. But his eyes kept following the shifting pastel reds of her crimson velvet gown with the long, loose skirt. Once, the dumpy Gladys with her birdlike vivaciousness and the catlike pounce caught him looking while he stood talking to her and to Helen Kemp, the full-blown but not unattractive wife of the painter with the Vandyke beard. She promptly exclaimed with elaborate artlessness, "Doesn't Cristina look beautiful tonight?" Helen Kemp was saying, "I've always dreamed of owning a Fortuny gown!" For some incalculable reason Gladys saw fit to show her claws. "Of course I couldn't ever wear one. One simply has to be tall. Still, in your case, darling—" and Gladys' tone professed to work a miracle of charity—"I know you'd look stunning in one. . . ."

He left them to their mysterious feminine bickering and joined Piggot and George Kemp. At the far end of the room, he noticed out of the corner of his eye, Geoffrey was still fixing highballs on the carved oak cabinet beyond the piano—still inconspicuously but unmistakably acting as host, as he had done when Peter had gone up to him for a drink and there had been time enough only to exchange a few words because of all the people hanging around.

There was the usual exhilarating texture of party voices talking all at once. Jim Hopper, the man from the curio shop, was just finishing a story about a French chambermaid, ". . . *mais, non, madame, c'est le chauffeur qui me l'a dit*—eet ees ze chauffeur who told me so!" He had started listening too late to catch the point, but he laughed with the rest because Cristina was coming up to him with a smile, a plate of hors d'oeuvres in each hand. There was a flicker of mischief in her eyes.

"Did you remember the house?"

"Remember it?" he floundered. "But I've never been here before."

"Yes, you have. About three weeks ago, late one afternoon. I happened to be watching a robin on the lilac bush through the window there when I saw you looking in over the wall."

He knew that he had blushed. "Oh, that! I looked in because I recognized your car from having seen it downtown. I was just passing by."

"You looked all around at everything like a detective, as if you were hunting for a criminal," she teased.

"I was just curious. There aren't many people who drive Italian cars. I guess I was pretty impertinent, staring like that. I'm sorry."

"Don't be. It was fun watching you when you didn't know you were being observed—you looked so intent. And I was fascinated when all of a sudden you walked in at Geoff's the next afternoon."

"Did you tell Geoff?"

"That I'd seen you before?" She smiled playfully. "I don't tell Geoff everything."

He lost her again to the crowd. But to his delight, almost immediately after supper, Collard and Furfey and Gladys and the others were pressing her to sing. Once again from the first ravishingly clear note that floated from her mouth he felt himself carried away by her voice and the beauty of the songs, by the enchanting picture she presented sitting at the piano in the parchment-filtered light of the single lamp trained on the music rack, her pale skin luminous with gleaming whiteness against the suddenly black-splotched crimson of her gown. They kept her singing for almost an hour this time—Monteverdi, Cimarosa, Rossini, two Neapolitan songs—before she protested and made Praither take her place and play jazz.

He was in no hurry tonight to leave. He drifted out into the patio where a pleasant group had gathered around the charming portale fireplace. Jeanne Lauber, in still another mandarin coat, was defending astrology against Gladys' jeers. She was not coming off too well. Her muddleheaded references to the Chaldeans and to all sorts of pseudo-scientific lore were shrilly pounced on by Gladys. "Now surely, Jeanne, you can't believe that! . . ." To Peter's astonishment, Collard, the biochemist or whatever he was, sided with Jeanne. "Precisely because I'm a scientist!" he warded off Gladys. "It's part of the scientific method not to rule out any possibility. For all we know so far, there may be radiations from the planets to which we're susceptible at the moment of birth. It's a crucial moment in our biological career."

"Obviously," George Kemp joked before Gladys could continue the argument. "Just look at all the people trying to crawl back into the womb."

"That's you, Hutch," a handsome, middle-aged woman, who had not been at any of the previous parties, was saying to her pudgy, bald husband, who had a nervous habit of smoothing his black mustache. "Hutch," she explained, "wouldn't ever get up in the morning unless I waved a frying pan with ham and eggs over him. He sleeps all curled up and with the blanket pulled all the way over his head. He looks just like——"

"Let's not get technical, honey."

The banter kept on. Peter stayed for a while longer on the portale. He fell to talking with Dorothy Lambert and George Kemp until Dorothy began to feel cold and they all three of them went inside. He passed within a couple of feet of Geoffrey, heard him tell Mary Orr and a small crowd about some sort of picturesque religious procession in Brittany, took pleasure in his clipped speech and his arresting way of standing there in his double-breasted gray suit, and yet walked on to another group. He told himself that it was because of Geoff's pupil—annoyingly in evidence and never very far away from him—that he was avoiding Geoff. Yet he found himself compelled to go on watching him across the room for any sign of possessiveness, of telltale familiarity with Cristina's house. When he thought he saw some new proof of how thoroughly at home he was here, such as the unhesitating way he reached around the doorjamb for the light switch in the dining room when he started for the kitchen for more ice, he stiffened with resentment and at the same time glowed with pride.

Buell left. Praither was expertly thumping out favorite old musical comedy hits, with Chet Orr and the man who had the affected pronunciation and the loud tie and several of the women singing soulfully. The party was settling into pleasant midnight intimacy. . . . He drifted to the bookcase built into the center of the long wall, saw that half a shelf was taken up by Piggot's books and told himself that he must get hold of one sometime and see what it was like. There were shelves full of modern American and English novels by the authors the Greenwich Village crowd had always been talking about; there were rows of paper-covered French and Italian books. Courteline, Gide, Proust, Pirandello, Manzoni, D'Annunzio—he scanned the names of the authors and noticed a set of small, leather-bound volumes of Dante on another shelf just as Cristina came up.

Her lips were parted in a smile and her serene, white forehead gave the lie to her mock concern. "I hope you aren't shocked by my library. I've been reading a lot of detective stories lately. I've been meaning to take them down to the hospital, but I just haven't got around to it."

He said, "I've been admiring it—especially the Dante here."

"My stepfather gave me those for my fifteenth birthday." Her eyes suddenly shone with infectious gaiety. "He also took me to the opera for the occasion and to Maxim's afterward, which was infinitely more exciting at the time than owning the *Divine Comedy*. I was in boarding school in Paris and I'd been shut up for months. You can imagine what an adventure it was to be taken out for the evening by a man. We had dinner at Fouquet's, and I wore a dress that was very décolleté. The sisters at the convent would have been horrified if they had known." She took down the first volume and held it out for him to see. "It's a lovely set, isn't it?"

He opened the tooled-leather cover of the slim volume, passed hastily over the boldly scrawled inscription on the flyleaf, saw that it was a beautifully printed book, and said, "Yes, lovely." He turned to the first page. "*Nel mezzo del cammin,*" he tried to read. "Is that how you pronounce it?"

Without taking her eyes from his, with an indulgent smile, she recited, "*Nel mezzo del cammin di nostra vita . . .*" and went on for a few lines— for much too short a time! The Italian words became hauntingly melodious in her mouth. Her voice was even more deeply enchanting than when she had sung.

Regretfully when she stopped he slipped the book back into its place on the shelf. "Would there ever be a chance of hearing you read some of that?"

"Why, yes, if you like, but I don't think I read particularly well."

"But you do."

"You told me you didn't understand Italian?"

"I'd just like to hear the sound of it. Or I could get an English translation and follow along."

"As a matter of fact, I have a translation. It's up there somewhere on one of those shelves." She looked amused all of a sudden. "All right, we'll have a Dante evening sometime. Maybe you'll come to dinner, and afterward we can read. Let me know when you're in the mood."

"Oh, I'll be in the mood. The sooner, the better—before you forget."

She smiled back at him. "Would you like to do it next week sometime? How about Tuesday night?"

CHAPTER FIVE

Girl or Woman?

Let's not be adolescent! he admonished himself repeatedly in the course of the next few days. There'll be dinner, and then Cristina will read. What's there to be so excited about? The chances are Geoffrey is going to be there, too. But he tingled with excitement nevertheless each time he thought of Tuesday night. Cristina kept crowding into his mind. He found himself experimenting with titanium white and rose madder and Venetian red, trying to capture the white-petal texture of her skin on a corner of the canvas he was working on. He wondered suddenly while he picked up an armful of firewood from the pile outside what the perfume was which she used—a moist, delicate flower fragrance he had been unable to identify. He woke with a gay start each morning, hurried across the road for the cow pony, and rode hard for two hours because riding was something he associated with her. And he was filled with instant alarm on Tuesday afternoon when the barking of the two dogs next door made him look out through the studio window just in time to see the yellow Isotta turn into the yard. Cristina, a bright red scarf

97

wound turban-wise around her head, wearing a polo coat, was at the wheel; Geoffrey was beside her in the low front seat.

He hastily put down the palette and the brush, wiped his hands on a clean paint rag, slipped on a coat, and hurried outside. They were both already out of the car. Cristina was stripping off her driving gloves, greeting him with a smile. Geoffrey joked, "I thought I'd better get here before you were snowed in! Mrs. Day and I were invited out to lunch together, and it seemed a perfect afternoon for a drive." But no explanation why they had come in her car. . . . "We weren't at all sure whether this was the house."

"Oh, I was; I recognized Peter's car." Her tone mimicked the excuse he had given her last week; her eyes laughed at him. "I hope you didn't mind my coming along."

It was only a visit; she had not come to call anything off! But her very blandness disconcerted him. Had she perhaps forgotten about their date for tonight?

He took them into the house, apologized for the saddle in the corner of the kitchen. "We're building a shed, but my Mexican neighbor keeps finding more pressing jobs. It's all very primitive." He ushered them into the living room.

"You seem quite comfortable here," Geoffrey said and appeared not anywhere near so much at ease as Cristina who went up to the north window and exclaimed, "It's charming! What a lovely view!" She turned toward the easel and saw the half-finished picture. "We barged in on you when you were right in the middle of work. May I look?"

"It's an old Tesuque Indian," he said out of sheer embarrassment.

Geoffrey had walked up to the easel, too. "Is this your first attempt at oil painting?"

"No, my second one. The first one was even worse. Dave Buell's informed me that I'll never make a painter."

It enchanted him to have Cristina say indignantly, "I think it's a very good picture—don't you, Geoff? Dave must have been fooling. Oh, I'm sure he was!"

Geoffrey said coldly, "I don't see how anyone can make a statement like that after such a short time. Besides I don't agree with Buell at all. On what does he base his opinion?"

"He feels that I don't think in terms of paint."

"Did he expect you to after only two weeks? It takes years to learn to paint—most painters think it takes a lifetime."

Cristina was saying, "I like especially what you've done with his eyes and the forehead here, Peter."

"That's largely a matter of drawing—not so much a matter of paint," Geoffrey corrected her. "The head is certainly well drawn."

"Oh, Buell sort of thinks I can draw."

"That's very gracious of him." Geoffrey's voice was razor-edged, so that Peter had a delightful sensation that Geoffrey was contending with Buell for him and that by defending Buell he could make Geoffrey show his hand all the more.

"He feels I ought to go in for lithographs."

"There's nothing to prevent you from making lithographs and painting, too. There are a number of other men besides Buell who can teach you painting."

The duel was suddenly between Geoffrey and him. He said blandly, as if he were obtuse to what was at stake, "Oh, I think Buell's a good teacher. I'll stick with him for a while."

"You must suit yourself. Have you any drawings you have done?"

"Yes, have you, Peter?" Cristina urged.

He got out the half-dozen drawings and sketches he had made, handed them to Cristina one by one, reluctantly, and—for all his feeling that they were too trivial to show and that he could do so much better now—reveled in her enthusiasm and in Geoffrey's close scrutiny.

"I love the gaunt man with the horses. He's got the same quality as my San Ysidro—it's one of those charming native carvings," she explained. "Don't you think that's excellent, Geoff?"

"It's a good drawing." He was—Peter noted it—impressed.

They would not let him make coffee or get them a drink. They were not going to stay. Geoffrey appeared almost in a hurry to go. Although he looked very relaxed in his elegantly baggy gray tweed suit, there was a taut restiveness underneath the country-gentleman quietude as he sat on one of the brightly painted Mexican chairs. His hand brushed rapidly down the tanned furrows on the side of his chin with the nervous gesture Peter had noticed before. He gave the impression of being secretly poised to jump to his feet at the first opportunity and start saying good-by. His mist-blue eyes were remote—evasive. He said abruptly, right in the middle of Cristina's questions about Tesuque and the neighborhood, "Will you join us for dinner tonight, Peter?" only to check himself almost instantly and turn to Cristina with a half-impatient, half-apologetic frown, "Oh, I forgot, Tina; you're having Jeanne Lauber tonight."

"Yes, I'm afraid tonight's out."

Had she forgotten about the invitation? No, Peter told himself happily the next instant, for her smile had broadened and now not only included him but was meant for him alone and was saying, *Yes, indeed, we do have something important on for tonight.* But, then, what was all that about the yoga woman with her tipsy trances and her mandarin coats? Had Cristina invited a lot of other people, too—or had she lied to Geoffrey about tonight? He remembered her saying, "I don't tell Geoffrey everything," and felt dizzied by the dimension of guilty secrecy the evening had suddenly taken on. It lasted only for a fraction of a second. Cristina's serenely open glance had shifted back to Geoffrey, and his speculation appeared not only sordid and insolent but ludicrous.

"And tomorrow I'll be busy, and Thursday night there's the Oxnards'. Friday and Saturday are both out. We'd better make it next week—Monday if you haven't anything else on. . . ." And in the kitchen, on their way out when Geoffrey's eyes fell on the saddle again, he added, "Would you like to go riding with us Monday afternoon? You can bring along a change of clothes and clean up for dinner at my place afterward."

The invitation to go riding with them, so often already in Geoffrey's mouth, had at last shed its irritating indefiniteness. Monday at three at Geoffrey's house! He accepted with alacrity.

But it was not Monday that he was thinking of after he had seen them into the car and watched them turn down the road toward Bishop's Lodge. His thoughts kept leaping ahead to tonight. Only three hours away; at five he'd start getting dressed. Why had she made a secret of tonight? Was it just playfulness or a mild assertion of independence on her part or perhaps a perfectly innocent reticence, the subject of who her guests were tonight besides Jeanne never having come up between her and Geoff? *Was Jeanne Lauber going to be there at all?*

She was. He saw her as soon as Cristina pulled open the living-room door, curled up in the big easy chair by the corner fireplace, her feet tucked under her, her eyes bright above the highball glass pressed against the tuniclike black Chinese blouse. While the two tawny cocker spaniels, who had not been in evidence until nearly the end of Cristina's party on Saturday night and who today had come yapping furiously to the door, flung themselves back toward Jeanne Lauber, Cristina explained, "Jeanne wanted to join us when she heard that we were going to read Dante. Do you mind? I think she likes Dante almost as much as you do, Peter."

Was she making fun of him again, he wondered, with that disarmingly open smile, which was like a magician displaying his hands to show that there was nothing hidden in his palms.

"I adore the *Divine Comedy*," Jeanne Lauber purred in her husky, rapture-laden voice. "I feel I'm intruding, though."

There was nothing for it but to profess himself delighted to see her there. But behind his polite enthusiasm and the small talk he was drawn into by Jeanne when Cristina left them to go to the tile-inlaid iron table beyond the fireplace to fix him a drink, he rebelled. Had Cristina felt that they needed a chaperon?

Yet he had to admit after only a few minutes that Jeanne Lauber's being there actually made for a greater degree of intimacy between Cristina and him. A certain constraint—a stealthy sense of guilt—which would have tended to handicap him if he had been alone with her was somehow removed. He felt free to hold Cristina's glance an exhilarating fraction of a second longer than he would otherwise have dared, felt free to look at her almost as often as he liked and pretend not to be aware of the curve of her breasts under the clinging, dark-blue wool dress and to be looking only because there was something compelling about the attentiveness with which she sat listening to Jeanne.

He encouraged Jeanne to talk. He chaffed her on her acquaintance with what appeared to be a whole series of holy men in India. At moments— as when she told about a Tibetan funeral high on a mountain plateau at dawn and about the weird chants with which the priests called the vultures to come for the corpse exposed on a crag—he became interested in spite of his distrust of her lush mysticism and the distaste aroused in him by her splotchy skin and her untidy bobbed black hair. But most of the time his awareness of Cristina would hardly let him notice Jeanne; even the furniture in the room, which had been rearranged since the night of the party, mattered more.

It was exciting to look around and pick up hints of how Cristina lived and what she liked, and presently to follow Jeanne and her through the carved door beside the chest on which Geoffrey had fixed the drinks into the dining room. He had caught only a glimpse of it on Saturday night. He did not want to miss anything: the woven straw mats on the red-brick floor, the massive Italian table and chairs, the crystal in the red and green corner cupboard, the antique priest's cope tacked to the wall above the sideboard like a huge emerald brocade fan, the charming little fireplace, the flowers, and the beautiful old majolica candlesticks. He won-

dered how often Geoffrey had sat in this room with her, at Cristina's
right and facing the patio window behind Jeanne—or did Cristina not
sit at the head of the table when there were just the two of them? Did they
sit across from each other, and did she always smile so enchantingly at
the maid's little girl who was helping serve and who looked back at her
with adoring eyes? Was her tone always so frankly appreciative and
friendly in talking to the maid as now when Mercedes brought in the
soufflé? "Mercedes, you did make the oven behave! How did you do it?"

Jeanne Lauber, he noticed, hardly touched her food. She had brought
her drink to the table and she smoked and talked. She was telling Cristina
now about the horoscope she had cast for a friend of theirs, had worked
on for two days, and then had thrown away because her astral calculations
had shown nothing but disaster. "I don't know what I'm going to tell her
yet; I can't tell her the truth," she fretted. It appeared that she had known
from the beginning—from the unlucky woman's aura—about the tragic
destiny written in her stars. "I can always tell. Sometimes it's overpowering, and then I refuse to try even to do a horoscope," she said with the
somber gravity of a pythoness who shudders at the very thought of her
monstrous gift.

"What about my horoscope—good or bad?" he teased.

"I'd like to do yours!"

He could see from her clammy-eyed humorlessness that she was going
to insist. She was not only a fool with her occultism but a drunk and a
bore. Why did Cristina have her around? She wanted to know when he
was born. He gave her the month and the day and the year.

"Do you know what hour?"

"No, I've never been interested enough to ask. Is that important, too?"

"It's very important! Can't you find out?"

"I suppose I can," he said hurriedly, wondering whether Cristina's
appraising glance meant that she had sensed his embarrassment at the
mere thought of going to Mizzi with any question about his birth, wondering again how much she knew about him. He said brusquely, dismissing the whole subject of astrology, "What beautiful candlesticks! Are
they Mexican?" and succeeded in making Cristina talk about Italy..

It was pleasant back in the living room. They had coffee in front of the
fireplace. Jeanne Lauber had settled herself on some cushions on the
floor and was sitting Buddha-style and gazing with drowsy raptness into
the flames. Mercedes' husband came in from the portale with an armful
of logs. Mercedes collected the cups and took away the coffee tray. The
two spaniels had curled up each at one end of the settee and only blinked

when Cristina went to the bookcase for one of the leatherbound volumes she had shown him the night of the party. She handed him the translation she had lying ready on the little table beside her chair. "Where would you like me to start?"

"I'd like to hear those lines at the very beginning again."

"All right, you shall." She put out her cigarette and started to read. *"Nel mezzo del cammin di nostra vita . . ."* Almost instantly the enchantment seized on him again. He tried to follow along in English for a few lines, but the sound of her voice drew his eyes away from the page. The words followed one another with exquisite stateliness; they struck him as magically apt and persuasive and musical; he did not have to know what they meant to feel intoxicated with joy. He hated it when she stopped.

"That's the first canto. Could you follow it?"

"A little. I hope you aren't going to stop."

Jeanne Lauber, whose head had been drooping, roused herself and smiled with bleary beatitude. "It's wonderful, darling. Where does the part about Paolo and Francesca come?"

"That's in the fifth canto, I think."

"Do read that," Jeanne begged.

He turned to it in his translation and kept reading this time because his curiosity was aroused by the first few lines. He felt himself go tense with delicious expectancy as he listened for the Italian words—like the rich and tantalizing underside of a priceless tapestry—of the story of Francesca and her brother-in-law who, it appeared, had fallen fatally in love while reading about another pair of guilty lovers still farther back in tapestried time. There was a piquancy in brusquely denying to himself that there was any romantic parallel between the story and Cristina's reading it to him, in dismissing the story with condescending tenderness; for didn't he and Cristina have a chaperon, and weren't they after all— quite apart from Jeanne's being there—a little too grown-up and fastidious for any such maudlin maneuvering, and wasn't he able to look with perfect composure now at Cristina as she finished reading the last line? Besides, who had said anything about Cristina's being married to Geoff? Was she going to be, though?

"Isn't it wonderful?" Jeanne rumbled.

"Yes, it's lovely," he agreed.

Cristina turned to him. "Well, now have you had enough?"

Jeanne Lauber got ahead of him. "I can never have enough. Read some more!"

"Let me see—all right, I'll read the part about Ulysses. That's one of my favorites. The question is whether I'll be able to find it now." Cristina hunted for a little while, found it. "Here it is: canto 26!"

Once again he gave himself up to the spell, heard only Cristina's voice, and did not even try to see what the words meant. He noticed out of the corner of his eyes that Jeanne's head was dipping lower and lower, until by the time Cristina stopped reading there could be no question that Jeanne was fast asleep. Cristina had noticed it, too, and smiled. She picked up a bright Paisley shawl that lay folded over the arm of the settee and bent over Jeanne. "Jeanney, don't you want to go to my room and lie down?" There was only a sleepy sigh from Jeanne and no pretense this time of coming out at will and with bright eyes from some soul-restoring trance. Instead, Jeanne with a comfortable sigh abandoned her Buddha pose, uncrossed her ankles and drew up her legs under her and let her head sag against the easy chair. Cristina spread the Paisley shawl over her legs; then got one of the silk cushions from the settee and carefully placed it under her head. "Poor Jeanne gets hay fever," she explained loyally. "She hasn't been getting any sleep. Would you like some ice water or a drink? Melita has brought in ice."

He tiptoed to the tile-inlaid table with her and fixed highballs for both of them. They laughed softly once when the ice tongs clattered against the tray, and there was a tingle of gay conspiracy in their agreeing with a smiling glance to change to the chairs on the other side of the fireplace, so as to lessen the risk of waking Jeanne. Their muted voices spun a shimmering web of warm intimacy until it seemed as if there were no one else in the room. They talked about furniture. The subject had appealed to him as safely impersonal and yet tinctured with the promise of leading to information about Cristina's past and about Geoff.

"No, the chairs," she said, "are Italian. Most of the other things though are from Normandy. I used to have a passion for old Norman furniture before the War. I picked up literally tons of stuff on my honeymoon, and then almost all of it had to go into storage because things like the big chest and the cupboards and a *bahut* I have in my room were much too big for our apartment in Paris. They wouldn't even go through the doors," she said with an amused laugh. "The chest is an old vestry chest. We found it on a farm near Berneval where the people had been using it for storing grain. You must look at the carving sometime; they represent scenes from Genesis and they are sort of amusing."

"I didn't know you were married before the War."

"Perhaps it's because I haven't told you."

He was flustered by the indulgent laugh that accompanied the reproof.

"You sound mysterious. Is it something one is supposed to be tactful about? I can't imagine you ever having something to conceal."

"I hope I have, although a friend of mine claims that we ought to have the courage of our mistakes. I don't agree with him; I'd rather keep mum about mine. Wouldn't you?"

"I suppose so. I just meant I thought you were still in school in Paris at that time."

"Well, I was. That's why I got married—to get out of school."

"Did you elope?"

"Not exactly. I gave Mother an ultimatum: either she'd let me take an apartment with a governess I'd once had and study music seriously or I'd get married during Easter vacation."

"And she wouldn't let you take the apartment."

"Yes, she did, but I got married anyway."

There were fenced avenues and paths from which he must not stray. It would mean offending against the rules by which he sensed he would have to proceed, to try and ascertain how many months and years "that time" had comprised before the War. But it was perfectly safe to ask jokingly, "Love?"

Cristina shrugged. "Partly. And I'd have had to go back to the convent after Easter vacation to finish out the year, and I just couldn't face it. I felt I simply had to get away from Sisters and chaperons and blue uniforms, or I'd die!"

"Did you hate being in a convent so much?"

"It wasn't that so much, but I was seventeen and I didn't want to go on studying for the *bachot* when what I really was interested in was music. So I wired Mother—I was spending the Easter vacation with some friends of Mother's in Cannes, and Walter was there, too, of course—that she'd better give her consent if she wanted us to be married properly."

It was as far as he could go along that particular path. He tried a detour that looked vaguely promising. "What did you collect after you had enough Norman furniture?"

Her silver-gray eyes lighted up mischievously. "Plain, ordinary playing cards and books and writing sets and anything else that might entertain wounded soldiers—I'd joined the Red Cross at the beginning of the War. But as a matter of fact I'd given it up long before that. It was just one of those things that belongs to a particular period of one's life. Haven't you been all wrapped up in something and then you've suddenly wondered why you'd been so fascinated?"

"Why, yes, I suppose so," he said and reflected hastily that there had

been no period in his life when he had had time for some luxurious interest that had not immediately furthered his ambition or his work, unless
indeed he was willing to go all the way back to his childhood and count
the passionate joy it had been to him to sing in Herr Granini's choir at
the time. And not even that had been gratuitous: much of the joy had
been due to the fact that the choir had been an escape from the drabness
at home. No, what he'd really have to count would be his zest for hunting
wild flowers that one summer in the Tyrol—or possibly his frenzy of
devotion in studying Latin by himself when Rudi Martin, whom he
had adored, had been sent to a swanker school where Latin had been
taught. . . . He added, still with Rudi in his mind, "The sort of thing one
outgrows and smiles at afterward."

"I don't think it's a matter of 'outgrowing' so much as it is of just
moving in another direction. For instance, when I started to study voice
I lost all interest in running a house, but later on I became as domestic as
could be again. I've never had the feeling that just because I've changed,
everything that happened before was necessarily childish or ridiculous.
In fact, I was very glad I had all this oak furniture in Paris when I bought
the place here. It fits rather well into an adobe house, don't you think?"

"Perfectly. Have you had this house long?"

"Not very. I got it five years ago when I came out here to take care of
my father. He'd been sent to New Mexico by the doctors on account of
his asthma. Father hated being in a sanatorium, and I really wasn't able
to do a thing for him just staying at the hotel; so we decided to get a
house. Poor Father never did get to enjoy it. He had a heart attack before
I could get it ready for us to move in."

"I'm sorry," he said. Another avenue from which he had to turn back,
since presumably any talk about the house now that she had been reminded of her father's death would be painful to her. "Did you spend most of
your life in France?"

"In France and in Italy—yes, I guess I did. Mother took me to Europe
when I was six and put me in school after she and Father were divorced
and she married again. So school in St. Cloud is where I stayed mostly
until I got married, except for summer vacations with Mother and my
stepfather in Pistoia—and except for a flying visit to New York every
other summer, when Mother took me because I was supposed to spend
a few weeks with Father. It usually amounted to only a few days actually
because Mother hated having to make the trip in the summer and because
Father was always busy."

She told about herself with an air of humorous detachment. He learned that her stepfather had a *palazzo* in Pistoia that had belonged to his family for six hundred years, that Pistoia was not very far from Florence, that her stepfather's first names were Pier Luigi, that Pier Luigi was an affectionate, dashing fellow who had a great gift for enjoying life and for making people around him enjoy it, and that his great passion was racing cars. It was exciting to listen to her and realize that there was something more than politeness and good-humored indulgence in her lending herself to his questions, that she was almost eager to have him know about her. Was it because she was going to marry Geoffrey, so that she already thought of herself as his stepmother? . . . He gathered that she herself owned a *palazzo* in Florence. "It's a very small one; any old stone house with a coat of arms over the door is a *palazzo*," she explained with a laugh. But he was unable to get any clue whether she had bought it or had come by it as a result of her marriage, any more than he could discover how long the marriage had lasted or when she had got to know Geoff.

She switched their roles suddenly, with a mischievous air of "Your turn now!" It was he all at once who was doing the answering. He found himself telling her about Pittsburgh and the steel mills, trying to evoke for her the magnificent power and fierce beauty he had felt at night sometimes in the open hearth shed, glossing over everything he had been busy with since—batteries and radios and the plating process—as mere gadgetry.

"But if the steel mills were as fascinating as you make them sound, why did you ever leave?"

He cast about for an explanation that would also satisfy him. His first laboratory job, the one Dr. Aspinall had offered him that winter evening at Carnegie Tech, suddenly appeared to him as a dubious short cut which his ambition had made him accept.

"I guess," he half joked, "I was weak."

"I don't believe that." Her gray eyes seemed to be measuring him. "I don't believe it for a minute. I think there is something very strong about you," she said just as Jeanne Lauber woke with a soft start and turned her head in momentary bewilderment at not finding them where they had been when she fell asleep—just as he realized that it was after eleven o'clock and high time for him to go. "We must continue this on Thursday. I want to hear a lot more about Pittsburgh," Cristina said with flattering earnestness by the door when he thanked her for the evening. . . .

Thursday turned out to be, in fact, a mere continuation of the evening. It was as if the big crowd at the Oxnards' and the rather pretentious house on the piñon-wooded rise just north of town and the cheerful party bustle and the lavish hospitality existed only to provide a festive setting for intimacy. Nothing had been lost of the delicious tension of two nights ago, he realized as soon as he caught her eye and saw the swift smile with which she welcomed him across the room.

He chafed at having to stop and say "hello" to people in the half-dozen groups that separated him from Cristina, who was standing with Furfey and the man with the flamboyant neckties—he had on a mauve and black one this time—at one end of the huge picture window, which offered a magnificent view of the scattered lights of Santa Fe below. When Geoffrey—oddly eager for his company all at once, almost voluble—detained him to talk again about the botched painting he and Cristina had looked at and praised, about their visit two days ago, about the horseback ride on Monday, Peter took the first opportunity—Daisy Oxnard arrived with some house guests of hers—to break away. It puzzled him a little to note the stealthy sense of triumph that went with his sudden indifference to Geoff. But there was not time to worry about either his exultation or his callousness. Except for the full-bosomed chatterbox, with all the diamond spangles and the frizzled blond hair, who seemed to be one of the Oxnards' closest friends and who had captured him in a mesh of talk, there was no other obstacle between him and Cristina.

And then, just when he had escaped from the chattering blonde and was free to join Cristina, he saw—not ten feet away, talking to Hal Oxnard and another elderly man in a shaggy tweed suit and to several girls from the fast young crowd—Aleida Gibbs! She gave him a brisk little smile and, in spite of having almost immediately turned her attention to Hal Oxnard and the others again, stood poised somehow expectantly—in that self-possessed athlete's way she had—as if expecting him to come. He had stiffened irritably even while he grimaced with exaggerated pleasure and bowed. She looked decidedly pretty in the smart dark-blue dress she had on; he admitted it, but the fact only added to his indignation that she should be there at all. He had the same feeling he had had when he suddenly caught sight of her at the livery stable, that she was spying on him.

I'll have to write Anne before she does, he thought impatiently, and tell her about Geoffrey Middlemas; otherwise Aleida is just as likely as not to mention him in a letter, and Anne might in all innocence spill the beans! No need for Mizzi to know that Geoff is here and worry about all that again. . . .

He made his choice, looked quickly away from Aleida and took the two short steps to the picture window, where Cristina said warmly, "Why, hello, Peter," and Furfey shook hands. The dapper little man with the mauve and black tie and the stage-British enunciation nodded perfunctorily and at once went on with the story he had been telling about his dog. It appeared that his chow had a propensity for nipping people he didn't like and that he had a particular dislike for women in riding breeches. "You're the only exception, Cris-tin-ah," he said and chanted her name as if he were doing a recitative on an opera stage. "But, then, La-o has good taste: he is a Chinese aristocrat." He seemed enormously proud of his dog's accomplishment and he made the most of telling how La-o had nipped the pompous fat man who had been hanging around the hotel lobby for the past week.

Cristina laughed dutifully. "Was he very angry?"

"Apoplectic, my dear. He threatened to send for his lawyer in Detroit until the doctor told him to shut up. They had to give him a hypo to calm him down. It was really too ridiculous: he kept yelling, 'I hope sir, you're insured!' "

"Are you?" Furfey asked.

"Certainly—ever since La-o took a violent dislike to a woman from Tulsa in a vile red dress. We're both insured with Lloyd's against freaks and frumps."

"That's quite an outfit, Lloyd's! I wish——"

Peter seized the opportunity offered by Furfey's threatened disquisition on the problem of insuring pictures, to say quickly to Cristina, "I acquired a dog Tuesday, just after you left! A puppy came and adopted me."

She caught on instantly and half turned her back to Furfey and the little man, shutting them out. "Why, Peter, how nice! What kind of a dog?"

"Oh, just the neighbor's mutt." He gave a broad wink and got her to smile at the brashness of his deceit. "Isn't the view magnificent?"

She followed him toward the middle of the huge window that stretched from the floor to the ceiling and took up half the length of the wall. She looked amused at their escape. "Willy," she said, "can be rather a bore."

"He's lascivious!"

"Oh, not Willy," she joked, "unless you're referring to his taste in neckties."

"Ties and perfumes. And he has an affair with every vowel, hasn't he?"

"Oh, I must tell Ralph! Poor Willy," she laughed.

In an instant they were in tune again, exactly as they had been on Tuesday night. If anything, Peter felt bolder in his bantering, elated by the fact that she seemed to share his desire to stay clear of the crowd. He noticed for the first time that behind her exquisitely feminine placidity there was a strain of wild recklessness, and the discovery intoxicated him. She said instantly, "Oh, yes, let's! . . . ." when he suggested—not expecting her to take him seriously—that they get up on a fragile, antique settee and sit on its back in order to see over the heads of the crowd and watch the parlor trick one of the boyish-boisterous guests was performing on the floor. She merely laughed at his question whether she herself had driven over the treacherous mountain road above the Riviera where her husband had had a bad accident. "Of course, I did. It wasn't really bad except when it was wet. Walter had the accident only because he was tight!"

She could be callous, too. Some of the reddish rum cocktail had spilled from her glass on the silk upholstery when she got down from the settee. They both laughingly tried to rub out the stain with the flimsy cocktail napkins which they had dipped in ice water. When the spot refused to disappear even after he had surreptitiously fetched a handful of salt from the kitchen and had sprinkled it on the stain, she briskly pulled one of the silk cushions over it. "Oh, well, we don't care," she said impatiently, so that he had to laugh at her petulance and felt excited at sharing the guilty little secret with her.

There was even a tinge of cruelty in her callousness. Her comments on people tonight had a caustic edge, especially when he asked her about the handsome, somewhat florid man who had been doing the rather childish stunts on the floor and whom she seemed to know. She did not make any attempt to lower her beautifully distinct voice, so that Peter felt certain that several people around them could hear every word if they were listening—"You mean Dickie boy who's all loaded down with tweed? All I know is that he's from California and plays polo and golf. He also confided to me that he is a four-goal man and that the best polo ponies come from the Argentine. That's as far as we got."

"And who's the woman with the diamond earrings?"

"That's Mamma, I believe."

"I thought she was his wife."

"Oh, she's much too young for that! No, I've been introduced: that's Mamma all right. She's very much in the picture, I'm afraid."

It was quite true that the frizzed blonde exhibited an altogether too strenuous youthfulness and that there was something soft about the big fellow in the large-patterned tweed suit. Yet Cristina's tartness puzzled Peter. He said, "You seem to have it in for mother's boys!"

"I've got good reason to: I've been married to two of them. I seem to have a fatal attraction for the type; they just flock to me. Do I look so very maternal, good God?"

Now that she challenged him, he realized that he was seeing a new Cristina all at once. It was not exactly recklessness, he corrected his earlier impression; it was some secret exasperation about to explode, some anguish, that made her so different tonight. She was certainly drinking a lot: she had finished her second cocktail since he had been with her. Had she and Geoffrey had a fight? Once when Geoffrey had been about to join them, she had distinctly turned toward the window and talked faster than before. And in some indefinable way everything that she had said had somehow seemed directed against Geoff.

"All I know is that you look enchanting when you frown! That's reason enough for anybody to 'flock.' "

"You're very nice, Peter. I suppose you know that." But the tenderness in her glance quickly wavered, as if she were too weary or too preoccupied to be interested in compliments. "Do you think we could scare up another cocktail? I seem to need a drink tonight."

He was afraid of losing her in the crowd. "I'll get you one. You won't go away? I don't want to lose you to Dickie boy!"

"I'll be right here. I'll hide in the draperies if someone comes."

He headed for one of the maids who had just come into the room with a tray of cocktails before he noticed that Aleida was directly in his path, talking to Ralph Piggot and the sculptor who had been a biologist. It rekindled his irritation to observe that she was talking to them as if she had known them for a long time. He was almost certain that she had seen him, but he pretended not to have noticed her. A chubby man, gesticulating and taking a step backward just then from his group, so that Peter had to guard the empty glasses in his hand, gave him an excuse to change his course. He circled around to the right, got safely to the maid with the tray, and hurried back to Cristina who was still alone by the window in spite of the people to the right and left. Her eyes were saying, "You see, I'm as good as my word!" He handed her the cocktail and returned her smile.

"I've been thinking—" he picked up playfully where they had left off, determined to explore her mood—"seems to me that one of those boys would make an ideal husband, docile and considerate!"

"What makes you think that's what a woman wants? Oh, a certain amount of sensitiveness, yes! But no woman wants a marriage that just amounts to running a nursery for a husband who's nothing more than a spoiled child."

Peter glanced at the big fellow, who was surrounded by women, and made her look, too. "Dickie boy looks pretty grown-up. I don't know how good he is at polo, but he looks virile enough."

"Don't let the beard fool you. Walter had a firm hand with horses, too, and he was quite the man about town when I married him; but the least little thing that came up, he was on the telephone to his mother in Cannes. Being a high-goal polo player or a masterful industrialist doesn't mean a thing—believe me, I know. Even when we were supposed to be on our honeymoon, Walter——"

She laughed while she told about Walter's attempts to telephone to his mother from Spain, but underneath her laughter she was fiercely serious. "A woman hates to have to compete for her husband with his mother. It's just too hopeless and too humiliating." And presently she was telling him not only about Walter, who had obviously been spoiled and weak, but also about Ian, who had been a composer and lame and brilliant and possessed of an indomitable will except when it came to his mother, against whom he had been rebelling unsuccessfully all his adult life. "She was a former ballerina, a tiny Russian woman with hands no bigger than a doll's—but with the most terrifying vitality. She was a demon! Ian was just simply afraid of her. And she had control over Ian's money, so that he never did break away. . . ."

Why, he wondered, was she telling him all this? Was she merely giving vent to some resentments that had suddenly been reawakened—by Geoffrey perhaps—and turned into fears, so that she needed to take someone into her confidence; or was she warning him what sort of man she expected her husband to be? Her intensity tonight at once frightened and excited him.

She said, "I'm not playing mother again to any man. I've had enough of that."

For an instant while he shrank from her peremptory tone and the jagged intransigence of her gaze, he was aware of a sudden furious resentment against the fine wrinkles below her eyes and against her too slim ankles and legs whose slenderness struck him all at once as a deplorable thinness caused by threatening age. But the next moment the very fact that she was excitingly older than he and beautiful and that she was talking with such revealing openness about herself made him like a fuse touched by fire again. Was it Geoffrey who needed mothering? Hadn't Piggot said something of the sort?

He tried to joke and immediately had the sensation of venturing out over a swift stream on a plank which might carry his weight and might not. "Now, me, I'd make an ideal husband: I never had a chance to form any mother fixations. I didn't even know my mother when I was small."

To his relief she recaptured a degree of playfulness. "That in itself isn't any guaranty."

"That's right, honey! Nothing's ever a guaranty."

Their puffy, blatantly hearty host had caught her last word and deftly given it the lubricious iridescence of a vaguely bawdy joke. The man in the shaggy brown tweed had come up with Oxnard, and in a moment the two of them engaged Cristina in the sort of flirtatious, glib, middle-age banter with which elderly people could always put youth in its place, Peter felt irritably. Cristina, being a woman and having to be polite, sparkled and played up to them. There was no hope for the present of having her all to himself again. He sauntered away from them, half intending to join Praither and Dorothy Lambert on the other side of the room.

He ran right into Aleida Gibbs!

Her "Hello, Peter" was cooler by several degrees than the smile with which she had greeted him before. Her manner crackled with reminders that he had slighted her in favor of Cristina. "I didn't know you were still here."

"Oh, I'm out in Tesuque. I decided to stay a little while. How was Dallas?"

"Very nice, thank you. I've been back almost three weeks," she said coldly and made it into a reproach. "I see you've got to know some people." Her hazel eyes went to Cristina and managed to include half the room.

"Santa Fe is a very friendly place."

"It is, isn't it?" Even the few innocent words became somehow a lash in her handsome mouth. "How is the horseback riding?"

"I stay on most of the time now."

"That wasn't a very good horse you had that day." Scrupulously fair, but beyond that, cold.

"So I found out." Already there was nothing more to say.

"Excuse me, Peter," she begged silkily. It was true that the young chap who had been at the same supper table with him at Dorothy Lambert's party was looking for her with two cocktails in his hands.

He was not in the least sorry to see her go. Overbearing jane! About as safe to touch as an electric eel! Not one word this time, he thought wryly, about his coming out to Pecos to dinner.

He walked quickly over to Dorothy Lambert and—a little spitefully when he saw that Aleida was still only a few feet away, where she could not help but hear and see—put himself out to be doubly agreeable.

"I've never seen so many parties," he said. "Does this go on all the time? I don't see how people get time to do anything else."

Dorothy's eyes gleamed with guarded pride and lurking small-town discontent. "Do you feel that Santa Fe is particularly social? In Shreveport we used to have lots more things going on. Anyhow it's like this only in the summer and fall. After Christmas the whole town just shuts down. Oh, you have a few people in for dinner now and then, but that's all. Life gets horribly dull. All there is to do in the evening is go to bed."

He chuckled at her as she blushed. "I don't call that dull, given the right company!"

"You know what I mean. There's no theater and no music. . . ."

A minute later, when they were about to line up for food and had stopped to look at a bronze portrait bust of Hal Oxnard, he complimented her on her black lace gown.

"Do you like it?"

"It's charming. But, then, you always look as if you were modeling for some Fifth Avenue shop."

"It's just a dress."

"Maybe that's how it started out, but with you inside it's become a work of art. Most women look like hell in their clothes. They oughn't to be allowed to wear—" It was his turn to flounder and blush.

Dorothy laughed delightedly. "This time *you* put your foot in it!"

He grinned. "—anything but sackcloth and ashes for not being prettier. You know what I mean. Obviously the ones that look awful in them would look even worse without."

It was all innocent, but there was an intoxicating sense of adventure, as if flirting with Dorothy Lambert was a rehearsal for some infinitely more important encounter which was bound to come, no matter how long Cristina seemed to want to linger with Hal Oxnard and the other man. Aleida Gibbs, Peter noticed when his eyes returned from hunting for Cristina, had been observing his gaiety with Dorothy; she turned away with an expression of cold scorn.

He dismissed her with a mental shrug. What did he care what she thought? She might as well see that he was a little beyond college dances and nice little girls with diplomas clutched in their hands. . . . But he was in for another brush with her. Shortly after eleven the party showed signs of breaking up. The young crowd and even some of the older couples, like the Praithers, the Orrs and Dorothy Lambert and her husband, were going on to Bishop's Lodge to dance. Two of the girls and Dorothy insisted that he come along; and because Cristina and Geoffrey already had on their coats and had announced that they were going home—so that he was not missing any chance of talking with Cristina any more tonight—and also because he noticed a little mischievously that Aleida was going with the crowd, he went.

They joined forces with a small party that was already in progress at Bishop's Lodge, moved tables together, chipped in to keep the orchestra playing after twelve o'clock, made Praither go to the piano and accompany a husky-voiced girl who seemed to know all the latest songs, made up a boisterous party, had fun. He waited for almost an hour before he asked Aleida to dance. She danced expertly, her body obeying the least pressure of his finger tips with beautiful docility, as if—with her suave and utterly controlled gracefulness—she wanted to mock his secret conviction which dated from his week end in Northampton in the spring that she was the sort of bossy, athletic female who could be counted on to want to lead. It irked him to find that he had been wrong. She remained coolly aloof in the crook of his arm, responded with brittle politeness to his remarks, and made it plain that only good manners compelled her to stay for a second short dance. As soon as the music stopped, she faced with exquisitely insulting matter-of-factness toward the table where she had been sitting and forced him to take her back to the dark-haired young geologist with whom she had come to the Oxnards' party and on from there. Her bland "Thank you" was like the closing of a door.

He chuckled to himself as he walked away from her and presently danced again with Dorothy and felt her soft body more and more unreservedly close against his. Pity, Aleida disapproved! It wasn't his fault that maturity was more exciting than college-girl charm and prowess on skis, or that he found Cristina's conversation rather more interesting. . . .

In only three and a half days, give or take a couple of hours, he reflected pleasantly on the way home from Bishop's Lodge, he would be starting out for their horseback-riding date. Had there been some reason for Geoffrey's curtness in informing him that they were to meet at Cristina's on Monday instead of at the Camino del Monte Sol? No reason that could have to do with him—unless Geoffrey had resented his talking with Cristina for such a long time, which would argue a ludicrous degree of jealousy. No, the chances were that Geoff and Cristina had had some sort of spat. Those high-keyed, vaguely menacing confidences about the two men she had been married to in France had somehow seemed really about Geoff!

Cristina could be hotly scathing and coldly devastating in her wrath behind her beautifully modulated voice! . . .

CHAPTER SIX

"Did You Have To Do That?"

$\mathbf{T}$HEN he saw an entirely different side of her. . . .

He came into town Saturday after lunch. He happened to walk up Palace Avenue when he saw the yellow Isotta parked outside the Lamberts' house and Cristina with a big paper bundle and a carton balanced on top of it coming down the flagstone walk. She wore her tan polo coat and a gaily flowered white wool scarf slung peasant-fashion over her head and wrapped around her neck. He hurried up the flagstone walk to relieve her of the things and carry them to the car.

He pretended to look anxiously all around. "I don't think anybody saw you. I won't tell a soul. All you have to do is make a quick getaway."

She laughed. "I'm glad you came along. The carton was just about to fall off."

More bundles and cartons had already been piled into the back. A pair of children's rubbers stuck out of one box; a folded sweater lay on top of another.

"Are you planning to start a store," he teased, "or is it a scavenger hunt?"

117

"Neither. I'm collecting things for the priest at Santa Cruz. He has a lot of poor children in his parish who haven't enough clothes for the winter. Look at all I've got! Now all I have to do is pick up some groceries."

"Good! Which store are we going to rob? Where's Santa Cruz?"

"It's twenty-six miles north of here. It takes about an hour."

"How did you ever hear about that?"

"Oh, I ran out of gas near Santa Cruz last year and the priest there gave me enough out of his Ford to get me home. He's exceedingly nice and he looks after simply droves of children. Some of them are orphans and live with their relatives, but the relatives are poor themselves and can't afford to buy them rubbers or overcoats."

"Aren't there any orphanages?"

"No, this state is very poor, and the diocese and the archbishop haven't any money either. Father Hegge is the only one who looks after them and he does it out of his small salary. It isn't anywhere near enough. So ever since last year I bully all my friends for the clothes their children have outgrown, and I send out toys and things. It's my charity. Want to come along?"

"I'd better before you hold up a bank!"

They picked up two cartons of groceries at the store and then headed north, past his turnoff at Tesuque, past the turnoff to the Tesuque pueblo. He had never seen Cristina so carefree and young. She bubbled with mischief. They laughed at the fantastic shapes of the eroded rocks on either side of the road, at an Indian who waved to them, at the memory of the fat man at the Oxnards'. She asked him to drive the Isotta and then teased him delightedly—with that pretense of callousness she could put on—for driving too far in the middle of the road and for once grinding gears because he was not used to the right-hand drive and to shifting gears on his left. She was even more exuberant when they got to Santa Cruz.

He could not be sure which of the two, the rawboned, hearty priest with the jutting jaw and the laughing eyes or Cristina, kindled the other, but they both glowed. And the five boys, who ranged in age from about eight to fifteen and who somewhat shyly at first helped to unload the car, caught the contagion of festiveness as the cartons and bundles were lined up on chairs and on the floor beside the littered desk in the big, cluttered study of the gloomy adobe rectory.

Father Hegge himself had something of the child. His enthusiasm

as he pulled a pair of arctics out of a carton—"Just what Juan needs!"—
and held up a red wool coal—"I've got just the little girl for that!"—
was unabashed in its generous greed. There was an infectious warmth
about him. Just as he had welcomed Cristina as if he had known her
all his life, had seen her only last week, so his directness cut through
all other formality. Within minutes Peter found himself addressed by
his first name and did not mind at all. He felt even strangely flattered
by it.

Yet there was nothing remarkable about the priest except his enthusiasm for the boys. He showed off proudly a half-finished bedstead which
the two oldest boys were working on in a primitive carpentry shop in a
shed. He told them about one boy who loved to tinker with the Ford
and had kept the car running for half a year without need of repair. But
the one he was proudest of was a boy of twelve who limped and had no
family at all, having been left when he was a baby with a foster mother
who had since become too ill to take care of him. Juan was building a
radio receiving set.

It was like an annual report. He showed them the garden he and
the boys had planted that year—"The Spanish people as a rule don't
go in for vegetables, but I'm getting the boys used to greens"—and a
great pile of firewood they had sawed by hand, the one cow out in the
sagebrush, the primitive shower he had rigged up for the boys. "We
don't have running water here," he explained with a grin, "so we've got
to do the running. Oh, there's enough to keep us busy all day! Evenings
are a little bad, especially in the winter, because the boys don't like to
read. They aren't students."

And suddenly as he looked at the priest's large-planed, cheerful face
which showed no trace of sticky piety and noticed his worn cassock
with the clumsily mended tear and the pathetic odds and ends of wire
from which the crippled boy was constructing a radio set, a plan took
shape in his mind. He would at least put in a pump with a simple gasoline
motor, so that they wouldn't have to haul water in the row of buckets
he had noticed by the well! He could send to the factory and get a complete set of parts for a Hearn Junior and a repairman's handbook, so that
the little boy could have the fun of putting the radio together himself!
And at the factory in the storeroom there were half a dozen old lathes
and drill presses which he had thrown out of the shop last spring and
which were carried in the inventory at one dollar because they weren't
worth anything except as scrap: he could get Nichols to ship a couple of

them out. . . . He could already see Cristina's delightful surprise when she heard about it.

He asked, "Do they like machinery, Father?"

"That's all they dream about, cars and machinery. They have a long tradition behind them of doing things with their hands. There have been some fine craftsmen, especially wood carvers, in this valley. I guess the boys have got it in their blood."

The exhilarating consciousness of what he had planned made him match Cristina's high spirits on the way home, made him feel for minutes on end that they were deliciously isolated in a luminous web of happiness which only they could properly value and understand. They vied with each other in finding things to praise in the priest.

"He's very sensitive," Cristina said. "You can see that. Did you notice how gentle he was with the boy who started to look in the carton with the toys?"

"But he's firm, too. You can tell he doesn't speak more than once."

"Of course not. Those children are devoted to him."

"He's one of the festive people."

"Festive?" she queried. "Oh, I think I know what you mean!"

"You should—you're like that, too. You give a holiday glow to everything around you. Between you and Father Hegge, you lighted up that gloomy rectory like two crystal chandeliers. It was like fairyland at the opera!"

"*Ce que vous êtes gentil aujourd'hui!* I've never seen you so gallant. Do you find life so depressing usually?"

"No, just drab and, I suppose, exciting occasionally, but not festive like this afternoon—that's a special gift like spring."

"Why, Peter, how charming! But now you've said enough. Did you notice the old shoes Father Hegge wore?"

"No, but I noticed his cassock. He must have mended that himself."

"How do you suppose we could get the dear man to buy himself some things he needs? If I sent him a check, he would only spend it on the children again. And I wouldn't dare to mention anything about his clothes—that would be too insulting."

"Well, we could establish a credit for him at the clothing store. I could manage to run up to Santa Cruz again sometime in the next few weeks and broach it to him and sort of kid about it—tell him he couldn't have a monopoly of playing Santa Claus. I could say I had to get some things and wanted him to have some, too."

"Oh, yes, you must! That's just what we'll do. I'll give you a check and you must take it to the store. I don't think he'll mind if he thinks it comes from you."

"No, I don't think he will. That's what I like most about him—that there's nothing sticky or mealymouthed about him. I hate the pious unction that always makes me feel uncomfortable with most priests."

She gave him a sideways glance. "You sound as if you had a grudge, Peter."

"I have. I put in a year in a Catholic apprentice home when I was fourteen."

"Was it hateful?"

"Nothing but sickening piety and no food and no sleep. They used to make us get up at five in the winter in an ice-cold dormitory just so that we could go to an ice-cold chapel at a quarter to six. I still get chilblains when I think of it."

"How horrible! Was that when you were learning to make steel?"

"No, that was in Vienna when I was an apprentice in a hardware store."

"But why were you in that school or whatever it was? I thought you were living with your relatives."

"Well, it was toward the end of the War and everybody was starving. I thought if I went to live in the apprentice home which was run by a wealthy order I might get more to eat. I was wrong. At my aunt's we'd had three small slices of sandy corn bread and unlimited quantities of watery turnips a day. At the apprentice home we got two small slices and not even enough watery turnips to give one the illusion of having eaten something. Besides, by that time I was working twelve hours a day, wrestling with cast-iron stoves and wagon axles that weighed a hundred pounds."

"It must have been ghastly, Peter. How could you stand that?"

"Oh, I survived. Things always look worse when you look back on them or when they're still ahead. I was luckier than most. I always could tell myself that I had my family here in the U. S. where there was enough to eat and that I could join my mother if I wanted to after the War. It was like a window—I could look out through it every time the drabness threatened to get me down. And I'd already started to collect festive people, and they'd light things up."

"I think you are very brave. Had you ever thought that it takes two to make a *festa?* Just don't go finding too many of your festive people between now and Monday, or I'll be jealous." They were back in Santa Fe. She had stopped in front of the hotel to let him out. "Thank you so much for coming with me. It was fun, wasn't it? I'll see you Monday, then, at my house. . . ."

He went immediately, even though it was Saturday and almost dinnertime, to see about ordering an automatic pump for Father Hegge's rectory well and to arrange with the plumber for installing it. Then he sat down in the lobby of the hotel and wrote to the factory in Harrison for an unassembled Hearn Junior and the handbook and the necessary batteries. There was no hurry about writing to Nichols for the old machine tools, since they would have to come by slow freight and could not possibly get to Santa Cruz in time to make a Christmas present for the boys.

But he was thinking less of the crippled boy and Father Hegge than of Cristina in his eagerness to carry out his plan. Cristina would be pleased and that would be enough. She would look at him again as she had several times this afternoon with those teasing, velvety shadows in her gray eyes. He wondered half a dozen times during the week end whether their ride on Monday would bring a continuation of the carefree, playful mood of their trip to Santa Cruz or whether it was going to revive the rather startling intimacy with its sudden confidences that had been like jagged, vaguely threatening discharges of summer lightning on the night of the Oxnards' party.

It was neither!

Cristina was as smilingly serene and self-possessed as she had been exuberant and playful—and keyed up and in the grip of some subtle rancor—the week before. Nothing in her thrillingly clear voice made even the faintest acknowledgment of the trip to Santa Cruz or of her confidences about Geoff. There was a briskness about her, and her face and throat above the ruffled white blouse and the beaded chamois jacket had a lovely outdoor glow. Her glance when she replied to Geoff's suggestion that they ride to Hyde Park was so untroubled and eloquent of a long and thoroughly satisfactory mutual understanding, that Peter wondered with a twinge of disappointment whether he had not completely imagined the rift between Cristina and Geoff. She said, "Why, yes, Geoff, if you like. But it *is* seven or eight miles. It will be dark by the time we get there."

"It is rather late for Hyde Park," Geoff conceded. "We'll go there sometime when we can start in the morning, Peter. That leaves only . . ."

They decided to ride out to Santa Fe Canyon. It meant that Geoff would be retracing his steps at least part of the way, since they were headed for Canyon Road. After they had been riding about four or five minutes—Cristina on the fawn-colored thoroughbred and Geoff on the same black stallion on which Peter had seen them the first evening, and he himself on the brown mare Cristina's handyman had saddled for him—Geoff explained, "the horse I had engaged for you cast a shoe. It looked for a while as if I mightn't be able to find a horse for you. Fortunately Cristina was willing for you to ride the mare."

"You make it sound like a favor, Geoff. The one I'm worried about is Peter, not the mare. I'm afraid, Peter, you're going to have an awful time. Chiquita hasn't been ridden for months. She's got lazy and fat. Don't let her get away with anything!"

The mare seemed frisky rather than lazy. She had playfully nipped the fawn-colored horse in the rump a couple of times on the way out of the yard. She puffed out her belly every few steps and tossed her head and blew and blustered until the saddle creaked, but so far she had kept up and trotted docilely half a head behind the black stallion.

They were in the outskirts of town. A farm wagon driven by two wizened old Spanish women and coming toward them on the narrow road made Cristina's horse drop back of Geoff's. The mare needed no other encouragement to fall back, too, and stay beside Cristina's horse even after the wagon had passed.

"Have you been in this part of town before?" Cristina asked.

"I took a couple of riding lessons with a fellow named Davis out here. I never got a diploma from him, though."

"You ride very well."

"I stay on, that's all. I'm just glad we aren't going through town or I'd really disgrace you between my lack of style and my clothes."

"But what is the matter with your clothes?"

"Well, look at your elegant riding togs and Geoff's, too, and here I am in blue jeans and this old jacket."

"But I like—" She checked herself and pretended to frown. "If you're fishing for a compliment, you are not going to get it."

They had turned into Canyon Road. The mare had edged over to the side of the road to bite off a few belated sunflowers that were still in bloom. He jerked the mare's head back. "Not even if I bring you a sunflower like Oscar Wilde?"

"Not even then."

He allowed the mare which kept straining toward the sunflowers to drift to the edge of the road. He turned to laugh at Cristina. "Chiquita and I are going to sulk."

"Go ahead and sulk!"

In no time at all he had fallen a whole length behind Cristina, three lengths behind Geoff. Partly to show Cristina that he had control over the horse, and partly because Geoff's horse was breaking into a trot and Cristina's was following suit, he dug his heels hard into Chiquita's side. The mare made a couple more stubborn tries to pull over to the side of the road, then smoothed out her gait and caught up with Cristina's horse and then with Geoff's. For a while all three of the horses ran along peacefully side by side. But Chiquita's prankishness would not let her remain peaceful long. She nipped Geoff's horse slyly in the shoulder once, then changed from a trot to a lope and kept nosing ahead of the black.

Geoff's horse lunged ahead powerfully all of a sudden. In a matter of seconds the mare had been left hopelessly behind, but the big black kept charging ahead as if in a rage, and Peter saw that Geoffrey had a hard time keeping control of him. He hurriedly brought Chiquita to a stop, heard Cristina come up behind him, and only slowly allowed the mare to move forward again to where Geoffrey sat waiting for them after reining in his horse.

Geoff wore a faint frown. He said, "Try not to let your horse race if you can help it. This stallion is pretty high-spirited. He's apt to run away if another horse tries to get ahead of him."

It was a rebuke, and Peter was annoyed with himself for having laid himself open to it by not having sized up at once the temper of the black. He held Chiquita on a taut rein and they rode along in silence for a while, Geoff half a length ahead, so that it was awkward to talk to him. He dropped back to wait for Cristina who looked amused.

"I heard you went dancing on Thursday night after we left."

He could not tell whether her question had no hidden significance or whether she was with a few words trying to deny all importance to their trip on Saturday—or whether, on the contrary, she was trying to conceal from Geoff the fact that they had seen each other since Thursday. He made himself sound doubly playful in case Geoffrey was listening. "I wouldn't have dreamed of going if you hadn't gone home first."

"But I wouldn't have gone home if I'd known. I might have come, too,

if I'd been asked. I love to dance! Geoff, did you know that Peter and
Dorothy and a lot of the others went out to Bishop's Lodge Thursday
night? Did you have fun, Peter?"

Her deliberate attempt to draw Geoff into the conversation exasperated him. She seemed determined not only to blot out the golden
memory of Saturday but also to give the lie to the vibrant intimacy
that had been between them at the Oxnards'. Her whole bearing today
seemed to proclaim that only the very young were apt to take a
woman's confidences after several cocktails seriously. It was a betrayal,
he felt, of the tender, exciting and somehow exquisitely selfless mood
which had enveloped them like an iridescent haze last week and which
he had thought she, too, was treasuring; either that or it was sheer
callousness—some baffling feminine ability to luxuriate in a mood and
yet remain immune to it, so that she could calmly pretend now that her
passionate vehemence on Thursday had been a tantrum and nothing
more. Almost to punish her, he took advantage of Chiquita's renewed
friskiness to move up to Geoff and talk to him.

They had entered the mouth of the canyon and were riding along the
lush canyon bottom which was studded with asters and parched sunflowers that had long ago lost their petals and shed their seed but looked
autumnal and fulfilled rather than sad. The willows and cottonwoods
along the stream still had not altogether lost their yellow magnificence.
The pines that grew up the sides of the canyon were growing taller as
the road climbed. A sense of gaiety invaded Peter as they rode through
the forest peacefulness. He had already forgiven Cristina. A mere glance
exchanged at the ludicrous, squalling rage of a bird scolding them shrilly
for their intrusion, had sufficed to weave the spell again.

When they had gone a little past the ranger station where the logging
road had turned into a mere trail, they got off to let the horses rest before
they started back. They sat on a log and had a cigarette. They watched
a chipmunk—tail high in the air—run the whole length of a huge fallen
tree trunk and laughed at his imperturbable dignity. "No, it's too small
for a turkey," Geoffrey said a minute later when some big bird started
up noisily some distance away in the underbrush. "A grouse perhaps. . . ."

He hardly knew Geoff, Peter told himself as he watched him fastid-
iously scrape off a minute dab of mud from his boot with his whip. In
a manner of speaking, he knew Cristina much better than him. Geoff sat
there with his reddish face, lean furrowed cheeks, faint scowl—entirely

open to scrutiny and yet impenetrable somehow. An unmanageable, too-steady gray gaze which faltered and withdrew at times into the depths of the bluish-gray eyes, as if to reconsider, and emerged again with a sort of uncertain truculence. Square and brittle wrists. . . . He would have—Peter guessed—not very heavy arms, rather thin and slack-skinned probably. He might weigh around one hundred eighty pounds, but a lot of it would be flabby flesh in spite of the impression of trim leanness he conveyed.

It was fun to size him up like this while they engaged in pleasant, desultory talk about his progress with the portrait of the Tesuque Indian, about Praither's painting and his dogs, with Cristina listening smilingly—happily, as if they were both her sons.

Geoffrey asked, "Did you bring a change of clothes?"

"Yes," Peter said.

"Well, then, you can drive over to my house after you get back to Cristina's and have a quick tub and change."

"But why can't Peter use the guest room at my house?"

"I've already asked Rafaelita to heat enough water for both of us. Everything will be ready," Geoffrey persisted.

"Well, the guest room is there if you want to change your mind and if Peter wants to save himself the trip. As a matter of fact, you could join us after you'd changed and you could both have dinner with me. Why don't we do that?"

"No, we'll do as we planned. It's too much of a nusiance for you. We'll pick you up afterwards and have dinner at La Fonda."

"All right, but it seems like a frightful lot of running around." Cristina shrugged, adjusted the bridle around the neck of her horse, and got on.

They started back. Out of the corner of one eye Peter saw Geoffrey looking at him and he felt himself scowl. The certainty that he had just been deprived of an enchanting evening through Geoffrey's stubbornness exasperated him. At her house Cristina would probably have played the piano and might have sung if he had asked her hard enough. As it was, there would be nothing but dinner at the hotel, and after that he would have to say good-by!

He took a vindictive pleasure in addressing himself only to Cristina and in ignoring Geoff who was riding on ahead. But presently as they approached the mouth of the canyon where the road widened there was no more chance for talk, for all three of the horses broke into an eager homeward lope. Chiquita became frisky again and stretched out in a gallop that brought her up neck to neck with Geoff's horse. The stallion did not seem to resent the challenge to his primacy this time; he even let the mare stay ahead for a few seconds now and then.

It was exhilarating to pound along like this, side by side with Geoff, and feel that even without benefit of swank riding boots and a fancy leather quirt he could hold his own. He called in a burst of exuberance, "I thought you had a fast horse!"

As if the stallion had understood the taunt he suddenly lunged forward and gained half a length on Chiquita. It had become a game. Peter dug his heels into the flanks of the mare and was delighted to feel her respond. The mare was keeping up beautifully with the big black—for a while, and then all of a sudden Chiquita lost ground at an alarming rate and Peter felt fear that had come from nowhere climb up into his throat. He tugged hard at the reins and shouted "Whoah!" loud enough, he hoped, to make Geoff's horse slow up.

Behind him Cristina was coming up fast. She caught up with him just as he watched Geoffrey pull the head of the big black to one side and force him to charge up a wagon trail that serpentined up the slope and lost itself among the piñons. The strategy worked; the stallion was slowing up. Only, suddenly he swerved and charged down the slope toward the main road. Geoffrey hurriedly flung up one arm to protect himself from a pine branch—then from another one. The second branch made him duck so low and so far to one side that he pitched forward off the horse.

Cristina's fawn charged ahead of him up the wagon road. He drove Chiquita after it and lashed at himself to hold his anxiety at bay, "Goddam childish trick! Damfool childish stunt!"

Geoffrey was picking himself up from the ground when they got to the scraggly pine tree that rose above the piñons. He looked a little white along the side of his jaw, and a small vein just below his ear pulsed furiously. He felt his left shoulder as if it hurt and he favored his left leg. "I'm perfectly all right," he said while he reached all the way across his body with his right hand to brush the pine needles from his left hip and leg.

"Are you sure you didn't break anything?" Cristina asked. "I think you ought to lie down and not use your leg."

It was his contrition, Peter realized, that made him brush so hard at Geoffrey's hat which he had picked up from the ground. "I'll ride into town for a doctor and I'll get a car."

"I'm quite all right, I tell you," Geoffrey said testily. "If you will get my horse . . ."

They both started out after the stallion, which had stopped a few hundred feet away and was grazing as if nothing had happened. When they were only about seventy feet away, Cristina warned, "We'd better not ride any closer—we might frighten him." It was the only thing that had been said between them, and even the few impersonal words seemed to Peter to carry an ominous note of reproach. They got off their horses and led them slowly toward the stallion, letting them graze on the way. After several minutes of standing within reach of the stallion, Peter stretched out for his reins, patted his still steaming neck, and started to lead him along with Chiquita back up the slope.

Cristina stood tautly waiting where her own horse had continued to nibble at the tufts of grass. He half expected some congratulation—at least, a mild explosion of relief that the stallion had not kept right on running back into town. Instead she said, and her voice was angry and oddly flat this time, "Did you have to do that?"

The reproach startled him for one bewildered second and then made him exult. Her silver-gray eyes were not indignant so much as grave. Her whole manner as she stood there with the bridle in her hand proclaimed that she felt somehow involved in his childish stunt and at least partly to blame for it. Otherwise what right did she have to call him to account with that naked air of having a claim on him? She was as good as saying, You had no business acting like that; it might have cost us dear!

There was nothing to say. Decency seemed to require that he act and feel contrite, but deep inside himself he frolicked and mocked, Of course, I didn't have to do that!

His other, real remorse at the sight of Geoff's grimace when he tried to walk, made him simmer with solicitude. He offered once more to get a car. He suggested that at least Geoff swap horses and let him ride the dangerous stallion.

Geoff refused. "No, thank you, I'm used to him. Just give me a hand up, will you?" He got on stiffly and winced when in spite of help he had to put all his weight for a moment on his left leg.

It got dark before they were more than halfway home. It was an effort to hold the playful mare in check, but Peter forced her to stay a whole length in back of Cristina and Geoff. Only when they were almost at Geoff's house did he allow the mare to move up beside the stallion, forcing Cristina to drop back. He tried to apologize. "It was idiotic; it was dangerous! I should have known . . ." Geoffrey cut him short. "You haven't had much experience with thoroughbreds perhaps. Just as well. I prefer any other breed for a saddle horse. One can never tell what they'll do next."

Cristina gave no sign that she had heard. Except for asking now and then whether Geoff was all right, she had hardly spoken at all. Peter had had to content himself with an occasional sidelong glance at her doeskin jacket, the elegant tautness of the whipcord cloth around her slim knees, her shining boots, her gloved hand. There had been no opportunity to catch her eye. She seemed inexorably withdrawn. . . . When they got to Geoff's house she immediately took charge. She made Geoff lie down. She telephoned for the doctor and she made Geoff take off his boots. And she made a punishment out of her rebuff of every attempt Peter made to be of use. "The only thing you can do is to take Fawn with you and ask Agapito to put the horses in the corral. . . . No, don't bother about the car. I'll take a taxi when I'm through."

Geoffrey fidgeted under their concern. "I shall be perfectly all right. Rafaelita will be back at six to tend to the stoves. Sorry, Peter, about our plans for tonight. Tina, why don't you and Peter go on to La Fonda without me? There is absolutely no need for you to stay; Rafaelita will cook some dinner for me."

"Nonsense!" she said. "I want to hear what the doctor has to say. You may have broken something! Oh, Peter, you might tell Mercedes not to forget to feed the dogs. . . ." She was clearly anxious to get rid of him. It made any delay, any further offer of help, seem uncouth. He summoned an extra warmth to say good-by to Geoff and took himself off.

There was only the consciousness that it was her horse he was leading and the tingling memory of the moment when she had admitted that for that one instant she had felt closer to him than to Geoff with which to hearten himself after the coldness with which she had sent him away. Yet as long as he was still on the way to her house and after that lingering in her living room to give Mercedes the message about feeding the dogs and finally still able to look back from his car to catch another glimpse of her garden, it was enough.

CHAPTER SEVEN

Mimosa and Mint

HE LECTURED himself. . . .

He was making entirely too much of it! Supposing she had told him in a burst of second-cocktail intimacy what qualities she expected in a man; supposing they had happened to laugh at the same things on a number of occasions; supposing she had taken him to task rather startlingly for the accident—what was there in all that except perhaps proof that she meant to marry Geoff and already considered them all three united by a vague family bond? Hence, the frankness with which she could speak to him about those earlier marriages. They were as good as related, weren't they?

She would make an enchanting stepmother! Yet that was precisely it: all her charm was withheld, for she still seemed to hold Geoff's tumble against him, so that he was forced into an awkward constraint and an exasperating uneasiness each time he ran into her at Geoff's.

Geoff's shoulder was still in a cast. Some bone had cracked. It was nothing serious, but for over a week now he had had to stay in an easy

chair and keep very still. It meant that nearly every time Peter telephoned it was Cristina who answered him, and when he called at the
Camino the chances were that she was there, too, with her indefinable
air of reproach. Perversely enough, the times her yellow roadster was
not parked in front of the house and she had either already left or not
yet come, he missed her furiously. He was consumed by restlessness and
he was absent-minded while he sat and talked with Geoff.

He accused himself of hypocrisy and callousness and ingratitude, for
Geoff had been singularly good-natured about the whole thing. He had
not once complained about the pain or the inconvenience he had been
put to by the spill; and when Peter had again tried to say that he was
sorry Geoff had brushed the apology aside with a brisk "These things
happen. Fortunately it wasn't my right arm."

He usually dropped in at Geoff's around four. Rafaelita, the stout,
cheerful Mexican woman from next door who always showed up soon
afterward to tend to the stoves and start dinner for Geoff, brought in the
tray with the cups and the squat silver pot and the hot-water jug.
Geoffrey made tea. They talked—on the days when neither Cristina nor
Geoff's brash student had come—about painting, about tempera technique, about the artists in Santa Fe. They were both careful not to
touch on anything personal, as if even the most innocent question might
disturb the curtain behind which lurked the truth—each one's truth
from which the other must be saved—of Cristina's relation to Geoff and
the accident with the stallion. They avoided even speaking of the distant past until one afternoon when Peter noticed a handsome, old-
fashioned barometer hanging between the window and the front door.
He was quite certain that the banjo-shaped, yard-long mahogany board
with the glass tubes had not been there the day before.

The habit he had formed of watching the barometer during the summer of the preceding year while he had half quizzically and half seriously checked on the weather predictions of a night watchman they had
had at the factory in Harrison made him saunter across the room while
Geoff was busy hunting for a reproduction he wanted to show him in an
art magazine. The mercury column, in the slim glass tube which curved
at the bottom like an inverted shepherd's crook and ended in a thistle-
shaped mercury cup, stood at 23.72. The whole instrument was beautifully made. A thermometer paralleled part of the barometer tube; the cali-
bration and the numbers on the brass scale were unmistakably hand-
engraved; a fine line of inlaid satinwood ran within an eighth of an

inch of the edge all around the mahogany board. At the very top was another bit of inlay in the shape of a small conch shell. And just above the mercury cup there was a small brass plate with the maker's name. He read the tarnished lettering: *John Middlemas, Penzance.*

Geoffrey had seen him look. "That was made by my grandfather—your great-grandfather."

The same feeling that had once seized him when his cousin Franz on the train to the Tyrol had spoken of Mizzi's father, the stonecutter and builder, and had said "our grandfather," seethed in him now with its mixture of infinite gratitude and embarrassment. Now as then he felt suddenly admitted to a room—a house—where he had never hoped to be, but it was as if he were dressed with humiliating insufficiency. He asked quickly to cover his turbulence, "Did he make glass instruments?"

"He was a clockmaker. So was my father—your grandfather," he added tentatively, cautiously. "Father is retired now and lives in Exeter; he has sold the shop in Penzance. I've been a grave disappointment to him; I was to have been the fourth generation of clockmakers."

Peter said, "I've always liked barometers," and was relieved that Geoffrey did not pursue the subject beyond saying, "There is a grandfather clock that goes with the barometer. Someday I must send for it. Uh, here is the Ghirlandaio. . . ."

After that, each time he entered the room, his eyes went sooner or later to the sober mahogany board with the gleaming glass tubes. He came to memorize each brass bracket that held the two instruments in place. He felt jealous of Geoff for having it in his possession—unfairly, it seemed to him. He watched Geoffrey's clumsiness in unscrewing a paint-jar lid and told himself that his kinship with the man who had made the barometer was much greater than Geoff's and that by rights the barometer ought to be his. He told himself proudly: One grandfather who had quarried his own stone and built churches and bridges and barns, and one who had made clocks and beautiful instruments—not a bad heritage even if unavowed, even if he was not allowed to boast of it!

Yet he trembled that Geoffrey might again bring the talk around to his family. The continuity to which Geoffrey had so lightly referred with his "fourth generation of clockmakers" was like a wonderfully beckoning vista down an avenue in an ancient park, with Geoff the wrought-iron gate which at once invited and debarred. He preferred not to be tortured by any more glimpses through the gate.

It made him cut down on his visits on the pretext that Geoff's shoulder was now out of the cast and that he was practically well again. He had also the excuse of having to spend two days in Santa Cruz with the plumber while they installed the pump, and a third day to deliver the radio set and show the little boy how to put it together—no longer so joyous an errand, except for Father Hegge's gratitude and the shining face of the crippled boy, as it had promised to be, since Cristina's coolness did away with any chance of inviting her on a second trip to Santa Cruz to surprise her with the pump and the two faucets in the rectory.

And there was also the weather to give him an added excuse for not calling on Geoff.

Almost overnight the seemingly inexhaustible, dazzlingly blue-skied and golden-leaved autumn came to an end. One afternoon the leaves drifted down in a shower of yellow and gold and carpeted the ground like some incredible tapestry; then in the evening a raw wind rolled up the carpet, tore at the bare trees, left the pastures glistening in the morning with frost. Dave Buell said, "November, just about this time, is when we usually get our first snow. . . ."

It came the following afternoon after a morning of black clouds and furious gusts of wind, fell all that night until it lay a foot deep, turned the mountains and the whole valley into fairyland for a day, but then melted and made a slough of the road. By the following noon the sky was again lowering. It was a day to stay at home, but Gladys was giving a party and Geoffrey and Cristina had said they would go. He had no intention of missing the chance of getting her away from Geoff for a few minutes at least—of perhaps talking to her alone. He set out eagerly in spite of the boggy road.

Geoffrey was not even there. Cristina said, "Geoff hurt his shoulder again. He lifted some silly box in his studio. He thought he'd better stay home and keep his shoulder warm."

Peter had had to rescue her from the courtly fatuousness of the flirtatious judge, and from a relentless account of deep-sea fishing by a Belgian pottery maker who was new in town and who, in his ungovernable enthusiasm, had a habit of thrusting his round face right up against his listener's and subjecting his victim to a spray of saliva with each explosive consonant. Cristina rewarded him with a sigh of relief that raised her breasts under the blue silk of her dress. "Oh! One more minute and I thought I was going to drown! He's a dear, but I wish he wouldn't spit in my eye. I feel as if I'd been out in the rain. . . ."

She was as full of lurking laughter as if she had never scolded him. She even scoffed at Geoff's new injury. "I really don't think it's going to kill him. If it does, it's his own fault. I offered to bring him a hot-water bottle, and he wouldn't let me! Men can be as stubborn as mules."

He wanted to make doubly sure. "Have you forgiven me?"

The faint hesitancy before she smiled, as if it cost her an effort to make up her mind, lent the moment a delicious gravity. She said playfully, "I suppose I'll have to or you're going to sulk again. Where have you been this last week? We've missed you. Geoff and I were at your house day before yesterday, and not a soul around."

He grinned, delighted by her interest. "Oh, I've been working."

"Have you? It sounds like very peculiar work. I'm told you dash off north every morning with the plumber. You see, you've been seen! You didn't think you could do things in a small town like Santa Fe without being watched. A handsome young man, very eligible—a lot of young ladies have a vested interest in you."

"And the grown-up ladies?" he bantered back.

"The elderly ladies have a vicarious interest. They live through you."

"What do you mean—live through me? Haven't they any respect for sex?"

"Vicarious living knows no sex. Haven't you ever noticed?" She became half serious. "When we were in Portofino for the summer there were all the aunts and uncles of my stepfather and they'd all take an equal interest in every dance I went to. I'd have to report every morning on all that had happened. Mother used to say, they lived off me like parasites."

"I can still see leechlike eyes fastened on you when you go down the street."

"That's only your amiable imagination, *mon cher. Vous délirez, mon petit. . . .*"

Not only was she not angry with him any longer but her friendliness exceeded anything he had dared hope for. Her voice tonight had a caressing warmth which seemed to be there solely for him. She ate her dinner beside him on a Mexican settee in a corner where they could be alone and laugh, and she refused to be enticed by Gladys and the judge to a more comfortable seat. When the others nagged her to play, she played the Chopin ballade he knew that she knew he liked. Nonetheless her invitation while he brushed the snow from the windshield of her car took away his breath. . . .

The party broke up prematurely. Chet Orr went to fetch something from his car around half past ten and returned with the report that it was snowing hard. The information was greeted with a few careless laughs and seemingly ignored, but by eleven and in spite of Gladys' protests more and more people were putting on their coats. The cars were already covered with a heavy blanket of snow, and it was still coming down as if dumped from a gigantic trough. It was work to get Cristina's windshield so that she could see through it.

Mary Orr called from the next car, "Isn't this fun?" Chet Orr inquired, "Need any help? Cristina, want us to follow you out to your house?" Mary chimed in, "Oh, I think we should! It's going to be terrible driving tonight."

"You're both darlings," Cristina assured them, "but I wouldn't think of it. I've driven in snow before."

Chet was still trying to help. "What about you, Peter? You aren't planning to drive out to Tesuque in this?"

"I was thinking of it."

"You'll never make it. I know that road; it turns into one mass of goo in weather like this."

"I came in over it."

"Well, if we don't see you for a week, we'll send out a Saint Bernard."

"No, you mustn't try it, Peter. You'll get struck."

He yielded to their solicitude. "Oh, I might stay in town—go to the Fonda."

"But the Fonda is full! I heard the clerk turn away some people this afternoon. All the politicos are in town. Why——"

"You can come and stay in my guest room if you like!"

It had been said so gaily, so openly right in front of the Orrs, that it could not have sounded more innocent; yet Peter knew a moment of breathlessness that was succeeded by a rush of joyous and vaguely guilty expectancy. He said quickly, "That's awfully kind, Cristina. Thanks, but I think I can find a place. But I think I ought to follow you out."

"I'm glad somebody will! Peter, you're welcome to stay at our house. . . ." The Orrs wished them luck and left.

All around them people were warming up motors. Cristina had started hers. The windshield was already covered again with sticky flakes. The wiper refused to work. Peter cleaned off the windshield once more, jiggled the wiper to make it behave, only to have it balk again after a few halfhearted jerks. He said, "Following you out isn't going to do much good. Somebody may have to stand on the running board. I'll come out with you and take a taxi back."

"Oh, I wish you would, but I won't have you standing on any running board!"

They struggled out Palace Avenue through the blinding snow. Every few hundred feet they had to stop to scrape the windshield again. A couple of times they almost went off the road. They turned it into a lark. By the time they had the Isotta safely in the garage and Cristina was slipping off her black fur coat in the living room, they were both caught up in a mood of exuberant gaiety where a mere word, an inflection, could make them laugh.

There were still some embers in the fireplace. He had picked up the bellows and was pumping hard to get a half-burned log to catch.

"What are you doing?"

"I'm fanning old flames."

"Oh, I don't think that ever pays. You'd better put on a new log."

"It won't be the same passion then."

"I don't care. Sometimes a fire needs a change." Her eyes laughed back at him. "If you're going to be stubborn about the fire, I know just what we need—a hot toddy! How does that sound to you?"

"Perfect, but I'll have to start thinking about getting back. Maybe I ought to phone right now."

"But you'll never get a taxi to come out here in this weather, Peter! Now, why don't you stay? The guest room is all ready; we have to keep heat in it because of the pipes. You'll be all by yourself on the other side of the patio and you can sleep as late as you like in the morning, and after you've had breakfast, I'll drive you in. The only thing I haven't got is pajamas. You can have one of my nightgowns, though." Her eyes shown with silvery mischievousness.

"It'd be putting you to too much trouble, Cristina. If there isn't a taxi, I'll just walk."

"Why, I wouldn't think of letting you do that! You know, Peter, it's going to be much more trouble getting the car out again and driving you in than having you stay, and that's what I'm going to have to do! Are you afraid of what people might say?"

He felt that he was being prissy and that she was laughing at him. At the same time her openness made his hesitancy appear more and more of an impertinence—a leering imputation of motives which she would reject with indignant scorn. He said hastily, "I'd be flattered by what they'd say."

"Good, it's all settled then. You make yourself comfortable. I'll be right back." She slipped her fur coat back on, went past the piano and the carved chest into the dining room and out into the kitchen, made a brief clatter with some pans, came back into the room but only to head straight for the outside door and the portale. She returned after a few minutes, the two spaniels flinging themselves ahead of her through the door. "There," she said; "all arranged. I've lighted a fire in your room, and I think the water is boiling for our toddy."

He followed her out into the kitchen, admired the gleaming array of copper pans on one wall, watched her fix the toddy, and carried the tray into the living room. She poured the steaming brew. And all at once, sitting beside her on the small needle-point sofa, delightfully aware of the delicate, moist-scented perfume she used and of her ravishing pallor which was heightened tonight by the dark-blue gown gathered at her throat, he succeeded in throwing off the constraint that had kept him tense. A delicious sense of adventure tingled in him now that he had accepted the narrow limits which he felt Cristina's very hospitality had imposed on him. He relaxed. Being on one's honor, he told himself, yet yearning to touch, the freedom of innocence, could be exciting, too!

He joked, "All the same, Gladys is going to want to know why I didn't come back for the Chevvy. She was standing right there when I got in your car. I think she loves to assay possibilities."

Cristina laughed. "Is that what you call it?"

"Well, I have to be careful or I'll be tarred with the same brush. All I know is that she was doing a pretty thorough job tonight on somebody named Lily May."

"I've never paid much attention to what people say, have you? Life's too short. I'm afraid Gladys does like to gossip, but I can't help liking her. She's sort of cute. She always reminds me of a bird."

"A vulture, you mean?"

They laughed. They talked about Santa Fe, about Connecticut, about the two cockers who had curled up on the sheepskin rug and blinked when Cristina told where she had got them. Neither of them mentioned Geoff. Once Peter felt bold enough to compliment her on her dress. ". . . I love that sheen it has. Is that taffeta?"

"No, it's *matelassé;* it's a kind of rep. I'm glad you haven't become so American that you've forgotten all your European background. Only European men take any real interest in women's clothes."

"I was too young when I left Europe to know—does having a European background impose any other obligations?"

"Not if they are hardships, I'm sure. What sort of obligations did you have in mind?"

"Oh, I was just wondering whether one was expected to flirt." He made it sound playful and he took care to lean slightly away from her as he reached for a cigarette.

"Decidedly not. How about another toddy if I heat some more water?"

The time had flown. He got up hastily. "No, thanks. I'm afraid I've already kept you up."

"But it's been fun. All right, I'll show you to your room. Just a minute. . . ." She disappeared through the door beside the tile-inlaid table into the little hall off which opened her bedroom and some closets and a bath. When she returned she had a white wool bathrobe over her arm and a folded pink nightgown in her hand. Her eyes flickered with amusement as if she knew already what he was going to say. She allowed the gown to unfold and hang to the floor. "No? Look, it's not silk and it's got no lace on it. Oh, dear, I was afraid of that!"

He grinned at her rueful frown. "Thanks, I can manage without pajamas for one night."

"But at least you can use this! Surely there is nothing so terribly feminine about a flannel bathrobe."

"Of course not," he hastened to agree so as not to seem unappreciative.

"I'm afraid I haven't any slippers for you. The husband of a friend of mine forgot a pair of moccasins here when they were staying with me in July, and I had them around for months before I could send them to him. People are always leaving things like slippers behind. The trouble is I just haven't been entertaining any gentlemen lately."

Was that for his benefit? he wondered. Did she, for all her casualness, want to make quite sure that he was under no misapprehension about her relation to Geoff—or about his own role as a guest? He grinned politely at her joke while he held the door and followed her out around the corner of the patio, where the snow was piling up even under the portale, to where light shone warmly through a beige-curtained glass door. They stepped down into an appealingly friendly room with carved Spanish furniture, bright Indian drawings, a white bathroom gleaming through a half-open door, a corner fireplace. The bed was already turned down. Cristina threw another log on the fire which had burned down to coals. "Here is the reading light. I hope you can find something you like over there on the shelf if you want to read. There's a new toothbrush in the medicine cabinet. Oh, yes, and there's only a shower. If you want a tub you can use my bathroom in the morning. And don't be alarmed if you hear somebody poking around tomorrow: the hot-water heater is right next to your bathroom, and you'll probably hear Mercedes shake down the ashes. Mercedes comes pretty early and she won't know you're here." She smiled. "Do you think you have everything you need?"

"Good Heavens, yes! Home was never like this."

Her eyes flicked away from him. She took two quick steps to the painted chest at the foot of the bed and lifted up the lid. "Here are extra blankets in case you're cold. I don't want you to freeze." She came back and stepped up close as if they were about to dance and she expected him to put his arms around her waist. "Well," she said and tilted her face unmistakably, "good night!"

Before he could check himself he'd drawn back, all his earlier warnings to himself like a bristling wall of spears to make him pause. It had been no more than a fraction of an inch but enough for her to notice it.

She looked amused. "I was just going to kiss you good night."

He tried to make a hasty recovery. "I told you I wasn't used to the amenities." His lips were so numb from the consciousness of his blundering, that he was only vaguely aware of the softness of her lips. "Thanks a lot for everything."

"I hope you sleep well, Peter. See you in the morning!"

He stood tautly listening until he heard her open and close the door from the portale into the living room. The certainty that he must have seemed to her either a hopeless innocent or a presumptuous prig, made his face burn. What right had he to read all sorts of things into a simple kiss and then reproach her for his fancies with his prudish hesitancy. He lay looking at the flickering log in the fireplace and puzzling over her kiss. There had certainly been nothing maternal or sisterly about it, but neither had it been particularly passionate. Ought he to have put his arms around her and——

Nonsense! he interrupted himself. In that cosmopolitan crowd in which she'd always lived, a kiss didn't mean a thing! She was fond of him—sure. But that was exactly why she had done it, because she thought of him as Geoff's son.

Yet in the next breath he remembered her remarks to Piggot and Collard at the party—double-edged and swift—and he wondered whether any act of hers was likely to be unpremeditated and utterly innocent. Did she perhaps think him a dreary fool? Was she perhaps waiting for him? He couldn't expect her to go in for any cheap languor or coquetry! Oughtn't he to get up and go into the living room on some pretext or other? But suppose he had got it all wrong and she received him—no, not with any display of outrage or silly incedulity, certainly, but with what would be infinitely worse—with an indulgent "Now, Peter you be a good boy and go back to your room, and in the morning we'll have forgotten all about it"? No, it would be too humiliating! . . . He tossed in tortured indecision until it was far too late to venture into the living room on the pretext of looking for cigarettes—until at last he fell asleep.

He was awakened by the cautious, cheerful clatter of a shovel being dug into coal and then emptied into a stove somewhat beyond the wall. The morning sun kindled the beige silk curtains on the windows into laughing, golden gossamer. The cold air coming in through the one partly opened sash had an exhilarating edge. Somewhat to his surprise he felt nothing but happiness. He was exultantly certain that he had only barely escaped making a blunder which might have made it impossible even to stay in Santa Fe. As it was, Cristina and he were still friends. In a little while, as soon as he had thanked her and called a taxi, he would be on his way to town, and next time they met the very memory of his shying away from her innocent good-night kiss would give an extra fillip to their new intimacy.

It seemed much too early, with the maid only starting the fires now, to think about going into the main house. He forced himself to stay in bed a little longer before he took a cold shower and hustled into his clothes and opened the door to the portale. The snow out in the patio lay much deeper. Along the main part of the house past the living-room door there were tracks from the tunnellike entrance on the other side of the patio to what must be the utility room in the near corner —the maid's, obviously, who must be in the living room or the kitchen now.

When he ventured into the house he saw at once that his fear of being too early had been unnecessary. A lively fire frolicked in the cleanly swept fireplace; the chairs and the cocktail table and the Navaho rugs in front of it had been straightened since last night; the whole room had a crisp air of being wide awake. Cristina came in from the dining room with a plump terra cotta vase full of yellow chrysanthemums, gave an odd little start, quickly recovered herself and exclaimed, "Well, good morning! You were supposed to have breakfast in bed; we had it all planned. Mercedes was going to hear when you were awake while she made up my room! You must have been so quiet, she didn't hear you get up."

Cristina, wearing a thin red cardigan left unbuttoned over her white blouse and a flaring gray tweed skirt, looking paler and more at the mercy of the fine lines below her eyes than he had ever seen her and for that very reason exhaling an intoxicating sense of early-morning intimacy, came up to him and smiled.

"Do I have to go back to bed?"

"No, we'll forgive you this time and let you eat in the dining room. Come on."

The maid had stuck her head in from the hall that led to Cristina's room. She gave a deep-throated Spanish laugh when Cristina said, "He fooled us, Mercedes," returned his good morning, hurried ahead of them out into the kitchen, and presently returned to the dining room with a silver coffeepot.

There was another bowl of chrysanthemums on the dining-room table. A fire was blazing in the small, tile-framed fireplace in here, too. From where he sat he looked out through the long, low window on the snow-blanketed strip of garden between the house and the road. Around the corner of the table from him Cristina smilingly turned her profile to him as she poured the coffee, and he noticed with a little thrill of discovery that the lobe of her ear was pierced and looked touchingly naked without some sort of earring. The roguish-eyed, soft-moving, noticeably pregnant Mercedes came and went. . . .

All the gaiety and innocence of the winter morning seemed trapped in the room. The sun-glistening snow outside which had stilled the whole neighborhood and presumably the whole town gave him a luxurious feeling of time out—of dispensation from any ordinary schedule or plan—of holiday. His festiveness made him secretly delight in her arguments that he must stay until lunch, at least.

"Agapito says the snow is two feet deep and we'll get stuck. I'm sure he's right because not a single car has gone by today—I've been watching the road. In any case Agapito has to shovel the snow away in front of the garage before we can get the car out, and he also wants to get some of the snow off the dirt roofs because he's afraid they might leak. Now, why don't you make yourself comfortable here in the living room and do whatever you like? Perhaps you can find something to read. Mercedes is cleaning out a storeroom, and I may have to spend some time with her and out in the kitchen, but you won't mind that, will you? Then we'll have a leisurely lunch, and by that time perhaps the snow will begin to melt or perhaps some other cars will have gone over the road and made tracks for us."

He argued for form's sake, "I was thinking of my Chevvy at Gladys'."

"But can't you telephone the garage to get your car?"

"Why, yes, I can do that," he agreed.

It only added to the enchanting unreality of the morning that the garageman hooted at the idea of fetching the Chevvy from Gladys'. "Listen, there are about fifty cars ahead of yours I'm supposed to get started all over town. People've been calling in all morning; that's all I've been doing is answering the telephone. I can't promise anything. Tomorrow, maybe."

It gave him the excuse he had been looking for. Why not stay? He had already persuaded himself that it would take the garageman to start the car. His exuberance would not let him remain by himself in the living room, since Cristina had disappeared while he telephoned. He decided to help Agapito shovel snow.

He climbed up one of the picturesque, homemade, peeled-aspen ladders in the patio to the portale roof and found Agapito shoveling over the corner that held Cristina's room. The smiling handy man was perfectly willing to be helped. He fetched another shovel from the garage. Together they cleared the roof over the living room, then over the dining room and the kitchen, pausing now and then for a cigarette. The sun felt hot on one's back, but the air was still cold. It made it exhilarating to work, to pitch the shovelloads of snow down into the garden in rhythm with the handy man. He even derived a glow from observing the layout of Cristina's house from up here, as if he were gaining some new insight into her by noticing how the guest wing joined onto the main house, and looking at the other wing which contained the kitchen and the tunnellike entrance into the patio and some rooms which evidently were not used, since the chimneys were covered up with boards and rocks.

Cristina came out once under the opposite portale and called up,

"Peter, you've been up there for hours. Aren't you cold? I didn't get you out here to work."

He called down, "This isn't work. This is fun."

"All right, but don't stay too long. . . ."

When Agapito and he had finished on the roof, they shoveled a path from the house to the garage and started in on the driveway. Cristina came after him when they had cleared only about half the space needed for turning the car around. She insisted, "Now you must come in; you've worked long enough. . . ." In the living room, after they had had a cigarette, she said, "Do you think you can amuse yourself for about twenty minutes? I have to be out in the kitchen to see about our lunch. Oh, and here—I suddenly remembered I had this." She held out a tooled-leather toilet kit, still in its cardboard box. "I got it in Florence for Agapito's Christmas present. I don't think it can hurt it if you use it once, and you seemed so concerned over not being shaved. I just hope it's the kind of razor you like. And remember you can use my bathroom if you want a hot tub before lunch. Do you think thirty minutes will give you time enough?"

He was ready in twenty-five. It was a delicious lunch: onion soup, hot biscuits and vegetable salad, *zabaglione*. He was aware that even though Mercedes brought in the food with something of a flourish Cristina had prepared most of it. She said, "I hope you like Roquefort dressing," and "I was going to make *crêpes Suzette* in your honor, but I didn't have any brandy and without it they aren't anything. I did have Marsala; so you got *zabaglione* instead."

He praised everything, but not half so enthusiastically as he wanted to, because her rippling, silky, somewhat triumphant self-assurance made him shy. She had changed into a smart, red wool dress and had heightened the color of her lips and drawn back her dark hair more sleekly over her ears while he shaved, and she was very much the impeccable hostess—effortlessly, unobtrusively gracious, charmingly self-possessed. It was the consciousness that she had, no doubt, made onion soup and elegant Italian desserts dozens of times for other guests before—years ago when he had perhaps still been an apprentice or even a schoolboy— that made him feel flattered but also faintly ill at ease each time he noticed the grateful eagerness with which she accepted his praise. Was she being indulgent because of his ignorance or was she sincere?

He found himself equally disconcerned by the history which everything in the house seemed to have. He had been struck by the charming peasant china at breakfast, and she had said, "Oh, do you like it? It's from Quimper. I got that years ago, one summer when I was in Brittany. I wish I'd got more. . . ." He wondered again how old she was while they sat having coffee in the dining room and he watched the exquisite pallor of her face and remembered the tone in which she had said "years ago." Thirty-six—forty perhaps?

They lingered over their coffee until nearly two before they went out to look at the road. Agapito had finished shoveling the driveway all the way to the gate, but, except for the footprints made by Agapito and Mercedes when they had come from their own house in the morning, there was no sign that any one had traveled over the road. Agapito admitted— after his Mexican politeness had made him hem and haw for a few minutes because he had not been able to decide what answer they wanted to hear—that he thought the car might get stuck.

"Oh, let's try it!" Cristina said. "If we get stuck we'll just get Agapito to come with his team and pull us out."

"No, it's too risky. I'd be afraid to let you come back by yourself. I'll just telephone for a taxi." But it was not so easy as that: the taxi people refused to send a cab. And the garageman held out even less hope than he had in the morning that he'd find time to haul the Chevvy into the garage. . . .

"I'll walk in," he told Cristina when he came back into the living room from the phone in the hall outside her bedroom. "It isn't far."

"Of course, it's far. You might catch pneumonia. You don't even have rubber boots as Agapito has. Look, Peter, suppose you do go in and you can get your car started, what good will it do? You can't possibly get out to Tesuque today; you'll only have to stay at a hotel. Now, what's wrong with staying right here?"

"Nothing, except I can't just treat your house like a hotel and stay on and on."

"I don't see why you can't. The room is here, and I love to have you. And by tomorrow you probably will be able to go home."

"It's awfully sweet of you, Cristina——"

"But what?"

"Well, for one thing, I've got to do some shopping. I need pajamas and a shirt and things."

"Oh, I'd forgotten about that." Her face lighted up. "I know what we'll do: I'll ask Agapito to saddle one of the horses and ride in. He won't mind in the least. All you have to do is write out a list of things you

want and tell him where you want him to go. Unless you want to go in
yourself—but I don't think it'd be much fun to go horseback riding
today."

"No, I'm not aching for a ride. I'd much rather stay right here,
especially if you promise to sing."

"Blackmail?" Her eyes were amused. "All right, if you stay, I'll
sing! I'd better call Agapito before he goes home because I think he's
all through. You can use my desk if you want to write down what you
want him to get. . . ."

The telephone rang while he gave Agapito a note for the man in the
haberdashery shop and money for the pajamas and underwear and a
shirt and socks. When Cristina came back from the little hall, and after
she had sent Agapito around to the kitchen to consult Mercedes about
some groceries he was also to pick up, she said, "That was Geoff. He
wanted to know whether I'd got home all right. His telephone line was
down until just a little while ago. I told him you were here."

"Oh? . . . Is he coming over?"

Cristina's thin, dark eyebrows rose ever so faintly. "Not that I
know of." As if she felt that she had sufficiently corrected any impression
he might have had that Geoffrey was free to come and go in her house
as he pleased, she added leniently, "There wouldn't be any sense in asking him to come in this weather," and then immediately went on to
change the subject. "This reminds me of a snowstorm when I was a
little girl and Mother and I were in Chamonix. They had to dig deep
trenches in the snow for people to get to the stores and to church. Have
you ever been in Chamonix? . . ."

But it was he who kept putting questions after that, partly because
everything connected with her seemed to him touched with exotic charm,
so that he could not hear enough about her past, and partly because
he found it enthralling just to listen to the haunting clarity of her voice.
He learned that Switzerland was where her mother had come to know
her stepfather, that Pier Luigi had followed them to Chamonix when
her mother's funds had run low and she had looked for a cheaper place
to live than Saint-Moritz, that Pier Luigi was a count—Conte Pier Luigi
Sola Moncini. "It's an old title," Cristina said, "though Mother claims
she didn't care about that; but of course she did—Mother is an awful
snob. Grandmother always says it would have served Mother right if
she had fallen for a tourist guide."

It appeared that Cristina's mother was a romantic who had found

Cristina's father dull and life in America drab. He discovered that Cristina's grandfather on her mother's side had been a Boston banker and that her grandmother was Italian, so that all at once Cristina's exciting pallor and an indefinable softness about all her movements stood explained. "I adore Grandmother," Cristina said. "She gets more fun out of life than almost anybody I know. . . . No, she doesn't go to Europe much; she loves New York. She moved there after grandfather died. . . . Well, she stays at a hotel with a maid who's been taking care of her for years, and she plays bridge and she goes to lectures and to concerts and to the opera, and she has a lot of friends. . . ."

He heard about Cristina's father, who had been a big handsome man who smoked cigars—"Goodness, how I hated those cigars when I was a child because Daddy always smoked one when he came to kiss me good-night every time he and Mother were going out somewhere or when there was a party going on in the house!"—and had a passion for launching new enterprises that promised him a fortune or threatened to cost him the two cotton mills he had inherited. . . . He heard about a boat race in Cannes, about a brilliant young French playwright named Raoul, whom, it appeared, Ralph Piggot also knew. . . .

It was delightful to give himself up to the luxurious realization that he could continue to stay with Cristina through the long, lazy afternoon. But there were two of him! Even while he listened for the lovely cadences of Cristina's voice and tried to visualize her as a little girl in a Long Island house and later in Florence and in Paris and at Cannes, another Peter—the distrustful, jealous, timid and cynical half of himself—had ever since Geoffrey's telephone call been taut with remembering last night. *Had her coming to his room not after all been intended as an invitation to something more than a good-night kiss? Had he been naïve?* Everything she said suddenly became a taunt. He asked, "Was Raoul one of your beaux?" and she answered, "Heavens, no! Raoul is a darling, but he isn't very male." She said of her mother and stepfather, "No, I hardly see anything of them. Mother has some silly notion that Pier Luigi has a crush on me." And when he asked, "Has he?" she smiled mischievously. "Well, yes, a little—but it's nothing serious as Mother thinks. . . ."

He found himself increasingly restless as the afternoon wore on. The secretly more and more clamorous half of him, which kept weighing the advisability of trying to kiss her again, tortured him with a sharpened awareness of the lines of her body under her dress. Largely to escape the strain of having to sit still again and conceal his restlessness from her knowing eyes after they had both got up to turn on the lamps, he reminded her of her promise to sing.

He loved the mild light from the single standing lamp by the piano bench, the businesslike way in which she sat down to play, her brisk hunting through the album she had placed on the music rack for the aria from the *Matrimonio Segretto* for which he had asked. Out in the kitchen, Mercedes was already busy with dinner, making an occasional discreet clatter, as if to let Cristina know that she had returned from her own house. He went to close the dining room door after Cristina struck a chord and let her voice run up and down the scale, by way of warming up. She apologized, "I haven't sung for two weeks; I'll probably sound horrible."

She sang softly, easily, superbly. She sang the Neapolitan song he loved, two other folk songs, a gay aria from a Puccini opera, some Monteverdi songs that entranced him. The liquid notes flowed from her throat and floated on the air like streamers of gold; it seemed to him that he had never heard such pure sound. Even her erectness on the piano bench added to the spell. He stood a little to one side of the piano, in the shadows, where he felt free to watch her mouth and eyes, and her white forehead trust back out of the light, and the intoxicating rise of her breasts each time she took a deep singer's breath.

The Monteverdi song stopped so unexpectedly that he was taken by surprise. His pent-up enthusiasm could only grope for words. ". . . and I'm crazy about the aria. You aren't going to stop?"

"The Puccini—*o mio babbino?*"

"No, the Monteverdi, the one just before this last song. You aren't going to stop?"

Cristina had already got up and was folding the music on the rack. "Oh, I think you've had enough. And I have to talk to Mercedes about our dinner, or you won't get anything to eat." She mocked, "You'll be saying I enticed you up here to make you listen to me sing."

"I'm only mildly conceited. Anyway, I'm much too superstitious to brag about my good luck."

Cristina had paused at the corner of the piano, a mere arm's length away from him. He wanted to keep her there—smiling at him, waiting indulgently.

"You know, you're the only soprano I've ever seen who looks beautiful when she gets anywhere near high C. Most of them look hardly human above F. They look as if they were going to dislocate their jaws and they waggle their tonsils at you."

She laughed. "You're supposed to listen to singers and not look down their throats."

"I don't if I can help it. I close my eyes. But in your case—" he was at a loss how to go on, but his quivering uncertainty about last night, his suddenly imperious need to know how much she might have meant, made him indifferent to his awkardness and made him blunder ahead— "it's a joy to look at you when you sing. No, it's always a delight. Sometimes it makes *me* want to sing high C!"

It was half tribute and half plea. He had raised his right hand and he took the short step that brought him close to her. She had not moved. He had just time to see the velvety tenderness that had come into her eyes, the sudden attentiveness, the spine-tingling radiance that was like a further flowering of her smile, before her lips opened softly against his.

She was neither eager nor cold. The pressure of her lips told him that she was interested but it also apprised him that she was far from being rushed off her feet. The pliancy of her body when he drew her closer seemed merely courteous, so that he had an impression of unruffled, callous feminine knowingness which piqued his pride. It made him pretend more passion than he really felt when they were about to draw apart, and made him seek her mouth a second time.

She had still lost none of her self-possession when he obeyed the warning pressure of her hand on his arm at the slight noise beyond the dining-room door and finally did let go. But he had the satisfaction of noticing an intoxicating deepening in her voice—a huskiness almost— as she said, "Why Peter!"

"I adore you, Cristina!"

"Well, I'm relieved to hear that. I was beginning to think after last night that there was something wrong with me. You jumped when I tried to kiss you as if I had some loathsome disease."

Her banter reduced it all again to the innocuous level of last night's kiss. But certainly just now her lips and her body yielding to his arm had implied something more than that. . . . He seesawed between elation and uncertainty while he was in his room putting on the clothes Agapito had brought from town, all through dinner, and afterward when they were once again in the living room.

Cristina was teaching him Russian bank. He found it hard to keep his mind on the game. Once or twice he only barely resisted the impulse to rush around the card table to pull her up out of her chair, but the possibility that she might receive him with a look of inexorable astonishment kept him glued to his seat. And yet occasionally something

excitingly playful and intimate in her voice assured him of the unlikeli-
hood that mere graciousness had prompted her response before, quickened him with a sudden certainty of more to come. But at this moment
another problem rose to menace him. There was one question he had
to ask, an answer he had to have. When they stopped playing a little
after ten he finally found an opening.

"Yes, it's a good game," she said. "Ian and I used to play it all the
time."

Ian—her second husband, the composer!

"I thought all you did was run away from his mother."

She paused as if she had forgotten that she had told him the other
night about her tribulations with mothers' boys. She smiled belatedly.
"Oh, we did; but we managed to have quite a lot of fun besides."

"Then, you didn't mind being married to Ian?"

"Mind? Of course, not. No woman minds being married as long as
it is a marriage. Mamma just kept ours from working out, that's all."

He tried to match her light tone. "Then, poor Geoffrey still has a
chance?"

She looked ever so faintly startled. "I'd never dream of marrying
Geoff."

"Isn't he in love with you?"

"I can't help that. We're just friends." Her pointedly steady glance
weighted the words. "And that's all we'll ever be! We've known each
other for a long time, but there are certain things about Geoff I simply
can't stand."

"But you're fond of him."

"I'm very fond of Geoff. Only—" she had completely recaptured her
smiling poise—"I'm not going to marry him. Do you mind?"

He was aware of a baffling surge of resentment on Geoff's account at
the very moment when he felt himself lifted on a surge of joy that tri-
umphed over Geoff. His blood sang with expectancy.

"On the contrary! I don't care a hoot about Geoff. I've got better
things to do—I adore you, Cristina!"

She tilted up her face readily enough when he reached out for her;
yet there was, for her softness, a holding back. Her vaguely rigid
shoulders and the soft hand against his chest seemed to warn him off.
He revenged himself for the momentary irresolution she had forced on
him, by allowing himself a fleeting awareness through his finger tips that
the skin at the back of her waist rumpled into disconcerting folds. He
hastily slid his hand farther up her spine and increased the ardor of his

lips. Her breath finally came as fast as his. She made no attempt to conceal her quickened heartbeat but she suddenly pulled away from him. Her voice was excitingly husky again. "Really, I don't much care for being raped on the floor."

He was still not sure of her. "I know I ought to say good night! Suppose I remember after a while that I've forgotten my cigarettes over here—are you going to sick the dogs on me?"

She glanced at the two spaniels stretched out side by side on the rug in front of the fireplace. "Pimmy and Pam are much too fast asleep." She smiled. "If you give me about fifteen minutes before you start remembering, I might even come out and help you look. I might even let you sit beside my bed and have one last cigarette. . . ."

What possible concern could it be of Geoff's? None, he answered himself and pulled the last pin out of the new pajamas in his room. Wine-colored—how idiotic of the clerk! He had expressly asked for blue!

He dawdled over putting on the pajamas, putting on a new pair of socks, combing his hair. He hummed the lovely passage from the Monteverdi aria over and over again to give vent to his exultation and nervousness and to keep from thinking of the way her body had folded against his. He put his overcoat on over his pajamas, and went out into the portale and looked up into the myriad-starred, infinitely winking, deep-blue sky until the freezing cold forced him to go back inside. He waited until a full twenty minutes had gone by before he knocked on the living-room door, opened it. Even so, it was too soon.

The door which led into the little hall with the gay green-and-red cupboard on the left and Cristina's bedroom door, he knew, just beyond that, was still shut. Pimmy, the larger of the two spaniels, lazily raised his tawny head off the rug, blinked, and went back to sleep. The lights down by the piano had been turned out; the ash trays on the cocktail table had been emptied into the fireplace; the fire, he noticed, had been allowed to die down to red coals. He wondered whether Cristina was expecting him to knock on the hall door to let her know he was here, or whether she was perhaps even expecting him to walk right in—as far as the little hall, at least. He decided against either probability, since the door was after all firmly shut, but after wandering around the room for a few minutes he could not resist letting the poker with which he had pushed the embers to the rear of the fireplace fall against the fire tongs with a clang that made the two dogs jump. After that there was nothing to do but wait.

He went to the bookcase and glanced without really seeing them over the titles on two of the shelves. He came back to the fireplace and played with the dogs. He strained to listen for some sound from Cristina's room and finally was rewarded by hearing a soft scrape as of a chair being moved. Then there was silence again—a whispering, pregnant silence that seemed to make fun of him. Had he been mistaken about what she meant? Had she changed her mind about coming out at all? Still, she had left the lights on here in the living room. . . . He jumped at the sly click of a latch. He turned just in time to meet Cristina's eyes.

It was as if gaiety had flooded in with her from the hall. Her smile asked no forgiveness even though she said contritely, "I've kept you waiting frightfully, haven't I?" She had put on a white negligee—all filmy ruffles and flowing folds and haughty train—which somehow gave her an air of complacent, rather recent maternity and for some unfathomable reason made him think of Mizzi and sent a voluptuous shudder of revulsion over him. As if to reproach him for his thoughts, her dark hair, allowed to fall loosely from where it was gathered with a white ribbon at the nape of her neck, gave her an enchanting girlishness.

The silvery gleam in her gray eyes mocked. "You haven't even had a cigarette!"

"I was waiting for you."

She shivered playfully. "It's cold out here. I have a much nicer fire in my room. . . ."

Not only was there a cheerful fire licking up the chimney of the square little fireplace in the wall that faced the maple fourposter, but the whole room was warmly intimate, airy, and feminine without any cloying frilliness. The pillows on the bed had been propped up against the headboard below the silk-shaded reading lamp, and one corner of the yellow blanket and the top sheet had been folded back.

Cristina pointed to the green easy chair by the fireplace. "You must sit there where you can be comfortable."

"And where are you going to be?"

"Right here." She touched the yellow pouf with the toe of her white slipper, pushed it closer to the fireplace with one side of her foot, so that for a few seconds not only her bare ankle but also a fold of pink nightgown emerged from her negligee. "I love to sit where I can watch the flames." She bent over to brush some ashes back into the fireplace with a little hearth broom, and the delicate flower-moist fragrance of the perfume she used tingled in his nose. Her loose hair when she straightened seemed suddenly no longer girlish but so intimately feminine that his limbs went soft with an overmastering need to possess her.

He said, and his voice came out hoarse, "That perfume would make a chrysalis imagine it was a butterfly! Is it a flower scent?"

"Oh, the toilet water—it's mimosa. It's my favorite scent. Are you a chrysalis?"

"Not usually, but when I'm with you I sometimes feel as clumsy as something in a cocoon." He grinned. "You also fill me so full of heady ideas at times that I can soar and fly."

She had reached for the red-lacquer cigarette box on the mantelpiece and was holding it out to him. "Is that why you won't sit down? I don't want you to fly away just yet."

"When I get those hallucinations I always fly in circles: I come right back to you. Haven't you ever watched a butterfly? It just has to dance for sheer joy, like this. . . ." His hands described two playful circles in front of her and slid around her waist.

Her gray eyes had watched in amused astonishment. Her mouth when she lifted her parted lips tasted faintly of antiseptic and mint, and for a moment the fact that she had blandly used toothpaste made him feel that there was something connubial and calculated in her preparations for him. But his carping could not hold out against the dizzying warmth of her body under the filmy negligee. He heard first the cigarettes and then the lacquer box fall from Cristina's hands down on the rug. His blood sang.

"You make one soar right into the upper atmosphere; I'm getting dizzy spells. Could we settle on that mimosa bush?"

She turned slightly with him toward the mimosa-yellow blanket on the bed. "Aren't you changing the metaphor?"

He felt himself driven toward her in an ecstasy of urgency as she undid the two bows in front. "No, I'm not. You are my metaphor!" Words were only an obstacle, he thought impatiently behind his impetuously mounting joy when she let the negligee slide off her shoulders and arms and kicked off the white mules and let herself fall back against the pillows, so that the lace-edged V of her nightgown slipped partly down over one breast. She looked radiant.

"You mean, I exaggerate?"

The exquisite torture of having to keep his impatience in check for endless seconds longer was like the music of an overstretched string. "You don't have to: you are beautiful!"

Her eyes were luminous. "Darling . . ."

CHAPTER EIGHT

Journey into Christmas
and Back

$\mathbf{S}$HE said, "I'm glad. They've always been my best point. I'm rather proud of their being small. I'd hate to be one of those females with great, bulging breasts. . . ." She said after breakfast the next morning when they were at last rid of the maid and laughingly drifted into each other's arms, "And I'd promised myself not ever to fall in love again!" and, because her forthrightness froze him into flustered reticence and she noticed it, "Peter, you aren't afraid of me, are you? . . ." She said, "That's one thing we don't have to worry about! I've been to half the doctors in Europe—I can't have any children."

He said, unable to figure out from her tone how she felt about it and thinking it safer to banter than to sympathize, "You don't mind, I hope!"

"I used to mind awfully. I don't much now, especially when I see what brats some of my friends' children are turning into, after being the

153

most darling babies. I'm afraid I'm not really very maternally inclined. Children can be rather a nuisance, don't you think?"

"Of course," he agreed with false heartiness, to conceal his uncomfortable sense of being jockeyed into saying something he knew he did not believe.

Can one, he asked himself, be in bed with a woman, hear her cry out, watch her eyes melt with tenderness as she comes out of the exquisite swoon, and yet feel as remote and watchful as if one had only just met her in a crowded drawing room and she was still formidably sheathed in smiling self-possession and cool elegance? Could one play truant to one's own delight and gratitude?

A certain artificiality—half-stilted formality, and half-guarded watchfulness—seemed to him an inextricable part of their relationship. He attributed it to Cristina's sophistication and a sort of worldly callousness that went with it and to his fear of incurring her scorn by somewhat not measuring up. He almost liked the artificiality. Because of it, everything they said took on a special resonance, and everything they did become deliciously exotic, festive, unique. Some magic seemed to shape events to their wish. Even the weather and the garageman seemed to conspire for their benefit, by furnishing him with an excuse for staying still another night. Their running into Gladys in the grocery store when they drove downtown before lunch to shop and to see about his car, appeared to have been staged expressly for their merriment. One look at Gladys' shrewd, greedy eyes told them she had only been waiting for the chance to confirm her suspicions about the last two nights. As soon as they were rid of her, they looked at each other and laughed. "Half an hour," Cristina said, "and all of Santa Fe will know!"

"Maybe we ought to ask her out as chaperon?"

"And have everybody wonder whom we were gossiping about? No, thank you; I'm particular about the sort of reputation I get."

They found dozens of things to laugh about. The air seemed electric with gaiety. The afternoon was a shimmering bubble that enveloped them in a privileged world all their own. They sat in the living room after lunch and talked—or, rather, he derived an almost voluptuous pleasure from drawing her out about the past because each new shred of information enhanced his sense of possessing her, and Cristina lent herself with wry and yet zestful tenderness to his curiosity and talked about Italy and her stepfather and about an automobile accident in which she and Pier Luigi had been involved. They both had been thrown out of the car; they had lain for hours before help came.

He was shocked. "I thought your stepfather knew how to drive, I thought he drove racing cars."

"He does. But this was a light French car that belonged to our host, and Pier Luigi isn't used to anything but heavy, low-slung cars, and anyhow he is pretty careless when he's just driving along at what he considers ordinary speeds. Besides, this wasn't really his fault. We were coming back from Cap d'Antibes after a party, and there was a *camion*— a truck, you know—stalled right in the middle of the road. No lights or anything! All Pier Luigi could do was to turn out into the ditch and go through a fence."

"Couldn't he get help afterward?"

"He had a broken back! I had only a wrenched ankle and a broken rib."

"How long did you lie there?"

"About five hours. It happened around midnight, and there wasn't another car over that road until after dawn. Then we had to wait another hour before they could get an ambulance. But what I minded most was that Pier Luigi wouldn't talk to me. He kept passing out."

"But that was frightful," he said.

"Oh, that wasn't anything. In the French Alps one time, Ian and I rolled down sixty feet into a ravine. We turned over three times."

"What happened?"

"Well, Ian was racing up an icy mountain road and not slowing down at some hairpin turns."

"Why?"

Her tone remained dispassionate, amused, as if she were telling about the somewhat incredible carryings-on of a mere acquaintance. "He was trying to kill us both. It was just after Ian had asked his mother to join us again when we'd been trying to get away from her—and after he'd agreed that the best thing for both of us was to get a divorce."

"He must have been a maniac!"

She considered it. "No, Ian was very sane and almost too gentle. That's why he loved pigeons so; he'd raised them ever since he had been a little boy. You should have seen him with a baby pigeon that had fallen out of the dovecot one time. He made me get out of the bathtub and rush all the way out into the garden because he wanted me to hold it in my hands.

He said that feeling the wild little heart beat against his fingers was the most thrilling thing that had ever happened to him." She reflected for a moment. "Of course, pigeons can be ferocious. Have you ever seen them fight? They go absolutely berserk. . . ."

She had had an even narrower escape as a child, when she had taken her father's motorboat out into Long Island Sound and had drifted about in a storm for hours and got pneumonia and almost died. It appeared that her dashing, handsome father, whom she adored, had never had any time for her and that the adventure in the boat had been an anguished protest against his neglect. "No," she said, "Mother and I didn't get along even then."

Her playful recital of the occasions when she had narrowly escaped catastrophe and the picture she called up of a lonely little girl clinging passionately to a stray puppy and a turtle and to her friendship for a half-witted gardener's son because her parents had paid no attention to her, filled him with indignant protectiveness. Yet this nostalgic tenderness, which was tied up with his memory of a dark-haired little girl whom he had once seen with her governess in a florist's shop in Vienna when he was a boy, in no way diminished the subtle tendency of a small but treacherous part of himself to remain stubbornly immune to Cristina's charm and even to be critical. As far as that fractious, tiny part of himself was concerned, her childhood sufferings were merely another item in that precious inventory which his infatuation was driving him to make.

There were other items: his noticing that not only the Chinese vase which she took him out into the storeroom to see but also the Della Robbia angel over the bedroom fireplace and the priceless Etruscan perfume jar in the bookcase had been broken and glued together again; his somewhat startled discovery of the shelves of medicines and drugs and jars of bath salts in the carved cabinet in the bathroom where she had sent him for alcohol with which to fill the little lamp of the chafing dish; his discovery of the enchantingly naïve Mexican wood carving of San Ysidro—the patron saint of the Spanish peasants, Cristina explained—in a niche in the little hall outside her room.

He loved to hear her explain. While she stood beside him and told him the legend, the chunky little figure of San Ysidro in his black short-jacketed peasant suit and outlandish, high-crowned hat and the disarmingly rustic angel, who was dressed just like the saint and was guiding the two stolid oxen hitched to the plow, appeared even more charmingly austere and quaint than when he had first noticed them. When she stopped, it was as if music had stopped. And because he could not get enough of hearing her voice, he cajoled her into reading Dante aloud again; but she had barely opened the book when the telephone rang. It was Geoff. He refused to come over for dinner; he was coming for coffee afterward.

He arrived just as Mercedes cleared away the salad plates. He fumbled with the buckles of his galoshes by the front door when Peter joined Cristina who had gone to welcome him. He hemmed and hawed about coming into the dining room and he would not have any of the Bavarian cream Cristina had made during the afternoon for dessert. But once he had sat down at the table with them and lighted a cigarette, he almost flaunted an airy suavity, as if to demonstrate that he was in complete possession of himself and that everything was exactly as he wanted it.

Cristina was playing up to him. Her strained vivacity made her sound ever so faintly like a solicitous mother persuading a child that it has not been seriously hurt. "But you can't mean that, Geoff? What are the Millers going to do without a car?"

They were talking about the disruptions the blizzard had wrought. And then all at once while they were having coffee in the living room there were fewer and fewer things to say. Cristina proposed—a little too spontaneously, Peter thought—that they play Russian bank. It was Geoff who set up the table and got the little painted box with the cards. Little convulsions of jealousy tortured Peter when he saw that the game which he had thought a cherished possession shared only by Cristina and him was also shared by Geoff, who had clearly played dozens of times with Cristina before. His jealousy was appeased only by his realization that their playing cards at all was an evasion, a polite and somewhat anxious turning away from fact, which had been forced on them by his own new relation with her. It made him glow with such a sense of triumph that for several minutes he did not dare to look at Geoff.

There was a problem, too, in encountering Cristina's eyes. He had to deny himself any acknowledgment of their intimacy, any lingering tenderness—his glances had to remain impassive and merely polite. It seemed to him at moments as if they were all three walking the same tightrope, cautiously stepping around one another whenever they met but pretending that their balancing took no art at all. They joked and laughed; they teased one another about their cards and scores.

After they had been playing for about an hour, Cristina asked, "Do you feel cold, too, or is it just me? I think the fire is getting low. Peter, would you put on some more wood—perhaps one of these big logs Aga-pito brought this afternoon?" Almost instantly Geoffrey pushed back his chair and said firmly, "I'll do it!" with an air of asserting a prior claim and reminding her of his much greater competence to perform the chore, since he knew his way around the house. Cristina's tone, mild and implacable at the same time, kept him from getting up. "Peter will do it, Geoff! We've had to make a new arrangement since you were here. Mercedes and I decided that those red adobe bugs have been getting into the house in the piñon logs. We're making Agapito leave the wood under the portale. Peter knows where it is."

Behind him while he went to the front door to get a log Peter could sense the bafflement—and was it, hurt?—beneath Geoff's elaborately in-different "Very well." Cristina was aware of it, too. She said repentantly, "Geoff, I never asked whether you wanted a drink. Do help yourself. You know where everything is. . . ."

Geoffrey excused himself from playing any more at a little after nine. Cristina protested, "But, Geoff, it's early still!"

His reasons sounded rehearsed. "I don't like to keep the automobile out in the cold too long: the motor becomes difficult to start. And I'd better get back to my studio to check on the leaks in the roof."

They were all three of them eager to prove that there had been no strain now that he was about to leave. Peter, helping him into his coat and noticing the gingerly way he inserted his left arm into the sleeve, asked guiltily, "Is your shoulder getting better—Geoff?" He'd almost said "sir."

"Much better, thanks. It's been bothering me a bit since the storm, but that was probably a touch of flu. At any rate quite all right today." He buttoned his coat, and his face looked at once handsome and drawn in the bright light from the tin wall bracket Cristina had switched on by the door. "I suppose you'll be here for a few more days?"

"Not if I can help it. I've already imposed on Cristina too long. Be-sides, I'd better see whether my roof's got any leaks. I've just been wait-ing for the garage to fix the radiator on the car."

Geoffrey offered, with his hat already in his hand, "I'll be glad to take you out to Tesuque if you wish to go at any time."

"That's awfully kind, but they've promised to have the car ready to-morrow morning for sure."

He was—Peter noticed again—not given to shaking hands. He reached abruptly for the latch. "Well—ah—good-by." To Cristina he added, "I'll ring you tomorrow afternoon sometime."

"Yes, do that, Geoff! . . ." There was something mocking in her exuberance as soon as he had left. "I want a drink. . . ."

Yet if they both had a sense of being let out of school that first evening when Geoff left, they did not put their relief into words. Nor did they do more than exchange a brief, cautiously conspiratorial smile the next afternoon when Cristina came away from the telephone, for Peter was there again when Geoffrey called. He had stayed in Tesuque just long enough to start up the stoves and to work for three hours with new zest on the portrait of the Indian, and then he had hurried back to town to take Cristina to dinner at the hotel.

The little house in Tesuque became merely the place where he went to sleep, to change his clothes, to paint with great new bursts of energy that made him forget about everything but the picture he was trying to paint. A shadowy and not quite real part of his existence seemed to be spent in it, as if it were a dusky railroad station in which he drowsily waited for a train. The shining part of each day began at four when he set out for Cristina's house. The road into town could not be bad enough to stop him now.

Geoff seemed tartly aware of it. Two days after his other telephone call he was on the phone again, and Cristina was saying, "Oh, I'm sorry, Geoff, but Peter has asked me to have dinner with him." There was a pause followed by her smiling taunt, "Why, certainly!"

"Geoff wanted to know," she explained after she hung up, "whether I had to have dinner with you every night. Poor Geoff, I'll have to have him for dinner soon."

"Why?"

"Well, we had sort of got into the habit of having dinner together several nights each week. Suppose I ask him for tomorrow night?"

"I won't be able to see you then!"

"Of course you will. I'll ask you both and I'll ask Jeanne."

"She'll go to sleep again and stay all night!"

She smiled at his anxiety. "No, she won't. Geoff doesn't really like her too well and he usually brings her and takes her home." Her eyes became flecked with gay triumph. "That way neither of them will stay too long."

But it turned out to be Cristina who found the evening with Geoff and Jeanne a strain, even though all her hostess sprightliness went into making them stay on and on. When they had gone and he had returned—for, now that he was not Cristina's house guest any more, he felt it necessary

to leave even before Geoff and to go through the comedy of saying good-
by to Cristina and driving off, only to return laughingly half an hour
later—Cristina exploded with comical intensity, "Thank goodness, that's
over with. Have you ever known such an evening? I didn't think it was
ever going to end."

"Jeanne can be quite a bore with her Tibetan dogs and Tibetan-this
and Tibetan-that."

A mischievous flicker in Cristina's eyes made them both burst into a
deliciously guilty laugh. "Oh, but it wasn't just Jeanne! I thought I was
going to scream if Geoff strode around the room just once more."

It was not striding so much as a sort of absent-minded prowling,
Peter noticed when they were all three of them asked to dinner at the
Orrs'. An inner restlesness kept Geoff moving softly about their living
room, crossing to straighten a picture on the wall, ignoring the chairs,
stopping to examine the books on the shelf. Nor did Cristina's complaints about him remain the same. A few days later he dropped in at
teatime and was already there when Peter arrived. He sat in one of the
easy chairs by the fireplace and spoke hardly at all, forcing them to keep
the conversation alive. When he left, Cristina burst out, "Have you ever
seen anything as ridiculous? He sits there like a bump on a log. Why
come at all if he is just going to sit there and not open his mouth?"

His first deprecatory smile—in spite of his virtuous air of seeming to
say: Of course, you're exaggerating, Cristina, we both know that, and
I'm grinning only because you're so amusing about Geoff!—left him with
an uneasy sense of guilt. He could not conceal from himself that there
was a faint vindictive thrill in hearing her criticize Geoff, so that he
waited with secret impatience to hear her mention him again, in the half-
blushing hope that she might hint at some new shortcoming.

But it also flattered his vanity to discover one by one all the reasons
why she preferred him to Geoff. In the same way his pride in her was
swelled by hearing about all the famous people she had known in Italy
and in France and in New York and all the exciting places she had seen.
He was glad when people began to take notice of their relationship, as
when Piggot stopped him in the plaza and said with oblique knowingness
in his somber, suave voice, "I see my warning was quite unnecessary.
The mountain air agrees with you. You came, you saw, you conquered,
I'm told!" And it elated him when Buell scowled at his finished portrait
of the Indian and preached, "All right. That's as far as you can carry
that particular thing. Now are you going to start another picture or are

you going to sit around the rest of the winter and admire this one? You can't paint and bat around every night. I told you that in the beginning. Keep that up and you'll turn into just another dilettante."

It flattered him—though it also evoked a fleeting sense of guilt in him toward Geoff—when Gladys asked Cristina and him to a cocktail party and pointedly, rather embarrassingly, did not invite Geoff.

He became delightedly aware that not only Gladys and Dorothy Lambert but also Mary Orr and several other women who had merely been normally friendly and flirtatious before suddenly took an increased interest in him and that their voices when they talked to him now tended to become a caressing purr. On the other hand, Aleida Gibbs' coolness had turned into frigid scorn. He had only to join a group of which she was a part, for her to walk away—or, what was even worse, to stay and ignore him utterly. To get the better of his annoyance, he told himself that her haughty disapproval was really only another tribute to his success with Cristina. He almost persuaded himself of it.

He realized that his feeling for Cristina—he was reluctant to call it "passion"—lacked some ardent core, some innocent, uncritical recklessness. In that sense what he felt for her was nearly all shell—mere admiration, gratitude. Even Cristina's increasingly unconstrained tenderness spoke chiefly to his pride. It put him under a strain at times when her affection raced ahead of his, challenged him, and forced him to reply. She said, "Isn't it nice that we get along so perfectly in every way? Don't you think we're lucky, darling?" and he answered hastily, "Yes, wonderful."

"I just wish I weren't so much older than you."

"A couple of years!" he scoffed tenderly, to keep her from worrying about it. "You're awfully conceited about that."

"I wish it were just a couple. I'm thirty-six!"

"I'm so glad you are. I get bored to tears with sweet young things."

"That's twelve years."

"What of it? I've always been older than my actual age. I just hope you don't find me too young."

"I love you, Peter."

"I adore you," he always said quickly and he ardently bent over her, from a feeling that his kisses had to keep her from noticing that his love fell somehow short. Yet for all his rueful sense of not loving her enough there was his eagerness every afternoon to get into town to be with her, the zest with which he had begun to draw all at once, the elation with which he greeted each new December day when the sun kindled the snow-capped Truchas Peaks.

He told himself: *All right, I'm not in love with her the way I might be with somebody else—what's wrong with that? There are all kinds of love. She's a woman of the world, and we're having an affair. Maybe it's because I met her through Geoff and can never look at her without being faintly conscious of him, or maybe it's because she is older and has seen so much more than I, that I can't ever let go completely and have to keep some small part of me in reserve. But I admire her and I find her fascinating and I feel I want to make up to her for all the grief she has run into with all the men she has known. But I'm not going to pretend that I'm head over heels in love with her!*

And on Christmas Eve, in Taos, he suddenly had a suspicion that perhaps Cristina, too, had secret corners in herself which she concealed from him. . . .

They had decided to spend Christmas in the little mountain town about which Peter had known only that it lay some seventy-five miles to the north, up the Rio Grande canyon, and that it boasted a famous Indian pueblo and an art colony. It had really been Piggot's idea one evening when they had all had dinner at the hotel. Piggot had run into some friends down from Taos for the day and had been invited up for a party on Christmas Eve. "I understand the Christmas dances at the Taos pueblo are very picturesque," Geoff had thrown out. "Isn't it quite a trip in the winter?" Cristina had asked.

"Not bad," Piggot had said. "We can make it in four or five hours unless there is a lot of snow. If we go up in my Buick, we'll be perfectly comfortable. I feel that while one's out here one oughtn't to miss any of these things. After all, the Indian dances are unique. . . ."

Peter had noticed as they talked that it was somehow taken for granted among the three of them that they would spend Christmas together, just as at parties they displayed a kind of family solidarity by sooner or later seeking one another out. The years Cristina and Geoff and Piggot had known each other in France were like an unbreakable bond. It had suddenly been he who had become an outsider again, so that he had felt grateful to Geoff for asking before Cristina could, "Would you like to come with us, Peter?" The irony of Geoff's invitation had not even struck him fully until he had been alone together with Cristina afterward and she had laughed at the mere thought of their not being with each other on Christmas Eve, so that he had suddenly felt called upon to defend

Geoff's generosity. . . . Cristina had liked the idea of the Taos trip. "We could stop and wish Father Hegge a Merry Christmas," she had said. They had both begun to look forward to it.

They started at a little after eleven on the twenty-fourth. A festive expectancy rode with them in the car. The sky was overcast, heavy clouds hanging down into the canyon—somehow perfect weather for Christmas Eve, Cristina said and they all agreed. They talked gaily back and forth, Cristina up front beside Piggot, and Geoff in the other corner in the rear, with the thermos bottles and the hamper of food which Cristina had put up for their lunch between them on the seat. Geoffrey was exceptionally communicative and talked in his clipped voice about a month he had spent in Wyoming the previous year and about the difficulty of catching the character of the New Mexico mountains in paint. They were still discussing the geometric structure of the Sangre de Cristo range on the right when they approached Santa Cruz.

Father Hegge welcomed them with boisterous warmth outside the church even though they had interrupted him and about a dozen boys and girls in decorating the side altars and the deep-set windows with Christmas greens—even though he admitted that neither he nor his charges had yet had lunch and that he had a strenuous schedule ahead for the afternoon: a final choir rehearsal for Midnight Mass, the rectory still to clean up, confessions to hear after three o'clock.

He insisted on taking them to the rectory after he had left the children in charge of a nun who had been struggling with a wheezing parlor organ up in the choir loft. The moment they entered the somber 'dobe rectory he turned with a sly smile to Cristina. "I've something to show you. We've made improvements since you were here!" He led the way into the bare, drab kitchen and proudly turned on the faucet over the sink. He beamed. "Now what do you think of that? We've even got a second one in the room where we take our showers. And let me show you something else. . . ."

He took them into the study to the radio—satisfactorily assembled, Peter noticed—and turned the knob. "This morning we heard some fine music all the way from Kansas City." He winked at Cristina. "An angel has been here to help us out, one of the practical kind with plumber's tools instead of wings." He winked once more and turned to him, so that Peter felt himself blush. "Is that assembled the way it should be? Juan says it is, and it seems to work just fine."

Cristina was softly radiant. "So that's what those mysterious expeditions were! He wouldn't tell me about them!" She pretended to pout and to complain to Father Hegge, who chuckled happily, and to Geoff and Piggot, who made vaguely approving sounds; but when they all followed the priest to the other end of the study, she seized his hand and pressed it impulsively to her side. "That was a charming thing to do. I love you, darling!"

They still had to admire the Christmas tree and the little crèche the boys had made, and while Cristina and the others were busy discovering new things to praise in the clumsily carved and painted and yet gay figures of St. Joseph and the Virgin and the shepherds and the ox, Peter hurried out to the car to fetch the basket Cristina had packed with fruitcake and candy and all sorts of sweets, and the box of candy he himself had brought, and tried to sneak them into the closet where Father Hegge had shown them a little pile of presents for the boys. He hastily tucked the envelope with his Christmas card and the credit slip at the clothing store under the big red bow Cristina had tied on the basket handle.

He had not been able to do it without being seen. Father Hegge protested, "What's this? What's this? We've had our Christmas presents from you this year! Wait, I've something for you, too. . . ." He brought two little carved figures like the ones in the crèche, one of an angel and one of a shepherd with a staff. "They were supposed to be in the mail last Saturday," Father Hegge apologized, "but Juan's friend had painted his angel the same color as Juan's shepherd, so we had a little bit of a crisis getting a different color scheme for the angel. I think the angel was intended for you, Mrs. Day; the shepherd is for you, Mr. Domanig. I think I got it straight. . . ."

The primitive little carvings, and the inquisitive glances of the children when they looked into the church once more, and Father's "Merry Christmas—God bless you!" were like richer presents than any they could possibly have brought. Geoff and Piggot admitted as much when Geoff seemed to speak for both of them by saying, "Nice chap, that priest. Those children seem devoted to him. . . ."

And then they were on the road again which was dropping down toward the canyon bottom and the Rio Grande. When they reached the river they stopped at a tin-roofed garage in a sprawling little village to have the car checked and to eat their picnic lunch.

For the next hour and a half the road wound in and out among orchards and small, scattered ranches alongside the Rio Grande. The scraggly fruit trees and the cottonwoods and willows that grew between the boulders that formed the riverbanks, had a bleak starkness against the snow that reminded one of the bewitched landscapes in the illustrations to some German fairy tale. The river, which looked neither very wide nor very deep, gave a hint of savage power only in the foaming whirlpools around the rocks that stuck up here and there from its bed.

Occasionally they met another car. Once Piggot and he had to get out and put on chains when they hit an icy stretch. Another time they had to move several hub-high boulders that had tumbled off the steep slope on the right and landed in the road. The canyon walls were drawing in close and soared with frowning sheerness—for fifteen hundred feet, Piggot said—to the giant crenelations at the rim, cutting off the light, until the Gothic buttresses and the grotesque pulpits which the sand blasts and the water had carved out of the rock took on a somberly shadowed eeriness. Now and again, when the grandeur became almost too much to bear, so that one or the other of them had to call attention to it, or when some frivolous incident mocked one's awe, as when a covey of enchantingly graceful quail made their way unhurriedly across the road and forced Piggot to come to a halt, Cristina would turn around and smile at Geoff and him, and her glance would linger on him for a reckless fraction of a second in a tingling exchange of messages which only they could understand. It happened again when the sun broke through the stubborn clouds for a few minutes at half past two and briefly kindled the brown rocks into rose-red and made the crouching shadows become friendly and intimate; but this time Geoffrey gave a harsh little cough, as if he had caught onto their secret wave length and irritably wanted to warn them of the fact. Out of politeness—to soothe him—Cristina had to say, "Isn't it beautiful, Geoff?"

It became even more breath-taking. The road was climbing up out of the canyon. They slithered around icy curves, looked down farther and farther on the darkening river, all but cheered on the car which was beginning to boil from the long climb, labored up more rising straightaways and around more curves, and then, at last, lunged over the rim of the canyon and saw spread out before them an immense plateau, ringed by a majestic sweep of mountains some ten miles away. It was like coming out of a tomb into the light again. Up here the clouds did not hang nearly so low; one could make out each snow-splotched peak along the semicircular mountain chain. One felt as if winged with the sense of liberation and joy. Geoffrey sounded gayer than Peter had ever heard him, as he held out his silver case. "Magnificent, isn't it? Cigarette?"

The air seemed thinner here than in Santa Fe, although Piggot assured them that the altitude was the same. The landscape, too, was utterly different as they headed toward the mountains across the plain. In place of the rolling red hills studded with black-green piñon, there was a vast expanse of silvery sage sticking up out of the snow. Taos itself, when at last they came to it after driving through some outlying villages, proved a sort of provincial cousin of Santa Fe, with a charmingly rustic plaza inclosed by portale-fronted stores, with one magnificent avenue of towering cottonwood trees whose bare branches met overhead and formed a skeleton roof with a quaintly truculent, self-complacent air that seemed to announce it had always preferred its own staid sobriety to the effete elegancies of Santa Fe.

The cheerful bustle of Christmas shoppers was everywhere, even in the lobby of the surprisingly handsome hotel. They stayed at the hotel just long enough to look at their rooms and have some hot tea in the coffee shop while Piggot telephoned his friends. Then the Taos painter arrived and whisked them off to an impressive old Spanish house where another Taos artist and his wife were serving hot buttered rum to a couple of dozen friends before the dance. There was the usual party gaiety, and then, just as it was getting dark, they all crowded into cars and rode out through the cottonwood avenue and over a country road for a couple of miles to the Indian pueblo, which nestled against the foot of the mountains.

A ruddy glow of fires greeted them as soon as they came to the first few adobe houses and corrals and picturesque raised log platforms on which hay was stored. They passed by the side of an adobe church and came out on a vast open square that was cut in half by a fast-running stream. The sporadic glow of fires which they had noticed from the road was suddenly accounted for. Scores of neatly laid piles of pitch pine stretched in a double row from the church across the square, and a few of the bonfires had been prematurely lighted. One bonfire even flared on a fourth-story roof; for, on either side of the creek, high above the adjoining houses, there rose a massive, five-story apartment house. Each story was stepped back from the one below, so that the effect was that of a terraced pyramid. Ladders led up from one roof to the next, and small groups of Indians—wrapped in rich-hued blankets which still showed up distinctly in the failing light—stood on the flat roofs and looked oddly Biblical.

More Indians were coming out of houses around the square, emerging from alleys that led to houses farther away, crossing the bridges over the creek, gathering by the low-walled inclosure around the church. Jostling against them, milling around one of the fires to warm their hands, were perhaps a hundred Anglos and Spanish people who had come out from the town to look. Small boys—black-haired, bright-eyed—played tag and darted in and out of the crowd, climbed up on the inclosure wall. A steady trickle of Indian women went through the low, open double door into the church, where one could make out rows of kneeling figures by the gleam of candles and red sanctuary lamps. In the alley to the left of the church a dozen Indians appeared with ten-foot torches—so heavy that the men were barely able to balance them when they tilted them against their shoulders—made of pitch-pine sticks fagoted with baling wire. A number of younger men, with ancient silver and brass-inlaid muskets and some modern rifles, clustered around the inclosure gate.

There was almost too much to take in all at once. A few of the guns were being fired off experimentally here and there, and a pretty woman who had been at the buttered-rum party gave a little squeal when a gun went off just beside her, and several other people from the party laughed. Another woman was chattering to Geoff, "Every year I promise myself I'm not going to come out here again and freeze to death. There's never any telling with the Indians when anything's going to start. I think they do it deliberately. . . ." The plump Taos painter beside Peter assured her, "It won't be long now. The padre just went into the church. They can't start until he gets here. . . ."

The sight of several Indian women squeezing through the crowd made Peter long for a pencil and a pad to make at least some costume notes. The women looked chunky and thick-waisted but at the same time enormously alive and wonderfully paintable. Their plain, mostly light or dark-blue, cotton shawls, draped Madonna-fashion over their heads and shoulders, fell into exciting folds; their beautiful white deerskin boots, which came all the way up to their knees under the hems of their green or blue or even yellow dresses, cried out to be put down in paint. Like one of Cézanne's white tablecloths, he told himself—probably hard as anything to paint!

For a few seconds he had all but forgotten about Cristina, who was walking up ahead with Farrelly, Piggot's Taos friend. Cristina turned around, stopped, and waited for him. "Aren't you glad you came, Peter? Have you seen those stunning boots the women wear? I want to see the church. Do you think we can?" she asked Farrelly.

Geoffrey and some of the others followed them into the inclosure and up to the open door, and edged their way around a tin holy-water stoup

and along the rear wall into the corner, from which they had an untroubled view of the touchingly simple interior. There were no pews or chairs;
the congregation, made up almost entirely of women, was kneeling on
the bare wood floor. Behind the little altar, taking up the whole front
wall, was a beautiful old wooden screen, crudely carved and divided
into numerous panels that were given over to charmingly naïve repre-
sentations of various saints. A rather ambitious wooden arch over the
altar was wound with crinkly, pink tissue paper and hung with pink
tissue-paper bells such as one ordinarily saw at Christmas in the East in
the windows of small grocery stores and saloons. Festoons of pink paper
streamers and tinsel looped from corner to corner and crossed in the
exact center of the church, directly over a small table on which stood a
statue of the Virgin, decked out in lace and blue satin and all sorts of
finery. Everything about the church betokened devoutness and innumerable loving attempts to adorn: the lace curtains in the windows; the
freshly whitewashed walls that glittered with the tiny mica particles in
the white clay; the phalanx of votive candles flickering on the floor in
front of the communion rail; the baby-blue silk bows pinned to the wall
below each window; the homemade gold-paper stars suspended on strings
from the low choir loft beneath which they were all standing now.

The woman who had squealed before at the shot whispered much too
audibly, "Are they Catholics, or aren't they? I thought they were
pagans!"

Ruth Farrelly whispered back, "It depends. Some of them won't have
anything to do with the Church. It may be a matter of the clan to which
they belong. Our Clara is very devout."

The pretty woman, who was evidently only a visitor, persisted. "But
Clara was in the corn dance last summer, and that's their religion, isn't
it? Maybe they have a sort of pantheon, and they fit in all kinds of gods.
Is it really true that they murder babies if they aren't healthy?" She was
as indifferent to being overheard as if she were discussing animals in a
zoo. It was embarrassing. Fortunately the Spanish prayers, which the
Indians were saying and which they seemed to have started before the
white-haired Spanish priest, kneeling in his surplice at the altar, had
arrived from town, were coming to an end. Some old Indian men were
making their way up to the table with the statue of the Virgin. The church
bell began to ring. A lot more guns were suddenly being fired off. Farrelly took Cristina's elbow and nodded to his wife and Piggot, who were
nearest to the door.

When they came out, the whole square was aglow. The bright flames of the bonfires thrust high into the air. The great torches flared and stood lined up between the fires just outside the inclosure, along the path which the procession with the lace-mantillaed statue of the Virgin was to take. And presently the little four-foot statue appeared in the door, swaying precariously on its stretcherlike wooden platform when the four men who were carrying it hoisted the shafts up on their shoulders. Four other Indians emerged with an improvised canopy—nothing more than four long sticks, with one corner of a large white sheet tied to each one— which they proceeded to spread over the statue and carry waveringly. An elderly Indian, with a magnificent, hawklike face, a powerful body and an incongruous air of gentleness, was carrying the little wax figure of the Infant Jesus, which in the church had been seated on the arm of the Virgin. He held it tenderly cradled in his hands and leaning against his chest, and went to take his place in front of the man with the statue. The white-haired Spanish priest, who looked frail and shivery among the blanket-wrapped Indians and the chunky women who came softly surging out of the church after him, prepared to follow the canopy.

But it was outside the inclosure, in the bright blur and glare of the fires and torches, that something exciting was going on. "Look, darling!" Cristina was saying recklessly. "Do you see?"

The dazzling headdresses just outside the gate, sticking up above the heads of the crowd, caught his eye first. *Like bishops!* he thought with a joyous heart, such as he had not known since he had been a very small boy at the theater and had made the ecstatic discovery that the savage thicket of thorns around the Sleeping Princess was turning to roses before his eyes. . . . The tall, miter-shaped headdresses—some of gorgeous salmon-colored silk, some of yellow brocade, some blue or green or brown—glistened with tiny bits of jewelry that were pinned all up and down the front. Three or four bright-colored silk ribbons hung from the peak down the back of each man. A black fringe fell from the front rim over the forehead and eyes. A gay silk handkerchief was tied over the mouth and chin by way of a mask.

Half amused by his elation and his eagerness not to miss anything, he hurried with Cristina and the others to the low wall beside the gate for a better view. Each dancer held a three-pronged wooden scepter—or was it meant to be a stylized fan?—in his left hand along with a dainty silk handkerchief, and a rattle in his right, again with a frivolous bit of silk. An exuberantly gay, fringed, silk shawl was pinned to both shoulders of each man and hung down in back almost to his knees. At first glance that seemed to be all the dressing up the dancers had done. Then Peter realized that the sharply creased trousers and the colored shirts and the neckties and the unbottoned vests—all so remote from the ordinary apparel of the Indians—were also part of the masquerade.

There were exactly twelve of the mitered figures, drawn up six on each side of the gate, in a way like courtiers waiting for their sovereign. And then Peter saw that his imagination had run away with him. They were not waiting to do homage to the little wax figure of the Christ Child or to the statue of the Virgin: they already had a king! A dancer, who stood between the two facing rows, wore a tall turban of thickly packed red and yellow and white and pink roses sewn to its black frame that was as clearly meant for a crown, and he had two scepters instead of only one. His face was masked like the other men's with a black bead fringe and a silk handkerchief, and the same broad silk ribbons hung from his turban down his back; but, as if as a further mark of his king-ship, the shawl pinned to his shoulders was white and he had a delightfully bizarre pair of scalloped white lace leggings slipped over his black trous-ers, covering them between cuff and knee.

There was also a queen: a ten or eleven-year-old little girl in a starched white dress and white shoes and stockings and a miniature bridal veil over her head and shoulders, standing with downcast eyes beside the flower-turbaned king. There were even two clowns, one of them, got up in tattered white-man's clothes and a fiercely mustachioed cloth mask as a ludicrously stern old man, lorded it with a long whip and boisterous shouts over the second clown whose horns and painted burlap mask and slyly blind charges made him out a bull. And there were two Mexican fiddlers, who all at once began to play.

The two lines of courtiers moved forward between the two rows of bon-fires with an exquisitely stilted, skipping step to the archaic dance tune the two musicians scraped on their violins. The king and his child bride moved with the same series of stately little skips and glides down between the two files toward the canopy, then faced about between the last pair of courtiers and danced forward with them, just ahead of the Indian with the Infant Jesus and the canopy and the gentle, old priest and the two musicians and the encircling crowd of Indians. The procession was under way, to the accompanying stutter of gunshots and the crackling of the bonfires and the hoarse shouts of the clown with the whip.

After the procession had advanced about a hundred yards, the men who had been staggering under the gigantic torches planted them firmly in the snow, the canopy bearers came to a halt, each line of mitered courtiers doubled back on itself, went through a charming succession of dance figures in which the king and the little queen danced with each pair of courtiers. Then the procession moved on another fifty or a hundred yards before it stopped again and then moved once more, all the way around the big open place and across the bridge to the other side of the creek.

The pretty woman who had discussed the Indians so callously in church fastened herself on him, without letting go of a bulky Taos painter whom she had in tow. She wanted an explanation of everything, and the painter was trying his best to satisfy her. "Nobody knows what the bull is doing in the dance. I don't think the Indians know themselves any more," he was saying. "They have a tradition that Montezuma taught them this particular dance when he came up from Mexico to visit the Rio Grande pueblos. Presumably, the one with the crown is Montezuma, who's dancing with his queen and his courtiers. It's the only dance in which the Indians wear white-man's clothes—I mean, the only time they ever wear them is when they dance this dance."

"An anthropologist who was here a couple of years ago said it was originally a Spanish dance which Montezuma and the Aztecs learned from the Spaniards," Ruth Farrelly said.

"Of course it is," a thin-faced, scholarly looking man said superciliously. "It's a Spanish folk dance, and the Indians have simply taken it over and added a lot of things onto it."

The woman who had complained about the guns going off still sounded petulant. She was talking to Piggot and Geoff. "The girl is supposed to be Malinche—you know, the Aztec princess they gave to Cortez as a wife. At least that's what I've been told by our Indian girl. I've long ago given up trying to understand what anything that goes on out here means. . . ."

But one did not have to understand: all one had to do was look! The wonderfully gay costumes of the dancers and their exquisitely stately progress between the rows of bonfires made Peter tingle with joy. The fires high up on the roofs, the bright blankets picked out by the glow from the darkening adobe walls, and the majestic, white-and-black-patterned mountains against the deep-blue sky reminded him somehow of every picture of Bethlehem he had ever seen.

"Isn't it enchanting, darling?" Cristina asked. She had let Farrelly and Geoff and Piggot go on ahead in order to wait for him. She slid her gloved hand under his arm and down over his wrist, and her fingers snuggled possessively between his, much as Sibby's had used to do. No, it was Anne's hand—he quickly corrected himself, not wanting to think of Sibby—that had exuberantly possessed itself of his fingers exactly like this two years ago when he had come home unexpectedly from Pittsburgh and had gone to fetch her at the skating rink! He found himself wondering in one small corner of his brain how Aleida was spending Christmas down in Santa Fe.

He tried to dull himself to the consciousness of Cristina's wriggling fingers by wishing that Anne could see the ruffle-bordered miters jerk forward with each delightfully staccato dance step. Cristina's girlish impulsiveness, which contrasted so sharply with her squeamish insistence on walking around a small muddy place over which Anne or Aleida would simply have jumped, exasperated him. It was as if she had trespassed on some domain that belonged to Anne—to girls Anne's age.

He had to force himself to keep from jerking away his hand. As it was she had noticed the lack of response; her fingers went limp. "Darling, is anything wrong?"

"How could there be? No, I was just trying to get at my cigarettes." Repentantly he took firm hold of her elbow after he had lighted their cigarettes and said, "You look beautiful in the firelight, darling."

She squeezed his hand with her arm and looked radiant and happy again. "I'm so glad. Don't you think this is a lovely Christmas?"

"Perfect," he said and knew that she was bound to think that he was referring to her being there, when what he really was talking about was the festive glare of the torches and the last few barks of the guns and the lovely cedar platforms on which firewood and hay were piled, and to the magic black-blue of the sky. But at least he tried not to shut her out again from his joy while they lingered for some minutes after the procession had returned to the church, and a good many of the Indians and some of the townspeople had gathered around the dying fires to get warm, and the dancers had started in every direction across the square and disappeared into the narrow doorways that beckoned briefly with the cozy light of kerosene lamps.

He made an effort not to let himself think again of the young Santa Fe crowd during the drive back into Taos, past the festive rows of lighted candles in partly sand-filled, brown-paper bags which lined the edges of roofs everywhere, during the half hour at the hotel while they changed clothes, during the pleasant supper party at the Farrellys'. And presently it took no effort at all any more! Cristina was surrounded by a whole flock of men. Her exciting pallor and lithe, high-shouldered elegance made one of the women just behind Peter claw flatteringly, "She's got style, I'll say that for her. Which one of the three is she with, do you suppose? I wish I had a skin like that—no, I'll settle for the Persian-lamb coat." Her voice, when they were all singing Christmas carols around the piano and Ruth Farrelly discovered that she had a voice and made her sing some carols by herself, had never sounded more entrancing than tonight. He felt deliciously proud of her, just as he was proud of Geoff for becoming the center of attention for some minutes by telling about the morris dances and sword dances his grandfather—*John, the clock-maker!*—had still seen in Cornwall at Christmastime as a child; just as he was proud even of Piggot's crushingly well-mannered way of getting the better of an argument with a Taos painter about Indians, because Piggot practically belonged to the family.

Not only pride in possessing her, but also a novel and still shy tenderness stirred in him when, after they had at last come back to the hotel from a drive to a neighboring village to watch Midnight Mass at a bulky old Spanish mission church, he sneaked downstairs and left his Christmas present for her with the clerk, to be delivered to her in the morning with her breakfast tray. Even so, his new affection was no match for her brimming tenderness twenty minutes later, when he knocked softly on her door. . . .

"Do you know why I'm so happy tonight?" she asked. She had exuberantly raised herself on one elbow and was bending over him, so that her dark hair, in spite of being tied with a ribbon in back, fell over her shoulder and tickled his face, and the lace inset of her nightgown hung free from her beautiful, small breasts.

"Because that red-bearded genius invited you to his studio!"

"Because today I've settled something in my mind. I decided while we were out at the Indian pueblo that it doesn't matter about my being older than you. I think what counts is that we have so many things in common—and we do like all the same things. I think we're awfully lucky, don't you?"

She was so radiant that it would have been cruel not to match her ebullience. "Awfully," he said. "I'm lucky in any case."

"Sweet!" She let her shoulder sink down on the pillow, but kept her face turned to him. "Wasn't Geoff peculiar tonight?"

"Peculiar? Why? Because he wouldn't play charades?"

"That, and the way he hardly opened his mouth all night."

"But he did talk about Twelfth-night and the mummers and things."

"That's because Ruth Farrelly asked him and he couldn't help himself. I know those stubborn, silent streaks: something was eating him. He just froze that poor man who wanted to tell me about his harpsichord."

"Oh, the flaming beard—good for Geoff! He couldn't have hurt him very much: Barbarossa was still going strong when I joined you. He must have given you an exact account of every nail and every dab of glue that went into that harpsichord. He sounded like an awful phony."

"Not really, darling. He's just enthusiastic and a little bit of a bore. At any rate you weren't rude to him. I'm so glad you don't get moods and refuse to say anything for days, like Geoff. You know," she went on in the same breath, even though Peter failed to see any connection except that she was continuing to congratulate herself and him, "another thing I decided today was that you wouldn't like children anyway. I watched your face when that little boy was climbing all over you and his mother at supper tonight. I don't think you'd mind not having any little darlings around one bit, do you?"

He was amused by the interpretation she had put on the annoyance that must have shown in his face. His irritation had had to do with the embarrassing helplessness of the spoiled little boy's parents in resisting the young tyrant's demands. The little boy had ended up by being allowed to puff at a cigarette and to taste everybody's drink and by spilling cranberry sauce all over a woman's blouse. . . . But it did not matter that Cristina had misunderstood. It was Christmas, and he could not deprive her of any happiness! It was his turn to bend over her. "You're darling enough for me!"

She drew back into the pillow, luxuriously away from his kiss, and kept her hand on the back of his head. "Oh, we do have so much to be grateful for!"

"Cristina, you said you were tired. It's late; I ought to let you sleep."

She smiled and would not let him go. "Happy-tired, is all. I did think I'd die if I had to stand up much longer in that old church. But that's all over now. Anyhow, I'd never be tired enough to want you to go! Darling . . ."

Her abandon had never been so complete. It alarmed him somewhat. Her face beside him on the pillow wore the drowsy, faintly masklike bloom of utter happiness, but her pale eyelids would not lift. She seemed to have strayed into some secret, inner labyrinth of voluptuousness, from which she was reluctant to come back. He blamed himself for being inconsiderate and not taking into account her exhaustion after the long day. He pressed her fingers which had stayed limply in his hand, and almost pleaded, "I adore you, Cristina!"

The corners of her mouth softened still farther in a smile; her fingers curved ever so gently and pressed against his palm; her eyelashes fluttered on her cheeks. She murmured drowsily, "Geoff, darling!"

He lay very still, behind the unchanged rhythm of his breathing and his determined effort to keep the position of his hands and his body exactly the same, so as not to betray that anything was wrong. She had said "Geoff"—there could be no question about it! Was it only because they had been talking about Geoff just a little while ago and his name had still been on the tip of her tongue? Was it nothing more than a perfectly natural slip, since she had known Geoffrey for so many years and since she was bound to think of him as Geoff's son? Or was she—for all her pretended indifference and in spite of the almost condescending tone in which she sometimes referred to him—in love with Geoff? Or had she been?

She was suddenly awake. He knew it even before she spoke. As once or twice before when he had thought her asleep or wholly absorbed in something else she had been doing, she had seemed to read his thoughts.

"What is it, darling?"

"Was Geoffrey ever your lover?"

She was wide awake—middle-of-the-night awake—and her eyes were without some subtle protective daytime haze which would have allowed her to stall. She had raised herself on one elbow and was looking straight into his eyes. "What makes you ask that all of a sudden? I thought we had settled all that. No, darling—not ever! There's something about Geoff I can't stand. Maybe it's that he is a little like Ian and sort of can't make up his mind and keeps putting things off. I'm terribly fond of Geoff but I somehow couldn't ever sleep with him. I thought you understood that. All right?"

She started to bend down as if to kiss him, then changed her mind and let herself sink softly back against the pillow. Her head snuggled into the hollow of his shoulder.

"All right," he said and slipped his arm around her.

And it *was* all right. Somehow for all her sophistication Cristina could not manage even those innocent social evasions which had to count as white lies. He knew it was the truth. And it fitted in with a sort of virginal eagerness in Geoff's pursuit of her.

He turned to kiss her when he felt her hair press against his cheek and chin. His lips brushed over her temple and her closed eyelids. She was already half asleep again.

"Darling," she murmured and did not really finish the word.

"You've got to get some sleep."

She flung one arm across his chest. "I don't want you to go."

"Farrelly is calling for us at ten."

Her hands held him tight. "I don't care! . . ."

No, she hadn't really confused him with Geoff, he assured himself as he walked softly down the corridor to his own room. It was simply that she had been exhausted after the long day—the most innocent kind of drowsy mishap—nothing for him to lose any sleep about. He didn't: in a matter of minutes he was asleep.

But in the morning while Piggot and Geoff and he were having breakfast downstairs in the coffee shop, he wondered all of a sudden why Cristina had been so vehement about announcing that time at the Oxnards' that she was not going to play mother again to any man. If there was really something about Geoff which she could not stand, then why had she had him for a friend for so long? Why that edge of vindictiveness nearly every time she spoke of him? Granted that she had never let Geoff make love to her—he shuddered again at what for a moment last night had appeared as a possibility—but wasn't she after all a little in love with Geoff?

He realized as he watched Geoff butter a piece of toast and firmly put a dab of marmalade on it that the fact that Geoff had been in love with Cristina had played a large part in her fascination for him. The darkling remnants of his childhood rage against Geoff had welcomed that. But he realized also that he had felt free to enter on the affair with Cristina only after her assurance that she would never marry Geoff—that Geoff didn't stand a chance.

The sudden possibility that she might be in love with Geoff without even realizing it angered him. It was not only a question of male jealousy —though that was there, he admitted it to himself—but also of an unexpected protectiveness he felt toward Geoff. There were evidently limits to the secret promptings that pushed him toward revenge—limits to the extent to which he would allow Geoff to be hurt.

Was she in love with Geoff?

The question nagged at him all day long, made him feel vaguely harassed and preoccupied, so that there was a measure of hypocrisy in his gaiety with Cristina when she joined them in the lobby at half past ten—so that he felt himself inattentive in the very midst of the warm gabble of voices at the eggnog party to which they had been invited at a ranch house just out of town—so that he only half enjoyed the Christmas dinner at the Farrellys' and felt dulled to all the color at the Indian pueblo afterward.

It irritated him to look on as if through a haze at the enthralling Indian spectacle. The few stately dance figures executed by the dancers the night before proved to have been only a sample of all there was to see. There were the same mitered courtiers, the gay ribbons streaming out behind them as they whirled around, and the tinsel jewelry in their miters flashing in the sun. There were the same clowns and Mexican musicians and there was the same royal pair. But today the dancers went through an enchanting variety of convolutions and steps. There were times when all the courtiers would rest one knee on the ground while the turbaned king and his little queen with the downcast eyes would dance slowly up and down between the two rows. Then again the mummery king and his bride would sit side by side on a low bench and appear to be holding court. There was even a sort of Maypole dance in which each courtier held the end of a gay silk streamer tied to the top of a slim pole held up by one man and they all danced around the pole as part of a charming game with which royalty was entertained. There was all the delicious mimicry and captivating gravity of a tapestry account of a royal levee. And there was the majestic complacency of the snow-festive mountains smiling in the sun and the engrossing sight of the hundreds of Indians all around.

"Look at the two on the roof," Farrelly was saying. "Aren't they magnificent types?"

"Do you see the real old one in the navy-blue blanket?" Ruth Farrelly asked. "That's the governor. That black cane he's holding against his chest is the Lincoln cane. Lincoln presented one to the governors of all the pueblos when he signed the treaties with the pueblos."

"Look at that red blanket," the blond woman said. "Isn't that the most gorgeous red? And look at the purple one over there! . . ."

He hated to miss so much. He wanted to remember what he saw. It exasperated him to realize that because of his preoccupation his mind was like a troubled sheet of water which mirrored fitfully but in any case did not retain. It made him coldly resentful for a few moments of the fine lines at the corners of Cristina's eyes, which were very pronounced today. It made him side with Piggot and vote to start back to Santa Fe right after the dance instead of giving in to Farrelly's urging and staying over another night.

It was only when they were safely at the bottom of the steep, icy road that led down into the canyon and looked doubly treacherous in the fast-falling dusk, that the question of Cristina's being—or ever having been—in love with Geoff all at once ceased to trouble him. He was sitting up front beside Piggot, and Piggot was saying, "It's their serenity that I find remarkable. I don't believe there's one psychosis or neurosis in the whole pueblo. Have you noticed how quiet Indian children are? Their whole mode of life is healthier. . . ." In the back seat Cristina and Geoff were talking about some friends of theirs in France, and about some furniture of Cristina's which a storage company in Paris had lost, and then about some other friends in Ventimiglia.

Peter listened to them rather than to Piggot. A glow of triumph took warm possession of him as he heard Cristina turn down Geoff's suggestion that they all have dinner at the hotel when they got to Santa Fe. "It's sweet of you, Geoff, but I'm simply dead. All I want is a hot bath, and then I'm going to fall right into bed. . . ."

Suppose she had once cared for Geoff—didn't that make it all the more flattering that she should have chosen him over Geoff?

"Why, thanks," he said and turned around and looked at Geoff's square jaw and at the guessed-at mist-blue eyes in the uncertain light, "I think I'd better go straight home, too. If Ralph will let me off in Tesuque when we go through . . ." But even in the near-dark he could tell that a subtle disappointment had changed the expression on Geoff's face. A twinge of contrition made him try to lessen the rebuff and assure Geoff that he was not going to see Cristina again tonight. "I know I can't get the Chevvy started on a cold night like this, and I have a notion I might have a time finding a taxi to bring me back from town."

At the gas station in Espanola where they all got out to stretch, Cristina said softly while Piggot and Geoff were talking with the garage attendant, "I didn't mean you, darling, when I was talking about tonight. I just couldn't face sitting around for another hour or two and talking to a lot of people at the hotel. I'd love to have you come if you don't mind my being dull. You could stay overnight."

"I don't think I'd better. It's going to be after nine before we get to Tesuque. I'm pretty worn out myself."

"Then I'll see you tomorrow at five? . . ."

"Worn out," he chuckled when he had watched Piggot's car drive off and had let himself into the house. Suppose she had once cared for Geoff—she was his girl now! *I feel wonderful,* he told himself.

CHAPTER NINE

Fallacy of the Absolute

THE trick was to develop a healthy callousness, he told himself.

A nice, thick skin—that was the way to achieve the serenity Piggot was always talking about. That was how the Mexicans, who refused to be cheated out of today for the sake of tomorrow, managed to keep so cheerful—and the Indians, who appeared altogether amused by the white man's anxieties, so serene. That was how Larry Collard managed it—Larry, who didn't seem to miss his professorship at Harvard or his scientific prestige and who didn't seem worried over his t.b. as long as he could play around with a succession of pretty Spanish girls at night.

The whole landscape that spread out day after day before Peter's eyes preached that sort of philosophy. Under the brilliant winter sun the country had a bland spaciousness in which no single detail mattered very much and an almost defiant air of imperturbable ordered peace. I'm soaking up some of it, he congratulated himself.

He reveled in his happy new placidity which allowed him to take in

179

his stride both the affair with Cristina and the pretense for Geoff's benefit that it did not exist. It allowed him to chuckle after each encounter
with Aleida in the Fonda lobby or in the street at her curt nod and
vaguely disapproving frown. It made him indifferent both to Gladys' arch
probings and to Ralph Piggot's I'm-part-of-the-family knowingness.

He loved his daily routine: getting up mornings shortly after six just
as the sun was coming up; braving the cold outside to haul up buckets of
water on the creaking pulley from the well and to fetch in wood; starting
the stoves; breakfast, and after that, working at the easel right until
noon; then lunch and a walk; then a couple more hours of work until
it was time to get ready for the evening at Cristina's house. Sometimes
after lunch if it wasn't too cold he went to the pasture next door and
caught Crecencio's lively little pinto and went for a ride. More often
than not, Crecencio's and Josefita's youngsters rushed in after school,
wanting to be entertained and to play with the puppy—which was half
the time at his house and half the time at theirs—just as he was getting
dressed to go to town. Twice a week he went to Carol Praither's studio
up the road to learn how to operate the lithographing press and how to
draw on stone.

He had given up painting and gone in for drawing entirely. The exquisite black-and-white patterns that met his eyes everywhere made him
scorn color as lacking subtlety. There were the feathery hedges and trees
against the snow, the checkerboard of fenced pastures and furrowed
fields, black-stippled mountains and above the timber line the sharply
etched white triangles of the dazzling peaks—infinite gradations of
blacks and grays. The lessons that Buell had given him in drawing with
the lithographic pencil on the stone, which had meant nothing to him
before Christmas, now all at once fascinated him. There were some lovely
effects to be achieved if one worked with relentless economy and relied
solely on clarity of definition and beauty of line.

He drew a jovial, pear-shaped Mexican who played the trumpet with
a pickup orchestra every Saturday night in a little dance hall down the
road and who conveyed an infectious gaiety with every jiggling fold of
his butterball body and laughing face. He dropped in at a murder trial
in Santa Fe and sketched the mother of the young sheepherder who had
killed a man in a tavern brawl. The old Spanish woman sat all alone in
one corner of the room while court was recessed for lunch, her black
shawl pulled up over her head and miserably hunched shoulders, and
looked utterly stricken and bereaved. He drew an engaging old man who

walked every noon down toward Bishop's Lodge, his ancient body bent over his cane but his wrinkled face radiant with a childlike smile when he straightened up to say, *"Buenas dias, señor."*

He saw two small, old Indian women, no bigger than children and as alike as twins in their white deerskin boots and blue cotton blankets and black cloths full of groceries slung over their backs, trudging home on the highway from Santa Fe just a few yards behind a farm wagon that had passed without giving them a ride. He took them to the Tesuque pueblo, and through their grandchildren, since neither of them spoke any English, arranged to have them pose for him the next day. He was determined to catch something of their devotion, of the peaceful, inexorable spaciousness of the land, of the stubborn courage of old age. He made endless sketches on paper, simplifying, playing with the geometry of the forms, striving to catch the lyric mood of the two tiny figures on the highway, before he arrived at a drawing he considered worth putting on stone. Praither was enthusiastic when he helped him print. "It's got form and texture. Why don't you send it to the Pennsylvania Academy? You've got until next week."

He knew about the black-and-white show in Philadelphia. The painters had been talking about it off and on for the past six weeks.

"I'm only a beginner," he argued. "I'd never get in."

"How do you know? I think it's a hell of a fine print."

He consulted Buell, who snapped, "An artist's work has to be where it can be seen! Being a beginner has got nothing to do with it. If the jury turns it down, you haven't lost anything."

His hesitancy to expose the lithograph to the eyes of strangers had to do with a lingering trace of his childhood awe of authority—was it because a father had seemed such a wonderful thing?—and bore no relation to his own feelings about the picture. He knew it was good. It was the best thing he had ever done. It was better than anything he had ever hoped he could do. He defied anyone to put the two old Indian women and their whole humble and yet brave existence down more completely than he had done.

He remembered a charming story he had read somewhere about a great Renaissance painter who had by accident landed in the house of an artist in some strange Italian city and after examining and praising his host's work had said quietly, *"Anch' io son' pittore*—I, too, am a painter." It had always seemed to him at once the most exquisite modesty and the proudest boast. He looked at the pattern he had achieved in the lithograph and at the compelling forms, and thought happily, *"Anch' io son' pittore*—just like Geoff!"

His exultation and the prospect of surprising Geoff, who was sending a portrait head, by hanging with him in the same show, decided him. He picked out the best print, packed it carefully, and shipped it off. Then he tried to forget about it.

He succeeded so well that he let the opening day go by without even thinking about it. Furfey—officious and as usual morbidly concerned whether any of the other painters had stolen a march on him—brought it to his attention rather belligerently. Furfey came in late at a small cocktail party at the Orrs' with a folded newspaper in his hand, stopped only to say hello to Mary Orr, and challenged him, "Heard anything from Philadelphia?"

"Was I supposed to have? I sent a lithograph and all I know is that so far they haven't sent it back."

"You've won a prize! The New York *Times* just came in on the train." He unfolded the newspaper and thrust it at him. "Here you are—third prize in lithography!"

Cristina said with unguarded jubilance, "Peter, how wonderful!" Dorothy Lambert echoed her, "We must do something to celebrate!" Praither had seized his elbow and was saying, "What did I tell you, boy?"

He felt himself beam in spite of his effort to minimize the news. "It must be beginner's luck. It's just a fluke."

"Fluke, nothing!" Praither contradicted. "That was a damn' good print!" He turned to Furfey. "Anybody else get anything?"

"Nobody in Santa Fe. Sloan got first prize in etching, and Mike . . ."

"Aren't you happy, darling? I'm so proud of you," Cristina whispered when for a few seconds the others had turned to Chet Orr, who had come up and was being told the news by Praither. Furfey was already whittling down the significance of the prize by scornfully pointing out how hopelessly academic the jury was, so that, after all, the list of awards was exactly what one might expect.

Chet Orr nevertheless came over to pound him on the back. Geoff said quietly, "Congratulations! I didn't know you had got to the point of exhibiting. Was it the man with the trumpet you sent?"

"No, something I've done since—a couple of Tesuque——"

He was pounced on by Gladys who caroled shrilly, "Peter, I just heard! Aren't you thrilled? I simply can't wait to see your lithographs. Jerry says you're going to let him have some for the museum show."

"Why, yes, next month."

"Do I have to wait till then?" If Gladys was aware of the polite boredom written on Piggot's heavy-jowled face, she did not let it trouble her in the least. Her voice slid down several octaves and became a caressing, cooing baritone as she turned to Geoff, "Geoff, now you'll have to win something! You can't let Peter walk off with all the prizes!" Her tone made it clear that she knew all about their relationship and that for some incalculable reason she wanted to needle Geoff. She was not through yet. She cooed, "Cristina, don't you think it's just too thrilling?"

Dorothy Lambert hastily began to talk about old Mexico. Ralph Piggot caught his eye, and Peter followed him away from the rest.

"You're cutting quite a swath," Piggot said with that air of vaguely avuncular solicitude which Peter had come to detest because he felt himself exasperatingly helpless against it. "You're showing up the old man right and left."

"What are you driving at?"

"Well, first you take away Cristina from him and now you're demonstrating that he isn't even any great shakes as an artist. I'd say you're getting your own back with a vengeance."

It seemed too theatrical to bluster "I don't know what you're talking about!" Besides it admitted too much.

"I didn't know that Cristina was ever his to lose."

"They've been close for a good many years."

"That proves that they have never been very close, doesn't it? I should say that that's a clear case of—opportunity refused. Cristina considers Geoff a friend and that's all. And as far as the silly prize is concerned, I'm certainly not trying to measure myself against anybody on the strength of that. That would be a little absurd. Excuse me, will you, Ralph? I have to talk to Dorothy. . . ."

He could snub Piggot and turn his back on him but he could not walk away from what he had said. Utterly absurd! he railed to himself. Who had asked that amateur psychiatrist, with his pasty skin and the wrinkly pouches under his soulful eyes and his elephantine allusiveness and his slang and his "with a vengeance," to psychoanalyze him and to champion Geoff? The whole accusation was too ridiculous for words! Why, it was months now since the last feeble, conscious desire for revenge in him had died. Certainly, there were still occasionally those impulses from the past that had to do with hurting Geoff, but he kept those in check. And as for their coming at all, that was something he could not control any more than he could order his dreams. The point was that all he felt for Geoffrey now in his conscious mind was affection and—well, sympathy and respect.

As for that crackbrained idea of Piggot's, that he was trying to compete as an artist with Geoff, who was an established painter and had exhibited in London and Paris and New York, that was even more manifestly absurd. It took a writer to dream that up. It was just a wonder he hadn't mentioned the business of the stallion!

But even though he allowed his indignation to simmer and boil, he could not make himself forget what Piggot had said. It spoiled the rest of the party for him. That evening in the hope of discounting everything Piggot had said by finding his books exaggerated and dull, he borrowed two of Piggot's novels from Cristina and took them home.

He started with the little one with the faded cover, which had been published almost twenty years ago. It was the story of two Negro boys in New York, and of the tough East River gang to which they belonged, of a warehouse robbery and the chivalrous loyalty between the two boys. The tenderness with which the book presented the quixotic, touching idealism of the two young Negroes and the authority with which it pictured their slum families and the drabness of their existence from which there would never be any escape, took him by surprise. For a minute or two the book brought back vividly his own rebellion in Vienna against hunger and poverty and the fact that Mizzi and Geoff had deserted him— his joining the sinister Jerabek and his gang and stealing brass fixtures from half-finished apartment houses in the afternoons after school when he had pretended to be in choir class, and coming within an ace of breaking into shut-up villas in the suburbs—that one awful, hungry spring when he had been thirteen and everything had seemed black.

He felt almost indignant that Piggot with his fastidious, somber, sheltered air, which argued a childhood spent in boarding schools rather than slums, should know so exactly how childhood deprivation and misery felt. He asked Cristina, "How does Ralph come to know so much about Harlem and the reformatory and about Negro boys?"

"He was a reporter when he first came to New York. Then I think he was a social worker for a while. Have you started the *Daughters of Danaüs* yet?"

"Is that how you say it? No, I'll start it tonight."

It was the latest one of Piggot's books. It baffled him and he had to force himself to finish it. The title, he discovered, had been taken from a Greek myth about the fifty daughters of a legendary king, forty-nine of whom had killed their husbands because their father had demanded it. The novel itself dealt with three sisters, all of whom could be said to have brought about their husbands' death: the first by relentlessly driving her husband to become as famous a doctor and public figure as her father was; the second, by nagging at her husband for not being as sensitive and fine-fibered as her father, until the harassed husband lost his bearings and took to drink; the third, by torturing her husband with her adulteries, committed for no other reason, apparently, than to punish him for having dared to remain so impervious to her father's charm as to make her live three thousand miles away from him. The theme of the novel was presumably stated by a Greek waiter who looked over a terrace full of well-to-do, elderly women in a swank California resort hotel and commented to a fellow waiter, "American women bury their men!"

He could make nothing of it, and the book merely confirmed his belief that most novels dealt with a highly artificial world of rhetoric and fine-spun psychology, which bore next to no relation to reality. Only the suspicion that he might after all have missed something that had been there between the lines, and his stubborn curiosity about Piggot, made him tackle two more of his books. He skimmed impatiently through the shorter one, which was called *Pillar of Salt*. It turned out to be the not very savory account of a demoniac man—brilliant, sensual, possessed of an insane lust for power—whose unbridled self-indulgence had been encouraged step by step by his adoring mother ever since he was a child, until he ended up simultaneously at the top of his profession and in the criminal court for the corruption of minors. It was the doting mother who was the "pillar of salt"—Lot's wife, who had looked on evil so indulgently that in the end, and without being in the least aware of it, she had become evil herself.

The other book was even more unpleasant. It was almost entirely given over to a brutally dispassionate description of what appeared to be at first merely the somewhat morbid bickering between a man and his wife over the half-dozen cats which the wife insisted on keeping as pets. As the murderous struggle between the two grew in intensity, the woman's passion for her pets revealed itself more and more as a continuation of a childhood flight from human beings to animals because her parents had terrified her by their quarrels and had neglected her and only some cats had consoled her in her unhappiness. Her attachment to her pets was shown to be both a cause and a result of her childlessness and a punish-

ment to her husband for his failure to supply the sense of security she
had always sought. The man's loathing for cats, on the other hand, became a hatred for all of life. In the end the husband, trying to throw one
of the cats out of the car in a paroxysm of rage, managed to wreck the
car and killed himself; the wife became altogether the slave of her pets;
and the cats survived as undisputed masters of the house.

All four of the books had been bleak, and except for the one about the
two colored boys all of them had pictured women as bringing about
disaster and tragedy. American women, especially. At one point or another Piggot accused the American woman of willfulness, of a lust for
power, of calculated sentimentality, of not making an adequate return in
womanliness for the American man's drudgery on behalf of her material
comfort, of conspiring to keep American culture from achieving maturity. It was a ridiculous catalogue, he thought.

He said to Cristina when he returned the books, "He's hipped on the
subject. He must be a little touched. Sure, there are women like Gladys
and Jeanne, but why doesn't he look at Dorothy Lambert and Mary Orr
and the kind of homes they make for their families? There are millions of
women like that."

She defended Piggot. "Have you ever watched the cinemas, darling,
in New York? They're packed with women in the afternoon. And then
there are bridge clubs and women's clubs and theater matinees—that's
what Ralph means. Women haven't time to do anything but throw a few
things together for dinner afterward. You know as well as I do that in
Europe a woman of that class will spend hours cooking dinner or *déjeu-
ner*. Pier Luigi when he was in New York last winter said exactly the
same thing."

"I think he dislikes women. Has Piggot ever been married?"

"He was married to Naomi Devoe for years. The photographer. That's
how I first got to know Ralph—through Naomi. And he's had affairs
since—no, you're on the wrong track, darling. Besides, if Ralph were
like that, he wouldn't be saying the things he does; men who're like that
are so much like women themselves, they always get along beautifully
with women. I think Ralph's an idealist who wants to reform everybody."

"What I don't understand is why all the women make such a fuss over
him when all he does is insult them in his books."

Cristina smiled. "Darling, you aren't a woman. It doesn't matter what
he says in his books; there's something appealing about Ralph. He's sort
of sweet. Darling, did you know that one of your eyebrows is higher
than the other?"

"Oh, I've heard a rumor to that effect. But I'm not going to have it lowered."

"I wouldn't let you. I love it the way it is; it makes you look quizzical when you don't approve of anything, like Ralph's books. It makes you look just like my San Ysidro; one of his eyebrows is cocked like that." She pushed up his left brow caressingly with her finger tips until they both had to laugh. "Who told you it was higher? I want to know. I'm jealous."

He grinned. It was a game that had to be played even though his mind was still on Piggot. "Let me see—it must have been my sister."

She pretended to pout. "You are sure it was your sister? Did she tell you, too, that your eyelashes are indecently long and silky? Anyhow, I love them."

"And I love your eyes and your mouth. . . ."

Sweet? Rabid, pompous, a bore!—he later pursued his strictures of Piggot to himself. A novel, a work of art—he improvised a theory of art with which to punish Piggot for coming between Geoff and him—had to have joy in it, had to affirm the existence of joy, at least. Piggot, with his father-confessor eyes and his portentous air of pinning one down with his dazzling intuitions, might impose on a lot of indulgent women but not on him. That crack about revenge had been nothing but an impertinent shot in the dark, a naïve putting together of what looked like "two" and "two."

It wasn't so simple as that. Piggot didn't know what a trick it was to keep the forces of the past bottled up! For Peter found that he could no longer conceal from himself that in spite of his affection now for Geoff there was always a sly, uncontrollable part of him waiting for a chance to do Geoff hurt. Before he would realize it he would find his whole being usurped by a stealthy vindictiveness and would catch himself gloating over some discomfiture of Geoff's. It usually happened at Cristina's when Geoff barged in.

Geoff could not stay away, it seemed. He showed up around five at least every other day, or they heard his brusque rap on the front door while they were still finishing dinner in the dining room. Geoff would have a drink or join them for coffee, and they would all pretend that there was no strain and that they were being perfectly natural; and sometimes when Geoff stayed on and they played Russian bank or Cristina went to the piano and sang, they did succeed in creating an illusion of being happy in one another's company and having nothing to hide.

But more often than not a moody woodenness would take possession of Geoff. He would seem to withdraw. Cristina's heightened vivacity would be forced. They would all be isolated by their uneasiness until Cristina's exasperation over Geoff's monosyllabic replies would all at once make her seek out some sore spot and plant a politely poisoned barb. Thus she taunted him one evening with the slow pace with which he worked. "You mean they're going to have to tear up your studio floor? Why, Geoff, you won't be able to work for weeks—but, then, you won't mind that!" A few minutes later when Geoff got up to go, Cristina said quickly, as if her first taste of cruelty had whetted her appetite for more, "You don't both have to, Peter! Why don't you stay a little longer?" The usual pretense of leaving together to save Geoff's feelings had been rudely jerked aside like a shabby curtain that was no longer needed to hide anything.

The worst of it was, he told himself afterward, that although he had squirmed while Cristina had baited Geoff, he had yet been aware of an insinuating, malicious pleasure which his sense of guilt had presently turned into wild, somehow desperate hilarity as soon as they had heard Geoff start his car and Cristina's eyes had met his.

Sometimes after one of these evenings his contrition would make him hunt for an excuse to go to see Geoff the following afternoon. He would be all deference and there would be an odd joy in being with Geoff. They would talk together almost easily and Cristina hardly existed at all. He would feel himself swept toward Geoff on a surge of affection and pride. And then, all at once, some demon from the past—from his resentful childhood still—would stir in him and would make him want to hurt. He would be looking at a picture Geoff was working on and manage to find something wrong with it. "I like it. It's a beautiful composition. The only thing that bothers me is that shadow there on the rock. That blue makes a hole in those warm reds. I'm probably talking through my hat, but that blue bothers me. . . ." Or he would get Geoff to talk about France or about his years at the Slade School in London or even—cautiously— about his childhood in Penzance, only to jab suddenly, "It must have been charming but it doesn't sound very efficient or exactly healthy. . . ." Or he would all at once balk at some British expression. "Torch? What torch? Oh, I see, the flashlight! Here it is on the window sill. . . ." Or he would manage to strike at Geoff through his truck-driver protégé. "Oh, is he the one you're having dinner with? I hope he's had time since Saturday to take a bath. . . ."

But on one occasion Geoff struck back. Only the faint pulse along the side of his jaw and an extra stillness in his face showed that he had not missed a mention of a dinner party at the Orrs' to which he had not been asked. He allowed the silence to thicken between them as if what Peter had told him about the Japanese prints which Chet Orr had shown Cristina and Peter had reminded him of something a hundred miles away. He finally roused himself.

"Have some more tea?" He had picked up the pot. "I had been hoping," he said portentously, "that you would take my name."

He saw it only as Geoff's way of hitting back, of putting him in his place. A blind anger fumbled behind his momentary bewilderment.

"Well, sir, I believe you're a British citizen. If I did that, I'd probably lose my American citizenship and I've come to value it."

"I should think all that can be arranged. I don't know about the technicalities but I understand it's a very simple procedure and the papers can be drawn up in the judge's chambers. I can ask Judge Blair if you like about the matter of your citizenship."

Geoff had sounded increasingly placatory, and the indefinable note of pleading allayed Peter's fear; but the memory of his moment of panic and savage resentment at Geoff's daring to use *that* as a threat, continued to fan his rage. At the same time he knew a moment of triumphant joy: *This is Geoffrey Middlemas coming to me as if he were asking a favor almost!*

He said haughtily, using gentleness like a lash, " 'Domanig' is a good name. I've tried to bear it with honor. I've sort of got used to it. Thanks all the same."

Geoffrey looked away. "Well, I'm sorry . . ."

His triumph left a taste of guilt. A sort of penitence made him defend Geoff the next day when Cristina goaded, "Did you have an exciting time with Geoff?"

"Not exciting but—"

"I can imagine!" Cristina's beautiful voice made her delicate rancor for his having deserted her for Geoff for one whole evening sound playful without dulling its edge.

"—but very nice. He showed me the new landscape he was telling about the other day."

"Is it one of those picture-post-card-size things he's been doing all winter?"

"It's not so small. It's about twenty-four by eighteen."

"I think it's disgusting the way Geoff has been letting himself go. He doesn't get up until the morning is half over; he says so himself. And then all he does is to turn out those timid little pictures, just like that awful man with the beard who does nothing but potboilers."

"Cristina, you're being a little rough on him! He's experimenting; he's trying to develop a new style for himself. This country isn't exactly easy to paint."

"Oh, that's just an excuse. I've known Geoff for a long time. He's always been a little—ineffectual. He loves to put things off. And lately he's been getting worse—I mean, ever since he's been in Santa Fe. Everything he's done out here has been cramped and fumbling and—oh, just anemic. Don't you agree?"

"I don't know about that."

"Darling, sometimes you are just like Geoff. You sit there and you won't open your mouth. I can't tell what you think. . . ."

It was true about his often sitting there without saying anything. He had hoped she had not noticed it. The squirming silence coupled with an evasive grin had become his uneasy refuge when Cristina got too close— was crowding him.

It happened more and more frequently. He had learned to tell the danger signs: the cajoling playfulness in her voice and the tender speculation that came into her eyes. "I bet anything, darling, you'd love Spain. We could stay in Florence for a month and then run up to Paris, or we can go wherever you like. We needn't tie ourselves to any routine. It's only that this year I have to be in Florence sometime before fall because I ought to be there when the men put the new plumbing in. Any other year we'd be free as air. Don't you think we could have a wonderful time?" Her enthusiasm would sweep her along. "Isn't it lucky that you aren't a lawyer or a businessman, so that you always have to stay in one place? Not that I'd mind, but this way we can have so much more fun. And isn't it lucky, darling, that we have enough money to travel if we want to?"

The strain of remaining silent and relying on his grin to buy him off would become too great. He would agree as vaguely as he could, "Yes, of course," or he would rebel against some small part of what she had said, as if by taking exception to any part of it, he could dissociate himself from the larger implications as well. "I'm not so keen on traveling as you are, darling. To me this place right here is as fascinating as anything in Europe: the Indian dances, and the Spanish architecture, and the desert, and the mountains—I don't think I'd ever get tired of it."

"Oh, but that's why I kept this house on after Father died. This is my favorite place in the whole world. Only, I do think it's foolish not to take in other places that are beautiful too. I feel that life ought to be as rich as possible and not hemmed in, don't you agree? But nobody says that we'd ever have to leave Santa Fe if we didn't want to. . . ."

Almost anything could bring about Cristina's congratulatory glow— "Isn't it lucky that we're both so healthy? . . . Isn't it lucky that we like so many of the same things?" The implication was always the same: *we're made for each other if any two people ever were!*

The easy chair by the big corner fireplace became a blind alley in which he was trapped whenever she came to sit in his lap or on the arm of the chair or merely faced him from the settee. He smiled harder, drew back into his chair, and clung to his precarious silence because it seemed unforgivable to dampen her exuberance and because he felt that time would somehow reward him for not hurting her and get him out of the difficulty; because he was flattered by her feminine importunity which assumed that he was shy; because he took a cynical pleasure in his certainty that nothing she could say could make him want to marry her; and because, finally, there was nothing to contradict.

But silence was not his only means of evading her. As often as not, when he saw what was coming, he moved quickly to counterattack. He suddenly evinced an insatiable curiosity about her palazzo in Florence or about the convent school she had attended in Paris or about her stepfather's racing cars; or he suddenly burned with the desire to hear her sing; or he began hastily to tell her about the Skolloker laboratory because she had once asked about it; or he boisterously, with an air of just having had a brilliant idea, proposed that they play Russian bank.

They nearly always ended up playing cards. It was like a ritual to which they returned almost superstitiously—a drug for which they reached whenever boredom threatened to come between them, as it more and more frequently did. Half of him, Peter realized, hated the game. It seemed to breed boredom instead of banishing it. Yet it was the only pastime that was safe; for after the first few weeks it had seemed somehow affected to ask Cristina to read Dante out loud, and lately Cristina had on several occasions refused to sing. "Darling, not today, do you mind?" She would offer to play the piano for him instead, but her playing would almost invariably now leave him unsatisfied and faintly critical. He felt unappreciative and guilty of disloyalty and yet bored. He accused himself of ingratitude: Piggot and most of the other men lighted up like lamps when they talked to her! She was fascinating-looking; she was witty; she had style—he told himself and looked across at her exciting pallor and her tautly drawn-back, dark hair and at her beautifully modeled lips. His self-reproaches would whip up his passion. He would put down his cards and walk around the table and start to make love to her.

But even at those moments he was conscious of evasion, of holding back, of a troubling duplicity on his part. There was a lack of joy, of spontaneity, in possessing her; there was always the compulsion to turn out lights, to close his eyes and plunge into darkness and blind himself to her nakedness, the need to pull up blankets and to feel at least the filmy silk of her nightgown and the material of his pajamas between his chest and her breasts. The same tyrannical prudishness made him find fault with some of the nightgowns she wore: one in particular which was trimmed with a good deal of lace aroused an ungovernable loathing in him, and the only explanation he could find for his revulsion and secret rage was that the ecru lace had all at once reminded him of the tiny bit of the same kind of lace that had shown in the "v" of Mizzi's flannel dressing gown when she had come into his room in Westchester for a few seconds to wish him good night his second night in America. Another evening when Cristina had on a bedjacket and he discovered that it came only as far as her hips, a sudden fury made him go ice-cold inside and rigid and numb.

"Is that the latest thing?"

"It's a bedjacket. Haven't you ever seen one before?" Cristina laughed. "Don't you like it?"

"I hate it. It's like some sort of maternity blouse."

He was startled by his own violence and asked himself while she turned her head on the pillow to laugh at him: *Why am I taking on so? Why this ridiculous connection all the time in my mind between Cristina and my mother?* ... And suddenly he knew that deep inside himself there had always been a guilty awareness that in one sense, at least, Cristina belonged to Geoff, since Geoff was in love with her. It was no excuse for him that Cristina did not want to marry Geoff! ... And deeper still in the dark folds of his consciousness, Cristina always threatened to take on some aspect of Mizzi, to look like her and sound like her, so that he shut his eye in a flush of guilt and fled.

Cristina said, "Darling, what a puritan you are! And here I'm wearing my prettiest bedjacket for you. I'd have you know that this lace is real *point de Venise*."

She was at least dimly aware of the exasperating ingredients in his passion, which made him shy away from her. She teased one night when he was staying over and came in from the guest room, where he kept a pair of pajamas and a set of shaving things, and solemnly knocked on her half-open bedroom door, "You come in like a grand seigneur. I'm always afraid you're going to come in wearing gloves like Louis the Fourteenth's brother. I feel as if I'd forgotten to put on a dinner invitation 'Decorations will be worn.' "

"Why, am I so pompous?"

"You're very sweet!" She stretched out her arms. "My darling! . . ."

But the next afternoon she said, "Darling, sometimes I think you loathe me. Every time I come anywhere near you and try to kiss you, you back away as if I had some horrible disease."

"I guess I'm just not demonstrative."

She grimaced with comic despair. "Don't I know it! I just wish you'd be a little more affectionate once in a while, instead of letting me make all the overtures."

He thought himself lucky that so far she seemed not to have noticed that he always said, "I adore you, Cristina," in place of "I love you," to avoid telling a lie. He reproached himself with his lack of zest for making love to her: I ought to want to kiss her shoulders and her throat, and I don't! There oughn't to be this dutiful lechery. I'm as if paralyzed because she has thin arms and legs and those folds of loose skin in the small of the back that older women get, and because of her elaborate preparations for the night, so that I'm always reminded of somebody's mother—of Mizzi. The smell of toothpaste and all that heavy connubiality! And this is wrong, too: there oughn't to be all this analysis! I guess I'm just generally bored. . . . And he blamed it all hastily on the time of year, on the leaden grayness which ever since January infected everything in town.

The notice that the machine tools which he had ordered sent from the East had arrived came as a sudden relief. He had almost forgotten about Father Hegge and his boys. He went to look at the lathe and the drill press still in the boxcar in which they had arrived at the railroad yard, recognized a broken spoke in the carriage adjustment wheel of the lathe which he had had welded himself, and was seized by a sudden violent homesickness for the factory in New Jersey and the whole world of steel and machines. What the devil, he thought, am I doing out here fiddling with lithograph pencils and paint tubes and listening to a lot of jabber about nothing and worrying about nightgowns and how much Cristina really cares for Geoff? I don't belong out here. I belong with this. And without meaning to, his hand had slipped through the packing crate and brushed caressingly over the velvet-smooth guide rails of the lathe.

He drove out to Santa Cruz the same day, a little uncertain whether he had not let his enthusiasm in December deceive him about the priest— whether Father Hegge really wanted the machines. His uneasiness was allayed at once. Father Hegge welcomed him with a genial roar, and his warm brown eyes in the rough-hewn face shone with pleasure. After the doldrums of Santa Fe, he was as wholesome as a tree. His five charges who were out in the yard and the sheds doing chores came up to shake hands with Spanish sobriety but with considerably more laughter in their dark eyes than the last time Peter had seen them, so that he felt almost like a favorite relative. The crippled boy wanted some help with the motor on the pump.

"Juan has been taking fine care of our pump," Father Hegge praised after the belt pulley had been tightened and just before he sent the boys back to their chores. "He spends all his time with the pump or with the radio, taking it apart and putting it together again." Father Hegge chuckled while he put on water to heat for tea in the drab, barnlike kitchen. "The other boys watch him like hawks every time he touches it, for fear he mightn't be able to put it together again and they wouldn't have a radio. I can't tell you what a boon the running water and the radio have been. . . . Juan and his friend Hipolito manage to keep busy all right. It's the older boys who are a little bit of a problem in the evening. I've been trying to get them to read, but we don't have very good light. Well, we do the best we can. This is something Hipolito made." And Father Hegge proudly picked up a carved paper knife from his desk. "He's quite a fellow, that little Hipolito. Did I ever tell you how he came to be with us? He showed up one day after Mass with a little bundle of clothes and informed me that he was going to help me take care of Juan. Well, it turned out that his mother was a widow with six other children and that it was all right with her; so he stayed."

They all had their stories. The oldest of the boys was the son of a drunkard and had broken into two stores in Santa Fe and would have been sent to reform school if Father Hegge had not taken him under his wing. The next oldest boy was illegitimate like Juan and had been raised by his very young mother to believe that she was his sister and that their parents were both dead. It had worked until Filiberto had learned the truth from his schoolmates, and then the supposed sister had grieved and wasted away through one winter until she caught the flu and died.

And listening to Father Hegge's warmhearted account of so much childhood misery and such lean future prospects for the boys, a surge of indignation swelled in Peter. It was as if he were filling his lungs with air and tensing his muscles. By Gad, he could do something about that!

He told Father Hegge about the lathe and the drill press in Santa Fe.

"I should say we'd like to have them," Father Hegge greeted the news. "Why, that would be wonderful! But you are going to a lot of trouble for us. . . . Incidentally—I don't know much about these things—but with a lathe and that kind of a machine, doesn't there have to be something to drive them, a motor of some sort?"

"That's right, Father. I was thinking of putting in a small electric power plant."

"You mean there's a chance that we might have an electric light bulb here in the study?"

He felt almost shamed by Father Hegge's enthusiasm. He promised, "There'll be more than one. . . ."

He consulted the electrician in Santa Fe and the plumber and the garagemen and heard of a home generating plant that was for sale. It was bigger than he needed but it was cheap and in excellent shape. In two days he had wired the rectory with the help of an electrician and jack-of-all-trades he had found in Santa Fe, and at the end of a week he had not only installed the gasoline motor and the generator and the storage batteries of the power plant but he had also spent a day in Albuquerque to buy a motor for the drill press and the lathe and a set of bench tools for the little machine shop which he had set up in the shed for the boys.

Half the village turned up the last day on some pretext or other to admire the lights in the rectory and listen to the whispering of the lathe while he gave the five boys and half-a-dozen others, who refused to budge, their first lesson in using the shop. "Just a beginning," he explained to Father Hegge; "just enough to make them respect the machines and keep them from hurting themselves. We'll get a little farther next week." It was arranged that he was to come out for an afternoon each week. "No trouble," he silenced Father Hegge's qualms. "It's more fun for me than it is for them. Besides, I'm paying a debt. A man let me hang around his machine shop and taught me a few things when I was a kid, and I still remember how much it meant to me."

He had not exaggerated when he said it was fun. The week he had spent in Santa Cruz had seemed rich, and he had felt himself tingling with zest and full of the confidence he had known in Pittsburgh that he could tackle anything. The winter grayness of Santa Fe seemed even more gray and leaden when he came back.

It was exactly as Dorothy Lambert had said: in the winter the town became ingrown. The same faces were lying in wait from one living room to the next. People began to repeat themselves. Cristina said charitably, "I like to be bored by people I like!" but made use of every kind of feminine subterfuge to keep from being cornered by the white-haired judge or by Hal Oxnard with his superannuated playboy charm or by Furfey with his tirades against the art critics.

One got to know the various obsessions and hobbyhorses they had. Each one had his favorite tune which he produced as faithfully as a music box. No matter by how devious a path, Furfey always managed to get back to the subject of the sober, sensitive artist—himself—at the mercy of corrupt art dealers and venal museum directors who connived with the critics to saddle the museums with musty masterpieces or with outrageously valueless modern art. Hal Oxnard blustered about his diplomatic career and drew portentous international parallels from the most trivial happenings in his back yard. Jim Hopper missed no opportunity to proclaim the superiority of everything Indian over anything the white man had. Praither in one key or another proclaimed his manliness. Jeanne Lauber smiled, lowered her head, and was off like a homing pigeon for Tibet. Piggot—subtle, sallow, irreconcilable—took the American woman to task.

There were also certain fixed channels into which any conversation was sure to flow. Gossip was one of them. They did not call it gossip, of course; they exonerated themselves with their firmly altruistic or—at any rate—impersonal approach. There was the analytical, passionately psychological approach which pursued motives within motives, like nests of Chinese boxes, with relentless scientific zest. There was the self-sacrificing, I-only-want-you-to-get-it-straight approach which, however reluctantly, revealed the facts that people ought to know. There was the intrepid-eyed, I-never-say-anything-behind-people's-backs-I-don't-say-to-their-faces angle which made everybody feel virtuous, and the botanizing, isn't-human-nature-just-too-fascinating approach—Gladys'—which gave one unlimited license to conjecture and examine and suppose.

But there were also more innocuous subjects which came up for discussion with monotonous regularity during the after-dinner doldrums somewhere around ten o'clock. There was the matter of modern man.

"Modern man," Piggot said, "has no roots. The American has been so busy moving from one frontier to the next, from Ohio to Kansas to California, that he's never had time to put down roots. And now the machine age has cut us off from the past. That's why we have no art. . . ." They spent hours in agreeing in detail that there was no great creative ground swell in evidence anywhere. "I don't mean all that playing around with pattern and design that Chet was talking about," Gladys chirped. "I mean a real style, like Gothic or Byzantine. Why can't we have a new style, Ralph? . . ." It was always only a step from art to religion. Chet Orr said, "I'm not talking about going to church! How many people do you know, Grace, who you can honestly say have any real faith, beside yourself, of course?"

He was talking to Grace Wyatt, a gaunt, sharp-witted, lively woman of around seventy who lived in a beautiful old house on Palace Avenue with a whole platoon of servants she had brought from the East.

"A great many more than you think," Grace Wyatt snapped and jangled her battery of bracelets. Her eyes and her old-fashioned diamond pendant earrings flashed as she turned her haughty head with the tight gray curls to Chet. They were in the living room in Jim Hopper's house and she sat on a thronelike Spanish chair beside a Moroccan coffee table, with Geoff's student squatting with an expression of rapturous attentiveness on the red Navaho rug at her feet. She gave the impression of holding court and of being about to bestow great favors, as she nearly always did, which accounted somehow for the presence of hangers-on like Jack Fettis and, some people said, even for her popularity with the priests. She had been recently converted to Catholicism by a witty, middle-aged priest whom she invited fairly often to the elegant little dinner parties she gave at her house or even to lunch at the hotel. Peter's first glimpse of her, in fact, had been in the hotel lobby when she had hailed the patiently smiling priest with an imperious, breathless "Oh, Father Joslin, dear! . . ."

Peter liked her crustiness and even the coy echoes of girlish petulance from which she always retreated with a rueful wink of self-mockery, but he had sat with her and Mary Orr all through supper and he wanted a change. He wandered over to where Piggot and Larry Collard were examining Jim Hopper's collection of Indian dolls and fetishes on a set of shelves built into the wall.

The biologist was nodding at a phallic, smooth, black stone sticking up out of a small jar. "The lingam-yoni. How do you suppose Jim got all those *objets du culte?* He must have bribed a couple of medicine men. There is one of those feather dusters the Hopis use in the snake dance. What a lot of stuff the guy's picked up!"

Piggot barely looked. "Anal-erotic," he said. "The collector's temperament."

But it was impossible to escape the conversation in back of them. Grace Wyatt would not tolerate competition and had raised her voice. Both Cristina and Geoff were listening. Gladys looked like a gull about to pounce.

"I can't tell you all it's done for me," Grace Wyatt was saying just as Jim Hopper came in from the hall with Aleida and her chubby, chattering escort and two other couples who had all been at some ski-club dinner at the hotel.

He braced himself for the usual perfunctory "Hello, Peter" and a just-polite smile when Aleida started past him to join Mary Orr, but for some inexplicable reason Aleida's "Hello, Peter!" had a warmth of which he had never even thought her capable. The delicious turmoil stirred up in him by her friendliness made him afraid to look toward the couch for fear his glance might meet only the usual cool stare. Yet there had been no mistake about her smile. He wondered whether it was something Anne could have written to Aleida that could have been responsible for it; but, no, Anne had said in her last letter to him only a few days ago, "Aleida says she doesn't see anything of you. She says that you're all taken up with a fascinating lady from Florence who sings beautifully and drives a foreign car." It wasn't likely that Anne could have said anything to Aleida that would have suddenly made her change her opinion of him. No, the chances were that it was all just coincidence: Aleida had had something happen to her that made her feel awfully good and some of her surprising radiance had been turned even on him.

Gladys had waited but she was not going to be diverted from what she had to say. She pounced. "Grace, you don't mean that you believe all that about papal infallibility and those miracles at Lourdes?"

"Of course I do." Grace drew herself up. "My dear, when you've lived as long as I have—" and her imperious voice at once added ten years and took twenty years off—"you can believe anything."

"I know exactly what you mean," Jack Fettis blustered as if to challenge anyone to contradict Grace.

"No, you don't," she turned on him and immediately repented of her tone, "but you will some day, dear."

The memory of Aleida's smile and his irritation over Gladys' persistence combined to make Peter burst out before Piggot could take Grace Wyatt's part, "Grace represents the latest thing in scientific attitude: everything is possible! A couple of years ago, if a thing wasn't rational, it wasn't possible. Now modern physics has changed all that, and we've discovered that the universe isn't governed by our system of logic at all and that the only sensible attitude is to be ready for anything."

"Peter, you're quibbling," Gladys pouted.

The truck driver hunched his shoulders and persisted pigheadedly, "I still say I know exactly what Grace means."

"My God, he is going to be a convert, too," Furfey, coming up beside Collard and Peter, jeered. He was forcing them by the threat of poisonous confidences he was about to make to move with him toward the far corner of the room. It was the only way to keep Fettis and the rest of the large group around Grace and Gladys and Geoff from hearing what he might say. "Anything to get in solid with the old girl!"

Collard said coldly, "Oh, has he been getting in with her? I heard only that he was going to be her chauffeur."

"Chauffeur, nothing. She still has her chauffeur." Furfey's pale rabbit face twitched with envy. His voice had become a whine. "That boy is set for life. I wish I could get somebody to subsidize me."

Collard no longer bothered to hide his distaste. He drew back a few inches and ran his hand down the side of his lean jaw with ostentatious annoyance, as if Furfey's breath had soiled him. "More power to him, since he needs it. I understand that's why Middlemas got Grace to give him some sort of job, so that he could stay out here and paint." Collard looked amused all of a sudden. "Fettis will probably even get to paint her portrait," he said maliciously.

Furfey had a coiled look of striking back. "If he doesn't, I'm sure Middlemas will!"

Peter felt himself seethe with anger. He said, struggling to keep his voice low to keep Geoff who was still beside Grace Wyatt from hearing, "You're wrong. Middlemas painted her two years ago in Washington. He doesn't have to cadge portrait commissions."

"I was just saying what I'd heard. It doesn't make any difference to me," Furfey backed down hastily and looked away and then made out that he had to see Jim Hopper about something on the other side of the room.

Grace Wyatt gathered her white fichu around her shoulders and announced, "Well, I have to get up early tomorrow. You'll have to excuse me, Jim; I go to seven-o'clock Mass during Lent." She said to Fettis, who had scrambled with fatuous alacrity to his feet, "Would you tell Matthews, dear, that I'm ready to go? There is no reason for you to leave. . . ."

They did not stop talking about religion after she had left. Mary Orr asked, "Do you know what the Spanish people call Grace? Jack Fettis *has* gone, hasn't he? They call her 'Mrs. Padre Joslyn.' Faustina told me. Don't you think that's cute?"

"I think it's terrible," Gladys brust out. "Grace is just making herself ridiculous. All this business about saying rosary every afternoon, and getting all those religious magazines, and having Father Joslyn at every party as if she expected to convert us, too. I mean, it isn't as if she had always been so devout."

"I bet she was a gay gal in her time," Hal Oxnard chuckled appreciatively.

"All the same," Chet Orr said, "I wish I had what she's got. She claims she never knew what peace was until now."

"Oh, you don't either, Chet!" Gladys protested. "Who wants peace? I don't want to be a slave to anything, do you?"

"I don't know, I sort of like Father Joslyn," Daisy Oxnard said. "He's intelligent. I think I'm going to ask him to my next party if he'll come."

Larry Collard said sardonically, "We're right back in the nineteenth century: drawing-room Jesuits—rich old girls like Grace who don't know what to do with themselves—fashionable conversions and de luxe editions of St. Augustine."

Geoff said, "As a matter of fact, I don't believe Father Joslyn had as much to do with Grace's becoming a Catholic as one of the Franciscan friars who is attached to the Cathedral, and he is a very retiring man. I don't think he's ever been in Grace's house except once last fall when she was ill."

"Oh, I know the one!" Dorothy Lambert said. "He has a birthmark over his right eye. You remember, Mary, he was there when we went to see Grace that time."

"I have an idea that he's a very remarkable chap." Geoff pursued his diversion as if determined to steer the conversation away from Grace. "I pass him sometimes in front of the hospital, and it always gives me a lift to see him. There is an amazing serenity about him, a sort of gaiety."

"But do you feel that that has anything to do particularly with his being a monk?" Cristina asked, and Peter noticed her voice had the tautness it always had when she was getting ready to taunt Geoff.

"I sort of feel it does."

"How do you know he wouldn't have looked like that anyway? You're just being sentimental, Geoff. You're probably thinking of the Ghirlandaio picture you like so much of the old man with the wen."

"I'm thinking of the beauty in his face." There was the faintest note of asperity in Geoff's voice. "I should like to paint him sometime."

"Do you feel that serenity is a necessary concomitant of saintliness?" Piggot asked. "I've a notion that only the very naïve saints are serene and that the others go through hell most of the time."

"Well, I don't picture a saint as transfigured every minute of the day; still, there must be moments of intense joy and a general gaiety. I'm thinking of St. Francis of Assisi."

"Oh, St. Francis is all right," Cristina said, "but what about all those horrible little child saints the guides insist on telling you about in half the churches in Italy? I fail to see the intense joy in being tortured when you are twelve years old—or in hearing about it. And then they show you those nauseating relics that are supposed to work miracles. I think it's all horrible."

"And if you join the Church," Gladys echoed her, "you've got to swallow all that. I don't see how Grace could; it's just too humiliating!"

Piggot said slowly, "If one has nothing else to cling to, one might be willing to humble oneself."

"Who said there is nothing else? Look at Jeanne," Gladys appealed to Jeanne Lauber, who sat in one of her innumerable black mandarin coats on the floor beside an Indian drum and looked up with blissful blankness, as an exhibit. "There was Buddha and Confucius and I don't know how many other great religious leaders. I don't for one moment believe that God revealed himself just to us."

Just as before he had been impelled to take Grace Wyatt's part, so now he could not resist the impulse to defend Geoff, but not so much against Gladys as against Cristina's faint sneers. He was also aware of a defiant need to prove to Aleida that he was not so much at the beck and call of the "fascinating lady from Florence" as she thought.

He said almost joyously, "That's a sort of doctrine of multiple revelation: God revealing himself equally to the Hottentots and the Easter Islanders! That particular belief can be carried to extremes. Where would you stop—with the men in the jungle, or did the monkeys have a revelation, too? Besides, even if it were true, I consider our running to the Eastern philosophies a pitiful abdication. I'd just as soon take dope."

"But what have you got against the East? Everybody knows they're away ahead of us in philosophy. After all, Jesus was born in the East," Gladys said triumphantly.

"But Christianity—the Church as we know it—is a Western phenomenon. It's got the genius of Thomas Aquinas and I don't know who they all were but they were Western men——"

"Oh, Duns Scotus and Albertus Magnus and Abelard and St. Bernard." Piggot helped him out.

"Yes, those—built into it! I'm a Western man and I want to go to hell in a Western way."

"Why do you all talk as if the Catholic Church were the only Church," Mary Orr challenged. "You can be a Christian without being a Catholic, I hope."

Piggot thrust up his jaw and obviously meant to answer. Peter was relieved. It was one thing to squelch Gladys, and another to hold forth on philosophy.

"Because I for one," Piggot said, "don't believe in patched-up premises in philosophy. Grace did what she had to do. Your convert usually comes such a long way that nothing will satisfy him but an absolute solution. In Grace Wyatt's place I'd have acted exactly the same way. I'm an addict, too, of the fallacy of the absolute—of the Gothic rage," he added with a sudden deprecatory grin that lent a surprising boyishness to his saturnine face.

"That's all completely over my head," Daisy Oxnard complained. "All I know is that if you're really in trouble, the ministers always tell you that you must have faith; but suppose you can't believe in all those things the churches tell you—suppose you don't have any real faith in God! How do you get to have faith, Ralph?"

Piggot hesitated. His dove-blue eyes shifted rapidly from side to side as if hunting for some escape. "Faith," he said cautiously, "is already a matter of grace. Some few lucky ones are born with it, and the rest of us have to struggle for it. I think that in its purest form faith is a virtuosity of the spirit that's granted only to the saints: they are the only ones who can get far enough off the ground to have any direct perception of God. All that most of us can do is to act as if we had faith by practicing the lesser forms of it—faith in life, in the virtue of human effort, in the inherent value of work. . . ."

It ended the discussion. People started to move around. Jim Hopper was taking orders for drinks. Hal Oxnard laughed. . . . All at once Peter found himself facing Aleida and he saw to his delight that something of her first smile was back in her eyes and playing around the beautifully modeled lips of her wide mouth.

She said, "You haven't come to see us."

"I've meant to but—"

"You just haven't got around to it!" The same gaiety which with a single remark wiped out the months when she had barely condescended to speak to him frolicked in her hazel-colored eyes while she watched him fumble for an excuse.

He plowed on stubbornly, "——I've been working pretty hard."

"I saw some of your work. As a matter of fact I saw a lot of it."

He wondered whether she had been east without his hearing about it. Had she seen the lithograph at the Pennsylvania Academy show or had she by some chance got to know someone at the Hearn Laboratories in Harrison?

"Where—in Philadelphia?"

"Oh, much closer than that." She clearly enjoyed teasing him. "In Santa Cruz. I saw the electric lights and the pump and the lathes and the radio."

It was so unexpected that it was like a present.

"I had no idea you knew Father Hegge."

"Do you think you're the only one who knows nice people? Father Hegge used to be in Pecos, and we saw a lot of him. We still take him things for his poor. My father says he attracts the poor as honey draws bees. He is a darling, isn't he? Father calls him the Franciscan Menace." She nodded to the geologist who was summoning her from the doorway into the next room, and said, "Yes, Bill," but she did not go. . . . "I think it's wonderful of you to do all that and to teach those children once a week, but don't you ever do anything but work? Do you ever go skiing?"

"I don't know how."

"I thought skiing was the favorite Austrian sport."

"I guess it is. I just never learned."

"Aren't you going to?"

"I hadn't thought of it."

"Are you afraid?"

In an instant her playful challenge had called up the scene at the livery stable. He started to bridle and checked himself. He told himself impatiently, I got off on the wrong foot with her, but that's no reason for

staying on the defensive for the rest of my life. She's a nice girl. Anne
dotes on her. She's even exciting!

He said cheerfully, "Afraid of falling down, you mean? I'm ready at
any time to give a demonstration that I can fall down as gracefully and
as gallantly as the next guy."

"You don't have to fall down. Anne doesn't."

"Anne had a good teacher. When do I get a lesson?"

"Tomorrow if you like. I'm going out to Hyde Park. . . ."

He could hardly believe the next day that it was he who was alone
with her trekking through the snow to the sunny slopes. She had delightfully become somebody utterly new, and as a result the whole day
had the quality of a dream—the startling vividness, the magic freshness
that gave a bloom to everything, the constant sense of surprise. She
was not at all the Aleida he had expected to find—bossy on her skis,
patronizing. Whether she taught him to walk or to sidestep up the
hill or just to use his poles, she did it with a matter-of-fact helpfulness
that took the sting out of her being in a position to teach. Yet he was
what only a few days ago he would have considered humiliatingly de-
pendent on her from the moment he had put on one ski and tried to put
on the second one. It kept sliding out from under him. Aleida who had
watched him struggle with it for a few seconds came simply over beside
him and fastened the binding.

She taught him how to walk and how to snowplow and turn. She took
it as a matter of course when at first he fell down at every try to turn.
"You're doing fine!" Her directions were brisk and to the point. "Keep
your shoulders level—keep your knees bent—keep the poles out! . . ."
There was not much chance for talk. The climb back up the knoll and
the problem of not losing his balance on the way down kept him busy
and out of breath. And after about an hour Aleida left him to practice
by himself while she climbed the steep slope beyond a tongue of spruce
trees on the right to do some skiing herself. When she had disappeared
behind the trees he practiced furiously, impatient with his slowness to
learn. He saw her come down just once and the breath-taking beauty of
the slim, navy-blue figure in its silent glide over the sparkling snow
made him all at once understand Anne's enthusiasm for her friend. He
wanted to shout to her, but he was awed both by the vast, velvety expanse
of snow that spread like skirts over the majestic slopes and by Aleida's
expertness.

Instead he climbed higher on his own tame knoll. He went faster on the zigzagging traverses across the slope, and when he fell down now at any turn it was because he tried to make it too tight, too spectacular. Once at his most daring he hit a bump just as he was going into a turn; he lost his balance, realized that the tips of his skis were hooked and hopelessly tangled up, turned a cartwheel, then felt his right ski come off and to his dismay saw it skitter faster and faster down the hill toward a clump of brush far below.

He started to slide and limp after it on his one ski just as Aleida came swooping around the tongue of spruce trees on the right. She executed a beautiful turn. Her skis kicked up a fine spray of snow.

"What's the matter?"

"I lost my ski. It decided to go look at the world by itself."

"Oh, I was afraid you had hurt your ankle. Down there in the brush? That happens to everybody. I'm always chasing a ski," she said with a laugh. "I'll get it." She leaned on her poles and in an instant was gone.

It astonished him once again that instead of feeling humiliated he was only warmed and delighted by her help. She was full of exquisitely simple, gracious gestures, he told himself a few minutes later when she made it sound like a favor if he would eat another sandwich which he was ravening to have.

She poured more tea for them from the thermos in the lunch basket she had brought.

She asked, "Do you like it?"

He held up his half-finished sandwich. "It's delicious. I like it even better than the other kind."

"Not the sandwiches; you've already praised those twice. The skiing!"

"I'm crazy about it. At least, I like it in theory."

She smiled back at him. "You'll get to like it in practice, too. You're doing fine." She turned the side of the basket to him that held the cookies and the fruit. "You know, you ought to get a parka and ski pants. They keep the wind out better and they don't get so wet from the snow."

He looked with amusement at the sodden splotches on his yellow corduroy pants. "I don't propose on my next attempt to spend quite so much time in the snow."

She persisted. "When you begin to ski well, you'll want to look nice, too."

"I leave that to you. . . ."

He could, too, he told himself. She looked charming in the navy-blue ski pants and the jacket which she had left unbuttoned at the throat where the white scarf was tied and in the gay red-and-blue knitted cap. He tried not to admit to himself his pleasure in the bird-swift glances of her hazel-colored eyes or in her pink glow.

They talked of Anne, of Smith, of Santa Cruz, but carefully not of Cristina or Santa Fe. It was part of the brisk, glass-blown perfection of the day that she should be as eager as he to protect their outing from any intrusion from the world of every day.

She said, "In a way I'm just as glad the others didn't come. You would have had more fun but you wouldn't have practiced so much."

He said, "I couldn't have had more fun, but it must have been an awful bore for you. I wish I weren't so slow."

"You aren't slow. You were doing fine. You should do more of this."

"I'm planning to if I can get more free tutoring."

"I might charge you next time—yes, I think I'll charge you a lot," she threatened playfully. "But you won't need to buy any skis. You can keep these as long as you like. They're an extra pair my father has and he never uses them anyway."

He liked the feeling as of an almost live bond with her which the skis gave him. "Thanks, I'd like to very much. And I'll get myself some decent ski boots by Saturday, and then maybe I'll do better next time. . . ."

But there was no next time!

On Thursday afternoon when he returned from giving the weekly machine-shop lesson to Father Hegge's boys and called Cristina from Tesuque to tell her that he had had to change a tire and would be late, he thought he heard her say to someone with her in the room, "On the other table, Aleida." He could have sworn that she had said "Aleida." Yet in the same breath he assured himself that it must have been some other name: Cristina hardly knew Aleida Gibbs! When he had told her about the skiing lesson with Aleida—"She's Anne's best friend. I was supposed to look her up months ago. You know how sisters are about their friends!"—she had not even known where Aleida lived.

Friday afternoon when he stopped at the post office for his mail there was a note from Aleida to tell him that she was sorry but that their skiing date for Saturday was off. No explanation why she could not come; nothing about another day instead; an inexplicable brusqueness after her gay warmth just two days ago.

He managed to get her on the telephone. He pretended not even to be aware of the guardedness in her voice or of anything peculiar about her note. "What about Sunday or Monday? I need my lesson," he joked.

"I'm sorry, Peter, but I can't go."

"How about the end of next week?"

"I'm afraid not, Peter." She seemed to be having a struggle with herself and to feel that she owed him something more; but though she started out boldly her voice soon faltered again. "Something has come up . . ."

"Does that mean our trip to Santa Cruz is off, too?"

"Yes. I'm sorry, Peter." She gave the impression of reaching out desperately for an excuse, any excuse. "I may have to go away. I may have to go to Dallas again. . . ."

He was certain all at once with a furious certainty that it was Aleida who had been in Cristina's living room when he telephoned. Something had been said that had brought about this baffling change. He could not ask Aleida what had been said, but he could ask Cristina!

He rushed in a cold rage to Cerro Gordo Road. Cristina gushed, "Why, darling, how lovely! You're early."

He forced himself to let several minutes go by before he asked, "Was that Aleida you were talking to yesterday when I telephoned?"

"Yes, Aleida was here yesterday for tea. What makes you ask about that all of a sudden?"

"I thought you hardly knew her."

"I don't. We happened to run into each other at the hairdresser's yesterday and we found we had several things in common. For one thing we discovered we both knew Father Hegge; so I asked her over for tea. Was there anything wrong with that?"

"No."

His effort to force her by his patience to betray herself and tell him what he wanted to know bore fruit. She said, "You never told me that you had asked Aleida Gibbs to go to Santa Cruz with you."

"I didn't think it was important enough. It wasn't much of an invitation. She said she'd like to see sometime what I was teaching the kids, and I said if she was interested I'd take her along some Thursday afternoon."

"You nevered offered to take me along!"

"You never said you were interested. You said machinery bored you."

"A girl still likes to be asked!"

"What did you tell Aleida?"

"I told her nothing. What should I have told her? We had tea and that's all."

"Well, it's odd that she should have seen you yesterday and then told me today that our date to go skiing tomorrow was off."

"I had nothing to do with that. Why should I have? You can go skiing all you want for all I care. You can go every day if you want to."

"That's what you said when I told you I wanted to make a stab at learning how to ski. Anne's friend was willing to give me a few lessons and that was that. . . . That wasn't what I was asking. Did you tell her about us?"

She bridled. "For whom do you take me?"

"Did you tell her about Geoff and me?"

"You *are* insulting! Do you think I'm Gladys that I go around tattling about my friends' private affairs? In any case I didn't have to tell her—she knew."

"Then what did you talk about?"

"Frankly, I don't see that it's any of your business, darling. Or if you really must know, why don't you ask her?"

"Because I barely know her and because I'm asking you."

"All right, I'll tell you. We talked about horses: Aleida is going to let me have a colt from her mare. And that's practically all we talked about. Now are you satisfied?"

It was ridiculous, of course—he admitted it to himself—to expect to pin her down. As if a woman like Cristina did not have a hundred subtle feminine ways of letting another woman know that she was in possession without putting her claim into words!

But whatever Cristina had managed to convey, Aleida did not turn chillingly scornful again as before. She merely became remote, with something faintly reproachful in her manner which seemed to say each time they met in somebody's house or in the street, "You are somebody else's property, remember? We've talked together as long as we should now; we've got to think of Cristina. I'm sorry, Peter. . . ." Some remnant of the friendliness which she had first shown him when she found out about his trips to Santa Cruz had survived; and invariably it was Father Hegge and the boys whom they talked about when they met.

It turned the weekly trips to teach Father Hegge's boys into a secret ally, a bond. Cristina sensed it, too. She said, "Do you have to run out there all the time?"

"It's only once a week. I'm trying to teach these kids something so that they can make a living here at home."

"Why is that so important? They can go somewhere else and get a job. Maximiliano goes to Wyoming every winter to herd sheep."

"Why should they have to go somewhere else? This is their home. Their whole life is tied up with this valley. If they go somewhere else they'll lose their roots and they'll just drift around like a lot of other workmen one sees in the big cities. I want to help them do something that'll bring them in enough money so that they can stay here where they belong."

"Why be so emphatic about it? You are just compensating."

"What do you mean—compensating?"

"Well, you're always for the underdog. You are trying to get even. You see the whole world as either underdogs or evildoers."

It was the first time she had ever even vaguely referred to his illegitimacy. He asked and his voice warned her off, "Get even for what?"

"I don't know for what but I can guess. You are trying to get even with Geoff."

"That's ridiculous. I'm not saying that it wasn't there, but I've got over that long ago. I simply don't like waste. If I can help those boys to develop any mechanical bent they've got, I'm going to do it; and if they need a few machines, I'm going to see that they get them. I don't see where Geoff enters into that."

"I think he does or you wouldn't take on so about it." But she clearly felt that she had gone as far as she dared. She tossed her head. "For all I care you can go to Santa Cruz twice a day. Do you want to play Russian bank or not? . . ."

CHAPTER TEN

Strikingly Pretty Tonight

BUT it was not only the trips to Santa Cruz that were an escape. He played truant even when he was with Cristina, and she noticed it.

She said, "You aren't listening. If you're going to look at that maga-zine——"

"Of course, I'm listening. Claude Blackburn's wife had a château in Auvergne!"

"Her brother did. It wasn't hers until her brother got killed in the War. . . ."

Who cared? Always these chichi genealogies and those lavendered details from the past. Always all those stories about older people, as if to hypnotize him into believing that that was the generation to which he also belonged. He rebelled: *Hell, I was still in grammar school then! I'm young. She's already done and seen everything; but not me—I haven't even lived yet.*

She said, "I went out into the corral today to look at Chiquita's foot.
210

The horses are getting awfully fat. How would you like to go riding tomorrow afternoon?"

"I ought to paint."

"Oh, well, I can ask Jeanne; and Gladys always wants to ride. Darling, let's not go to the Kemps' tonight. It sounds so dull. I'll tell them that I'm still having trouble with the pump and you're fixing it again."

In the beginning, when with a sort of prankish perverseness they had sometimes started to make love just when they had been supposed to get ready to leave for some party, Cristina had often said jokingly, "Darling, we simply have to get up. What a bore! I know what—let's call up and say both cars have broken down and Pimmy has the jaundice," and he had fallen in eagerly with her exuberance, and they had concocted some excuse and had laughingly stayed at home. She was waiting for him to kindle to her suggestion again.

"But we said yesterday we were going to go. I think we owe it to the Kemps. We didn't go to their other party last month."

"I really don't feel like it tonight. You go, darling," she urged. And he went, happy to get away.

He was always escaping from her now. He arrived late in the afternoon because he had worked at his easel until nearly four, and he left earlier and earlier in the evening because he had to get up early the next morning to paint! It was an excuse. So was his playing poker with Praither and a group of Praither's friends one night a week.

He did work. One of the results of the prize he had won in Philadelphia had been an offer by the director of the art museum to give him a one-man show in the fall. The problem was to have enough drawings and lithographs by September to fill the walls of even the small alcove he was to have. But he learned a good deal from his drawing of the two old Indian women with which he had won the prize. He simplified and trimmed down to the lean, sinewy essentials and found that there was a knack to doing it and all sorts of rewards: one could achieve elegance and tautness and power and a sense that there was more than met the eye. One could also work fast and with gratifying results. Except Buell everyone had nothing but praise for the new lithographs.

Buell took one look at a drawing of three pentitente crosses on a bleak hilltop, with a mangy dog chasing two sheep across the barren knoll, and jeered, "Nice work! You're getting to be as good as one of those fashionable Paris dress designers: small proportion here, large proportion there—it couldn't be prettier."

It was like a cold shower. "What do you mean?"

"Just what I said. It's so goddam slick, it belongs in the five-and-ten. You'll sell a million. Why do you bother to put it on stone? I'd have a zinc cut made: you can print more that way."

"I was stylizing the forms. Isn't that all right?"

"So I see. Know what all this reminds me of? A fine, buxom woman squeezed into an old-fashioned corset! A corset isn't style. You had more style in the first couple of things you did last fall. Here," and he tramped in his muddy boots over the white rug to the drawing of the roly-poly trumpeter tacked up beside the window. "This is simple and straightforward, but it's got something. You weren't trying to be clever there. It's an honest statement of what and how you felt about that man. That's your style! When I look at that I don't have to retch. . . ."

He knew Buell was right: his heart had not been in any of the recent drawings. Buell was not given to eloquence, but his indignation had said as clearly as Piggot's elegant vocabulary could have done that a work of art was an act of worship and praise, was always revelation, perhaps even prophecy, and that it was born of passion and reverence; whereas he had relied on esthetic titillation and technique, just like most of the full-fledged artists who were around. Except for Buell and the academicians, who were too naïve to be tortured by any doubts about their work, Peter told himself, hardly any of them really worked: they fumbled, and they fiddled with different techniques, and they faked. Most of them were as if partly paralyzed by a sense of futility and gloom. There was Praither, with his childish running away from work, with his incredible craftsmanship and always somewhere in every picture some impish touch that mocked the whole and was like a signature of defeat. There was George Kemp, with his abstractions and his endless color experiments. There was Hutch, who wanted to paint like the Chinese. There was Orr—and a dozen like him—who strove sincerely enough and who knew how to paint but whose work was like an airplane that couldn't get off the ground. There was Furfey, who was obsessed by the symbols of success rather than by any problem of paint. There was finally Geoff, who fumbled like the rest and was scared.

What ailed every one, the others as well as himself? Why couldn't they look at a landscape or an apple and see it and paint it as passionately as Cézanne? Why were they all hoping for some illumination from a new technique? Wasn't it precisely the love affair with the apple—as George Kemp had called it in talking about the same thing as Piggot last fall—that brought about the unique, intense vision which alone could give rise to a valid new technique? Wasn't any reversal of the process proof of sterility?

In a way, he told himself, they were no different from the young would-be artists in Greenwich Village; they were older and had seen more, that was all. Where Sibby's friends had been to Paris and to Italy and Spain, George Kemp and his friends had been to out-of-the-way places in China and Peru. They had been the guests of Tartar chieftains, and they had been attacked by reindeer herds somewhere near Stavanger Fiord, and they had fished in some Transcaucasian river where Georgian shepherds put weighted sheepskins in the stream to collect the gold flakes washed down with the river mud—Jason's Golden Fleece, no less! They had won prizes and their pictures hung in museums and their names were in *Who's Who;* but they were somehow still as insecure and as unfulfilled as Sibby's friends. They were even surrounded by the same crowd of gushing, know-it-all hangers-on. The only difference was that the New York dilettantes had talked by the hour about all the masterpieces they were going to paint and write, while these gray-haired ones, who bore themselves with such vast assurance and bored complacency, all talked like grandfathers although they had never fathered anything.

In his sudden craving for something solid to cling to he turned to the native culture all around him. He went during Holy Week and watched the penitente processions from the morada—the grim, windowless, adobe chapel where the members of the flagellant brotherhood held their secret devotions and flogged themselves—to the three stark crosses on the hill. It was dangerous to sketch openly during their services. Praither had warned him that the members of the society retaliated swiftly for any attempt to treat them as freaks—people had come close to getting killed. But there was nothing to prevent his memorizing the gaunt Mexican carrying the big cross, the shriveled man playing eerie melodies on the homemade shepherd's flute, the pugnacious-looking man whirling his wooden noise maker, the two men who were lashing their bare backs, the man who was reading aloud from a prayer book. There was nothing to prevent his hurrying to the car now and again to jot down a few hasty notes. He had gone back to drawing again, but humbly this time, determined to catch the truth of what he saw.

He watched the bright-eyed little girls with their gay new hats, pink or baby-blue, on Easter morning on their way to church. He went to the wedding party at Crecencio's and Josefita's the following day: Josefita's mother, whom he had thought of as ancient but who looked surisingly vivacious all at once and turned out to be after all only forty-one, was getting married again. He brought his present and squeezed into the crowded house, where the bride—all black silk and demurely lowered lids over her gleaming eyes—and her bravely grinning new husband and dozens of relatives and friends sat stiffly on chairs and benches around the walls of the best room, where everyone sipped solemnly from his little glass of homemade wine and now and then ventured to whisper some shy remark, where everyone took his turn at a long table that groaned with food and then sat in starched formality again through the rest of the afternoon—until at last it was time for the *baile*, the wedding dance at the dance hall down the road, and some of the stiffness melted away and there was laughter and fun.

The more he saw of his Spanish neighbors, the more he valued them. He liked their humor and their refusal to be rushed. He saw the decency and comeliness and the surprising richness of their lives. He enjoyed working alongside the men cleaning out the irrigation ditch instead of hiring a man to do his share of the work, as Buell and Praither did. He helped Crecencio mend his fence. It was the example of Crecencio, busy with his plowing and with lambing and a hundred things around his ranch, that filled him with a sudden need to exert himself physically. He started a little garden of his own in the front yard, where he could haul water from the well if there was none in the irrigation ditch. He took to getting up an hour earlier, so as to have time to ride. He watched the first few dandelions spring up and the scraggly plum hedges turn into a miracle of pungent-scented white lace and he discovered the patch of wild purple iris along the creek. Gradually an exuberant sense of spring infected him.

But the joy that swelled in him each morning made him only more reluctant to return to Cristina in the afternoon. He concealed his daytime glow at once guiltily and jealously. His buoyancy, he realized at last, had to do directly with his secret feeling of escape. There were afternoons when he shrank from the moment when he had to start for town.

He was forced to admit it to himself: he was afraid of her—at least of the Cristina who was attempting to manage him, for, in order to blot out the memory of his more and more frequent moments of rebellion, he had come to think of her as possessed of two utterly distinct personalities. There was the Cristina of the exciting pallor and the aristocratically plain, dark hair and the silver-gray eyes and the quiet elegance that made one's glance follow her, the Cristina who was gracious and amusing and wonderfully considerate and whose voice was like a physical caress, the woman with whom he was almost in love; and then there was the other Cristina whom he had surprised one afternoon in the middle of a venomous rebuke of the expressman for not having brought some parcel a few days earlier, and another time when she had flown into a seemingly uncontrollable rage with a little Spanish boy for running over a tulip bed, the woman who could be oddly callous about people's misfortunes—"Oh, I can't be bothered worrying about that!"—and the next moment almost revoltingly sentimental about Jeanne Lauber's dipsomania and about horses and dogs, who indulged herself in alarming tantrums and scenes and threw ash trays across the room.

Yet in the end it was the gentle Cristina—the tender, exquisitely womanly one—of whom he was most afraid. After one of her cajoling, playful, all but irresistible speculations about marriage and all the fun they would have, she would suddenly falter as if all at once overcome by distrust of his silence which she had for the past half hour interpreted to suit herself. All her gay confidence would collapse and she would complain, "You don't really want to marry me. How is it that absolutely nothing I do ever comes out right? Other people get all the breaks—no, it's true, everything I've ever wanted has slipped right out of my hands."

Her despondency would make him feel more at her mercy than her bullying; he would feel that the least he could do was to comfort her. He would pretend to close his ears to her self-doubt, scoff at it indignantly, make fun of it even while he remembered all the broken vases in the house and the cakes that had refused to rise and the fancy casserole dishes she had burned after putting in hours cooking them and her own accounts of all the accidents in which she had been involved; so that each time, after he had succeeded in teasing her out of her mood of self-distrust, he would find himself secretly trying to answer the question she herself had raised.

Had things always gone wrong for her, he wondered, because she brought a romantic dream to bear on life which either mangled men or made them run from her—as now, when she confronted him with her preconception that he was going to marry her? Did she, too, belong to the category Piggot had labeled the other night "the American Madame

Bovary" and had described as compounded of unbridled willfulness, too many trips with Alice through the Looking Glass, a frontier dream of chivalry, and merely twittering glands? Was there such a thing? Piggot was inclined to be rather absurd where women were concerned. . . .

Or had things turned out wrong so often for Cristina only because of a succession of bad breaks? But he was inclined to reject any belief in consistent bad luck; he persuaded himself that he had long ago formed a theory that the victim always bore part of the blame for whatever happened to him. Was that where the answer lay? Had she provoked her bad luck, just as now when she was trying to make him jealous at any cost? For she was not only flirting with the old judge and making Geoffrey go riding with her nearly every afternoon, but she was also perversely inviting Geoff's student along with Grace Wyatt and Jeanne Lauber and Geoff and the judge on Friday evening, which was his poker night.

When he turned around at the next party and flirted with Dorothy Lambert and with a sultry Texas girl who was visiting the Kemps, Cristina registered awareness of it at once. "Did you have fun with Miss Fort Worth?"

"Why, yes. She told me about her twins."

"I should have guessed they were quadruplets—she's so bosomy."

"Oh, they aren't hers: it's one of her horses that had the twins. She's married, but that's not what we talked about. She told me about the palominos she raises and about Arabs and quarter horses. Very interesting."

"I'm glad she can talk about something. All she did at our table was sit and sulk."

"Oh, she's quite articulate; she went to boarding school in the East."

"Why, how nice for you! That must have been like old home week!" She pleaded suddenly, "Darling, let's not ever go in for making each other jealous. That's horrible."

Yet at the very next opportunity, Peter noticed, she herself was flirting again. It became another count against her in his mind, like the wrinkles at the corners of her eyes, like the bad luck that was dogging her, like her exasperating vindictiveness toward Geoff.

It was a tug of war between them for Geoff. He had begun to see a lot of Geoff largely because he felt much more at ease with him—less guilty —ever since Cristina and he had resumed their rides—yet there was still a brittle guardedness in their relationship which the most trivial occurrence could crystallize.

Late one afternoon while he was waiting for Geoff to get ready to come to dinner with him at the hotel—Cristina had gone to Denver for a few days with Mary Orr to shop—he drifted without thinking across the room to the mahogany-mounted barometer he had come to love. He saw that there was dust on the glass tubes and blew it off, and he straightened the banjo-shaped board which hung a little askew. He failed to hear Geoff come in from the studio until it was too late to pretend that he had not been looking at the handsome instrument. Geoff said quietly, "Why don't you take the barometer? The walls are too crooked in this house, and it should hang straight to register accurately. I really haven't any place for it."

His embarrassment over having been caught unawares made him sound colder than he meant to be. "No, thanks, I wouldn't know what to do with it."

When they got to the Fonda dining room, Geoff still smarted from the rebuff. He took it out on his student, who came into the cantina a minute after they did and took the little table next to them. Fettis had greeted Geoff exuberantly and presently offered, "Why don't I come and sit with you?" Geoff pushed the forks and knives farther out on either side and said more harshly than Peter had ever heard him speak, "You'd better stay right where you are. This table is barely big enough for two."

Jack Fettis cringed, flushed, and looked on the point of blubbering. His coarse-skinned moonface which had turned plum color was swollen with hurt. He ordered a sandwich and coffee, clearly cutting his dinner short, and immediately began to gulp down his sandwich when it came. He kept his eyes reproachfully down on his plate or on the opposite side of the room. When Geoff addressed him once with contrite friendliness to ask how Grace Wyatt was, Fettis flushed an even deeper brown and choked on the few words he squeezed out. He left soon afterward, his ungainly shoulders hunched up under his loud-checked shirt as if he were carrying a cross.

Geoff's testiness, though hard on Fettis, had been as good as a thunderstorm for clearing the atmosphere. They were able to look at each other again and grin. At one of the large tables in the center of the room the Belgian potter who always had tiny, glistening bubbles quivering on his lower lip when he talked was enthusiastically explaining to his bored-looking wife, to Collard, the Texas girl and the Kemps that the flower seeds he had planted that morning were twice as big and twice as productive as any other seeds. A minute later he was sputtering about the unique excellence of his house in Carmel.

Peter caught Geoff's eye. "He's off again!"

Geoff grinned back. "My mother would have said, 'All his eggs have two yolks.' "

At once Peter's ears felt taut with alertness. He chuckled, "How amusing!"

"It's an old Yorkshire saying. Mother picked up a lot of them when she was a girl. There was another that would have fitted our friend. She used to say, 'The least boy always carries the biggest fiddle.' Though that's not the same thing perhaps."

It did not matter one bit. All that counted was to keep Geoffrey talking and Peter succeeded in that. He learned that Geoff's mother—*my grandmother*, he told himself once—had come from Yorkshire, had had certain tart north-country ways that had kept her a stranger in Penzance, had died when she was still young—when Geoffrey was only eight. To Peter's delight, Geoff was willing to be led on and to talk about Penzance—about St. Michael's Mount, an ancient castle and monastery on a towering island rock to which one could walk out from the shore at low tide; about a fishing village named Newlyn and another called Mousehole, where Geoff had gone on his bicycle; about marshes along the Marazion road, about the palms which, astonishingly, thrived in the gardens in Penzance, and the granite houses, and the statue of Sir Humphrey Davy in front of the Market Hall. "Penzance," Geoff said and somehow managed to include him in it, "has always been an inventors' town. . . ."

They drove out to Tesuque after dinner in the Chevvy. Geoff had wanted to see the recent drawings he had done and was full of praise. He admired the garden in the front yard and the first few tulip spears that showed above the ground. They went for a walk along the wild-plum hedges before Peter took him back to town. They laughed together in the car. They had never been so close.

Yet the very next day the lurking tension between them sprang to life again and forced them apart. He stopped at Geoff's to pick up some lithography paper which Geoff had insisted the previous evening he must come and get. Geoff had the paper all ready for him, a fist-high stack of it. "Most of it is Italian," he said. "I've found it very satisfactory. These small sheets come from old Dutch folios I picked up in Amsterdam. They weren't cut out very carefully, but you might be able to use some of them."

He felt embarrassed by the size of the stack and especially by the little pile of end sheets from old books. Praither had talked about the priceless-ness of old Dutch paper only the other day; it was practically unobtain-able now and wonderful for making prints.

He balked. "I couldn't take all of that; it's much too much. I'd be robbing you."

"You're not robbing me. I haven't done any etchings or lithographs for years; the paper has just been lying here. You might as well get some good out of it."

Some demon made him rebel at the mere possibility of becoming too obligated to Geoff. "The Dutch paper is too valuable; you might want to use it some day. I'll take the Italian paper with thanks."

Geoff's handsome black eyebrows beetled in annoyance. "Suit your-self. Leave what you don't want. There are some pieces of cardboard and over there is some string if you want to wrap it to take out to your car. Excuse me for a minute—I haven't had a chance to look at my mail. . . ."

They were both to go to the Orrs' for a drink; it was almost time to leave. When Peter had finished tying the paper between the cardboard sheets, Geoff looked up from the letter he had been reading by the window. "All ready?" He seemed to have had good news and to have got over his annoyance. He held out the letter.

It was written on Grace Wyatt's stationery—"Los Pinos" printed at the top—in a squat, heavy hand and it was from Jack Fettis. He was complaining about Geoff's curtness at the hotel. "Last night in the cantina . . . and that kind of thing hurts. . . . You've been a fire by which I've warmed myself and a light. . . ." There was more in the same vein. *One long whine!* Peter characterized it to himself and realized that his impatience with it was due as much to the blatant adulation of Geoff as to the tearful flatulence of the style. He handed the letter back to George. "A little lush."

Geoffrey bridled. "Not at all. A perfectly nice letter."

In an instant they were miles apart again. And as if the perverse demon that had prodded him still was not satisfied, Peter felt impelled to reach out and help Geoff with his topcoat although he knew—or was it pre-cisely because he knew—that he resented being helped. Geoff jerked the coat collar irritably up over his left shoulder, which was still somewhat lame from his fall from the stallion. "I'm not decrepit," he said frigidly. "I am quite capable of getting into a coat by myself." Yet only minutes later in the front yard at the Orrs' when they had to step across an irriga-tion ditch, Peter was tempted again to seize Geoff's elbow to help him across. He just barely checked himself in time. There was evidently no limit to the stubborn vitality of his old hate.

Ralph Piggot, with that exasperating knack he had of seeming to read one's thoughts, presently showed that he, too, was aware of it. He arrived in Tesuque one afternoon. "I was out for a drive and I thought I'd drop in—unless, of course, you're busy. . . ." He wanted to see the recent drawings and was even more enthusiastic than Geoff over one of a penitente brother who had carried a crucifix cradled in one arm in the Good Friday procession. "What an astonishing face! Did he really look like that?"

"Yes, pretty much. I've had him pose for me since. He faced the rest of the *hermanos* every time they stopped along the road to pray. He held the crucifix for them to see, and the wind blew his hair like that. I didn't have to fake anything."

"He couldn't look more like some ascetic saint if you had."

"He's the village idiot—according to Praither. I haven't found him so stupid. At any rate there was something beautiful about the way he knelt there on the ground in the high wind, with his head bowed beside the crucifix."

"You've caught it. I'd like a print of that if you're going to turn it into a lithograph. I mean I should like to buy one. . . ."

They talked about painting, and in no time Piggot was back on the subject of the rupture of some vital connection between modern man and his past. "We all have to make our peace with our past and with our destiny," Piggot said, and then without warning, "That's one thing Geoff has failed to do. Of course all this has been pretty rough on him."

"Oh? . . ." He looked hard at the somber, sagging, pouchy face to gain time. "What has been?"

"You."

Uneasiness kept him from being as acid with Piggot as he would have liked. "Are you his champion?"

"I'm Geoff's friend and I like to think that I'm yours and Cristina's as well."

"I think we've discussed Cristina before. I'm not her guardian and I'm not responsible for her likes and dislikes."

"I wasn't thinking of Cristina. What I had in mind was Geoff's hope that you might agree to some public acknowledgement of your relationship."

Piggot's tact was even more exasperating than his impertinence. Only his earnestness and the fact that he was Geoff's friend, who had to be considered as a sort of emissary whether Geoff knew he was here or not, kept Peter from putting a brusque end to the talk. He said sharply, on a warning note, "I don't need any favors from Geoff."

"You would be the one to bestow the favors. Has it ever occurred to you, Peter, that when a man gets to a certain age and has no family he's apt to be lonely and apt to long just as desperately for a son or a daughter as he does for a wife? I happen to know that Geoff had been thinking about you for a great many years. That's why I'm saying that recent events have been rather hard on him."

It was amazing how profoundly satisfying it was now that he had condoned Piggot's bland assumption of intimacy, to go on arguing with him. It was like adressing Geoff himself. He said slowly and savored his indignation, "His thinking stayed on a very academic level. I never heard about it. In any case it all came pretty late in the day. Has it ever occurred to you that things might have been pretty rough on me? When I was fourteen my one ambition was to kill Geoff. It took me years to get over all that hate."

"Are you sure you are over it?"

The sheer gall of him! He picked up the cigarettes from the magazine table and offered them to Piggot with an attempt at smiling nonchalance to prove to himself that he still had the upper hand. "You know," he said, "you're delightful, Ralph. Now I'm supposed to feel guilty because I haven't been shedding tears over Geoff's loneliness."

There was not even the beginning of a smile in the brown eyes. Piggot only scowled. He drew reflectively at his cigarette. "It's much easier to be hard than strong. I understand that you've pretty much had to make your own way in the world and I can easily see where charity would appear as weakness to a self-made man."

"I'm not stupid enough to think of myself as self-made. I've had to learn to stand alone, which isn't the same thing. I've had a lot of help and I've been grateful for it. In fact I went so far in my gratitude that I turned every older man who was kind to me into a sort of substitute father. It isn't much fun to have to play games like that—about as much fun as to have to hunt for your father."

"We're all looking for our father. Modern man is orphaned in the universe. We all feel that we're entitled to some paternal shelter and to a wall to our backs that used to be there. As a matter of fact you've been lucky: you've always had the luxury of having one simple explanation for

everything, one single villain to your piece. You've always had a dragon
to slay."

"You mean, I've had all the breaks?"

"Philosophically speaking, yes."

"Next time I lose an arm or a leg, I'll send for you to tell me how
lucky I am. . . ."

How glib and mellow they all sounded, including Cristina! he thought
sardonically that night. It was one of the times when he had an oppressive
feeling of being caught in a lush, dense forest where the proliferating
foliage cut off the sun and the sky and made it hard to breathe, so that
he had an almost overpowering impulse to slash his way out of the dank,
green twilight at any cost. They were to have gone to a piano recital at
the Museum and to the Oxnards' for a drink afterward, but Cristina had
a slight cold and in any case did not very much want to go. "I hate to
listen to second-rate pianists; I'd rather listen to my own playing. But,
darling, you must go!"

She had been out riding with Jeanne that afternoon and she did not
seem to have much of a cold, but she drank more than she usually did
and kept nervously lighting fresh cigarettes, and Peter recognized the
mood of wild recklessness with which she had on several occasions lately
tried to hide the fact that she was depressed. He refused to go to the
recital without her even though he dreaded the mood. They played black-
jack after dinner in front of the corner fireplace. It was a game he himself had only recently learned from Praither's friends and had taught to
her. Russian bank had become somehow too tame for them, and though
the chips were for pennies and nickels and dimes they played with an
unconfessed, smiling vindictiveness that made their winnings and losses
run quite high at times. It was one of the nights when it seemed impossible for her to win even once; his pile of chips had become embarrassingly
big.

She finally managed to win a few rounds. It even began to look like a
modest winning streak; a couple of his stacks of chips moved across the
table to her. He teased, "Are you laying up treasure for yourself?"

"Alas, my treasure is fast melting away."

There was no missing the overtone. The accusation was there behind
the smiling wistfulness that claimed it was all in jest. He felt clawed
by guilt. It was a relief when she pleaded a headache and refused his
offer to stay with her.

It was after ten, but still not too late—as Cristina insisted when she
had sent him away—to drop in at the Oxnards' and because anything

was better than being alone with the memory of Cristina's reproach, he went.

It was not a large party, so that he could lose himself among the other guests, as he had hoped. Almost the first thing he noticed when he walked into the Oxnards' big living room, was that Aleida Gibbs was sitting beside Larry Collard on the fringe of the loosely grouped crowd at the upper end of the huge picture window. It was the second time he had seen her with the biologist, and he was aware of a sharp stab of resentment. She looked strikingly pretty tonight in the sequined white bodice and long blue skirt that made up her dress, and there was an air of smug intimacy and cosy separateness from the rest of the crowd in the way they sat side by side on the low, upholstered bench at the base of the plate-glass window. He wondered whether she had again come in Collard's car, as she had to the Kemps'. . . . He went out into the dining room, made his and Cristina's apologies to Daisy Oxnard for not having joined her party at the recital, was given a drink, noticed a man with a bristling, blond mustache and a sun-reddened bald head whom he had not seen before, and sauntered back into the living room.

Gladys, who seemed to be bossing some sort of discussion, thrust out her bird face at him. "Peter, you're just in time. You know everybody, don't you—Bertille—and Aleida Gibbs?" Aleida's nod and her "Hello, Peter," were party-friendly and polite. Gladys bubbled on, "We've been talking about all the different personalities everybody has, how we all are an entirely different person to different people—I mean that we actually present a different side of ourselves to everybody because the chemistry between people is so——"

"That's not what we were talking about," Jim Hopper complained.

"Yes, it is, Jimmy; that's how it started. I want Peter to have the whole picture. Anyhow, then Freddy said that we all have a certain image of ourselves, of the sort of person we like to think we are, and that we don't ever truly see ourselves when we look in the mirror." Gladys' voice rippled and soared and slid expertly up and down scale. Her protuberant eyes snapped with exhilaration at holding the center of the stage. "And then Ralph claimed——" she said and paused histrionically for breath—"that everybody has some secret fiction he lives by, like Napoleon believing he was a demigod and could do anything. Bertille says her fiction is that she washes dishes only because she likes to, and Freddy says his fiction is that his tummy is invisible, so that he can go right on eating all he wants to. What is your fiction, Peter?"

Aleida was looking at him along with the others, and the consciousness of her expectant eyes taunted him with his inability to think of something amusing to say. The moment was so like the one when he had been ignominiously at the mercy of her gaze outside the livery stable after he had slid off the horse, that he felt again stripped of every shred of decent pretense and utterly exposed. Half a dozen other occasions when she had always seen him at some slight disadvantage were like spotlights that turned their glaring beams on him. The lovely day at the ski course was as if it had never been; her enthusiasm over his trips to Santa Cruz had lost all reality; only the virulent memory of Cristina's having her to tea and warning her off remained.

He fought off a sudden poignant regret at having somehow forfeited her youthfulness. *First there had been Sibby to stand between him and her, and now Cristina—there was no help for it!* He felt swept along on a sudden wave of recklessness.

"My fiction is courage," he said.

"Oh, that's charming," Gladys chirruped as if he were a child that had said something bright, and Bertille added with almost equally exasperating literal-mindedness, "I don't believe it; I bet you got lots of guts. . . ."

He was furious with himself. He had spoken with utter disregard of how it would sound because in his mood of bleak desolation and sudden sharp-sightedness he had seemed to be making an important discovery about himself and because for a moment there been a perverse pleasure in not caring whether everybody knew. The only blessing was that Gladys turned almost immediately to Piggot. "Now, Ralph, I simply must know what your fiction is!"

He was out of the limelight at least. He took a cigarette and risked a glance toward the window seat. Aleida was smiling—a radiant, friendly smile that was unmistakably meant for him. It was as if they were at Hyde Park again, and Santa Fe and Cristina's claim on him had ceased to exist. She was wonderful even when she wasn't on skis! For a moment it did not even matter that Aleida sat beside Collard and had probably come to the party with him. He grinned back and then forced himself to look away, so as not to seem to presume on her generosity—she had after all merely meant to let him know that he had a friend in the room! What, he wondered while he sat half turned away from her, had happened to the young doctor to whom she was supposed to be engaged? Not that it could conceivably mean anything to him when she was getting married and where. There was one way of finding out, of course: he could write Anne tonight.

As he sat listening to the talk around Gladys, doubt assailed him about Aleida's smile. He had imagined most of it! Next time he looked at her she would be remote again and Cristina would be between them like a haze. But when the discussion broke up and he lost sight of her and then saw her again—with the bald man with the blond mustache; already in her tweed coat and saying good-by to people near the arched doorway into the hall—the smile for him was back on her face. Her eyes made him come up to her.

"Peter, I don't think you have met my father. Father, this is Anne's brother, Peter Domanig."

The blond man held out his hand. "Oh, yes, I've heard about you. How's Anne?" He had a firm grip. His voice was low-pitched, pleasant, male. He looked to be about Praither's age, somewhere around forty-five, but he was much less high-strung and jittery, more vigorous. He declined to let himself be thanked for the skis. "They'll do you more good than they will me. You just keep them or give them to somebody else. I've got another pair and I don't even use those. How do you like Tesuque?"

They exchanged the usual bits of information. At the end Aleida's father said cordially, "If you ever come out to Pecos look us up!"

"Yes, do," Aleida echoed him. And while it was true, Peter told himself, that she had no choice and had had to say something of the sort, she might have sounded merely polite, whereas her invitation had been warm. Nor had anyone compelled her to smile again when she had nodded good-by.

Her smile had given him the most extraordinary lift. So had the discovery as she had stood beside her father that she had exquisitely modeled brows and that there was something exciting about the petal-like glow of the skin below her eyes. So had the fact that she had left with her father and that Larry Collard had stayed behind.

He made up almost gratefully to the biologist. "I suppose you know Mr. Gibbs. . . ."

"Edmund? Yes, sure I do."

"I just had an invitation to look him up. What kind of ranch has he got?"

"A very fine one. Right on the Pecos River. He runs five hundred head of cattle."

"He doesn't look like a cattleman."

"Oh, they come in all sizes and colors, but I guess I know what you mean—no, he hasn't been a rancher all his life. He started out to be a lawyer in the East; then he inherited this ranch and couldn't find the right man to manage it."

"He seems like a nice fellow."

"Ed's a good guy. He's a two-fisted drinker and he's read a few books."

"Do you see much of him? He doesn't seem to go to many parties."

"He hasn't been going out much since his wife died. I run out to Pecos a couple of times a month, and we get in a little chess."

"You mean your Spanish girl friends let you get away that long?"

"Now and then I get a night off. . . ."

But what good was all this information to him? What did it matter who saw Aleida and when? He certainly would never be able to take up the invitation and see where Aleida lived. Cristina would be waiting for him tomorrow afternoon and every afternoon. . . .

CHAPTER ELEVEN

The Indians Have Roots

HE FELT trapped.

Cristina's exotic pallor and taut, fine-boned elegance which could still rouse his passion, the aura that clung to her of persistent, unaccountable misfortune in the past and his reluctance to add another hurt, but most of all her importance to Geoff—were like so many strands that tied him to her.

He got a glimpse of just how greatly she mattered to Geoff. The evening before they were all to go to an Indian dance, he ran into him at the garage. Geoff was wearing his riding breeches and boots, but he explained, "We didn't go riding today. Tina had an appointment with the dentist this morning and she didn't feel up to it afterward. She may have to have some teeth out, poor dear. Frightful for her to have to lose teeth when she is still so young. . . ."

And suddenly the concern in Geoff's eyes and the tone in which he had said "so young" made him see what torture it must be for Geoff to have to stand by and watch him constantly being preferred by Cristina and

227

not even returning her love. Yet Geoff must hide whatever he felt for fear of not being entertaining enough and perhaps losing what little he had of her.

He remembered the beautiful bunch of red roses Cristina had had on the piano a week ago and her gay explanation that they had been sent by Geoff. "They're in honor of a secret anniversary!"

"I didn't know you had any secrets with Geoff," he had said rather tartly.

"Oh, you'd be surprised! We've known each other for a long time."

"And it runs to red roses. Very passionate. I thought you couldn't stand him."

"Darling, you mustn't be so literal. I love Geoff. I'm terribly fond of him."

He remembered the dozens of errands and problems with which she still turned to Geoff almost instinctively.

They were, he told himself, like three figures chasing one another around and around on some ancient Greek vase: Cristina with her arms outstretched after him, Geoff desperately reaching for Cristina, and he himself pursuing Geoff. The fact that he wanted to escape the pattern on the vase only added to his sense of guilt.

Every minute with her now was pregnant with the menace of some reproach from her—spoken or, what was even worse, without words. She gave a violent little start sometimes when she had not heard him come up behind her, so that he was alarmed and cloaked his contrition in a cruel kind of surprise—"Goodness, how nervous you are!"—or in an equally cruel solicitude—"What makes you start like that, darling?"

She tried to sound as if she were joking. "I'm afraid of you."

"What nonsense!"

"You're so cold, darling. I actually have nightmares about you! Last night I dreamed that I was downtown and that I had to walk around and around the plaza with a ball and chain on my feet. I was fearfully ashamed and I tried frantically to hide the ball under my coat, so that people wouldn't see. I was in a frenzy, I was so mortified."

She sounded amused enough for him to dare to treat it as a joke. "Where did I come in?"

"You? You just laughed and walked away."

"It must have been one of the days when I forgot my boy-scout oath. I don't quite see what the ball and chain have to do with us." It was ironic that *she* should claim to be the prisoner. . . .

"It's just that I hate this sort of life we're leading—constantly having to make excuses for not going out to dinner alone or for not having people over in the evening. People are talking! Don't you think I know?"

"What do you care? People are going to talk, no matter what we do...." Indignantly he thought: she's lived a pretty fast life in Europe— she says so herself—and has never given a hang what anybody thought; why suddenly all this concern about people? ... "You shouldn't have such violent dreams!"

"I can't help it. I'm always dreaming that you're either shoving me off the roof or kicking me down some stair or pushing me out of a car. It's horrible!"

"It's defamation of character...."

He tried to tell himself that she was being hysterical, but her night-mare anguish found a guilty echo in him. It added to his uneasiness. It made him stiffen and draw into an invisible shell before he could check himself each time she came to sit on the arm of his chair, so that she had cause for saying, "There you go again. I must learn never to touch you."

"It's just that I wasn't expecting it. I was afraid I'd spill the drink on you...." He multiplied excuses, but he made no move—as he had done formerly—to draw her back against his shoulder and reassure her with caresses and words. He realized that there were dozens of things she did that made him impatient now: he hated it when she wore the Fortuny gown because he had persuaded himself that the velvet bodice and the long, trailing skirt made her look haggard and old; he shrank when he saw her twist the end of a new cigarette into her silver and ebony holder because he knew in advance exactly how she would blow out the smoke in long, slightly affected puffs; he waited tensely each time she mentioned Geoff, to see whether she was going to be caustic again; he was secretly indignant—because it reminded him again of her age—when she told him about her teeth....

"No, only on one side—up here where I have a bridge. It's really only two," she said, "but that's bad enough. He isn't sure they have to come out; he wants to watch them for two or three weeks. I had a ghastly time sitting and thinking about it all day. I almost came to Tesuque to see you this afternoon."

"Why didn't you? I could have tried to cheer you up. After all if it's all over to one side it won't show one bit; and you said yourself it's only a question of two teeth. I knew a fellow who had all his teeth knocked out playing football when he was in high school. It isn't anything tragic. Besides, it may all turn out to be a false alarm."

"Do you really think so? Oh, I keep hoping it is! A dentist in Cannes scared me the same way one time and he turned out to be wrong, thank God! I won't take this man's word for it anyway; I have a wonderful dentist in Paris who's always taken care of my teeth. It'll just mean that I'll have to leave here much earlier than I had planned. Thank you, darling, for cheering me up."

He returned the pressure of her cheek against his and said, "I haven't even started yet. Wait till I go after that dentist's teeth! . . ."

He stood in front of the small mirror on his kitchen wall the next morning—still naked, and his chest and legs still tingling from the cold well water he had splashed all over himself in the rubber tub—while he was getting ready to go into town to pick up Cristina for the trip to the Santo Domingo pueblo. He filled his lungs full of air until his chin touched his chest, and thrust back his elbows and whipped his fists over at an imaginary opponent a couple of times, and approved of his shoulders and arms in the mirror, and told himself: *I've run away twice—first from Corinne in Pittsburgh, and then from Sibby. Granted that Corinne was a simpering boarding-house queen who wanted to turn me into a replica of her former bookkeeper husband and that Sibby was a case of belated calf love which I found I had outgrown almost as soon as I got into it, still the fact remains that in each case I wrote a letter and you might say ran away. This time if I run, I lose Geoff. This time I've got to slug it out!*

He had no great desire to see the Indian dance in spite of Mary Orr's bullying—"It's tremendous! You can't imagine what it's like to see hundreds of Indians dancing all at the same time. There's something about the rhythm that gets right into your blood. I keep hearing that drum for weeks afterward. You simply must go, Peter!"

He had bantered, "You'd be surprised at all the things I can do without. I'm a mountain of incuriosity where the Indians are concerned."

"Don't let Jim Hopper hear you."

"He's heard. I buy a fifteen-cent Zuni ash tray off him once a year to prove my devotion to the Indians."

"What about Cristina? *She* wants to go."

He had grimaced. "There it is. . . ."

Cristina not only wanted to see the dance but she had let them in for a picnic lunch with Grace Wyatt and the carful of people she was taking down. The prospect of having to spend an hour or more with the truck driver protégé and with the priest, whom Grace had asked along and whose presence invariably imposed a certain constraint on everybody when there was only a small crowd, had had most to do with putting him off.

The only thing that reconciled him to the trip was that Larry Collard, whose car had broken down, was to come in the Isotta with them. It cheered him that Collard was not going to Santo Domingo with Aleida; but quite apart from that, he had come to like Collard more and more in the past few months. The fact that Collard not only was a scientist but had held a professorship commanded a secret respect akin to awe from him, which neither the artists nor Piggot, the writer, did. There was also a fascination about Collard's throwing away his life by not staying in a sanatorium, since it was hard to believe that he was so sick that there was no help for him. His looks belied the reports that practically had him six feet under the ground. He had the easy, big-framed, masculine assurance that Praither was always trying to prove he had, and he was healthy enough to stay up half the night indulging his apparently insatiable taste for the company of Spanish girls half his age and for Mexican dance halls. "T.b. makes them sexy as hell," Hal Kemp said. . . . He was quite as intelligent as Piggot, without Piggot's pontifical air of settling every problem for good. He had proved on closer acquaintance to have a tart, gusty humor that was a relief after the artists' stodgy earnestness; Peter had liked him ever since Collard had turned away from one of Pettingill's prissy-voweled disquisitions on the subtleties of linden-flower tea and had said, "Guy smells like a pet coon!"

It was a pleasant drive. The Santo Domingo pueblo proved to be about halfway between Santa Fe and Albuquerque. After they had gone some twenty-five miles, Collard made Cristina turn off the highway where a crude wooden marker pointed out the road. It was little more than a pair of tracks winding across the desert up and down arroyos and sand dunes. They passed the Kemps, who had pulled off to one side to let their dog out for a run. Chet Orr had said, "What I like best about the spring corn dance is that it's exactly the same dance as on the fourth of August but you don't get all the tourists you get then. There's usually just a handful of white people and that's all." It did not look like that this time. Nearly the whole artist crowd had talked about going down, and in the Fonda lobby that morning a flock of fashionable tourists, who had interrupted their spring migration from the swank Arizona winter resorts to New

York to hang around Santa Fe for a few days, had been clustered at the desk inquiring about transportation to the dance.

They came to a railroad track, a water tower, a few shanties, and a creek lined by cottonwood trees. Their road veered from the railroad track and the creek into the desert again and meandered on for more bumpy miles. They drove around some black rocks and suddenly they all heard the drum—an imperious, low thudding that seemed to come out of the earth. Instinctively Cristina speeded up, but not for long. The road dipped down into a basin, and they caught up with Grace Wyatt's big old Cadillac which was barely creeping along, so that they were forced to slow down to a crawl. They had one endless mile of it, in the course of which the muffled pounding of the drum grew gradually higher in pitch and more insistent; and then suddenly they could see the big adobe church beyond some towering cottonwood trees and a great sprawling cluster of squat dobe houses, from beyond which came the sound of chanting along with the throbbing beat of the drum. One sensed the existence, beyond the rows and clusters of houses, of a great open square.

They pulled up beside the Cadillac in the open space below the church where about a dozen other cars were parked—greeted Grace Wyatt and Father Joslin and Gladys and Jack Fettis, and started out with them along the one wide street that clearly led toward the center of the pueblo. It was after eleven. They had decided to watch the dance for half an hour or so before they had lunch. Father Joslin, who was walking on ahead with Gladys and Geoff's student, was acting as guide. Grace Wyatt had taken possession of Cristina. Grace's chauffeur was bringing up the rear with a couple of camp chairs under each arm. Collard glanced up toward the church, with its wooden gallery across the front and the two rearing horses painted on the wall above the huge door, and said, "I hope the padre is *persona grata* today. Last time I was here the Indians had just had a row with their priest and made him get out. They wouldn't let a priest anywhere near the pueblo. These Santo Domingans are a rough bunch."

"They look it!" The few Indians they passed, Peter saw, were not friendly like the Tesuque Indians, or handsome like the ones in Taos. They were short and chunky, and they had broad, Mongoloid faces and a disconcerting way of looking past one with their black, shiny-pebble eyes, as if they were not aware of the white man's presence at all.

"The time you get a taste of how tough they can get is when they catch anyone trying to take a photograph. Last August some smart boy was trying to take a few shots with a Leica he had inside his shirt. The *Koshares*—you'll see them: they're the fellows who weave in and out among the regular dancers and are supposed to be the spirits of the ancestors who supervise the dance—jumped on his camera and then on his nice new panama hat, and it looked for a while as if they'd beat him up. Not that I blamed them much. The dances are part of their religion, and I don't like wise guys. Here we are. . . ."

They had come into the upper end of a huge dusty rectangle that stretched on and on between two rows of houses. Down near the center of the long plaza, a round dobe structure that looked like a fort and had a long ladder slanting up through a hole in its flat roof, and the dense crowd of Indian spectators on either side of the drum-shaped building, prevented Peter from seeing the men who were producing the eerie, deep-voiced chant. More Indians were crowded together on the roofs of the houses and under the crude portales in front. The pueblo looked bigger than the one at Taos, poorer, ugly, stark. Something like pity welled up in Peter at the desert drabness that lay over everything—a pity that seemed immediately thrust back at him by the haughty self-sufficiency and aloof power proclaimed by the chant.

The vibrant beat of the drum, which kept strangely ringing on like an organ tone, as if the hard-packed clay ground acted as a sounding board, and the deep-throated male voices seemed to Peter to engulf him in a sea of sound. It seemed even a little difficult to breathe in the sound-thickened air. At the same time Peter's legs carried him forward with a bouncing eagerness that also was born of the sound.

They got closer to the round building with the ladder and began to catch glimpses over the heads of the crowd of what was going on. Four long rows of dancers stretched down the plaza, a row of women alternating with a row of men. The women were in black dresses that left one shoulder bare, and there was a curious green board fastened on each one's head like a foot-high tiara. The men were naked except for a white ceremonial kilt of some thick, woven stuff, and they had bunches of bright green feathers tied to their glossy, long black hair which was cut in bangs and hung down loosely in the back just like the women's. To the left, at the far end of the farthest line, was the drum—a big one, such as people liked to get for coffee tables. It was heavy enough to make the drummer lean far back to counterbalance its weight as he held it by the leather handle with his left hand. Just beyond the drum clustered the men who were doing the chanting, a group of at least eighty or a hundred Indians huddled in a loose circle, dressed in bright-colored silk blouses that hung outside their white trousers like pajama coats. And then there were the men Collard had talked about, the spirits of the ancestors, painted all over with white and yellow clay and with black stripes to suggest a skeleton, and with only a loincloth around their middle and bunches of dry cornhusks tied to their clay-whitened hair.

Cristina turned around to see whether he and Collard were coming. Peter smiled at her with guilty alacrity, because he realized that for minutes he had been completely oblivious of her, but when Jack Fettis too picked that very instant to turn around, his dislike of Geoff's pupil made him look away and turn to Collard. "I didn't know the Indians went in for forts."

"That's a kiva—one of their underground ceremonial chambers. Over there is another one, down by those houses. See the ladder sticking up? As I understand it, the public is divided into two big clans, the summer people and the winter people, and each one of them has a kiva."

Father Joslin and the others were heading toward the side of the plaza, toward the houses, and then walking down past the crowded portales. They waved to the Orrs and Carol Praither, saw the Kemps on one of the roofs on the other side of the plaza, and found Geoff, Piggot and Jeanne under a portale where there were comparatively few people, so that they were all able to squeeze in, and Grace Wyatt's chauffeur even found room enough to set up all four of the campstools he had brought for the women.

By standing behind Jeanne Lauber, who was sitting on the low adobe wall of the porch beside several Indian women, Peter was able to see perfectly. He was glad that there were a number of Indians between him and Cristina and the others, so that he did not have to talk. He still felt nothing but annoyance at the insistent pounding of the drum. His vague disgruntlement made it hard to pay any attention to the dance. His eyes roved from the bright-colored shirts of the chorus and the woven red belts the chunky, shapeless women had around their middle, to the two white girls on the roof on the opposite side of the plaza and to Jim Hopper who was coming down the ladder from another roof.

His eyes kept on taking in isolated details. A dobe stair, he saw, led up to the roof of the kiva; an elderly Indian was just going up it and then down the slanting ladder through the hole in the roof. The men dancers had some kind of bushy-tailed animal pelt fastened to the kilt in the back. The women were barefoot and held a little bunch of spruce sprigs in each hand. Spruce seemed to be of special significance in the dance: the men not only had a few sprigs tied to each arm with a white band, but they also held a small bunch of it in their left hand—to balance the gourd rattle in their right.

Jim Hopper was crossing the plaza down below the far line of specta-tors. A few minutes later he appeared in front of the portale and threaded his way between the Indian women and children in front to say hello to Grace Wyatt, Cristina, Father Joslin and the rest.

The four long files of dancers were drawing closer together. The pitch of the drum and the rhythm of the beat changed abruptly; the chorus, still chanting, faced toward the west. It was clear that some new figure of the dance was about to begin. Peter felt a stirring of curiosity. The four files broke into four parts, and presently in each one of the four segments the four lines fused and formed one single line, but so that men and women alternated in the new file which doubled back on itself and became a circle. The four big circles broke up and became straight lines again in an intricate evolution that arrayed the dancers like an army in an ancient Chinese picture Peter had once seen. At no time did the dancers miss a beat. Their whole weight came jarring down on one heel with the little skip and kick that made up each step with trancelike regularity.

He asked Hopper, "How long do they keep that up?"

"All day, but there are two complete teams and they take turns. The summer people dance for a while, and then the winter people take over. You can see the second chorus and the dancers down by the other kiva— see them? The thing to be here for is the close of the dance at sundown when both groups dance together."

"I didn't think they could keep it up for very long, especially those kids." For at the end of each of the four lines when they were parallel again, there were children tapering all the way down from nearly grown boys and girls to little tots about whom Gladys and Cristina raved— "Aren't they darling? Look at the little boy at the end, Geoff! Larry, have you noticed the one at the end? Isn't he sweet?"

"Even an hour of it at a time is pretty strenuous," Hopper said. "There was an ex-football star from Stanford here a couple of summers ago who bet he could keep up with the Indians. He got groggy after half an hour or so. Of course that was in August, and it was hotter then."

It was hot enough. The two thousand feet they had dropped down into the valley soon after they had left Santa Fe made a difference; the sun beat down on one here as if Santo Domingo were a thousand miles farther south than Santa Fe, or as if suddenly it were no longer just spring but the middle of July. Cristina had long ago taken off her gray wool coat, and Gladys was complaining of the heat and of thirst. Father Joslin ran his finger around the inside of his Roman collar, and Geoff, who had been standing out in front of the portale in the full sun, dabbed his forehead with his handkerchief. Only Grace Wyatt, whose gray curls peeked out under a blue, silk-trimmed hat and who wore jiggling pendant earrings and a blue serge coat and looked exactly as if she were about to start out from her hotel to have lunch somewhere in New York, did not seem to mind the heat. "Are you hot, dear?" she asked Cristina. "It can't be too hot for me. I'm *frileuse.*"

"Hot?" Gladys shrilled. "I'll say it's hot."

"Now isn't that funny—and I'm not hot at all. Here, dear, feel my nose. . . ." And Cristina had to let her hand be raised to the tip of Grace Wyatt's nose.

They watched again until—without warning, without the white man's need to round out a conclusion and taper off, with the calm abruptness of an animal lying down to rest—the dance came to an end. The drum simply stopped. The chorus broke up and the bright-shirted men began to walk toward the kiva in no particular order. The dancers, men and women, still more or less in their four lines followed along behind. But within seconds after the drum had stopped, another drum down at the right on the other side of the plaza took up the beat. The second group of dancers who had been waiting in the alley between some houses came out into the square, the man with the drum and the chorus at the head, and moved up toward the place the others had just left. In a matter of minutes the new dancers had lined up; the chorus had begun to chant; one of the dozen or so supposed spirits daubed with black and yellow clay stopped to fasten the spruce twigs that were coming loose on a little boy's arm, working with a sort of priestly concentration and with somewhat surprising gentleness. Then as abruptly as the other group had stopped, this new one began to dance.

There were turtles painted in black on the backs of two of the spirits of the ancestors, and fishes on the backs and thighs of several others, Peter noticed. He asked Jim Hopper about them.

"Fertility symbols, and the fish are supposed to suggest rain to the cosmic powers, just like the long fringe that hangs down the right leg of each man from his belt, and the sea shells the men wear. The *tablitas* on the women's heads have to do with rain, too. Those steps that are cut in them are standard Indian shorthand for clouds."

Everything was symbolic, it appeared: the evergreen, which stood for life; the foxskins that dangled down each man's back from his belt; the skunk fur with which the men's deerskin boots were trimmed in back, the sleigh bells fastened below the knees to the men's legs, the little bunches of green parrot feathers tied to their hair, the fact that the women danced in bare feet.

"What about those long strings of red beads around the men's necks— what are those?"

"Coral."

"How did they get that?"

"From California—possibly Old Mexico. The pueblos have been trading with the Indians down there for hundreds of years. That's how they got their macaw and parrot feathers and the Aztec banner they use in the summer dance. . . ."

Gladys had spotted the members of the string quartet who were stopping off in Santa Fe for a few days and whom she had somehow corralled for the supper party she was giving after the dance and bullied into promising to play. Three of the four men wore spectacles and all of them looked almost touchingly out of place with their musicians' gentleness and their solemn blue serge suits among the tweedy tourists. Gladys insisted on rushing off and bringing them to the portale where they smiled and squirmed under her introductions and attentions before they could finally excuse themselves and drift away.

"Nice fellow," Hopper said about the musician who had looked a little like Schubert. "I hope he didn't mean he was going to write down the music now. The Indians are death on that."

Grace Wyatt was asking, "Are you hungry, Father Joslin, dear?" She consulted Cristina and Gladys, "Lunch, dear?" She summoned Geoff without inviting Piggot or Jeanne with the bland highhandedness of old age. "Jim," she explained while the chauffeur collected the camp chairs and she marshaled her guests with one last glance like a general reviewing his troops before she took Geoff's arm, "has a favorite place. He says there are no snakes. . . ."

Jim Hopper made them drive back toward the tiny railroad junction they had passed. On the far side of the creek was a stand of young cottonwoods, all feathery and on tiptoe still in their spring green. It was a charming spot. Grace's chauffeur, who had slipped on a white houseman's jacket, set up the camp chairs again, brought two big picnic hampers from the Cadillac and even a bucket with three bottles of meticulously swathed and chilled Rhine wine. There were chicken and salad and fruit and cheese, and there was the delicious wine which Grace shipped out from her cellar in the East; there was also the chauffeur to wait on them, and a white tablecloth and a chest of silver, so that it was all much more like lunch in a French garden than a picnic even though most of them sat on the two traveling rugs Jack Fettis had spread on the ground.

Fettis was in his element. He could—in between toadying to Grace and clumsily flirting with Cristina whom he persisted in calling "Christine"— in the guise of looking after Grace Wyatt's guests, subtly turn himself into the host to whom one was somehow beholden for food and drink. He was up and down like a jumping jack passing things after the chauffeur had been told to have his own lunch and had withdrawn to the other side of the Cadillac. He alternately smothered Geoff with doglike devotion and solicitude as if he were the aged Titian, and boisterously thumped him on the back until Geoff's stiffening shoulders discouraged that. He patronized even Grace's guest of honor, the priest, in his exuberance. And he sulked like a scolded puppy when Jim Hopper and Father Joslin started to talk about the Indians, so that his newcomer ignorance of the subject shut him out.

Jim Hopper was telling about the Indians' belief that the Rio Grande Valley was the vital center of the earth and that the ground all through Western New Mexico was potent with some vital magnetism which the dancers invoked with their feet. "They believe that the powers that regulate the universe live somewhere underground right here."

"I thought the Indians pumped the pep into the earth—" Fettis had to show off what little he had learned—"like when they run races in the winter to strengthen the sun. That's how a guy at San Ildefonso explained it to me."

"It's both. The way the Indians look at it there is a vital current that flows in both directions between them and the earth. They charge the earth like a battery when they dance, but power also flows back into them."

Fettis' carrot-thatched head was thrust up at an angle that promised more bickering, but Father Joslin forestalled him. "Wasn't it Antaeus who drew his strength from the earth?"

Jim Hopper grinned. "You've got me. I wasn't in school that day."

Gladys, sounding like Piggot at his most portentous and humorless, went off on some dreary world-saving tack. "But Antaeus had faith in the earth; that's why he could draw strength from it. The Indians still have that kind of faith, and we haven't. I think white people have lost all contact with nature and things, Father Joslin, don't you agree?"

They all agreed that the Indians had an almost fierce sense of reverence for nature and all living things. Collard, twisting the stem of his green Mexican wineglass between his slender fingers, told about some herbs he had asked an Indian medicine man to bring him from the Truchas peaks. "All I wanted was a couple of handfuls, just enough to identify the plant and maybe make a rough analysis. Instead, he brought me a whole bale. There I was, with the couch looking like a hayrack and all kinds of beetles coming out of the herbs and starting up the walls and across the floor. But was I allowed to take the stuff out on the trash pile and burn it? Not much. Some spirit—either in the herbs or up on the Truchas peaks, I forget which—was going to be mortally offended if those herbs weren't treated affectionately. They had to be given decent burial in a fresh mountain stream. I had to trundle all the way out to Pecos and find a spot in the river where nobody was likely to disturb that fodder before the Indian was satisfied."

"That's exactly what I mean," Gladys stridently took possession of the story; "the Indians actually practice love. All we do is hate."

Father Joslin had remained cheerfully unperturbed. "That's not what our Lord taught: He commanded us to love."

"I know, but nobody does. Look at the different denominations: they all hate one another."

Unexpectedly, considering his usual gentleness, Jim Hopper sided with her. "I'm a little inclined to agree with that. I believe that God exists only to the extent that we love one another."

"What an amiable heresy!"

"Why is it a heresy, Father Joslin?" Gladys challenged him.

"Because that would make God the creature of our virtues, whereas God doesn't depend for his existence even on our love. He would still be around even if we all turned into black monsters of evil."

"But you do agree, Father Joslin," Gladys persisted, "that the Indians have got something we haven't?"

It was easy to see why Grace Wyatt was so devoted to the priest. He had a ready laugh, an open glance and a warm, male voice, and he was good-natured and deft, as now in eluding Gladys' argumentativeness. "Oh, there is a lot that's good in some of the pagan religions. The pagans are quick to let you know about it, too." He chuckled. "I found that out when I first went to China as a missionary. While I'd been in the seminary, I'd had dreams of carving out great chunks of heathendom and bringing

them all into the Church. But when I got there I discovered they were trying to convert me!"

Cristina was all charm. Her voice was vibrant again as it had been in
the fall. "Who won, Father?"

"Well, you might say the Almighty did: I made a few converts, and all
that my Chinese friends could do with me was to make me appreciate their
poetry. But it wasn't for lack of trying on their part; the Chinese can give
a chamber of commerce pointers on bragging when it comes to their
culture."

The tension brought on by Gladys' tactlessness had been relaxed. They
talked about the difference between American and Chinese turquoise now.
But Peter found that there was still some unpleasantness in store for him.
He helped Fettis and the chauffeur take the picnic hampers back to the car.

All at once Fettis said, "You don't like me, do you?"

It was like Fettis to drive one into a corner, Peter reflected irritably. He
said, "Do you expect everybody to like you? I don't."

"Is it something I've done?"

He seemingly had no shame; he wasn't housebroken yet. And yet
Peter felt a stirring of sympathy for him. He said as casually as he could,
"Forget it. What do you care whether I like the way you draw, or not?
Everybody has his own style, and that's that."

Fettis' exuberance was enough to revive Peter's antagonism. "Hell, is
that all? I don't mind if you don't like my work. I like your lithographs,
but that's all right. . . ." He was irrepressible. Fortunately they were
joined by the others and there was no more chance for Fettis to elaborate
on his declaration of love.

There were a good many more cars parked outside the pueblo than
when they had left. The summons of the drum was much more irresistible now; the wide, irregular street that led into the plaza was like a fun-
nel sucking one into the square; the sun blazing down seemed to mock
at the white man's certain enslavement to the insistent sound. But the
magic was not so compelling as all that after all! Neither Grace Wyatt nor
Father Joslin was coming back into the pueblo—Grace claimed she was
tired, and Father Joslin had some work waiting for him—and at the last
minute Gladys decided to go back with them, to check on the preparations
for the string-quartet concert and the Spanish supper she had planned
for the evening. "Just chili and beans," she called after them from the
car. "Don't forget, come right after the dance! . . ."

The spectacle had not changed in the time they had been gone, except that the more blinding glare of the sun made the bright colors of the silk blouses of the chorus appear metallic almost and that the occasional sharp gust of wind, which raised sudden yellow clouds of dust, gave an odd edge of defiance and flintlike obstinacy to every movement of the dancers' hands and feet.

They were able to squeeze in among the Indian women and children and tourists under the portale again, and there was even room to set up the two camp chairs Grace Wyatt had made them take, one for Cristina and one for Jeanne Lauber, who with her ridiculous Chinese parasol stuck out at an angle just under the edge of the portale roof was taking up enough room for two. Peter and Collard stood behind them for a while. Then, when Jeanne repeatedly raked their chests with her parasol and all but poked Collard in the eye, they moved to the other side of the pine post next to Cristina. Geoff and Fettis and Jim Hopper were wandering down the plaza to cross to the other side and get up on one of the crowded roofs.

It was hardly possible to miss the new arrivals among the white spectators. They were nearly all the type of hard-enameled, wearily elegant wealthy tourist who could be seen arriving at the Fonda almost any afternoon to kill a few days. They were—from force of habit, because they were so used to chasing perfect golfing weather around the globe—already in midsummer clothes. One of the two young women a little to the right of Collard was vigorously—the gold coins on her gypsy bracelet tinkling on her wrist—rubbing sun-tan lotion on her face. On the roof across the plaza two girls sat with their legs folded under them and displayed most of their handsome, tanned thighs under their short skirts. The two men standing behind the two girls looked thoroughly bored.

Nor were some of the older tourists any less conspicuous through their obvious lack of interest in the Indian dance. A tall, slender woman in a striking white cape, with an exotic hood of the same thin white wool as the cape pulled carelessly up over her washed-out, blond hair and over her ravaged face and restless eyes, was coming down along the houses, eying the spectators through a lorgnette. A twinkling, pink-cheeked, potbellied man, who was at least three inches shorter than she, followed about two steps behind. To Peter's horror, the woman stopped short when she saw Cristina and then rushed toward her with a histrionic gasp of delight. "Darling!"

Cristina's enthusiasm was controlled. "Nancy—I wasn't expecting you until Saturday. How nice!" All the same she had to respond to Nancy's kiss on each cheek.

"Roberto has to be in New York on the sixth. Besides, Tucson was getting frightfully hot. You remember Roberto, don't you?"

Roberto had livened up. His name was Smith, and there was nothing in the least exotic about him. All he wanted, Peter gathered presently, was the right company and a country-club porch and a nice long drink. Peter also learned from listening to Cristina and him that he and the haggard blonde had come to Arizona from Reno and that they were married only a few months.

There were introductions, the Indian women and children around them looking on with sidelong fascination while Nancy with her showy cape and her brittle assertiveness continued to hold the center of the stage. She was offered Jeanne's campstool, refused it and Cristina's, too, and insisted on standing beside Cristina's chair where she cut off the view of half-a-dozen Indian women behind her against the wall. Peter and Collard were stuck with Roberto, who wanted to talk.

Nancy and Roberto both talked! Peter pretended to make a choice and to listen to Nancy, whom he did not have to answer since she was addressing herself to Cristina, and from whom he could gradually edge away and pretend that she was a complete stranger to him. The maneuver did not save him from having to listen, though.

She seemed to feel obliged to give Cristina an exact account of everything she had done since she had sailed from France last fall—apparently, some months after Cristina had. She talked about stores in New York, about a ranch in Reno where she had stayed, about some man in Paris named Nicky who—to judge from her tone and from the fact that she presently mentioned him a second time—was considered by her to have some sentimental claim to Cristina's interest. With almost the identical knowing undertone lining her crisp society voice, she inquired about Geoff and then Ralph. "Why, Cricri, how too perfect! I can't wait to see the darlings." She trained her lorgnette on the ladder near which Geoffrey and Piggot were standing now on the other side of the plaza. "Roberto, Geoff and Ralph are here!"

As if to keep her from probing further, sidetrack her, Cristina asked in her most caressing tone, "Where did you ever find the lovely cape?"

"But you've seen it, darling. I had the most divine Arab run it up for me last spring in Marrakech. So useful. It's exactly like a burnoose, except for the weight." If Cristina's question had been intended as a warning, Nancy had either missed it or—which was more likely—was deliberately ignoring it. "Cricri," she asked—and Peter's French was up to it and made him look woodenly toward the dancers—"*lequel?*"

Cristina seemed after all not reluctant to point him out. She turned around after only the briefest hesitation; her silvery-gray eyes had the soft radiance which they usually had only when she was about to give herself to him as she asked, "Peter, do you have the keys to the car?'

He had to enter into the comedy. He fumbled in his pocket for the keys and was aware while he was doing so of Nancy's brash scrutiny through the lorgnette. "Yes, I have them."

"Thank you, dear. I just wanted to make sure." Her eyes let go of him with a caress.

He tried to put his attention on the dance; yet he found it as difficult as before, even though Roberto had given up hope of drawing Collard into any sort of sustained conversation and had dismissed Jeanne Lauber as unrewarding, too, and had just about resigned himself to a glum silence. For a few minutes Peter succeeded in losing himself in the dance by following the vigorous steps of the grimly painted spirits-of-the-ancestors, who appeared to be at liberty to dance anywhere between the four rows of men and women and whose dancing had something wild and vaguely terrifying about it. Then two of the *Koshares* suddenly interrupted their dancing and headed with sinister purposefulness toward a plump, elderly woman who was scribbling something on a tiny scratch pad. One of them tore the pad out of her hand, shredded the paper into little pieces, and let the wind carry them away. The other one possessed himself of the woman's little silver pencil, and—with the same solemn, savage thoroughness as his companion—twisted it, broke it and then stamped the pieces into the ground. After that, Peter found it impossible to keep from listening to Nancy again.

She was telling Cristina about some woman she had run into on the train—Suzette, whom they had both known in school and who had been on her way home to Paris from Japan. "Cricri," she said with a kind of venom in her voice, "it's too absurd: she's going to be a grandmother in July! *Figure-toi—la petite Suzette!* Do you remember the time she went to Soeur Monique when we had eaten all her *caramels moux*, and the time we scared her with the story about the rattlesnake?"

But, then, they were even older than Suzette, who was to be a grandmother in July, and Cristina was as old as this woman with the haggish eyes and the sunken cheeks! Cristina must be older than she had said, Not that that mattered by itself. . . .

His anger turned against Nancy, with her lorgnette and her white cape. What a frump! Why did Cristina constantly have people around her like Jeanne Lauber, who must have been sipping steadily from the thermos bottle in her raffia shopping bag and who looked blissfully befuddled again, or like Gladys or Grace? Was she trying to start a home for freaks?

He moved around in back of Nancy's husband and went to stand behind Collard and the girl who had been rubbing lotion on her face and arms before. He stayed there even after Nancy summoned Roberto and the two of them went out into the sun to join Piggot and Geoff. He stayed partly from a vague desire to punish Cristina for the frumps, and partly because the rather generously exposed breasts and the baldly inquisitive glances of the second of the two girls beside Collard had aroused his interest.

The dancers out in the hot sun had doubled their rows and gave the effect again of a massed Oriental army moving relentlessly into battle. It occurred to Peter that it was the tapestrylike intensity of the spectacle—the powerful treading of the men's legs not producing one inch of forward motion—which had reminded him of an old Chinese print he had once seen of an army descending a misty mountain road. There was, he told himself, enormous power behind all that restraint; Jim Hopper wasn't altogether wrong in making such a fuss over the Indians. One had the feeling that there was a great deal one ought to be able to learn from them; though what exactly—power, serenity, faith?—it would be hard to say.

Collard took half a step backward to stand beside him and glanced toward the roof on the other side of the plaza, where the two girls were still showing off their sleek legs, and said, "No wonder the laundries are going broke!" They were still grinning at each other when Ralph Piggot, who had either missed the Smiths or already escaped from them, leaned over the three squat Indian women in front of the portale and said almost angrily, as if he expected to be contradicted, "It's beautiful enough to make one cry!" His somber eyes were at their most soulful as they swept on from them to Cristina, who agreed, "Yes, it's beautiful, Ralph." Piggot straightened up, nodded like a schoolmaster who is content with his class, and walked on past the portale toward the upper end of the square.

Peter's eyes raced ahead of Piggot and scanned the horseshoe of spectators. *Aleida apparently had not come!*

The two girls on his right were talking about deep-sea fishing off the coast of Mexico, about a party given by the American consul in Guaymas, about some people they had expected to meet in a place called Mazatlán. There could be no question that their elaborate air of unconcern at being overheard, their pretense that neither Collard nor he mattered any more than the Indian women to them, was part of a campaign to capture Collard's attention and his. Collard proved he was aware of it, too. He held out his pack of cigarettes to him with an amused wink; but to Peter's surprise the amusement turned into an eager smile when the girl with the coin bracelet asked Collard for a light.

At least they were not crude. As soon as the girl had got her light she said coolly, "Thank you," and turned back to her friend to go on discussing a hotelkeeper in Guaymas who had failed to provide her with a decent boat. . . . No doubt, Peter reflected, in Long Island this summer when they'd be watching a tennis match or a polo game, they'd be talking about the corn dance in New Mexico—which they had hardly seen. All the same, if he were free—here without Cristina—it would be rather fun to see whether there was anything at all behind the brittle languor, the expensively simple clothes and the fussed-over skin beside a certain amount of tepid sex. But he was precisely not free like Collard, who for once was showing an interest in women not Mexican and who was striking a match now for the other girl's cigarette. Irritably, on the pretext of wanting to take off his coat, he stepped away from Collard and the two girls, closer to Cristina, and with his coat under his arm stared out at the dance.

It was gaining more of a hold on him all the time. The throbbing insistence of the drum seemed to travel through the ground directly into his feet and legs and up into the pit of his stomach. The turquoise-colored *tablitas* on the women's heads and the bunches of spruce in their hands seemed as familiar as if he had seen them all his life. The *Koshares* dancing with sudden passion and a trace of impatience—ancestors returned from their powerful god-world to teach their stumbling offspring the magic rites on which depended their life—somehow gripped one's heart. But what stirred him most was the chorus—the hundred or so elderly men in their bright-colored silk blouses and wrinkled white cotton pants, their arms stretched toward the western horizon and their hands gently hauling at the air, as if they were trying to draw down rain from the few infinitesimal clouds in the sky while the haunting chant rose from their throats.

It was incredible, Peter told himself, that he should feel so awed. Sleigh bells—garish shirts made of rayon probably—wooden tiaras that looked as if they had been cut out with a fret saw by a child—pajama pants! What gave it all such an air of majesty that it never occurred to him to smile? They were in earnest, that must be it—not with the deadly, neurotic seriousness of the white man, but with the utter and serene commitment of a magnificent animal faith. They were addressing the great powers of their universe—the sun, the clouds, the fertility of the earth—with complete confidence that, properly entreated, those powers could be swayed. Here were people with roots—Piggot ought to be satisfied! Though what good the Indians' way of life could do the white man was a little hard to see. All Piggot or anyone else could do was envy them and find out where the white man had gone wrong—no, how he could go right again, since everyone seemed convinced he had gone wrong. But how could one find the answer that reconciled a naïve faith like the Indians' with the machine age? There were no illuminations and no revelations any more these days. All the white man could do was to envy the Indians if he was so inclined and admire their art, like this dance."

Cristine and Jeanne had had their heads together for several minutes under Jeanne's bamboo parasol. Cristina's eyes beckoned him to her. "Jeanne," she said, "would like to go back with us. What would you think of starting back?"

Just when he was getting the feel of the dance and really beginning to see things! Why, they hadn't been here an hour yet! ...

"Now?"

"I'm getting sort of tired, aren't you?"

Just like Grace Wyatt, who was an old lady and had to have a chauffeur carry cushions and chairs for her! "No, but if you'd like to go ..."

"They are just doing the same things over again. I think we've seen it all, don't you?"

Like hell they had! Certainly the other team was waiting by the upper kiva, clustered on the outside stair and at the front of it, like a cast waiting in the wings to go on, and certainly they'd go through the same figures and steps as the group that was dancing now; but only someone who had seen the dance a great many times would remember the details well enough from one cycle to the next to be aware of any repetition. Besides, he had wanted to see the two groups dancing together at the end. ...

"Yes, of course," he said, "let's go."

"I don't suppose Larry will want to go yet?"

No, Collard did not want to go. Why should he when he was having a good time with the two girls he had picked up? Neither was anybody else leaving now, Peter fumed to himself as he walked behind Cristina and Jeanne with the two old-lady camp chairs hanging from his hand by his side. People were still arriving, getting out of a touring car, when they got to the Isotta. Even Aleida might still come.

Cristina wanted him to drive. They put Jeanne in the other corner of the front seat, and as long as they were bumping over the rough trail that cut across the desert, she kept chattering away to Cristina and saved him the necessity of having to talk; but once they got out on the highway, she promptly fell asleep and he was alone with Cristina. She said, "You didn't mind too much, darling, my taking you away?"

"No, it's perfectly all right. What do you suppose made you so tired?"

"I guess I didn't sleep well the last few nights. I always wilt in the sun. . . ."

He kept on silently bickering with her: when had they been out in the sun?

She went on, "I thought I'd lie down for an hour when we get home. I've asked Nancy and Roberto in for a drink when they get back."

"Tonight? What about the concert at Gladys'?"

"I don't think I'll go. I don't much feel like chamber music after that drum, do you? Besides I'm sort of all in from the heat. I'm going right to bed after I've given Nancy and the others a drink. I'm sorry to be such a washout, darling, but I just don't feel up to it."

"Then why are you giving a cocktail party?"

"It's not really a party. I'm just having the Smiths and Jeanne and I told Nancy to ask Geoff and Ralph and I thought I might ask the Oxnards to drop in. Don't you think Nancy is sort of fun? Roberto is rather dim but he's a good egg. Did you like them at all?"

"Not particularly."

"Oh, I'm not crazy about Nancy either, but I've known her all my life and I've got to make at least a gesture while they're here. Darling, you don't have to stay if you don't want to."

He could hear the plea behind her professed indifference: she would want him there for Nancy's sake. Well, he was not in the mood after that magnificent dance for either Nancy's affectations or for the flippancies of a cocktail party. It just happened that for once he would much rather go to Gladys'! If Cristina was too tired to listen to music, then she had no business having Nancy in. . . . He hardened himself. "If you don't mind, I'd rather not. It'd be pretty much of a rush. I'd have to dash out to Tesuque to change my clothes for that kind of crowd. Where did she get that 'Cricri'?"

"Oh, that was my nickname when I was in school. Nancy is the only one who still calls me that."

"Who is Nicky?"

"He's an old friend of mine in Paris—somebody I've known forever."

"She didn't sound as if he was just a friend."

She laughed 'way down in her throat. "He proposes to me once a year and he writes me every week. I owe him a letter, as a matter of fact. Nicky handles all my business affairs for me."

"Do you like him?"

"Oh, Nicky's a dear."

"But you didn't want to marry him?"

He felt jealous, not on his own account—he was willing to take an oath on it—but on Geoff's. He had never felt so coldly detached from her as now. It seemed incredible that she should not notice it.

"I may yet," she flirted. "Who knows? Darling—" she went on impulsively and sounded a little like a maiden aunt—"why don't you go to Gladys' by yourself. They say it's a very fine quartet, and you'll have fun."

He made only a perfunctory attempt to match her strained generosity. "I hate to go without you. But if you really don't think you want to come, perhaps I will. . . ."

CHAPTER TWELVE

Conclusions are Expensive

THERE was the usual crowd at Gladys', except that the four musicians whose music stands were already set up on the other side of the fireplace and who were somewhat awkwardly circulating among the other supper guests added an unaccustomed note of restraint and expectancy, and except that—Peter saw with a start of pleasure—Aleida was there. His delight was instantly damped by jealousy: she was with Collard again.

He ran into Piggot just inside the dining room. "I take it the party is all over, or didn't you go to Cristina's?"

"I take it your headache, which Cristina told us about, is much better!"

"My headache wore a white tent."

"I can sympathize with you somewhat. Nancy is not one of my major joys in life."

"Where is Geoff?"

"I believe they all intended to have dinner at the Fonda."

"Cristina, too?"

"That was my understanding. . . ."

Piggot's elaborate indifference made it clear he was being discreet. It only added to the resentment Peter had been nursing against Cristina ever since her friends had turned up, that she should have changed her mind about being tired. Some of his irritation crept into his attempt to bait Collard, who had come for second helpings with a plate in each hand. "What happened to the red-snapper girls? Wouldn't they take the hook?"

Collard grinned. "I had to throw them back."

"Too young?"

"No, barnacles."

"You looked as if you were having a big time."

"I'm easily amused." One could not resist Collard's grin; it was hard to believe he was sick. "The trouble is that I'm just as easily bored. . . ."

There was the usual talk, except that everyone was still keyed up from the dance and somewhat on edge from the dust storm which had blown up in the middle of the afternoon and was still sucking and pushing at the windowpanes.

"This wind," Mary Orr complained, "I wish this darn wind would stop. Every afternoon now for a month."

He had sat down between Dorothy Lambert and Mary Orr, opposite Praither and Helen Kemp and the musician with the Schubert face. He had stopped to say hello to Aleida on his way out of the dining room with his plate, and her response had quickened him with delight. But the consciousness of being tied to Cristina had instantly soured his joy, had made Aleida's smiling-eyed warmth appear as nothing more than kindness continued over from the other night, had made him unwilling to take her invitation seriously and squeeze into the snug group in the already crowded little alcove to which Collard had returned.

"It's killed all my new plants," Helen Kemp echoed Mary Orr.

"Oh, but you do have the most beautiful patio!" Dorothy Lambert comforted her. "You know you do."

"It just isn't worth it, Dorothy! Of course I know darn well that tomorrow I'm going to start all over again. . . ." Helen had been listening with one ear to her husband, who was telling a story about the feminine admirers of some supposedly highly amorous novelist. She called across to the fireplace, "George, I won't have you telling that story!"

George was evidently used to the byplay. He went on happily. ". . . publisher said, 'Madam, if all the women who want me to publish their memoirs of their life with Trowbridge were laid end to end, it would be the first time for——' "

"George, you're disgusting."

Kemp chuckled. The others laughed.

The musician with the thick glasses inquired politely what sort of flowers Helen raised, was questioned about his own garden in New Rochelle, about the success of the tour the quartet was on, about the number of hours he and his colleagues practiced each day. More and more, as people finished their coffee and the Spanish girls collected the dessert plates, the four musicians seemed to grow in stature and to become the center of each group. The lean cellist by the window explained that they had decided to play a quartet by a Spaniard named Arriaga because the music promised to clash least with the Indian music they had been hearing all day.

"Arriaga?" Jim Hopper asked. "Never heard of him. What is he— one of the moderns like De Falla?"

"He was a contemporary of Beethoven's," the violinist said. "He was born in 1806. He died when he was only nineteen."

"Nineteen!" Helen Kemp gasped. "That's younger than Schubert."

"At nineteen," Mary Orr said, "I was still practicing scales."

"Of course, Mozart——" Praither began but was cut short by Gladys who turned to the violinist with her most birdlike simper. "Do you think, Maestro, we . . ." She shepherded the musicians to the bedroom where they had left their instruments, made George Kemp and the rest of the group by the fireplace move to the lower end of the room, unnecessarily hushed everyone while the musicians were still arranging the music on their stands and adjusting the two floor lamps.

An entirely different kind of hush took possession of the room, seemed to emanate from the musicians and to return to them in softly beating waves when they raised their instruments and sat there with poised bows. It came as a relief and at the same time as an exquisite assault on one's expectancy, like the abrupt start of a laughing, sun-glistening shower on a May afternoon, when the first violinist gave a faint bob of the head and when suddenly sound silvered the air. As several times before, Peter noticed again how swiftly the impression of awkward, helpless gentleness that most musicians usually gave changed into an imposing air of authority the instant they began to play.

He kept watching rather than listening. Only a tiny, obedient part of his mind tried to snatch at the music as it flowed past and informed him that this quartet by a Spaniard he had never heard of had the enchanting elegance of Mozart and something of Haydn, too. But most of his attention rebelled against the very loveliness of the sound: what folly to ask them to listen to these delicate arabesques and coy oppositions and dainty advances and retreats after he and the others had been exposed to the powerful, bludgeoning rhythms of the Indian drum and chants all day long?

Yet gradually and in spite of his rebellion the music wove its spell over him. One passage after another spoke to him, made him want to hold onto it, escaped him like a playful bird. He found himself suddenly in league with the music against his own inattentiveness, indignant when the first movement proved very short.

He scowled involuntarily when Gladys whispered something to Mary Orr after the men had started to play again. There were deep-throated, stately phrases this time that succeeded one another with almost religious solemnity, for all that the plump first violinist had called the movement a minuet. There must be some mistake. There was nothing of the dance about this. Only, what difference did it make? This melodious gravity was ravishing. Oh, and here it came: here was something that was airy and gay! Now the stately cello-led measures again. Perhaps one of those ancient Easter dances in Spanish cathedrals—Jim Hopper wasn't the sort of person to make up that kind of thing even if it did sound incredible— could be danced to music like this. Ah, no, really, this was all much too short!

He prepared himself to enjoy the last movement. It added to his pleasure to see that Aleida was listening attentively. In an instant he was completely caught up again in the delightful pattern of sound. Why, this was beautiful! And to think that the man had been only nineteen. What a miracle genius was! . . . The beat of the Indian dance which he had felt sure would stay in his blood for days had receded until it seemed weeks since he had heard the drum. The amazing thing was that this music, which had seemed almost frivolous at first, should be able to hold its own against the memory of the Indian chants that had stirred him like a dark muttering deep down in the earth. But who *said* that this quartet, this white man's magic, was slight? It was airy and elegant, yes; it was the product of the subtle brain and of fastidious emotions rather than of the dark voices of the blood, but it was not weak. It had the same strength as a beautifully designed suspension bridge or an exquisitely lacy Chinese sculpture carved out of the hard white jade! It had the civilized man's strength.

The others echoed his enthusiasm over the music and his wonder at the composer's youth while they stood around and lionized the four musicians who presently excused themselves with the plea of being exhausted from the long day in the sun. Even after they left, the mood in the room retained a certain gravity.

"He might have been as great as Mozart," Praither said. "If he could write music like that at nineteen——"

"Only fifteen!" Gladys squeaked. "That's all he was when he wrote the quartet. All I can say is: where does that leave the rest of us?" A second later Gladys' voice had slid down several octaves. "Jim, where are you going with my statue? Don't think I'm going to let you take that back."

Jim Hopper was carrying a small Chinese teakwood statue, his hand cupped under its base. He came over to Gladys with it. "I'm just trying to show Hutch something. Look at the headdress!"

They all looked at the pointed tiara with its exquisitely carved, scalloped edge. From where he sat, Peter could not make out whether the eight or nine-inch-high statue was of some Chinese goddess or of Buddha.

George Kemp said, "What about it? It's a halo."

"But it isn't. Look at it! It's not in back of the head. It comes right up from the middle of the head; it's exactly like the *tablitas* the women wore today. That's what I wanted to show Hutch." He went off with his statue to the alcove.

On the studio couch, Yvonne Miller, talking to Piggot, Chet Orr and Lily Praither, was being very serious. "Europeans used to say that the American girl was brittle. I think that now as an entire nation we are getting brittle."

"How do you mean—brittle?" Chet asked.

"Well, don't you think we are, Chet? People all seem to be growing a hard shell, and pretty soon you get the impression that's all there is— shell. You go to a cocktail party, and everybody is shouting at everybody else and being desperately bright, and it's all on the surface; nobody is really talking to anybody. Take advertising on the radio—all that deliberate attempt to make people feel insecure and put the stress on externals——"

Peter missed the rest of it because Dorothy Lambert was talking to him. He picked up the thread of the conversation on the couch again when Gladys said indignantly to Piggot, "You always blame everything on women. I don't believe they run the country! I don't believe it for one moment."

"They control two thirds of the wealth—that's what counts."

"Now, don't say again—the way you did in that horrible book—that they're all widows because they made their men work themselves to death!"

"There are certain statistics by the insurance companies."

"But that doesn't prove that the wives—" Yvonne Miller got ahead of Gladys—"were responsible for all the stomach ulcers and heart attacks. American men are ambitious by themselves. Maybe it's because executives, for instance, don't have long-term contracts, the way they do in Europe, and never can feel secure in their job; but in any case it isn't just because their wives want to keep up with the Joneses."

Gladys had been waiting impatiently, with her bird-face thrust out. "And what's the reason, Ralph, that American women are as willful and selfish as you claim they are?"

"Historically it began with the fact that in a frontier society the woman invariably becomes the custodian and interpreter of culture; the man's too busy making a living to examine cultural values. He accepts——"

"I don't agree with you, Ralph! If American women are bossy, it's the fault of the men—because they're weak and can't assert themselves."

Piggot looked as if he were stretched on the rack of his own patience. "The docility is inculcated in them at their mothers' knees. It's part of our cultural climate. It's what I'm talking about."

"Why don't you blame fathers, too?" Yvonne challenged Ralph. "If girls are spoiled, it's their fathers who are doing it. Why, when I used to ask Hutch to take me east to see my family, I wouldn't even get an answer; but let Phyllis say something about wanting to see New York, Daddy, and we couldn't start packing soon enough."

"The American father-daughter relationship is a very special chapter. It's been said that fathers go to their daughters for the affection they don't get from their wives."

"Oh, tommyrot, Ralph! Really . . ."

Dorothy Lambert was not interested in listening. She was too happy with her children and her lawyer husband to bother theorizing about family relationships. She wanted to tell him instead about her little boy's confiding to her while she put him to bed just before a dinner party, "All this partying can't be good for Daddy's asmic. Daddy has to go to bed, too. . . ." "It's what he'd heard his grandfather say," Dorothy explained. "Phil has asthma. . . ."

He kept on catching odds and ends of talk from the couch. Chet was asking Ralph, "When did all this happen? When did this fatherlessness begin?" and Piggott answering, "Sometime in the nineteenth century when people turned their backs on every sort of orthodoxy, when everybody was carried away by the Great Optimism. It hasn't hit us in this country with the full impact yet because we've been too prosperous to be aware of any loss. . . ."

He heard Yvonne Miller protest, "Do you expect us to grind our own corn and weave blankets and plaster houses because the Indian women do?"

"No, but——"

Hutch said, "Why not? We'd all be a lot happier if we lived more simply and didn't have all those gadgets to worry about. . . ."

In one form or another, not only Piggot but Chet and nearly all the painters joined in a nostalgic litany of longing for some other civilization or at least for some bygone age. Peter glanced once toward the alcove and saw that Aleida and Collard were half listening, too, and that Furfey was coming toward the fireplace with a dolefully cantankerous air of bursting with what he had to say. His weak chin sagged petulantly. He whined, "I wish I had lived in the Renaissance, when there were patrons and there was a place for the artist. No wonder artists find it so hard to create. I hate this age!"

Willy Pettingill, wearing an almost quiet tie for once but reeking of perfume and mouthing his vowels as usual, tried to go Furfey one better in spiteful extravagance. "What did you expect? You aren't of any importance in the machine age. All you are, Furfey, as far as the average, solid citizen is concerned, is a parasite—a dilletante. You're lucky they don't put you in jail. Of coure we don't grow any Grecos or Rembrandts that way, but who cares? I don't think we'll get any great artists any more. I don't see them around."

Partly because Aleida was listening, and partly because he still felt belligerent from his set-to with Gladys, and partly also because Furfey's and Pettingill's whimpering exasperated him, Peter felt irresistibly drawn into the argument. He said, "I don't think that all genius has suddenly dried up. I think there are just as many great artists now as there ever were."

"Where?"

"In the laboratories."

"Painting pictures, I suppose?"

"No, being brilliant scientists and engineers."

"Of course you might say that the scientist is an artist in a way," Chet Orr said indulgently.

Pettingill pouted. "Frankly I don't see any relationship."

"I don't either," Furfey echoed him.

For a moment Peter felt at a loss. His very dislike of the two men and his growing impatience with the eternal talk about the shortcomings of the machine age, got in the way of his impulse to show up the hollowness of their complaints, their squealing impotence and sulky-child refusal to face their own times.

"The process," he said, "of creating something, whether it's in the laboratory or the studio, seems to me the same."

"You mean there isn't any difference between a chemical formula for some silly new plastic and the Beethoven Ninth?"

"I wasn't talking about the product. I said that the creative process that's involved in inventing a new machine and in composing a symphony or painting a picture is the same. In either case you start out with a problem you want to solve. There is just as much intuition in the hypothesis of a scientist as there is in the first glimpse an artist has of what his picture ought to be. After that they go through the identical period of drudgery: the scientist has to test his hypothesis, and the painter has to translate his vision into paint.

"From the alcove Larry Collard, showing that he—and perhaps Aleida —had been listening, threw his prestige as a scientist into the scale. "I think he has a point."

Pettingill said peevishly, "Suppose he has, what is he trying to prove?"

"I'm saying that a lot of potential artistic genius may be taking the form of scientific genius nowadays because the temper of our time is scientific and technological. A man like Leonardo might never have painted a single picture if he had lived in the twentieth century; he might have spent all his time in a laboratory or a drafting room. The same thing would be true, I think, of a lot of other artists who proved that they were just as talented engineers as they were painters."

"All right, I grant you that Giotto and Michelangelo were also engineers, but that was secondary: they were artists first. What makes you think they wouldn't be artists first nowadays?"

"The fact that everything in our civilization encourages a man to become an engineer rather than an artist. A little boy nowadays is going to play with toy airplanes and automobiles and not with a toy palette or an easel."

"But that's what I've been saying," Furfey sputtered. "Everything's the machine and St. Extrovert! Nobody has any time for art. It's a horrible age."

"But that isn't the fault of the machine."

"Then whose is it?"

"Everybody's!" He felt suddenly a little flustered by the silence. They had stopped talking not only by the fireplace but in the alcove. Aleida's eyes looked very large in the mellow light. There was nothing for it now but to go on. . . . "The philosophers', the artists', the educated people's, even—" he tried to joke—"the women's."

"Now, really, Peter," Gladys rumbled, "don't you go like Ralph blaming women for everything."

"Well, they are the ones who buy pictures and go to concerts and set the intellectual tone of a civilization. I was just trying to say that we all are to blame."

"And what are we supposed to do?"

"Not run away from the machine."

"Not run away from it!" Pettingill taunted. "Don't make me laugh! Why, we live by the machine."

"I know, but we treat the machine as something distasteful, as a necessary evil."

Pettingill gave another delicate snort. "Why, the machine runs our lives! We're swamped by gadgets."

"I wasn't talking about gadgets. I was talking about machines."

"What's the difference?"

He felt nothing but blind anger for a moment at so much obtuseness. On the other hand there was no reason to be angry with the others. They were perfectly willing to have him squelch Pettingill if he could.

"If it saves sweat, it's a machine. If it's a handy little thing that makes a click, it's a gadget." Mary Orr beside him gave an appreciative little laugh, and he felt encouraged to go on. "There's all the difference because a gadget is essentially frivolous, a mere aping of the function of the machine, whereas the machine has freed us from drudgery, has let us conquer space and time and the law of inertia."

"All right, suppose we have a lot more free time now—what have we done with it? All we do is go to more movies and listen to more tripe on the radio."

"But that isn't the fault of the machine, that we haven't grown up to our opportunity. The machine in itself is neither good nor bad—though we treat it as if it were half enemy and half rebellious slave."

"Who does?"

"Well, women do fairly often, and men do. Have you ever watched people yank at some lever in a perfect fury without first making the slightest effort to find out how a machine works, without trying to understand its limitations, without any sense of how much human genius has gone into perfecting it and making it into a fine tool for a specific purpose?"

"What do you want us to do—salaam every time before we get into the car or plug in the electric percolator?"

"No, but I think that until we become aware of the true role of the machine in our civilization, until we treat science and technology as neither magic nor something degrading, we'll never evolve any great art of our own because we'll be fighting ourselves as a civilization—we'll be split right down the middle. Physically we'll live by the machine, and philosophically and aesthetically we'll scorn it."

His fervor made him feel a little guilty because part of it, he realized, was not altogether honest. His irritation with Cristina and his impatience with her society friends this afternoon were also seeking a vent in this diatribe against Pettingill and Furfey and all the fastidious, anemic artiness they represented. But he found he could not stop now.

"For instance, if you go into a steel mill in Pittsburgh and if your mind isn't made up in advance that it's all monstrous and ugly, I defy you not to be carried away by the spectacle. To me an open-hearth shed has some of the grandeur of a cathedral; there is something majestic about a 150-ton ladle that hangs from a crane so high up under the roof you can hardly make out the man in the cab, pouring molten steel into ingot molds! It's a triumph of human achievement. It's got the same kind of vitality as the Indian dance today; it simply happens to be the white man's way of asserting himself. Yet when you go into the houses of the people who own chunks of those steel mills, all you see is simpering little pictures that belong to another century and another civilization. You get sticky French pastoral scenes and saccharine eighteenth-century English portraits, and if the people are really big stockholders—Botticellis and Rembrandts—the farther removed from our reality, the better. There is nothing to celebrate our triumph! Aesthetically we're disowning the thing that feeds us—we're fouling our nest."

"Then you prefer a steel furnace to a Botticelli?"

"A Botticelli painting is wonderful. What I object to is our nostalgic lechery for another age and practically forcing any artist to think and feel with the mentality of another century. I think the corn dance today had power and made one feel that it was great art because it dealt with

the sun and rain and fertility—all the things that keep the Indian alive
and are important to him. And when Botticelli and Rembrandt painted,
they expressed their own culture and not their great-grandfathers'. But
our artists can't express our culture because our mythology, or metaphys-
ics, or whatever you want to call it, refuses to take account of our reality,
of the means of our well-being. That's why I think our art is false, and
that's why we haven't been able to create a style of our own and are
constantly copying the style of some other civilization. That's also why
I think so many artists are experimenting with new techniques in painting and in music—because they have nothing to say and are desperately
hoping some new technique may miraculously supply them with a vision
and a message."

"I know," Orr said. "What we need is roots like the Indians'. We have
to get back to the land again."

It was a digression, and a dangerous one, because it thinned out everything he had said!

"Going back to the land—puttering in a garden or running a few cows
on a model ranch and pretending we lead the simple life—that isn't going
to help. We cut those particular roots a long time ago. It isn't we who
work the land any more; it's the steel tractor that does the work. Steel
and the tractor are our real roots, and they also come from the earth."

"From the factory, you mean," Furfey jeered. "If there's anything
more cold and artificial, I'd like to see it."

"Certainly, from the earth: the iron comes out of the mines, and the
steel's made with human sweat, and the machine is full of our dreams.
The man guiding the plow is a sentimental concept for second-rate poets;
it has nothing to do with our civilization any more."

"What would you like us to do," Pettingill asked: "go to Pittsburgh
and paint blast furnaces and smokestacks?"

The prejudice was formidable. They hated the machine with all the
loathing and fear of the thin, tubercular-looking French girl he had overheard saying to another girl in the Paris subway, *"Trîmer dans une
fabrique—ah, non, tu sais, j'aime encore mieux faire le tas!"* A man at
the hotel had translated it for him: "Slave in a factory? Not me, I'd
rather go into the streets!" It had stuck in his mind because the fierce
passion of the girl had spoken so eloquently of a childhood spent in the
shadow of those incredibly gloomy European factories which hulked like
penitentiaries on the outskirts of big cities—in the shadow of the misused
machine!

"Painting the steel mills isn't important, but being aware of them is. I feel that unless the blast furnaces, the laboratories and the power dams enter into the picture we have of ourselves, instead of our pretending they aren't there, we'll continue to be without roots and everything we're going to do is going to be phony and wrong. It's like the war in 1914 when people were acting as if the men were engaged in a series of medieval battles that could be fought according to the rules of chivalry, and when as a matter of fact each man was up against a machine and not just another man. I think it was because of this essential dishonesty that the years between 1914 and 1918 were so vile. A modern war has to be fought efficiently in terms of the machines that are being used if the war isn't to be altogether criminal."

Gladys was scandalized. "By 'efficiently' I suppose you mean, more ruthlessly?"

"I mean unsentimentally and therefore more humanely. I think maybe the next war will be that way: hit as hard as you can and bring about an end as quickly as possible, and therefore kill fewer men and cause less suffering."

Gladys returned to the attack. "But if you are so against art, Peter, why haven't you drawn a lot of machines and wheels and things? All those beautiful lithographs of yours are of Indians and Mexicans."

"Because I've been dishonest, too," he said. "Not because I've drawn Mexicans and Indians—it isn't a question of the subject an artist picks but of his approach to it." He tried once more to make clear what he meant. "It's a matter of our coming to see that science and the machine represent thousands of years of human striving and ingenuity, and that scientists and engineers and some industrialists can just as truly be heroes as the Homeric warriors. The same courage and the same endurance are involved; it's just the battlefield that's changed. I feel that unless we learn to understand and honor what our modern world has achieved, we'll never have a philosophy for our time nor an art of our own."

He saw the hostility in Furfey's eyes and added defiantly, "A machine isn't cold and antihuman just because some anemic poet says so. A mechanic walking through a shop will unconsciously run his hand over a beautiful piece of machinery the way a horse fancier will pat a horse."

"I can see what you mean about a mechanic being crazy about a motor," George Kemp said. "I understand that. But when you say that my being aware of a lot of machinery and junk is going to improve my painting, I don't know what you're talking about. Am I supposed to start studying the quantum theory at my time of life?"

"No, but I think that children ought to be taught something of the history of science and ought to be made to understand some of the benefits of modern technology. They ought to know that the invention of the cam or the discovery of induction have been infinitely more important to our well-being than some silly war a thousand years ago."

"I don't know what a cam is," Yvonne complained, "and I bet I couldn't understand it if you explained it to me, Peter."

George Kemp said, "I can't see where anything that has to do with technology can have any bearing on art. The two things are diametrically opposed."

"But I don't think they are opposed. That's only what the sentimentalists have made us believe. You have the same rules of elegance and economy in mechanics as in painting: the more efficiently constructed a machine is, the more graceful and aesthetically satisfying it is. On the other hand all the elements of a great painting function as superbly as the wheels in a fine machine! The only things that are diametrically opposed are the way we live—refrigerators and airplanes and the radio—and the way we make believe in our art we live. And a man from Mars would probably find our handling of international affairs remarkably quaint and sadistic, too."

"What difference could technology make in international affairs that it hasn't already made?" Jim Hopper wanted to know. "We use science every way we can to destroy one another."

"That's just it: we use science the way you'd expect a little boy to use a slide rule or any other precision tool. If we ever grow up to our ingenuity, I have a notion that more and more people in each nation would think it a disgrace to let millions go hungry for lack of farm machinery and dams. Piggot told me that the whole Mesopotamian basin was crisscrossed by thousands of miles of irrigation canals five thousand years ago. Until we see that it's absurd that we with our modern tools can't do as well as people five thousand years ago, and until we're determined to turn the world into a garden and consider it an insult to our dignity to let people in Asia or anywhere starve from drought while a few hundred miles away big rivers are flooding cities—well, we haven't grown up to our tools."

Piggot, who had hardly opened his mouth all evening, said slowly, "That's the Tower of Babel philosophy as opposed to the City of God."

"Ralph's come alive," Gladys caroled expectantly, but Ralph did not go on to explain, and Peter was not sure what he had meant.

He felt that he had made a fool of himself. He had let his irritation with

Cristina betray him into a stupid argument. He had merely succeeded in temporarily silencing Furfey and Pettingill, in inducing in the others a certain flattering thoughtfulness and in harvesting a number of encouraging glances from some of the women who liked him well enough to have been warmly on his side even if he had argued the exact opposite.

People were getting up and were all talking at once with the final burst of vivacity that meant the party was coming to an end. Yvonne Miller and Gladys both summoned him at the same time—"Oh, Peter!" and "Don't you go away, young man; I've got a bone to pick with you!" Gladys was fortunately prevented from leaving the fireplace by George Kemp, who insisted on keeping his audience intact, and Yvonne could be put off with a grin. He clung gratefully to Dorothy Lambert, who was willing to talk about nothing more serious than her roses and his attempts at gardening and who promised with innocent coquetry which they both knew did not promise anything, "I'm really still coming to see your house and the flower bed. Next week for sure!"

Helen Kemp was again going through her loyal-artist's-wife routine of keeping the spotlight on Kemp. "Don't be vulgar, George!"

"I just want to finish telling this story to Glad. So the Mammy asked——"

"George, I'm going to take you home. You're drunk!"

Ralph Piggot came up to Peter. "The rose invariably disowns the dung heap," he said.

"Does that come under the heading of wisdom?"

"It comes under the heading of what one learns," he said with his saturnine scowl and went on.

The group in the alcove was breaking up. Aleida, he discovered with an almost painful rush of joy, had been standing a little behind him on his left, waiting for Piggot to go. Her hazel eyes had warm golden depths. Her light-gray jersey dress with the gay brick-red design knit into it around the neck and at the bottom of the skirt made her look more charming than he had ever seen her before.

"I liked what you said."

He felt himself blush and at the same time go warm with pleasure. "I talked too darn much."

"I didn't think so. It was all new to me and exciting. You made me want to see the steel mills."

"I wish I could show them to you."

The golden lights in her eyes wavered and withdrew. He had reminded her and now himself of the afternoon when Cristina had warned her off. He started to ask, "Did you——" just as she said hastily, "I saw your new machine at Santa Cruz. Father had to look at some cattle in Dixon and I drove up with him and on the way back we stopped in to see Father Hegge. I hope your ears burned. Father Hegge just raved about you." Her eyes suddenly held a new shadow. "Are you planning to start a factory at Santa Cruz?"

"No. What makes you think that?"

"Oh, all those machines. I know it sounds silly after what you said tonight about facing up to the machine, but I'd hate to think of a lot of factories in the canyon."

He was relieved. "Small chance. The cost of shipping takes care of that. By the time you'd paid the freight for bringing in raw material and shipping the finished product, you'd have priced yourself out of the market. Besides, there's no power, no railroad, no labor pool—not anything a manufacturer would want. That's what makes it so hard for the Spanish people to make a living here. That's why so many have to go to California for work. What I'm trying to do is to teach some of the boys enough about machinery to revive some of the old Spanish handicrafts on a modern scale for the Anglo trade right here in Santa Fe."

"Oh, it sounds exciting. What kinds of handicrafts?"

"Well, I've found an old German blacksmith who's willing to teach them ornamental ironwork: grille gates, latches, all kinds of braces and stands—the sort of thing every Anglo who builds out here wants for his house. Then Father Hegge's dug up a fellow right in Espagnola who's going to teach half-a-dozen kids who are interested how to make Spanish furniture. There's certainly a demand for that. Two or three of the boys who like to carve may be able to make a good living out of it eventually. In the meantime we'll try and sell everything that's good enough at a bazaar a couple of times a year. Later, if it all works out, we might try to scare up somebody to teach them tinwork and maybe even leatherwork. Oh, we've got lots of plans!"

Her hazel eyes had kindled again to gold. "Oh, I think that's wonderful!"

It made him sing inside; it also made him shy. He asked quickly, "Did you go to Santo Domingo?"

"We got there just when you left."

"I didn't see you; I must have been blind."

"We were parked under the cottonwood trees. We had to get water out of the stream for the radiator. As a matter of fact you passed by quite close to us. I almost . . . called." There was no missing the sudden check in her voice. Cristina had come between them again! There was an awkward little pause. "Well, good-by. . . ."

Her coming so close only to draw away again filled him with bitterness. It was all Cristina's fault! His rancor and a vague sadness still warred with his sense of disloyalty to Cristina the next day. The sense of guilt won out. It made him feel penitent and oddly conciliatory by the time he went to Cristina's at five.

She came across the patio behind the two ecstatically racing, jostling spaniels to meet him. She had not stopped to take off her gardening gloves and she still held the trowel in her hand. She wore a frilly white blouse and a rose-colored skirt with halters which were boldly intended to give her a piquant girlishness—and did, largely because she appeared altogether soft and docile and dewily mysterious today. The familiar moist fragrance assailed him as if he were smelling it for the first time. He felt himself melt with tenderness as she folded against him and murmured, "I'm so glad you're here." But she did not stay relaxed in his arms. He felt the little premonitory stiffening of her waist and arms. "I hear you were very eloquent last night."

"I'd hardly call it eloquent."

"Yvonne and Gladys said you were. They couldn't wait to call me this morning at crack of dawn. Come and see the tulips, darling." She took his hand, but the confiding-little-girl mood had already lost its magic for him. He had to make an effort to return the pressure of her fingers as she led him toward the semicircular flower bed around the shell-shaped basin of the fountain in the far wall. "They said you were simply fasc-in-at-ing!"

" 'Tight' describes it more accurately."

"It's funny that you're never eloquent when you're here. I'm lucky if I can get two words in an evening out of you."

"Oh, now, darling, you know that isn't true. They're beautiful," he said and hoped to get her to talk about the tulips instead. "I like those dark-red ones especially."

She said perfunctorily, "They are big, aren't they? You know, if you hadn't been so horrid about helping me entertain Nancy and Roberto yesterday afternoon, I might have liked to go on to the party, too."

"But you said you didn't want to go to Gladys'. You said you were going to bed. How was I to know you'd change your mind and end up at the Fonda for dinner?"

She flared up. "I had to entertain them, didn't I? They're my friends. It seems to me that if you could go to Gladys', you could have come here, too, and not left me to cope with them all by myself."

"You said you were just going to give them a drink and pack them off to the hotel, and that I didn't have to come back if I didn't want to. Well, I didn't; I'm not very keen on Nancy. And it wasn't as if you had to cope with them all alone. Ralph was here, and you had Geoff."

She made a motion as if to stamp her foot. "I wish you'd stop cramming Geoff down my throat. If I'd wanted Geoff, I'd have married him years ago." She glanced at the bright-colored wicker chairs by the portale fireplace with an air of having changed her mind. "I think we'd better go inside. I had a brainstorm that it might be fun to have our drinks out here, but it's much too windy."

The faint twitch of her knee under the rose-red skirt when she had all but stamped her foot, so far from igniting his desire for her, as it would have done a few months ago, had succeeded only in making him aware of the contrast between her childish temper and youthful clothes and the taut, tired skin around her jaw. There were moments when her face was almost ugly, he reflected hostilely as he followed her down the two steps into the living room.

His silence seemed to worry her. She said, suddenly contrite, "I'm sorry, darling. How was the party last night?"

"It wasn't any kind of party. It broke up before eleven o'clock. Everybody was tired from the dance. We just ate and sat around. You didn't miss a thing."

"Oh, I know, darling." She had turned on the lamps even though it was still light. The tautness had gone out of her face. She had changed to a new mood. "Wait till you hear what I've planned!" He had handed her her drink and he was about to go to the chair where he usually sat, across the cocktail table from her. She reached up and seized his sleeve. "Don't be so damn' remote! I want you close." She patted the couch beside her. "You aren't angry with me?"

His ostentatious concern not to spill his drink and the business of offering her a cigarette provided him with an excuse for not sitting very close. "I never was."

"I wouldn't blame you if you were. I don't know what makes me blow up like that. It's perfectly silly, isn't it? Let's not talk any more about last night! Darling, what would you say to our taking the trip on the Chili Line tomorrow instead of next week? Hal Oxnard says there's a quaint, old hotel in a place called Alamosa where we'd stay tomorrow night, unless we decided to go all the way on to Denver. Then the next morning we'd take the train back. Hal says it's an absolutely beautiful trip, and there's one place 'way up high where they always stop the train for a while and let the men get out and fish. Roberto is simply dying to go. Don't you think it'd be fun?"

Her mention that Roberto was to come along alarmed him. It was a question of a trip on the narrow-gauge railroad which wound picturesquely, so everybody said, through the high country in the northwestern part of the state. The jaunt had originally been proposed by Geoff, and the party was to have been made up of just the three of them and Ralph. He stalled, "Who all's to come?"

"Just Nancy and Roberto—I have to do something for them while they're here, and this is just perfect since Roberto likes to fish—and the Oxnards and us. We got it all planned today at lunch. I'm so glad I asked the Oxnards last night. Hal and Roberto hit it off just beautifully."

"What about Geoff? He was counting on going with us."

She exploded, "Oh, darling, don't be so damn' difficult! Do you think I enjoy planning things for Nancy and Roberto to do? Geoff's got all summer to take that trip. He wouldn't enjoy it one bit. I happen to know that he doesn't particularly care for Nancy."

"Neither do I."

She threw back her head and thrust out her chin. "All because of Geoff! I wouldn't think of interfering with that honeymoon of yours. All right, I'll ask him. What I don't understand is this sudden passion of yours for him. I should think you'd feel just the opposite after——"

It was the first time she had ever threatened to refer to his relationship with Geoff. He went cold and tense inside. "After what?"

"After all you've said."

"What have I said?"

"You didn't have to say anything. I could guess."

"You may have guessed wrong."

"Like the time you raced his horse—look, darling, let's not fight. I said I'd ask Geoff."

"And I don't like that kind of favor."

"All right, then, don't come if you don't want to! I'll ask Jack Fettis to go."

"More ice?" He picked up her glass and went to the tile-inlaid wall table to freshen up their drinks. It was strange, he told himself while he listened to the maid begin to set the table in the dining room, how indifferent he was to her mention of Fettis—how completely she had failed if her intention had been to get under his skin. Let her take anyone she liked. . . . He went back slowly to the fireplace and saw her take one last, furious puff before she fiercely crushed out her cigarette in what was obviously a determined effort to regain control of herself. He pretended not to have noticed, gently set down her drink in front of her because she was busy snapping open her compact, and sat down in the chair.

Cristina said guardedly, like a snail poking out a delicate feeler from its shell, "I've been thinking of going east with Nancy and Roberto next Monday and maybe sailing with them. They're going to stay in New York for a couple of weeks."

"I thought you weren't going to Europe until September."

"I want to get to my own dentist in Paris."

"How long are you going to stay?"

"I can't tell yet." Their voices sounded to him as if they were talking to each other in a cavernous cellar, across an indeterminate distance, in the dark. . . . "It depends on how long the men in Florence are going to take, putting in the new plumbing. Once I go, I'm certainly going to stay on through the winter."

"What about the house here—are you going to close it?"

"Mercedes will do it. She's done it once before." There was a pause that seemed to hollow out the space around them, that emptied it of everything except themselves, so that Cristina's voice when she went on was startlingly raw and near. "Would you come to France with me if I went now?"

"I'd sort of counted on putting in the summer in Santa Fe."

"Well, would you come if I waited till September?"

There was a vein of desperation somewhere underneath the ostentatious brusqueness with which she had asked the question, so that it seemed unbearably cruel not to give in to her silent appeal. It was only the consciousness of making her pay for some prolonged insult to Geoff that gave him the courage to meet her eyes.

"No."

"Darling, there's one thing I've got to know." Her fingers twitched convulsively as she reached for a cigarette in the red lacquer box. Mercedes had opened the door from the dining room and was about to come up the length of the room, greet him and inquire whether she was to start serving dinner, as she did every night, when Cristina stopped her abruptly. "Mercedes, could you hold dinner for a little while? I'll let you know when we're ready."

She sat looking straight ahead, past him, until Mercedes had not only closed the door into the dining room but the second one out into the kitchen as well. She still had made no effort to light her cigarette although she held the lighter in her other hand. Her eyes when she turned toward him were naked in their anguished insistence.

"Darling, do you love me at all? Because I do you!"

There was no escaping it.

"I love you, but I'm not in love with you."

"You could have told me that before!"

How could I? he thought.

She sat without moving for a succession of endless seconds, her silver-gray eyes dully fixed on the bookcase behind him, just about where the Dante volumes would be.

"Thank God, this life isn't going to last forever!"

Her shoulders sagged. Her whole body seemed to wither and go dry. There was something infinitely desolate and reproachful about the single tear which started down her cheek from her left eye. She said with a gallant affectation of disgust in place of despair, "O God!"

He found it impossible to sit still any longer. He went to the couch and stood irresolutely beside her for a moment, torn by the desire to comfort her and the fear of saying too much and undoing all the painful honesty of the last few minutes. He finally sat down on the edge of the couch and touched her back.

"I'm not worth all this agony."

"Are you telling me?"

She flung herself into his arms, stayed for a moment, then shook her head violently and with her hands still grasping his arms pushed herself away from him.

"I'm all right now, darling. I'll just marry Nicky and settle down to being a banker's wife—or maybe I'll marry Geoff and be your step-mother, or is that incest?" She reached for her handkerchief in the pocket of her rose-colored skirt and brusquely dabbed at her eyes. "You'd better go now."

He hesitated awkwardly. "If there is anything I can do—if I can close up the house . . ."

"Mercedes will tend to it. Please, go."

The urgency in her voice warned him that she was using her last shred of strength to keep from breaking down. She had drawn herself up very straight and stood with her head thrown back. Peter glanced away from her faintly quivering nostrils in contrition, only to find when his eyes

slid down her side that the fingernails of her right hand were digging so
hard into the palm that her knuckles showed white.

He bit back his aching sympathy for her and started for the door. Just
before he opened it he said, "Good-by, Cristina," and waited for the sound
of her voice while he fumbled with the latch. She did not say anything.
He closed the door softly from the outside and all but tiptoed along the
portale and out of the patio to his car. Even after he was already halfway
to the plaza he realized all at once that he was barely creeping along and
still driving as if he were stealing out of the yard of an invalid who had
to be spared all noise. He stepped on the gas but after a very few seconds,
from a feeling that he needed leisure to think, he slowed down again.

He still found it difficult to believe that the few seconds between them
added up to an irrevocable break—that the end could have come about so
quickly, so easily. His thoughts kept absurdly flitting back to the pajamas
and the toilet kit he had kept in the guest room. If only she remembered
to clear out the bureau! Still, Mercedes had seen them there often enough
before. . . . Perhaps Mercedes would take them for Agapito, which would
be fine.

It seemed heartless to be even aware of the stealthy elation stirring inside him. He hastily, guiltily, made himself think of the way she had
looked, standing there in front of the couch. He promptly winced at the
memory. It must have cost her a tremendous effort to show so little of
what she must have felt. She had quite literally kept her chin up. "*Tenue,*"
she had called that once, good form. "There is a way of doing these
things," she had said. It was abominable to have to inflict suffering like
that on anyone; yet to go on being dishonest with her would have been
even more inexcusable.

I wish, he defended himself, *she hadn't taken on so about me. After
all we were supposed to be only having an affair! That's how it started
and that's all it was ever supposed to be until Cristina suddenly began to
get different ideas, and then I made it clear that I didn't want marriage.
She understood that, too! She said at least a dozen times, "I know you
don't want to marry me," and I never denied it. I'd just try to take the
sting out of my refusal by trying to take the blame and always saying
something like, "It isn't that; it's just that I'm not settled enough yet to
get married. I've got to be free until I know what I'm going to do."*

And yet he squirmed with wretchedness inside at the thought of her
suffering. To get away for an instant from the ache of his remorse, he
turned to blame Cristina again. If she was so set on getting married, why

did she have to be so arrogant toward the older men who wanted to marry her—toward Geoff especially?

If I did use her to get even with Geoff—I don't like admitting it, but there was a grain of truth in what Piggot said, and those dark impulses deep inside me drove me without my being aware of it—so did she use me to punish Geoff for not being the sort of man she wanted him to be. I was the improved version, I suppose! Why, she couldn't have been bitchier to Geoff except toward the very end when she started to play him off against me. She never once considered how desperately he is in love with her and she must have known that long before I finally caught on to it. Why should I let her go on and needle Geoff with me? After all, he is my father; he means more to me than she!

He felt an irresistible desire to see Geoff. He turned off Alameda and headed eagerly for Canyon Road and the Camino. The elation which had troubled him by its furtive presence before now stirred in him quite boldly, and he let it stir. *I'm free,* he thought exultantly. *I could even drive out to Pecos and see Aleida if I wanted to and if it weren't dinnertime....* He worried all of a sudden that Geoff might have gone out somewhere and he stepped hard on the gas.

Geoff was home. He did not altogether hide his astonishment. "Come in. Delighted to see you." He wore a handsome old tweed jacket and a gay red foulard cloth around his throat, loosely knotted and tucked inside his open shirt. The elderly Spanish woman who cooked for him stuck her head into the room from the passageway that led to the studio to pick up a wastepaper basket from beside the desk. Geoff was clearly planning to have dinner at home.

Peter said hastily, "I was wondering whether you'd like to come to the Fonda for dinner with me. I know it's a little late to ask you."

"I wasn't intending to go out. I worked in the garden all afternoon and just took a quick shower and put on some old clothes. Let me consult Rafaelita to see what she has in the house—unless you have some special reason for eating downtown. You'll have a whisky and soda in any case...." He disappeared into the passageway and was gone quite a long time. When he returned, carrying a tray with glasses and a bowl of ice and a soda bottle on it, his face wore a pleasant grin. "Rafaelita thinks she can stretch what she has in the icebox so that there'll be enough for both of us. Would you like to stay?"

"I'd like to very much."

"That's settled then. I don't eat much before seven-thirty. Rafaelita cooks dinner for her own family first and eats with them before she comes over here, and the arrangement suits me perfectly because I got used to having late dinner in France." He talked along smoothly as if to gloss over the unexpectedness of the visit.

Peter took the cue and, watching him drop a couple of pieces of ice into each glass, kidded, "I thought you considered it one of the deadlier sins to put ice in whisky!"

"Quite right." His eyes flickered with amusement; he was in good spirits today. "I was talking about whisky, though. What you're getting is not quite in that category. I was trying to kill the taste. Here you are. . . ."

They went out into the garden to look at the new fence Geoff had put up to keep the neighborhood dogs out of his flower beds. They looked at the iris in bloom. They talked about the relative merits of peat moss and leaf mold from the mountains for protecting seedlings from the parching west wind. Only once did Cristina come into their talk. Geoff asked, "Speaking of the mountains, have you heard any more about our proposed trip?"

It was the first time that Geoff had even remotely acknowledged that Peter's relationship with Cristina might be closer than his; and coming as it did now ironically at the very moment when it no longer referred to fact, Geoff's admission of defeat was like a lash.

"We may have to go by ourselves. Cristina has decided to make the trip tomorrow with the Oxnards because she wants to take the Smiths. I happened to see her just now for a couple of minutes."

The desire to soothe Geoff's feelings, to efface as much of the memory of his one-time triumph as possible—the sudden need to make up for the hurt he had caused Geoff had become irresistible. He said with a humble air of knowing that he was not telling Geoff anything new, "I suppose you know all about the possibility that she may go to New York and sail with the Smiths?"

"Yes, she telephoned this afternoon. Tina offered me her house to live in for the next year."

Nothing in Geoff's tone gave any clue as to what he intended to do.

"Are you going to do it? I mean, move into her house?"

"My lease here runs until September."

"Oh, you're staying the summer, then?"

"I may stay even longer than that. But I may also go to France for the winter. It depends on how well the work goes. In any case I have an option to buy this place."

Then Geoff was not going to go traipsing after Cristina—not immediately at any rate. He felt relieved, as if Geoff's statement of his plans for the summer was proof that his hurt over Cristina had healed. He also felt that it was his duty to satisfy Geoff's inevitable desire to know about Cristina and him. He said with a happy sense of presenting Geoff with a gift, "I've been toying with the idea of buying a place in Tesuque. No France for me. I like it here."

The barest flicker of Geoff's eyelids showed that he had taken in the full implication of the words. His angular, high-colored face became extraordinarily mellow and warm. "That will be very pleasant. We'll see something of each other. . . ."

They went back into the house and talked briskly, gaily, with an exhilarating sense that a monstrous obstacle between them had been removed, about a dozen trivial things. Once while they were having dinner Geoff offered, "I have a good deal of furniture stored in New York which I'm going to have sent out. They're mostly things I picked up in France. There may be some pieces you'll like."

He was happy that this time everything inside him prompted him to accept an offer of Geoff's with gratitude and warmth. "Thanks very much. . . ." But because he realized that this was far from enough to wipe out the memory of his churlishness when Geoff had wanted to give him the barometer, he added, "But what I'd really like, if your offer still stands, is that barometer."

Geoff's face lighted up. "We'll put it in your car right now." He strode across the room to the barometer and took it down from the wall before Peter could protest, "Oh, I didn't mean right this instant," went to the kitchen for a cloth to dust its back, then went to the studio for an old Navaho blanket in which to wrap it, and carried it out himself to the car. "There's no reason why you shouldn't have it now. There, I believe it'll be safe like this."

It was almost, Peter reflected with a surge of affection, as if he were doing Geoff a favor by accepting his gift. And there was a startling pleasure in having the rough-textured sleeve of Geoff's tweed jacket brush for a moment against his hand and in noticing the faint scent of lavender soap that clung to his cheek. Yet when they had finished securing the barometer against any jolt on the back seat, Peter found himself reluctant to return to the house. Nor did Geoff ask him to stay. It was as if they had both been rendered shy at the same moment by the sudden overpowering awareness of the warm current between them. Geoff averted his eyes rather brusquely and his wave was almost frosty when Peter backed the Chevvy out into the Camino del Monte Sol.

He drove very cautiously, the barometer on the rear seat seeming like a newly found, wonderfully important and well-disposed, fragile old relative who could not be transported too tenderly. The inscription on the tarnished brass plate, "John Middlemas—Penzance," kept dancing before his eyes. A delicious serenity that was only broken into now and again by a somewhat uneasy elation that had to do with his freedom from Cristina enveloped him like a dream.

When he got out of town the virtuous glow that had been growing in intensity ever since he had left Geoff's house finally insisted on exploding into words. He congratulated himself: *Silly how I used to hate him all those years and made a dragon out of him when all along he's been a simple, frail human being who desperately wants to be loved. Funny, too, how I graduated from one stage to the next in trying to make myself his equal, always thinking I was getting myself ready to take my revenge but actually cheating myself out of my hate, until finally there was almost no hate left—except for that business with Cristina, of course. At that rate a fellow can start out full of murderous hate and end up a blooming saint!*

Something like alarm at his unbridled exultation made him check himself: *All right, let's have no play-acting! He's my father. I like him— period.*

Yet his elation would not be controlled. It drove him, after he had carefully hung up the barometer in the living room and rubbed the brass plate until it shone, to go for a walk on the hills behind Bishop's Lodge. Even that did not still his exuberance. Bits of music kept going through his head after he went to bed. It was a long time before his happiness would let him go to sleep.

CHAPTER THIRTEEN

Hate Has Another Face

What in hell has happened? he asked in angry bewilderment.

The buoyancy and the virtuous glow, which had seemed like permanent rewards, had faded to nothing in only three days. He blamed it on his near-dread of running into Cristina somewhere and on having to slink in and out of town and constantly having to keep an eye out for the yellow Isotta and on having to inquire from Piggot and the garage mechanic whether she had gone on the Chili-line jaunt with her friends, because his very fear of facing her again had saddled him with a compulsion to check on her whereabouts. In spite of the furtive trips to Santa Fe, he felt imprisoned in Tesuque and chained to the house.

I'm getting claustrophobia, he told himself. *If she is going to leave, then I wish she'd go!*

But Monday afternoon when Gladys twittered in the plaza, "Oh, you're still here, Peter. I thought you'd gone to New York, too," the relief which he had promised himself failed to materialize. Gladys went on twittering, "It was just luck that I ran into Cristina and her friends in the Fonda this morning and got to say good-by to her. I hadn't any idea she was leaving. How long is she going to stay?"

There was no relief. For one thing there was the curiosity in people's eyes. He could counter Gladys' probing with curt nonchalance—"I haven't the faintest idea, Gladys"—to let her know that the break between Cristina and him had been final enough and that Cristina's plans were no longer of any interest to him. But that did not do away with the subtler questionings and the discreet silences each time Cristina's name came up in his presence anywhere, nor with the sudden spate of invitations which showed only too plainly that the women thought him in need of sympathy, so that he came to dislike going into town almost as much as he had hated to stay away from it before Cristina had finally left.

Yet if he was without an invitation for an evening he felt unbearably at a loss for something to do at the hour when he had formerly started for Cristina's house. And it was not only the emptiness of those evenings by himself that troubled him, but also a gnawing sense of remorse that during so many hours he had spent with Cristina lately he had not made her happier. The fact that their affair had been bound to come to an end did not enter into it, he accused himself. People had to give one another all the happiness they could as long as they had the chance and if they professed to be something more than enemies or mere stray acquaintances! He saw it as a sacred human duty all of a sudden and winced at the thought of how far he had fallen short.

To add to the bleakness that surrounded him everywhere, he discovered that Aleida was gone. She had gone east to visit an aunt. She had left two days after their talk—after Cristina had lurked behind some innocent remark! Was it because of Cristina that Aleida had left, or was it sheer conceit on his part to imagine that she had been interested in him simply because he had suddenly come awake to the golden lights in her irises, the exquisitely textured skin below her eyes, her honey-colored hair, the way she held herself. He had no means of finding out. He could not go after her and ask—he did not know her well enough for that. He could not ask Anne to ask—there were limits to the commissions one entrusted even to a devoted kid sister. All he could do was wait until she came back—if she didn't get married first to her doctor beau in the East!

He drifted into the habit of spending entire evenings with his Spanish neighbors up and down the Tesuque road. He stopped off to chat for five minutes or for half an hour if he met one of them while he was out horseback riding. He joked with them, listened with delight to their accounts of charming old native customs still remembered by the older people but already dying out, felt flattered by their confidences and their invitations to supper. He even tried to help them with their problems, as when he was able by hiring a good lawyer to keep a small rancher from losing all his sheep to an unscrupulous merchant over some shabby technicality. They came to him with letters to write to some mail-order house because they had been sent the wrong thing, or they merely needed a ride into town. He did not grudge the time. He was grateful to them for giving him something to do.

He could not get himself to paint or draw any more. The mere thought of picking up a pencil filled him with distaste. He told himself, I've argued myself out of it! And it really was as if at some point in the course of the argument that evening at Gladys' house he had killed all his interest in art. His last drawing, which was less than two weeks old, seemed as remote as if he had done it years ago.

He bullied himself. Why take on about it? I've never really cared for painting for its own sake. I've always used that freak talent for drawing I've inherited from Geoff to please or impress somebody. This time it was to impress Geoff. No wonder my puny attempts at art have always struck me as slightly self-conscious and insincere. No wonder I was so eloquent the other night when I tried to prove that our art has no connection with the rest of our lives!

Almost as if to live up to his own preaching, he turned his attention to anything connected with mechanics and machinery. He put in two whole days working with Father Hegge's boys on a broken-down car which he had bought for them to give them a chance to learn about auto mechanics. He threw himself into some stubborn technical problems raised by the plumbing-supplies manufacturer in Dayton to whom he had leased his chrome-plating process the previous spring. He toyed with the enticing offer the Dayton man had made to him again to join his firm. He looked at the technical magazines which had been piling up month after month and not only went through them carefully but even studied the advertisements. But when he actually thought of himself back in harness, wrestling with manufacturing and marketing problems once more, his desire to go back wilted instantly.

Nothing that he could think of to do tempted him. He sat in the Fonda one noon having lunch with an amusingly arrogant young dilletante, who sounded like an Oriental prince when he made the waitress take the fish back to the kitchen a second time. He thought, *I've really arrived! Now*

I can sit here in the middle of the day like any young waster who's never done a lick of work in his life and never will and whose chief occupation is to bully waitresses whose feet probably hurt.

A grayness infected everything. Even his shy, new affection for Geoff, which had filled him with such a joy, seemed like something that could be overdone. They had made a habit of having dinner together every Wednesday night, but beyond that, except for parties to which they both had been asked or chance encounters in town, he had all but avoided Geoff.

There was one exception. Peter ran into Geoff outside the hardware store. Geoff was putting a new floor in his studio and he was doing all the work himself. Peter offered his help.

They worked for four days side by side, putting in new joists for the ones that had rotted out, nailing on a subfloor, and finally the floor. They worked briskly, happily together. It was as if Cristina were in the room and they were both determined to prove her wrong. The fact that Geoff had clearly put off replacing the sagging studio floor as long as he had been able to was part of the proof: he had given the lie to her accusation during the winter that he was welcoming the upheaval in his studio to keep from having to paint. And it was also because of Cristina's harping on Geoff's laziness, Peter felt, that Geoff now tapped in each nail with fierce concentration and a stubborn sort of emphasis and would not even take time out to smoke a cigarette.

Nor did Peter himself succeed in shaking off an intense awareness of Cristina and of her attempts to set him against Geoff. It was as if each time he passed Geoff a bundle of oak boards or handed him the can with the nails he was saying to Cristina, "Do you see how wonderfully we get along together?" And it was still Cristina who was proved in the wrong by the waves of regret that swept over him at the thought of how wretched he had made Geoff during the past few months. "So unnecessary," he thought. "Why do we do these things? Why did I have to torture him? I didn't really want to at all. I've liked him all along! . . ." In the evening while they sat in the living room or strolled out into Geoff's patio, Peter's affection swelled at times until he felt an impulse to touch Geoff's coat or at least brush against his sleeve—almost as if he were a little boy again. The sudden sound of Geoff's voice would fall on his ear like a caress.

The four days with Geoff were both an atonement and a joy. But when they were over he was suddenly plunged into a bleaker loneliness than before. His very memory of the four happy days made him shy—afraid of crowding Geoff. Grayness settled on him again.

He got a letter from Anne, who was in the throes of preparing for her final exams and all excited about a vacation trip to Europe she and two other Smith girls were going to take. She answered his carefully casual inquiry about Aleida's engagement to the young doctor in the East: "That's all off. I thought you knew. Aleida broke off the engagement right after Christmas. All Bill thinks about is his career. He's really awfully stuffy. . . ."

What difference, he thought, can it make to me? Just because she went skiing with me once doesn't mean she cares for me; she'd have to do that much on account of Anne! I've no right to go after her. She probably thinks me pretty low after Cristina's claims of ownership. All I can do is wait and see how she acts when she gets back. I don't think there's much hope. . . .

He went to parties as he had always done, but he felt like a sardonic spectator. He made conversation, grimaced politely, flirted, but could not enjoy himself. It was as if a harsh, white light had been trained on all the social jockeying and maneuvering that went on in the wings, so that he suddenly saw too much. He observed, without wanting to, the jumpy-eyed watchfulness of some of the merchants' wives when they were at one of the big crushes given by a wealthy summer resident to see which of the other merchants or lawyers or doctors had been deemed patrician enough to be asked, to note which of the artists were important or amusing enough to count with their hosts, to gauge who had to be included in the party they were going to give the following week.

It produced the same wry amusement in him to trace Louella Furfey's obvious intent, at a party the Furfeys gave, not to leave out any well-heeled visitor or resident who might possibly buy one of Furfey's pictures and to invite only the elite of the plaza crowd and only those artists who did not push too hard for sales and thus need not be feared as competitors. Only the very wealthy and the artists who were either too poor or too wrapped up in their work to care about their social standing, seemed free from snobbishness.

There were times when his disillusionment blinded him to any friendliness and laughter, and all he remained aware of at a party was a curious, velvety jungle ruthlessness. He watched a New York architect, whom everybody knew from previous summers, make a glossy entrance at the Oxnards', shake hands with a suave flourish and sound like an ecstatic cello, glitter and bubble like an overflowing champagne glass as he swooped from one long-lost friend to another. Peter watched with increasing loathing while the architect caressed poor Jeanne Lauber with a question and pretended to listen breathlessly as his eyes darted about the terrace in a rapid survey of the other guests. The man said, "Oh, really?" seconds after Jeanne had finished answering, smoothly excused himself and rushed over to Helen Kemp—"Helen, darling!"—and thrust his back at poky little Hutch Miller, who had been talking to Helen and whom he had evidently long ago placed as unimportant.

There were many like the architect, and all of them had something of his callousness. People's eyes were always slithering between the temple and the tip of the ear of the person they were talking to, searching for somebody more important. "Somebody less boring sometimes," Peter corrected himself; yet he knew that his first censure had been right. He surprised a look of utter desolation in the eyes of a woman who had been pitifully hovering on the edge of a hilarious group that ignored her. He watched the desperate attempts of inept ones like this woman to fasten onto some guest who was a little less dull—or scared—than they were. He watched the features of an elderly man's face fold for a moment into a grimace of sheer hate when a woman edged away from him with a mumbled "Excuse me, I've got to see. . . ."

The discovery of so much scheming and unhappiness at what professed to be occasions of carefree gaiety filled him with nausea. He came to feel the need after a party to blot out the memory of it and he often drove to some Mexican dance hall or other on the outskirts of town, where there was sometimes a charmingly formal wedding dance going on and where there was always a passionate preoccupation to make the moment yield all the happiness it could. The innocence and courtlike decorum of those dances as much as the prettiness of the Spanish girls enchanted him.

For a moment he thought he was almost cured. He felt sure that he had grown the thick skin he had been longing for.

The evening at the Oxnards' started unpromisingly enough. He sampled the Pernod *frappé*, found that he disliked the sickeningly sweet anise taste as much as before, and turned to the affected young writer beside him who had recently brought out a volume of short stories which everybody raved about and no one seemed to understand. "How do you drink this stuff?"

The glib young genius immediately struck a pose and doled out his words like nuggets. "The forefinger, old boy, the index; like the noble Romans—the vomitarium, you know." Greenwich Village with a touch of Soho, presumably! Peter winced at the staleness of it. . . .

To the right, a tweedy, ruddy-faced summer resident was so engrossed in entertaining a group of women that he kept depositing his cigarette ashes in the ice-packed caviar bowl on the hors d'oeuvres table behind him; he finally buried his stub in the caviar, too. The women whom he had been regaling with his wit pretended to be convulsed by his black finger tips, and he preened himself on his blunder as on an exploit.

The party was turning out like all the rest, and he began to look around for a way to sneak out. He got as far as the hall, only to run into Jim Hopper, who wanted to continue the discussion about art and the machine age. Before he knew it he had let himself get more carried away than he had intended to in telling Hopper about the courage and imagination involved in Theodore Skolloker's early experiments. He mentioned Edison and Faraday, when all at once the latest house guest of the Kemps, to whom he had not paid much attention so far except to notice that she had a full-blown handsomeness and wore a low-cut white gown trimmed with tiny tufts of what appeared to be swan's-down, bore down on them and demanded in a richly feminine voice, "Jim, who is this fascinating man?"

He bantered with her, put her lush forthrightness down to a new technique, and did not mind too much when presently Hal Oxnard and his tweedy pals came buzzing around and carried her off; yet he had been flattered enough by her interest to change his mind about leaving and stay on.

It was half an hour before he saw her again, this time with Larry Collard, who had just rescued her from an intense little man. "Oh!—" she was gasping to Collard—" oh no, not that! Darling, you were in the nick of time." Her tone spoke of depths of intimacy. Then she saw Peter, majestically ignored mousy Lily Praither to whom he had been talking and descended on him—"I've been looking all over for you!" Lily Praither had already turned to Helen Kemp. Collard grinned good-naturedly and effaced himself. . . . Out in the garden on the other side of the lilacs, she was saying, "Is that your car? Darling, I suppose I'd better have my wrap—it's in Daisy's bedroom. And you might grab a drumstick or a ham; I know there's no food in Helen's house. . . ."

She had vitality and warmth, but the memory of Cristina was still too fresh. He did not offer to follow her to Colorado Springs, where she was going the next day to stay for a month. It was either too late or too soon! . . .

What in hell is wrong with me? he kept asking himself.

It was as if all the vaguely enticing vistas that had always lured him forward into the future had suddenly revealed themselves as painted cardboard frauds. He had no zest for anything. It was as if he had seen it all before.

It must be that now that I no longer hate Geoff, he told himself, *now that I've made my peace with him, there's no longer anything to strive for, I've become what Piggot would call an integrated person. I don't hate anybody, but life's become a bore. Or is it because Aleida isn't here, and there's no telling how she feels about me, that I feel like this?*

From sheer boredom and a little because he had neglected Father Hegge's boys for two weeks, he drove to Santa Cruz one dazzling, smiling Sunday morning and arrived soon after the beginning of High Mass. He stood in the back of the adobe church which was gay and somber at once with the bright dresses of the little girls scattered among the dark clothes of the women and men and with the sun bursting in through the small windows and frolicking on the gray walls. He was a little startled by the slow-moving and somehow luminous devoutness of Father Hegge, who was so full of high spirits and so ready to laugh outside of church.

It turned out to be Corpus Christi Day. Before the Mass was quite over a few of the Spanish men began to collect banners that were leaning in a corner by a side altar up front. Four of the men brought out a touchingly simple gold-cloth canopy held up by its four white sticks and took up their stand in front of the communion rail. Some twenty little girls in white dresses and veils were being marshaled by two nuns up by the front pews.

Presently the men with the banners of the various religious societies— the first, bright-crimson one labeled in gold letters "League of the Sacred Heart"—started down the center aisle, and people from the pews fell in behind each one. The little girls in white began to strew flowers from the small baskets in their hands so enthusiastically that it did not look as if their supply of petals would last even until they got out of church. Father Hegge, the monstrance in his hand, was already waiting under the canopy held high over him by the four men.

Politeness had forced him to stay where he was by the holy-water stoup while the procession filed past him out of the church door. One by one the tawdry silk banners went by, and even the rear pews were emptying. He had meant to squeeze into the corner until every one was outside, but when the Spanish men around him crowded in behind the last banner they forced him to move along. He consoled himself that once he got outside he would be able to slip away and lose himself among the spectators he could already see.

But he had not counted on the familiarity with which at least some of the men had come to look upon him after seeing him go in and out of the rectory all winter and spring. The man carrying the blue-and-gold banner just beside him suddenly handed him one of the blue silk cords that hung down from the crossbar. "You want to help?"

To refuse would have been a grave discourtesy. He took the cord and drew himself up straight and admonished himself: I'm not going to slouch and make myself small! This isn't going to hurt me. It means something to the Spanish people whom I like and to Father Hegge whom I like enormously!

After a few minutes his solemnity gave way to secret merriment. He looked up at the blue banner and saw that the gold letters said "San Luis de Gonzaga," and that the painted oval on the banner showed a devout young man with a cross clasped to his chest. It came back to him from his childhood memories of going to church with Aunt Kathi that the picture must be of St. Aloysius of Gonzaga, the patron saint of male purity.

He chuckled inside himself at the incongruity. But already, he realized, he had fallen victim to the charm of the unevenly straggling procession, the gaudy, brave banners, the discordant singing of some endless Spanish hymn that floated back from the strung-out lines in front like a tattered veil, the little girls in white just in back of him, the altar boys enthusiastically tinkling the altar bells on either side of the canopy, the young green of the cottonwoods that lined their path—the rustic piety that seemed to fill the whole June morning. He did not even mind having to go back into the church and all the way up front to the side altar before he was relieved of the blue cord.

Father Hegge said afterward while they were having coffee in the rectory, "It was nice of you to come up for Mass and for our procession."

"It turned out I let myself in for a lot more than that."

Father Hegge's eyes gleamed with puckish delight. "I saw you. You looked very well as an honor guard."

"Did you see what banner it was? It's a wonder I didn't trip and break a leg. The last thing in the world I'd lay claim to is to be a fit guardian of purity. It was an insult to St. Aloysius."

"Oh, St. Aloysius can take care of himself." Father Hegge was laughing at him. "You may be better than you think. Look at all the nice things you've done for us up here."

It was one of the pleasant things about Father Hegge, Peter reflected, that one could banter with him like this and that although Father Hegge knew about his Catholic childhood he had never once nagged to get him to return to the Church.

"Are you trying to trap me, Father?"

Father Hegge smiled back at him. "No need to do that. We all trap our-selves. By the way, I got a post card from a mutual friend of ours and a big box of candy for the boys."

In spite of himself his heart skipped a beat. He tried not to give himself away. "Oh, from Cristina Day."

"I forgot how many lady friends you have. No, it was from Aleida. A great big box of candy. You must have some before you go. We'll call in the boys in a minute—they're in charge of it. They want to talk to you anyway—something about the distributor on the car they don't under-stand."

"I'll help them if I can. Did Aleida write from abroad?"

"From Cleveland, I think. Let me see—I've got the card right here." Father Hegge went to his littered desk and returned with the card in his hand. "Yes, Cleveland it is. And she's promised to bring us some choir records for our phonograph when she comes back."

He played out the comedy which he knew could not fool anyone. "Oh? I didn't know she was coming back. I thought she was going abroad."

There was an unmistakable twinkle in Father Hegge's eyes. "She doesn't say anything about going abroad. I must tell her about our pro-cession today and the new banner bearer we have. . . ." Half an hour later when Peter left, Father Hegge was still in the mood to tease. "Next year," he said, "when you come up for the Corpus Christi procession you must carry one of the poles of the canopy. . . ."

That evening Piggot, who had watched the procession at the cathedral in the morning and with whom Peter compared notes while they walked back to the plaza from a dinner party at Grace Wyatt's house, had some comments on Corpus Christi, too.

"Corpus Christi," he lectured, "the love feast, the *agape!* One can't help wondering, of course, here in Santa Fe how much love the Spanish con-quistadores had for the Indians. In any case there was no hate—the Span-ish still had too much vitality for that at the time. It's only when a civilization begins to decay that it has to have recourse to hate. There appears to be a natural law that an organism which has lost its own inner drive can live only by hating some fellow organism. The second organism becomes its crutch. If it is destroyed by the first organism's active hate or if it collapses for any other reason, the first organism no longer has anything to hold it up and it falls flat on its face. Rome went downhill fast after it had got Carthage out of the way. That's what hap-pens to nations quite frequently."

"And to individuals," Peter baited, catching his drift. Piggot with his exasperating knack for reading one's thoughts was putting into words the worry that had been troubling him during the last few days.

"And to individuals! Hate is the dominant note of our time."

"Suppose it is. Isn't hate really a groping for love?"

Piggot was not to be turned aside. "Possibly. I still call it hate. We're beginning to live more and more by a sort of spiritual parasitism. Perhaps it's the fate of a civilization that puts its faith in the doctrine of human perfectibility to descend gradually to the level of the louse."

"You've said that before about progress. What have you got against having faith in man?"

"Its essential arrogance—the *hubris* of the Greeks. Arrogance always aims too high and ends in failure. You get a vicious progression: failure breeds fear, and fear does away with the capacity to love, and when people no longer love they reach out for hate. And the chief trouble with hate is that we can't hate others without also hating ourselves—destroying ourselves."

Peter recognized the tune. Partly from impatience with Piggot's preaching and partly from recklessness and a furtive hope of help, he put an end to the pretense that they were still dealing in generalities. "I don't know that hate is so bad. I've stopped hating anybody. I love everybody now, including Geoff—I don't see that I'm any the happier for it."

"Of course, you aren't. Hate is the arch temptation of the black cherubim: it appeals to our lasciviousness. That's why when one gets rid of hate there is such a sense of emptiness. It's the hardest thing in the world to find something to love. One has to keep on looking, though, or one falls back into hate."

Peter's impatience with Piggot grew. If he knew so much why couldn't he say something that made sense? He said, "Theoretically I ought to be as happy as a clam. Actually I feel like going off to Africa or the Arctic somewhere or slugging myself with drugs."

Piggot stared past Dorothy Lambert's house. "Most of us are in that boat. We have no Holy Grail."

He wanted to sound caustic. "The trouble is when we've explained something we haven't explained it away. . . ."

If only there was something new! *I don't really want to take that little Spanish girl to the dance tomorrow night. She's charming, of course, but if I actually gave in to that brainstorm and married her, what would we talk about? It would only be Corinne in Pittsburgh over again. I could go to the rodeo with Mitch. I could go to Mexico. . . .*

In his boredom he was delighted when Father Hegge arrived all unexpectedly with Juan, the little crippled boy, the next morning.

"We've had breakfast," Father Hegge thanked him. His eyes twinkled. "This isn't a social call. You'll probably throw us out. I came to ask you a favor."

"Another procession?"

"I'm afraid it's something more difficult than that. I'm hunting for someone to take Juan to Denver to the hospital, and since you were on our way to Santa Fe I came to you first."

Father Hegge was looking him straight in the eye, half making a joke of it. But the little boy, who ever since Peter had brought him the radio and had shown him how to assemble it had glowed with devotion each time Peter had come to Santa Cruz, was politely looking away with precocious Spanish courtliness, so as not to embarrass him in case he wanted to refuse.

He said happily, "You're mistaken, Father. That's much easier."

Already the faint tautness that had been in Father Hegge's manner was gone. His eyes laughed. "We all make our own burdens. It would be wonderful if you could do it! Only I feel that this is an imposition. You've already done so much for us. Here's my problem: I've just heard from a doctor friend in Denver, who has offered to operate on Juan, that he has a bed in the hospital for Juan for the next four months. Juan had infantile paralysis when he was a baby, and his feet were turned in. Dr. Woodman is sure that he can straighten them. Juan is going to have a long siege, but afterward he'll be able to run again. I've promised him a letter every day if he's going to be a good boy and won't be afraid."

"I'm not afraid," the little boy said stoutly. "I brought my radio."

"The other boys are letting him take the radio along to the hospital, so that he won't be lonesome. That is, of course, if you're willing to bother with it. It's all up to you. I'd have taken Juan myself but I have two dying people in my parish whom I can't leave, and Dr. Woodman wants Juan now."

"All right, when do we leave?"

"Well, as a matter of fact we have Juan's bag and the radio out in the car—just in case you might want to go today. But we can put it off. I can bring Juan back tomorrow or the day after, whichever suits you best."

"When does he have to be in Denver?"

"Well, Dr. Woodman did say that he'd like to have him there by Friday, and since Dr. Woodman is doing it all out of the kindness of his heart——"

"You've got a lot of friends, Father," Peter teased.

"Oh, it's not me. Dr. Woodman is doing it for the love of God even though he says he doesn't believe in God. He's a little like you. All the same, it's the grace of God working in him."

"God's got a mighty capable assistant!"

Father Hegge had been fumbling in his inside coat pocket. He brought out a small envelope. "Here are twenty-five dollars which we've been saving for this trip."

Peter waved it away. "Spend it on the other boys, Father, or they'll envy Juan the fine trip he and I are going to have. . . ."

They took the afternoon train.

It was even more fun than Peter had expected to turn the trip into a treat for the little boy. He observed with delight Juan's wide-eyed wonder at the old-fashioned elegance of the quaint narrow-gauge train which seemed largely patronized by well-to-do ranchers going to Denver on business trips. He had bought a checkerboard for Juan, and he played with him all afternoon; then he took him into the diner and let him order everything his shy curiosity craved. He turned down an invitation after dinner to join some of the ranchers for poker because he did not want to leave the little boy. Instead of poker he lent himself happily to the boy's avid eagerness to hear about the world of science and mechanics and told him about Edison and Tesla and Faraday and about his own experiences in the steel mills and laboratories. And in Denver the next morning on the way to the hospital he bought him a history of invention and science which the boy proudly clutched to his chest.

CHAPTER FOURTEEN

Lost and Found

HE stayed over for three days and watched Juan come out of the ether and recover sufficiently to play checkers. Only then, and after he was satisfied that the doctor was kindness itself and that the little boy would be well taken care of, did he take the narrow-gauge train back to Santa Fe.

For a few minutes in Denver he had toyed with the idea of going east to pick up his car, which was still in the Thatchers' garage in Montclair and to spend a few days at home in Westchester. But a curious apathy once he had made sure that the little boy was all right and an unavowed fear that he might miss Aleida if she returned to Santa Fe made him reject the idea.

Traveling south through the green mountain country of Colorado was drearier than when a year ago he had been headed for Santa Fe in the train across the drab Midwestern plains. He had had a purpose then; now it was somehow as if he were slinking home. A place alone, the beautiful mountains, he reflected as the train slid through the quivering sunset haze in a high green valley, obviously did not make for happiness.

By chance the subject occupied him a second time that day.

He sat opposite a bald, pleasant-faced man of about fifty during din-ner. The man had a slight German accent, was well-spoken, and looked prosperous and at peace with the world and himself. They talked about the weather, about food on trains, about Denver, about hotels. By the time they had their coffee, they got along so well and had already learned so much about each other that they hardly needed to introduce them-selves. The man had a dairy ranch in Alamosa, just on the New Mexico line. He had been born in Switzerland and had come to America at twenty-one, right after he had finished agricultural school in Berne, to take a job under an uncle of his who had managed a big cattle ranch. He had married an American girl and had a daughter in college and a boy in high school and another girl still in the grades. And he was going to take a month's trip to Europe in the fall. . . .

They went from the diner to the observation car. Every once in a while their remarks had the startling intimacy and honesty that conver-sations with perfect strangers seemed to evoke on a train. The Swiss rancher said, "I had a notion when I was a young man that I wanted to be an engineer and do a lot of traveling, and here I am out in the sticks, breeding cattle. You wonder sometimes whether you've taken a wrong turn in the road somewhere along the way. Of course, when a man's got a wife and a family, he hasn't got much time for that kind of wonder-ing. . . ." He said, "That kind of woman who's all for show, all for dress-ing up and going to parties all the time, has never appealed to me. Oh, we both of us like a good time, and a man wants his wife to wear nice clothes. . . ."

Peter said, "I've only learned two things in dealing with men: never to drive a man into a corner, where he loses his self-respect, and to be scared to death of a man who's afraid. . . ."

He asked as they sat looking out on the fusing rails and on the darken-ing night closing in like cleft water on the bright wake of the train, "Are you going to take your family with you to Switzerland in the fall?"

The rancher shrugged. "It woudn't mean anything to the kids to go. They'd much rather stay right here. And my wife feels she'd better stay with the children this year, even though the two younger ones could stay with my sister-in-law and the oldest one is going to be away in college anyway."

After a pause in which he lighted a cigarette and drew on it pensively

for a little while, he said, "We took all three of them to see their grand-
parents a couple of years ago. They had a good time, but after all they
didn't speak the language and it woudn't have made much difference to
them if we'd gone to Sweden or to Italy instead. I can't blame them:
everything they know is right here. It's different with me. If I don't get
back once a year, I get to feeling restless, and, except for the war years,
I've gone every year. Of course my family is here and my business and
my friends, and I've got a pretty good life, but somehow it's never the
same thing as the country where you were born and raised."

He paused again and took a few more puffs on his cigarette before he
went on. "My oldest girl used to come to me when she was little and say,
'Daddy, tell me a fairy tale.' Well, I'd tell her all the stories I'd heard in
Switzerland as a child, and as long as she was little that was fine, but after
she started going to kindergarten she wanted to hear only the stories all
the other kids knew about, and what did I know about Mother Goose
and *Alice in Wonderland?* When the two younger ones came along it was
the same thing. You lose your whole childhood when you go to a new
country. . . ."

He was lucky, Peter reflected as he lay in his berth, when it came to
nursery rhymes. He mightn't be able to reel them off by the yard and
meet the exacting standards of a youngster—he grinned to himself—
who'd want every word about Humpty-Dumpty in its place, but at least
he wasn't altogether a stranger to them. He had Sibby Page to thank for
that, Sibby who had made him read *Alice in Wonderland*, and before that
his little sister, of course. It was Anne, with her whole imaginative childhood world still intact when he had first come, who had made it so easy
for him to take root in American soil. All the same, he was lucky never
to have felt that strong pull back to Europe which the Swiss rancher had
talked about.

I suppose, he thought, it's because I didn't have a happy childhood
such as he probably did in Switzerland, and because Mizzi and the road
to Geoff and everything I dreamed about were in this country, and also
because I just simply like it here. I enjoyed that short trip to Vienna last
year, but now I don't care whether I ever see it again.

As if to give the lie to his boasted indifference, his mind kept returning to random details of his visit last summer. He felt again moved to
tenderness as he remembered Aunt Kathi's solicitude about his health,
her fear that he was smoking too much and not getting enough sleep, her
endless simples and teas, her touching displays of respect, the cakes and

other delicacies—all of it embarrassing in the light of his intense dislike for her when he had been small. He smiled as he recalled her prognostication of a storm from the rheumatic pains in her back one morning when he and his cousins had started out on an excursion to the monastery at Melk: "You'd better take your raincoats. You won't laugh when you get caught out in the woods somewhere and get drenched to the skin. I can always tell with my back. . . ."

Just like the night watchman with the stump of his amputated leg at the plant in Harrison! Just like Cristina's two cockers that were supposed to become very nervous before a storm, he thought indulgently. · One wondered what particular organ it was in their case that gave them warning of an approaching storm; presumably they had a built-in electroscope that registered the "electricity in the air" the watchman had always been talking about.

Well, why not? It hadn't been disproved! . . . The night watchman might be as loony as they came with his theory about "the electricity" itching in his stump, but the odd thing was that he had been right almost every time with his predictions of a storm. And he had done his predicting before the barometer had shown any significant change. If it wasn't scientific to accept a theory until it had been proved, it was equally unscientific to reject it before it had been disproved. The funny thing last summer had been that Aunt Kathi had been right, too: there had been a terrific downpour while they were looking at the painting in the abbey at Melk. Coincidence could account for all the cases individually, of course, but when you took them altogether you got a surprisingly uniform correlation between claim and fact. There must always have been hundreds of thousands of people with rheumatism or arthritis or amputated limbs who claimed they had twinges and all kinds of aches when the weather was about to change for the worse. There certainly was such a thing as atmospheric electricity. How could one tell whether it had some effect on the nervous system, or at least on certain kinds of nervous systems or not? One would have to test!

And all at once he found himself wide awake in his berth and in the grip of a familiar excitement. It was like the moment when he had got his first clue to the new model of the alkali battery while he worked at Skolloker's, like the moment when he had hit on the record changer and on the dodge that led to chrome plating—like the crucial moment that had been at the beginning of all his inventions. A sense as of an unsuspected door about to open in what still appeared a blank wall quickened him.

One would have to reproduce the electric charge of the atmosphere before a storm—ionize the air—and see whether such an electric field had any effect on test animals! Better still, try a powerful positive charge and also a negative charge, step each one up indefinitely and see what it did to the animals—whether it depressed them or exhilarated them or merely made them restless perhaps. Supposing a certain kind of charge proved to have a beneficial effect, one could take a patient who was critically ill, put him into an electrically conditioned room—much as one put a pneumonia patient into an oxygen tent—and quite possibly give his vitality that extra boost which made the difference between life and death.

Romantic? . . . What did anyone know about the effect of atmospheric electricity on the human constitution? Had anyone ever studied it? Not that he had heard! It was all still to be done. He would need a laboratory —his thoughts went racing on—*and a shop and his own power plant.*

That piece of property to the north of Tesuque would be perfect for a laboratory: far enough away from the village to insure privacy, and not too far from the road to make it hard to deliver any heavy equipment. He'd need an electrostatic generator or a big induction coil—he'd probably have to build all that himself—and he'd have to insulate the ionized-air chamber from the ground. Build it on a platform of hollow tile or glass brick. . . . But it could all be done! The biggest hitch would be the animals—he didn't know anything about laboratory animals. A heavy enough charge in the air might produce all sorts of chemical and physiological changes in their bodies; it would take experience he did not have just to know how to feed and take care of guinea pigs. *Larry Collard!* Perhaps he could get Larry to help—at least teach him how to take care of the animals or help him hire a competent research man.

He felt an intoxicating lucidity as he lay there and planned. Details fell into place as if he had been thinking about building a laboratory and setting up his research project for months. He did not fall asleep until he was exuberantly going over his plans a second time, and by then it was already dawn. . . .

He went to see Collard as soon as he got into Santa Fe. Collard was working for once—on the head of a young girl, which was beginning to emerge from a great chunk of golden-brown wood. He was good-natured about the interruption. "You couldn't have come at a better time. I was just about to quit; my little model forgot to come back after lunch. Let's go out into the patio. . . ." He was amiable and hearty in his well-bred, squash-club way until Peter explained his errand, when he immediately went on the defensive and became captious and remote. One could almost hear the shifting of the gears.

"I'll help you all I can, of course. Exactly what is this experiment you have in mind? I suppose you're talking about sunspots?"

"I'm talking about atmospheric electricity. At the moment I don't care what causes it; I'm just interested in finding out what effect it has on us. What about sunspots?"

"Well, there's a fellow who's been studying the influence of sunspots on climate—his name's Huntington. He thinks as you do that there is a definite correlation between climate and civilization. Not all climatologists agreee with him on his theory that sunspots have any effect on climate."

Peter had never known him so argumentative. He said, "But I'm not interested in climate and civilization. I just want to see what happens to the individual under certain conditions of the atmospheree."

"Same thing. If I'm not mistaken, Ellsworth Huntington claims to have found a correlation between sunspots and the suicide rate; and you're saying that it's the electric charge of the air that makes an amputee's stump itch. How do you know it isn't the barometric pressure or the humidity that makes rheumatics or amputees uncomfortable?"

"I don't know. But in one case, at least, a man with an amputated leg used to complain of discomfort hours before the barometer fell or before there was any change in humidity." He added hurriedly, "I'm perfectly aware that one has to have thousands of cases to prove anything. It just happens that I studied this one case very carefully for a couple of months: he was always right about storms."

"I was going to say, you are dealing with a few isolated cases."

An intangible softening in Larry Collard's manner restored Peter's confidence. He said, "Wait a minute! Isn't it true that invalids and cripples have always been complaining about bad weather because it intensified their particular ailments? I've read about it as far back as I can remember. There must have been millions of such cases in the history of mankind, and not just thousands. That means there's a vast amount of empirical evidence that all points one way. I think where there's smoke, there's fire."

Collard grinned. "Or, at any rate, a popular superstition."

"All over the globe? I doubt whether any reports that come from so many sources and are so uniform are all due to imagination."

"You'd be surprised how widespread and how stubborn superstitions can be. There's one other factor to consider: cripples and invalids of any sort are almost bound to be somewhat neurotic."

"When you've said 'neurotic,' you haven't said anything. Supposing a neurotic is hypersensitive to noise: that makes him a nuisance to his neighbors, but it doesn't mean that the noise doesn't exist. Now, here's another thing—you're a doctor, Larry, aren't you?"

"Yes, but I haven't practiced medicine except for one year as an interne, so don't ask me for any prescriptions. I'm more of a biologist."

"That doesn't matter. But isn't it true that more patients who are critically ill are lost between the hours of eleven at night and about six in the morning than at any other time? Is that a fact or is it a superstition?"

Collard's lean, handsome, but somehow weary and ravaged face softened again in a smile. "Yes, that's true. It's also a fact that you get most of your births during those hours. It seems to be a period of low ebb. Do you claim that's due to atmospheric electricity, too?"

"I'm not claiming anything—that's why I want to run some experiments. But there's a possibility the degree of ionization of the air is quite different at night from what it is during the day. If that's so, then the low ebb you were talking about might very well be due to that difference."

"And, of course, that difference would be due to the sun. We're back to the sunspots again."

"Yes, if there's any regular variation in the atmospheric charge, it's bound to be caused by the sun. At the moment I don't much care what causes the electric charge, whether it's the sun or humidity or wind friction or cosmic rays. All I'm interested in is whether atmospheric electricity affects an animal organism in any way."

"You're pretty sure it does."

It was his turn to grin at Collard. "Well, I have a hunch. At the same time I'm keeping an open mind. If I find anything, good! If there's nothing in it, that's that."

"How are you planning to produce your electric field?"

"That's one of the things where I need your advice. The method is going to depend on how much room a cage with the guinea pigs will take up while they're being tested. I was thinking of a big condenser which I'd hook up to a high-voltage source of power. I'd simply step up alternating current and then rectify it. Another possibility would be to use an electrostatic generator or an induction coil, but I've a notion that the noise of machinery in the room or sparks would upset the guinea pigs and introduce an extraneous factor into the experiment."

"That's quite true. Incidentally white rats would be a little better for what you have in mind."

"Well, there you are. You see I don't know the first thing about laboratory animals. I wouldn't know about feeding them or keeping them from getting sick. Do you think I could get a biologist to take care of all that?"

"I think I might be able to persuade some young research assistant to come out. You'd probably have to guarantee his salary for a year and pay him a few hundred dollars more than he'd get at some college in the East, because this would be a sort of blind alley for most of them from the point of view of their academic careers."

"I'm perfectly willing to pay what's necessary. But would one of these fellows be able to examine the tissues of an animal and tell whether there had been any changes?"

"I don't know what changes you have in mind. If you mean degeneration of tissue, he should be able to tell that. It depends on how competent a man you get."

"What I had in mind was this: supposing I place those white rats you mentioned in a highly charged field, just before the breakdown of the air, before you get the miniature lightning between the two condenser plates, and supposing I delay the breakdown and keep the rats exposed to the terrific electric tension for a long time—isn't there a possibility that there may be some chemical or other changes in the nerve tissue of the animals? I mean, nobody has ever tried the experiment—how does one know what to expect? There may be all sorts of changes, organic or chemical or—I don't know what you'd call them. In any case, Larry, if there were changes, you yourself would be able to tell them, wouldn't you?"

Collard grinned again. "As a matter of fact electrical nerve impulses were what I was working on before I came out here."

"Damn it, Larry, you've just got to help me with this! I don't want to drool over a coincidence, but this one is too pointed to ignore. You're probably the one man in ten million as far as my project is concerned."

In an instant Collard had withdrawn into some remote, inner fastness where one could not follow him. He spoke as if across a moat. "Why do you suppose I'm out here? I've got a couple of years at most. You'll have to excuse me. All I'm interested in is in having a good time."

He felt cowed by Collard's bitterness and suddenly embarrassed by his own boisterous health. It lasted only for a moment, and then his high spirits reasserted themselves. He felt powerful enough to galvanize Collard back into health. He bullied, "To hell with predictions like that! How can the doctors tell? The way you tear around every night, there's nothing wrong with you that a pretty Spanish girl and a Mexican dance hall can't cure. You might as well do a little honest work and show me how to be scientific while I make an ass of myself."

Collard's eyes hardened with hostility, and Peter thought he had gone too far; then Collard sat up in his deck chair and pushed the cigarettes toward him on the low, stretched-cowhide table. "I'll think about it, but I'm not promising anything. I'll let you know in a couple of days. There'll certainly not be any difficulty about getting you a reasonably competent man for your laboratory." His tone became conversational and sprightly again. "Supposing you find you were right in your hunch, what do you intend to do then?"

"If there's a correlation, the next step would be to study the amount of charge carried by the atmosphere at various times of the day and night, before and after storms. Then, I'd have to find out what the optimum charge is when it comes to the human organism. As far as I've been able to find out, nobody has ever paid the slightest attention to atmospheric electricity, tried to measure it or anything else. What beats me is how medical men could have ignored the subject for so long."

"There are more pressing research projects perhaps. We aren't even getting on very fast with those." The faint shadow that passed over Collard's face showed that he was thinking of his own disease. "Of course one can never tell where a piece of research like yours may lead. . . . What happens when you've found this optimum charge?"

"Then I go to work and try to design some simple, efficient apparatus for producing a charge artificially in a room. If it turns out that all one needs to do is ionize the air, it oughtn't to call for too expensive a machine, and every hospital would easily be able to have a number of rooms where the critically ill could get the benefit of the charged air until they've weathered the crisis. As I said, each room would be like an oxygen tent."

Collard looked amused. "And presumably if it doesn't cost too much, one would be able to sell this euphoria generator of yours to a few million homeowners!"

Peter grinned back at him. "Very likely—eventually. Only, I wouldn't have any monopoly. Since I can't take out a patent on a natural law, every electrical company would be free to design its own model and peddle it. I'm much more apt to go broke on this little project than I am to make a lot of money. Anyhow, all that's still a long way off. Right now what I want is to get going with the research."

Collard hesitated for a moment. He said thoughtfully, "There's a chance you may have hit on something."

Peter had got up. "We'll find out. Meanwhile, I'd better dash out to Tesuque and see whether I can still get hold of a piece of property that would be an ideal location for a laboratory. Wish me luck. See you in a couple of days! . . ."

But two days later it was Collard who sought him out in the bank while Peter was busy counting out the cash for each of the seven members of the family who had owned the property he bought. Collard teased, "I see you travel with your gang."

"We just finished at the lawyer's, signing the deed. I now own a hunk of land, a handsome view, a lot of prairie dogs, and part of a creek."

"That calls for a celebration, doesn't it?"

"No time."

"How about running out to the house anyway when you get through? There's something I want to show you."

"All right, Larry, if you won't mind if I don't stay very long. I have to see the well driller at two; then I've got a session with the contractor; then building supplies; and then I've promised to take these people home. . . ."

At his house Collard, after pouring a drink and insisting on drinking to the laboratory, picked up a handsomely bound old book that lay face down on the arm of an easy chair. Collard turned several pages before he found what he wanted. "This is Boswell's *Life of Johnson*," he said. "By sheer accident I ran across a couple of passages last night I thought might interest you. Here's the first one. Johnson says in 1758: 'Surely, nothing is more reproachful to a being endowed with reason, than to resign its powers to the influence of the air, and live in dependence on the weather and the wind for the only blessings which nature can put into our power, tranquillity and benevolence. . . .' Then in 1775 Boswell says about Johnson: 'He had, till very near his death, a contempt for the notion that the weather affected the human frame.' "

Larry Collard grinned slyly. "Boswell doesn't agree with that one bit, of course. He's a *grand nerveux* and he's always griping about the weather; so he's delighted with his entry for August 2, 1784, when Johnson writes in a letter: 'The weather, you know, has not been balmy. I am now reduced to think, and am at last content to talk about the weather. Pride must have a fall. . . .'"

What did all that ancient drivel have to do with what he was after? Peter wondered. And yet he listened more and more happily. Something about Collard's manner in reading the passages filled Peter with certainty that Collard had made up his mind—favorably. He said, "I didn't know Jonson lived as late as 1784; I thought he was a contemporary of Shakespeare's."

"Oh, you're thinking of Ben. This is Dr. Johnson—Samuel Johnson, the one who wrote the dictionary."

Always, Peter reflected luxuriously, delighting in his vagrant thoughts, these gaps that dated from the time when he had been in a mill instead of in a high-school class! But what did it matter? What mattered was that Collard knew all about laboratory animals.

"As I said," Collard went on, "there's a chance you may be onto something."

"Does that mean I can count on you?"

"Did you know Aleida was back?"

He wondered whether his face had betrayed the start it had given him. "No." He must keep cool. What right had he to appear more than just politely interested? "Did she come back alone?"

"As far as I know she did. Whom was she supposed to bring?"

"I thought her cousin might be here again." Was Collard merely teasing him by keeping his decision in suspense, or did his mentioning Aleida mean more than that? A thin band of anguish tightened around his chest. "Will that make any difference to your decision—Aleida's being back?"

Collard's playful tone filled him with enormous relief. "Why, not at all. I just happened to mention it because I remembered it."

"Then I can count on you?"

"For what it amounts to, yes. I can't promise how long I'm going to be around but I can help you get started anyway. I imagine it's going to take you a little time to get your laboratory actually set up."

The thought of Aleida was like a secret thread of joy, a steel spring, inside his confidence. "Don't take any bets on that. When I knuckle down, I get things done. . . ."

CHAPTER FIFTEEN

Gentian Meadow

PETER listened while he wiped his hands on a bundle of cotton waste. Through the glass-brick corridor that led into the testing room came the voice of the young driver who had brought out the paint and more lumber for shelves from the building-supply company. "What the hell are those big copper sheets?"

The grumpy old carpenter said testily, "Keep your damn hands off those. That copper shows every fingerprint. If they're all smeared up, I get the blame. They're condenser plates if you must know."

"Condenser plates!" the driver protested noisily against being imposed on. "That size? Who are you kidding? I know what a condenser looks like."

"You asked me, and I'm telling you. If you want to know any more, go ask somebody else."

"And what the hell are all those wire contraptions out in that other room?"

"Cages."

298

"Cages? What's he going to do—raise chickens?"

"You can ask more questions than anybody I ever saw. They're for the rats."

"What rats?"

"White rats," the carpenter said with the weary authority of the insider. "They use them for testing."

"First, it's going to be a radio station; and now it's a menagerie. This is the screwiest place I ever saw," the driver gave his considered opinion.

Peter was amused. He tossed the oily waste in the steel bin between the lathe he had been uncrating and the drill press that was already set up, and went out of the shop to the portale where the contractor was waiting for him. One of the Mexican helpers had already started brushing linseed oil on the corbel and on one of the posts that supported the portale roof.

The contractor straightened up from measuring the sashes that were leaning against the wall and squinted up at the painted corbel. "I can put more stain in it," he offered.

Peter had stepped out on the sagebrush to get a better view. "No, that's all right. By the time he gives it a second coat, it'll darken some."

"Most people would like it darker, but you're the boss." The contractor had come out to stand beside Peter; he glanced toward the two men who were starting to lay the red flagstones at the lower end of the portale and said a little pompously, "Yep, that's going to look all right." He turned to go back to his measuring but stopped for a second to sniff the air. "Smell it? When it gets to be near the end of August, you can always tell fall's in the air."

Left by himself, Peter looked down the row of portale posts once more. *Lucky thing he had listened to Geoff about the portale!* Geoff had said the first afternoon he had come out to look, "Even though it is to be a laboratory, that's no reason for not sticking to native architecture," and he had added, full of his recent interest in building, which dated from his buying the house on the Camino, "Besides, it isn't only a question of looks—a portale helps to keep the inside of the building cool and protects the wall. . . ." The flagstones were perhaps an extravagance, but not too great a one, and after all something he could afford; and the laboratory would serve him for a long time. Even if it turned out that there was nothing in his hunch about the atmosphere, there were any number of practical things for him to go to work on.

His eyes traveled down toward Tesuque and swept over the lacy clumps of wild asters and the laughing array of sunflowers along the road. *It was*

almost fall; he had been too busy to notice it! A blue roadster that looked
very like Aleida's was coming up the road from Bishop's Lodge. It was
still too far away to make out faces behind the flashing, glistening windshield, but he could tell that it was a man who was driving and that there
was a girl beside him in the car. *Not likely anyway that Aleida would
come to see him, even though she had been excitingly friendly two days
ago when he had run into her for the first time since she'd been back.
There had been only the faintest shadow of reserve between them from
last spring and they had talked for a full five minutes in front of the grocery store about Anne's letters from Europe and about her palomino colts
and about his plans. Unfortunately Mary Orr and Gladys had come along
and had taken her away!*

The blue roadster failed to turn off the road by the big tree and to
come up the slope. He caught a sideways glimpse of the car: it was *not*
Aleida's father or even Collard at the wheel, and the girl was a woman
with red hair!

His jagged disappointment told him how eagerly he had hoped that it
might be Aleida. He suddenly knew he had to see her.

He walked back under the portale and said to the contractor, "I've got
to run out to Pecos. I don't think anything is going to come up; Fred
know's what he's supposed to do about the shelves. If I'm not back when
you go, just leave the keys under the keg."

He stopped at the house to put on a clean shirt and begrudged even
the ten minutes it took him to clean up. The few miles to Santa Fe had
never seemed so long. He felt better after he had got to the other side of
town and was actually on the Pecos road. His very impatience to get there
now, his uncertainty as to the exact location of the ranch and his half-
amused confusion at the thought of how to explain his sudden call after
he had let the whole summer go by were shot through with gaiety.

He passed the first few scattered houses and was about to stop at a small
ranch beside the road to ask his way when he saw another blue roadster
coming toward him from the huddle of adobe dwellings that were obviously the center of the village. He told himself quickly, to stave off another
disappointment: *I've got blue roadsters on the brain!* But this time it *was*
Aleida and some other girl in a yellow fiesta dress!

He honked and waved, stopped, and hurried across the road to where
Aleida was pulling up. She smiled and softly thrust her elbow and arm—
left bare by the charmingly puffed short sleeve of her green muslin
dress—out of the window as she took her hand off the wheel.

"Hello," she said. "What are you doing out here?"

"I was about to look for your ranch."

"Why didn't you telephone? We would have had the mayor and a special committee out to welcome you."

"It was supposed to be a surprise."

"It would have been that in any case," she managed to reproach him and filled him with delight. "Jane, this—" she turned to introduce him to the appealingly youthful and eager girl beside her, who, he learned, was her cousin and who looked young for a college junior. "It's too stupid!" Aleida exploded. "The first time you come to see us we have to have an appointment in town! Jane has a fitting for some clothes she wants to get in time to take back east with her. And Father isn't home, or I'd say you might want to wait for us at the ranch."

"It doesn't matter," he said. "I'll try another time."

"You know, we almost came to see *you.* Jane's been wanting to see Bishop's Lodge, and I've been terribly curious about your laboratory. Larry says you are doing the most fascinating things. But I suppose it's all so secret that no outsiders are let in," she teased, and Peter was enchanted to see how much laughter there could be in her hazel eyes.

"Why don't you come out after the fitting?"

Her eyes consulted Jane's for a second. "All right! We'll dash on ahead. We'll see you in Tesuque about five. . . ."

He dawdled as much as he could on the way back, but even so had a long wait. He kept glancing out the big machine-shop window every few seconds to watch for a sign of the car. At a quarter to five he could not stand it inside any longer and on the pretext of inspecting the painter's work came out on the portale. At a few minutes to five he at last caught sight of the blue roadster. He hurried toward the rough bridge they had built over the arroyo.

Aleida pulled up, smiled, and again rested her elbow and arm on the window ledge. "Is this as far as one's allowed to go?"

He noticed again what beautiful arms and exquisitely turned wrists she had. He smiled back at her. "Without an escort," he said. "I came to keep you from going to the right because there's a lot of broken glass over there we haven't had a chance to clear away."

"I thought you had changed your mind," she teased, and the golden flecks were back in the depths of her eyes. "Is that the laboratory?"

"No, that's a machine shop. I'm afraid there isn't really much to see in there, but if you want to walk through it——"

"Of course we do. We want to see everything. That's why we came!"

Peter had never seen her so gay or so secretly and intoxicatingly attentive to every word he uttered once he had taken them into the building, so that from sheer flustered incredulity and delight he addressed himself almost solely to her cousin, who seemed dewily—he was struck again by the effect Aleida had of making other girls seem immature—like a child alongside of her, even though there could not be more than two or three years difference between them.

He took them through the shop, the little powerhouse, with the Diesel and the generator already embedded in concrete, through the testing chamber which he privately referred to as the "static room," through the cheerful little gallery where Collard's rats were to be housed, and through the handsome room that was to be Collard's office and laboratory. Then he showed them the well house and just beyond it, on a slight rise, the place where the contractor's children had found a lot of Indian arrowheads.

Aleida exclaimed at the view. "Aren't you going to build anything up here?"

"I thought it would be a good place for a house sometime."

"Aren't you going to have a house?"

"Well, right now all I'm trying to do is to get the laboratory under way," he excused himself.

It was Aleida's cousin, who had taken off her red-and-green kerchief and stood for a moment tossing her straw-blond hair, that asked with flattering reproachfulness, "Won't you be at the Santa Fe fiesta at all?"

"Well, tomorrow I have to finish setting up equipment in the shop, so that Saturday I can turn out some braces we have to have. And Sunday I'll be busy all day laying out cabinets and shelves in the little room I showed you where we'll do the testing. I'm afraid I won't get much chance."

Aleida said as he walked with them to the blue roadster, "We were going to ask whether you'd like to join us Monday on a ride up to Panchuela Creek. Jane has never been in the high mountains. Will you come?"

Even while he hesitated and talked and tried to make up his mind, he had time to be amazed by the startling closeness that existed between Aleida and him today, so that they seemed quite inexplicably to be alone with each other, and the little cousin hardly there at all. "Darn it," he said. "Monday I've got the Diesel man coming from Fort Worth. We've been having trouble with the motor, and I've been trying to get him for two weeks."

"But you can't work all the time!"

It was as much the nudging, young-girl charm of her cousin, waiting for his answer as if the success of her whole visit in New Mexico depended on it, as the tantalizing prospect of spending a whole day with Aleida, that abruptly made him decide.

"All right, I'd very much like to come."

"Oh, grand!" Jane burst out eagerly.

"Could you be in Pecos by seven o'clock? We could all have breakfast at our house, then drive to Cowles where the horses are going to be waiting for us, and get started about nine. Jane and I are going to put up a picnic lunch."

"What do I bring?"

"Nothing except a fishing rod if you like to fish. I'm going to take mine. There are loads of trout in Cave Creek."

"How about a saddle? Shall I bring mine?"

"Not unless you'd rather have your own. John—our Indian—is going to take the horses and saddles up to Cowles on Sunday. Seven o'clock won't be too early for you?"

"Heavens, no! That just means leaving here at six. I'm always up that early...."

But because he was scared to death that he might oversleep, he had told Crecencio to wake him Monday morning at half past five, only to be already shaved and dressed when Crecencio came over from next door. It was the first day he had taken off in more than two months, and the feeling of having been let out of school grew in him the closer he got to Pecos and then to the place, three miles above the little store, where Aleida had told him to begin watching for the gate to her father's ranch. He saw the blue roadster drawn up in front of an adobe house with a long portale some three hundred yards off the road long before he came to the iron cattle guard and the shingle announcing "Gibbs." For just a moment as he drove through the gate and headed down the bumpy, private road, the adobe ranch house struck him as disappointingly unimpressive and drab. Then he saw the charming patterns made by the morning sun under the portale, the cottonwood grove to the left beyond the house where a small herd of cattle was grazing along the river, and on the other side of the Pecos the pasture land sloping up the wooded hills that walled in the valley, and he laughed at himself for having expected a picture-book ranch house after a whole year in New Mexico, and the mood of festive anticipation took possession of him again.

They had not heard him arrive. He stood at the big screen door, saw the cheerful wicker and cowhide furniture spread out with inviting carelessness all up and down the portale, smelled the exhilarating morning freshness in the air, dimly made out the large, brick-floored hall through the screen and saw that it got most of its light through a leaded-glass window at the opposite end, and could not resist listening for a few seconds to the voices that came from the room on the right. He heard Aleida ask, "Father, are you sure you brought them in from your car?"

Mr. Gibbs sounded vastly good-natured, amused. "As sure as one can be about anything of the sort. I'm not taking any oaths before breakfast, though."

"Rosita, they must be in the closet!"

The throaty Spanish voice presumably belonging to a maid buckled with protest. "O.K., I look again, but ees not there."

"Jane, be a dear and help Rosita."

"I can't; my hands are all sticky with the goop from the sandwiches. Who needs ponchos anyway—it isn't going to rain." Jane's voice was suddenly full of mischievous hilarity. "Why don't you go yourself? There's nobody in the hall."

"I'll get even with you later! . . ."

The exchange had been boisterous, affectionate, gay. It was the first time Peter had ever heard that particular quality in Aleida's voice. He hastily jangled the cluster of camel bells beside the door and wondered whether Larry Collard or Aleida's father was coming on the trip. Mr. Gibbs came to the door. He was in city clothes and clearly had no intention of going on any all-day horseback ride. "Come on in! You'll have to excuse us—we're a little late this morning. One of the dogs tangled with a porcupine, and we've been pulling quills out of his mouth for the last hour."

"I like that!" Aleida protested from somewhere in the big living room on the right. "All you did was watch and hand out advice. I'll be out in a minute, Peter."

Aleida's father grinned. "That's right; this wasn't my day for surgery. Aleida—" he explained—"got blood all over herself, and she's had to change. I hope you don't mind eating in the kitchen—we always have breakfast there."

Jane, in riding breeches and gleaming boots and an immaculately ironed white blouse, joined them and was at once dewily self-contained, tartly virginal with him—as with an elder sister's beau who was no longer fair game, Peter noted with amusement—and delightfully determined not to be ignored. They went through a handsome dining room, out through a neat butler's pantry into a sunny kitchen where a plump Spanish woman was busy at a massive coal range, and a smiling girl of about fourteen was washing a few dishes at the sink, and where a table with a red-and-white-checked cloth and a vase of zinnias on it was already laid for breakfast in the alcove that adjoined the butler's pantry. Peter was introduced to the cook and her daughter, was shown the two canaries in a cage, was given a tall glass of orange juice by Jane. Everything in the house, he noticed, was straightforward, generous, relaxed.

Aleida came in through the pantry door while they were still standing around. She was dressed like Jane, except that she wore a rough gray and red wool shirt, almost as if she scorned to impress him by the clothes she wore today. She greeted him, excused herself for being late, made them all sit down, and was presently being teased by her father again. They had breakfast and talked about the Labrador retriever puppy that had been hurt, about porcupines, about a skunk that had got into the chicken house and had carried off a porcelain nest egg, until Mr. Gibbs excused himself with a genial "I hate to leave you, but I have to be in Las Vegas at nine. Have fun! . . ." There was not going to be any fourth! Peter helped take out saddlebags stuffed full of thermos bottles and food and a bundle of slickers to Aleida's car, and went with her to look at the injured puppy which lay on a saddle blanket in the garage and growled and wagged its tail and seemed to be getting along all right, and then they were off, too.

It took an hour to drive to Cowles and nearly twenty minutes more to get over the two miles of sharply rising forest road to the ranger station, where the horses were. They spent another half hour saddling up and chatting with the ranger and his wife before they finally started up the narrow logging road. Yet Peter had no sense of delay, for even the drive in Aleida's car had already been touched with the enchantment of a childhood outing, partly because there had been the excitement of climbing steadily and of watching the wooded sides of the valley gradually closing in, and partly because he had been lifted by an exquisitely mingled sense of protectiveness and privilege in sitting with the two of them in the front seat, Jane between Aleida and him, talking quietly, lightly now and then because there was no hurry, because he had the whole day still ahead of him.   •

They rode single file, Aleida's sorrel immediately plunging into the lead and the businesslike pinto Peter had drawn, not seeing any reason to expose himself needlessly to scratching branches, falling in behind Jane's gray. Almost as if by agreement, Aleida and he allowed Jane to make all the discoveries and call their attention to some gigantic spruce or to the chipmunks that were scampering about everywhere or to some particularly charming spot along the rushing creek. Once, after they had been on horseback for about half an hour, Jane complained of a ringing in her ears—"It's a kind of singing. I feel sort of all lightheaded, don't you?"—and was informed by Aleida that they were already up over nine thousand feet. Jane exulted, "Wait till I tell Roger. He's always bragging how high he and those brats climbed in the Sierras last year. I want to go all the way up, as far as one can go. I feel drunk."

But there was something intoxicating besides the altitude, and the singing was deep inside him. There was the increasing number of slim, silvery aspen trunks shooting straight up to their feathery tufts of infinitesimally rustling leaves. There were the great, shaggy pines and the crowded spruce trees that were so bemused in their own shadow as to appear almost black and the asters and the belated bluebells and a dozen other kinds of wild flower which he could not name along the creek and the trail. There was the rich silence, full of suppressed chuckles and whisperings, broken now and again by the silver-shrill call of some bird that seemed to make fun of them—broken, too, when Aleida or Jane or he spoke and the whole forest seemed to be listening. But above all there was his renewed astonishment that he should be here with Aleida and this rather charming cousin of hers, quite matter-of-factly answering Aleida and looking at her oval face haloed by her wide-brimmed Stetson when she twisted around in the saddle and asked whether this was anything like the Alps— as if they had always been accustomed to talk so simply to each other, as if there had been no winter and spring just passed when she had disapproved of him, as if there was no need any longer between them of Anne, his sister go-between.

A wild turkey started up with a tremendous clatter of wings and disappeared in the half-dark of the spruce branches. A cottontail eyed them solemnly from the top of a hummock and then scudded off in such sudden panic that they all had to laugh. More and more the forest brightened as aspen crowded back the somber evergreens, their white trunks no longer merely graceful up here but majestic as they shot up to the tremulous green roof overhead. The open strip along the creek widened and became a small meadow every now and again, so that Peter was able to ride alongside of Jane. He got her to tell him about her winter at Leland Stanford and her plans to go to New York after college and get into theater management. A couple of times Aleida dropped back and joined in their talk; then the trail would become too narrow again, and she would pull away from them and ride on ahead once more.

It was while they were all three side by side on a strip of lush mountain meadow that stretched out ahead after they had topped a rise that something blue in the grass here and there caught his eye. Deep blue— not like any other blue—strangely familiar. It could not be wild iris: it was too late for iris, even up here where everything was several weeks behind; besides it was not the same blue. That incredible purple tint— nothing like violets!

He reined in his horse and pulled it around in back of Jane's. He had a feeling of holding his breath as he headed the horse toward the nearest patch of blue. Even as he swung himself out of the saddle, the constriction in his chest, the hesitancy which would hardly let him dare believe, exploded into joyous certainty. *Gentian!*

In an instant he was transported back in time to the moment when as a boy he had walked out with Franz onto the meadow below his grandfather's quarry that one precious summer in the Tyrol. The violent joy he had experienced then at the discovery that his grandfather owned something as rare as a meadow on which there grew gentian—so much more wonderful even than the quarry or the forge or the forest or the water conduit which that other Peter Domanig had built—vibrated in him again. Grandfather's meadow, which had been nearly encircled by granite palisades and almost overpoweringly fragrant with the scent of mint and wood strawberries, and this sunny one, with Aleida and her cousin riding slowly toward him across the warm-smelling grass, fused and became as one. He felt an impulse to reach out and embrace not only the patch beside which he was crouching on the ground but the scattering of blue all along the creek.

He looked up at Aleida and said, not even attempting to bridle his enthusiasm, "It's gentian! Did you know it was here?"

Her hazel eyes flickered with mischief. "Why do you suppose I brought you and Jane up here? Wait till you see my favorite spot when we get to Cave Creek."

Jane had got off her horse and was bending over beside him. "Gentian —is that what they are? Oh, aren't they beautiful!"

"I didn't know they grew in this country," he let himself babble on.

"These are the first ones I've seen since I was in the Alps as a child. I'm going to pick you some."

"Peter, just a few! They'll wilt if we pick them now."

"Just a few," he promised and—like Jane alongside him—went on picking the exquisite purple flowers until he had a small nosegay which he handed up to Aleida—proudly, full of secret delight at having something to give her that was wonderful enough to express his gratitude to her for bringing him.

"They're lovely," she said and tucked the stems carefully into the slit between the two top buttons of her red-and-gray wool shirt. She gave him a mischievous smile as they headed the horses back toward the trail. "Of course they grow in this country! Didn't you ever see any in the East? They grow in Connecticut."

"Not real ones."

"Fringed gentian—yes, real ones."

He reveled, in his exultation, in contradicting her. "I don't believe one word of it."

"Of course there aren't so many, and they aren't so beautiful as these."

"I should think not! They're probably dogtooth violets. Why, gentian only grow where it's high, like here or in the Alps." *In a rare and wonderful place like this!* he added inside himself.

Not only had this meadow with its incredible wealth of black-purple blooms winking from the rich mountain grass, sentineled all about by laughing white aspen trunks, been waiting for him like an inheritance held secretly in trust for him until precisely this moment by some invisible guardian, but also this day was one in ten thousand. It was one of those days when the past and the future existed only as a pale shadow region around the triumphant present—when every moment seemed memorable and the hours stretched out in golden serenity, so that he found himself inclined one minute to move softly and all but hold his breath for fear of upsetting some delicate balance in the day, and wanting to race his horse and sing for joy the next.

It was as if he had inadvertently swallowed some fabulous drug. The most commonplace, predictable happening immediately took on the magic uniqueness and vitality, the haunting beauty of a scene in a rare Chinese print. Every experience became a new peak of delight. They came on five plump and preoccupied pheasants which remained so unperturbed among the trees that Aleida's cousin was able to get within a few feet of them with her camera before they fluttered into some underbrush. They discovered a tangle of raspberry vines jeweled with berries at the bottom of a ravine. They arrived at Aleida's favorite spot, a small meadow along Cave Creek that was a purple riot of gentian. And then there was the final climb to still another meadow up over the top of the Divide.

There was no end to his joy. There was the pleasure of watching Aleida's sure-handed competence as she unpacked the lunch; his sharper pleasure when she leaned forward to hand him the aluminum cup with coffee just as he sat down and he caught a glimpse of a dainty silk strap and intoxicatingly white skin through the "v" of her rough lumberjack shirt; the deliciously lazy hours after lunch when Jane and he lay on the grass and looked up at the sky while Aleida went off to fish. There was the exciting gallop across Horsethief Meadow until Aleida pulled up short and showed him the magnificent gray timber wolf who had paused to stare at them from the edge of the wood. There was the charming moment when Jane began to look tired during the fast ride down to Panchuela Creek and Aleida and he exchanged a half-amused, half-alarmed glance as over a child and hastily stopped for a rest. And there was his sudden realization that although nothing had been said between Aleida and him that had not been casual, there was yet between them an exhilarating sense of intimacy.

It seemed part of the dreamlike magic of this day, on which anything could be expected and nothing foreseen, that Aleida should assume as a matter of course when they got back to the ranch that he would stay for dinner. "Of course, you're going to stay. You've got to help eat the trout!" Part of the magic, too, that the relaxed graciousness he noticed again in everything about the house should make him feel as if this were already the dozenth time he was sitting in the living room pleasantly talking with Mr. Gibbs over a drink while the two girls had gone off to change. And still part of something not to be explained that when he finally left at ten he should agree so eagerly to come to Aleida's farewell party for Jane, as if he had not been in the habit of instantly saying "no" to any invitation in the last two months.

The dominant note—he told himself that night in Tesuque, indulgently remembering what Piggot had said about hate as he reveled in his memory of the day and felt himself swept along on a tide of affection not only for Geoff but for Mr. Gibbs and for Aleida's cousin, Jane—*is the need to love, same as it's probably always been. Hate is only the panic of those who can't manage love. . . .*

Everything was changed. Two nights later he looked around the Gibbs Ranch living room at the familiar faces he had been seeing at parties all of last winter and spring, and wondered how he could possibly have felt acid about so many charming people last June. Suppose Roz Trappan did cultivate the more successful artists and was particular whom she had to her parties, and suppose Louella Furfey did try to help sell her husband's pictures—what was that but healthy feminine ambition and wifely loyalty? What was wrong with a little innocent snobbishness? It added zest to life and made things exciting for women. He had been ridiculously exaggerating in June when he had seen it all as vicious. He had completely ignored the warmth and generosity constantly in evidence, as now when Hal Oxnard beside him was offering the use of his big car to Praither, who hadn't any money and needed to get his pictures to a show in New York which Dave Buell had arranged for him at his own gallery. "Why don't you take our Cadillac and just pile all your pictures in the back? We never use the old bus. Save you all the bother of crating and shipping. . . ."

He did not hear Praither's answer. On Peter's left Aleida was asking Mary Orr, "Won't you have a highball, too, Mary?" He had been unable to keep his eyes from following Aleida in the stunning, sequined blue tulle dress all evening. She said to Mary, as she jiggled the empty glass pitcher she had picked up from the tray on the coffee table, "I'll get some in a minute!"

He asked quickly, before the tweedy young rancher from Las Vegas who had been sticking like a burr to her ever since dinner could get ahead of him, "Can I help?"

"You certainly can. Remember: four highballs, two with soda for Pitch and Daisy, and the two with plain water for Larry and the Judge. Where's your glass? . . ."

She did practically all the work after they got to the butler's pantry. He had only the delight of watching her deft grace as she reached up into the cupboard for more glasses, pulled open the door of the icebox, turned on the faucets in the sink. He complained, "There isn't anything for me to do. I don't know why you had me come out here."

She turned to him with the bowl of ice in her hand. "You can put soda in those two. Maybe I wanted your company."

The laughing gleam in her hazel eyes reminded him of the golden dust on the wings of a butterfly he had once seen. Exultantly his glance lingered for a second on the exquisitely tender skin in the soft hollows above her cheeks and swept up to her thick honey-colored hair. "Did you really?" he asked and took the bowl from her and set it on the table.

In an instant they were in each other's arms. There was no need for words. There was only the glorious awareness that she crowded against him as hard—as joyously—as he did against her. *Not just passion*—he found time to think, *not just silly pride of conquest. This was joy!*

Wonderful minutes, after which she pulled away gently. "We'll have to take in the drinks."

Her ruefulness and instant, eager response when he refused to let her go made them both smile as their lips met again. He joked, with a glance at the highball glasses on the table, "It takes time to crack the ice."

She laughed back. "It also takes time for it to melt, and it's half melted now. They'll come out looking for us."

"I suppose we'll have to go." He opened his arms reluctantly and stood aside while she turned to the table and reached for the pitcher. He poured soda into the two highballs Aleida had put to one side and then took the bowl with the ice out to the icebox, exchanging a smile with her when they passed each other by the towel rack. Aleida was already arranging the highballs on the tray. He stood behind her and looked down at her fluffy, amber-brown hair, not quite daring to bury his mouth and nose in it.

"Aleida?"

Her beautiful alertness, the serene expectancy with which she half turned her head, filled him with joy and made things easier. "Yes, Peter?"

"Do you know about me and Geoff?"

"That he is your father? Yes. Gladys told me. This is an awfully small town."

"And you don't mind?"

"I think it's exciting. I'm so glad that you found him and that you had to come to Santa Fe." She turned her head back to the glasses on the table with enchanting sudden feminine withdrawal. Her voice came—rich and soft—as from some lovely secret retreat. "When you're in love with somebody, everything about them is beautiful."

He bent his head until his lips and the tip of his nose touched her hair. *How wonderful*, he thought. *She knows all about me and Geoff. There is no need to explain and cringe. She said, "When you're in love!"* In his happiness he slid his hands under her arms and then over her breasts.

"Fresh!" she said. She put the last highball on the tray, twisted around in his arms, and was intoxicatingly against him again.

She said, "I've always wanted a wedding. I can hardly believe it—I suddenly don't mind in the least not having one. Aunt Milly is the only one who's really going to mind. Father won't care—no, let me finish! Your work *is* important, and I don't want you to take time now for a trip and for building a house. Besides, it would take at least three months to get ready. We'd probably have to wait until Christmas, so that Anne and my cousin and our families could come, and Christmas wouldn't be a good time anyway. Aunt Milly would want us to wait until spring, and —do you know what—I don't want to wait!"

He said, "There's another thing: that business about Geoff and me."

"But I've told you, angel, I don't care."

"I know. It's swell of you, but if you're going to have those three kids—"

"*We* are going to have, darling!"

"—it wouldn't be fair to them. Geoff has offered to adopt me—that seems to be the procedure—and I think I better take him up on it. It's going to be a nuisance about my name. I don't want to change it. I've got some standing as an engineer. It's going to be sort of awkward."

"I know what let's do: let's hyphenate the two names! The Spanish people always have the names of both their parents."

"Domanig-Middlemas?" he tried out the sound of it rather dubiously. "It sounds a little ridiculous. No, I'm afraid it'll have to be 'Middlemas.' Do you mind?"

Her eyes laughed. "No, Mr. Middlemas. . . ."

Geoff said, "That won't give your mother much time to get here."

He grinned. "That's the idea. That's why I'm not going to write her about it until the last minute. Aleida and I have decided we don't want a lot of family complications."

"I shall be perfectly willing to keep out of the way."

"No, we don't want that. We've talked it all over: we're all going to live here, and Aleida and I would rather have you there. What we're planning to do if I can get my research project well enough under way by then, is to take a couple of months off next spring and stop off for a week in Westchester on our way to Europe. Aleida has never been in Europe."

Geoff said slowly, "I hope you're also planning to spend some time in England. Your grandfather would very much like to see you. . . ."

"Isn't it astounding that we can be here—in October."

"And like this!" She laughed and made her finger tips perform a miniature gallop up his ribs, where he was ticklish.

"I had to break the ice this morning in the dog dish, and I bet we wouldn't have had a car today if I hadn't drained the water out of the radiator. Gad, darling, you're beautiful!"

"You just keep right on thinking so. Do you know what let's do? Let's hurry down to the creek and take a cold plunge."

"Like this?"

"Of course not, silly—though I don't think there's a soul within miles of here. Hand me my blouse, darling—and don't lose my gentian!"

"Hasn't it been wonderful—finding a gentian and two raspberries?" he exulted.

"As wonderful as last time we were here?"

"Not even any comparison . . ."

They were back at the gentian meadow—or rather, above it, in a sun-splotched clearing among the laughing aspen. *Like an enchanted palace in a fairy tale*, he thought and looked at the countless slender silver columns and the deliciously tinkling, golden foliage that roofed the endless arcades.

"That creek is going to be icy," he said. "Do you think you ought to go in the water?"

"I love it cold. Darling, I'm disgustingly healthy. You'll just have to get used to it. Come on!"

He picked up the cigarettes and matches and his tweed topcoat and Aleida's leather jacket and followed her to the young trees at the edge of the wood, where the horses were tied. Suddenly the suggestion of a lilt in Aleida's walk and his discovery once again of the exquisitely feminine curve that sloped from her slim neck down to her shoulder, made him quiver with a kind of awe. *Gioia!*—everything inside him sang with the word Cristina had taught him without giving him the substance, so that until now it had been an empty chalice—*this is joy! Thank you, Lord, for her, for this tree—this flower—this sky—this land—for everything that has nourished me. . . .*

They had reached the horses. Aleida untied hers and got on while he was still busy tying her jacket and his coat to the back of his saddle with the saddle strings. When he had got on, too, Aleida gave him a mischievous glance, headed her horse down the long slope that led to the creek, and called out gaily, "Let's race!"

For an instant he was about to dig his heels into the flanks of his horse and follow her. Then he chuckled to himself and jerked the head of his horse to the right and plunged down the sharp declivity which offered a short cut to the meadow and creek.

In a few seconds Aleida's voice came in shrill outrage through the trees. "Oh, you stinker—wait till I get you!"

The rustling trees seemed to nudge each other and to whisper delightedly at her throatiness.

He laughed for joy. He reined in his horse and called, "I love you, Mrs. Middlemas!"